PRAISE FOR *WINNER TAKES ALL*

"Sandra Kitt is a writing legend, and *Winner Takes All* proves that when it comes to great story-telling of the most romantic kind, she has the gift."

—**Brenda Jackson**, *New York Times* bestselling author

"Sandra Kitt is back with an emotional punch, delighting us with two strong but somewhat mismatched people. Along with falling in love, they each must deal with family issues, and the complications of a huge lottery win. It's a page-turner you don't want to miss!"

—**Lori Foster**, *New York Times* bestselling author

"A warm-hearted story of old flames, new loves, and a clever and nuanced plot reflecting current issues with sensitivity, warmth, and wisdom."

—**Susan Wiggs**, #1 *New York Times* bestselling author

"Skillful, silky writing, interweaving Jean and Patrick's past mistakes with hopeful futures. I especially loved the twist at the ending and the generosity of Kitt's characters."

—**Nancy Thayer**, *New York Times* bestselling author

"*Winner Takes All* is heartwarming, life-affirming, page-turning romance at its best!"

—**Brenda Novak**, *New York Times* bestselling author

"Charming, multilayered, thoroughly entertaining tale, in which readers are the real winners. Prepare to fall in love."

—**Farrah Rochon**, *USA Today* bestselling Author

"Delightfully entertaining and deliciously romantic story of second chances and family drama!"

—**Debbie Mason**, *USA Today* bestselling author

"Sandra Kitt writes beautiful stories about fascinating characters I would love to know in real life. *Winner Takes All* is romantic, tender, emotional, and compelling."

—**RaeAnne Thayne**, *New York Times* bestselling author

"Sandra Kitt is always a must-read! One of the original trailblazers of Black romance is back!"

—**Kwana Jackson**, *USA Today* bestselling author

"Sandra Kitt delivers a tender, love-conquers-all romance. Complex interracial couples, past and present, show how things have changed—and stayed the same—but finding the *one* is all about fighting for each other. Emotional, impactful, heartwarming."

—**Jennifer Ryan**, *New York Times* bestselling author

"From the first page to the last, this book is a reminder of why I love Sandra Kitt's writing: her words are poised, elegant, perfection."

—**LaQuette**, award-winning author

THE TIME OF YOUR LIFE

SANDRA KITT

sourcebooks
casablanca

Published by Sourcebooks Casablanca, an imprint of Sourcebooks
P.O. Box 4410, Naperville, Illinois 60567-4410
(630) 961-3900
sourcebooks.com

Cataloging-in-Publication Data is on file with the Library of Congress.

Printed and bound in the United States of America.
VP 10 9 8 7 6 5 4 3 2 1

Fill your life with experiences, not things.
Have stories to tell, not stuff to show.
—*Anonymous*

CHAPTER 1

When Eden Marsh came through the heavy main doors of the Guild Society, just a few blocks from the Department of Labor in Washington, DC, she was greeted by a hollow silence and a reminder of why she was there. A solemn acknowledgment of the recent passing of a man who'd had a profound effect on nearly everyone who'd known him, including her. She advanced to the center of the large lobby, with its Italianate marble floor, feeling herself beginning to give way to the emotional significance of the day. Eden took a breath to clear her head, determined that her personal sense of loss would not take away from the purpose of the day. To celebrate Everett Nichols.

Alone in the austere hallway, she felt drawn into the grand first floor salon, off to the right, by evidence that the room had been set up for some sort of event. Eden frowned as she glanced into the room. The dark and formal setting had been laid out with all the trappings for a reception. Or a meeting, or some sort of celebration. A table at the end of the room displayed a variety of glasses for an open bar. Two tables on the longer sides of the room were set up for buffet service, awaiting the delivery of food. It was everything she'd ordered for Everett's affair. But this was not the room she'd booked.

It was a distinctly masculine room, meant to be used by society members, once solely men, to welcome guests, business associates, family visiting for a few hours for an event, or just a place for members to gather to reflect on their good fortune, having achieved Masters of the Universe status.

Everett would hate it, Eden thought.

"Hello, are you Eden Marsh?"

Eden turned to the voice and the short, slender man approaching her. "Yes. Mr. Madison?" She shook his hand.

"Nice to put a pretty face to the voice on the phone," Mr. Madison said in an effort to be friendly. "As you can see"—he waved into the salon—"everything is ready. I'll have the catering staff bring in the refreshments shortly."

"But not here," Eden said clearly.

Surprised, the manager frowned. "Excuse me?"

"This is not the room I was originally shown. This is not the room I wanted. I chose the renovated reading room on the second floor. The room that the club commissioned Mr. Nichols to redesign and renovate several years ago."

The manager's expression turned to one of guilt, but he quickly recovered. "I'm so sorry. But that room is being used for another function. I believe our *director's* secretary," he said with emphasis, "asked to use it for her daughter's bridal shower. In any case the grand salon is our most popular rental space. It's so historic."

Eden shook her head, her gaze expressing a sort of "gee, that's too bad" gesture, as she opened her satchel and pulled out folded papers. "I'm sure it is, but it's not what I agreed to. I have a signed contract, Mr. Madison. It clearly says that the reading room will be set up for a memorial service lasting two hours for seventy-five guests." Eden held out the document to the flustered Mr. Madison. "Would you like to see it again?"

"No, I remember the contract, but…"

"Good. You just need to transfer the refreshment setup to the second floor. That shouldn't take too long." Eden looked at her watch. "The guests will be arriving in under an hour." She smiled sweetly at the manager to soften the blow of her digging in her heels. "I'm sure you can explain to the bridal shower party about *my* agreement. They can use the salon. It's big and cozy…and historic. Thank you for doing this," Eden said with self-deprecating politeness, not allowing the club manager to attempt more excuses.

"Of course," Mr. Madison conceded, giving in to the utter charm with which Eden made her case. He turned away to do her bidding.

Eden was alone again, with the silence of the building and the odd stillness that hung in the air. She immediately forgot Mr. Madison, confident that he wouldn't dare ignore the signed contract…and risk the consequences.

She continued to the wide staircase and climbed to the second level. The landing opened right in front of a bright room with high ceilings, its late-twentieth-century furnishings more in line with the earlier styles of the salon. No chrome and glass here. But it was modern and comfortable, one wall entirely devoted to an enormous built-in filled with monographs, atlases, and attractively bound series and sets. It wasn't a library, but definitely a reading space for club members that was bright, relaxed, and uncluttered.

Everett didn't like clutter, either. *Keep it simple* had always been one of his mottos.

Eden sighed and blinked, focusing. Here, there were three round tables set up for a luncheon. The tablecloths were pink, and there was a large, ornate bouquet in the center of each table. This layout was what the club manager had expected to function for the bridal shower.

Eden heard sounds beyond a partition at the end of the room, and two young men in black slacks and pristine white shirts, waitstaff, appeared with a rolling service cart.

"We're here to move the flowers downstairs. We'll be back for the tables in a sec," one of the men said.

"Thank you. I know this is last minute, but could you hurry? My guests will be arriving soon."

She watched as the two men quickly loaded the cart with whatever would fit and headed back to the discreetly placed service elevator. Eden returned her attention to the room, quickly assessing if there was a need to rearrange furniture. She was relieved that there wasn't. Maybe just repositioning some of the chairs into small clusters and placing the small side tables conveniently for glasses and plates. She began to do some of the moving on her own.

The manager reappeared and rushed to assist Eden when he found her attempting to shift a club chair so it faced the center of the room.

"Ms. Marsh, please. You don't have to do that. My team will take care of everything."

"I don't mind," she responded agreeably. "I can move a chair."

"Yes, yes," the manager said with a nervous chuckle. "I can see you're very capable, but I don't want to add a line item on the contract that includes coverage for injuries."

She stepped back and turned to look around again. Satisfied that it was all coming together, Eden headed for the staircase.

"Ah…is there something else?"

"I just want to check how things are going in the kitchen. I don't want my food platters to end up as hors d'oeuvres at the shower."

"But…"

Eden was already halfway down the stairs, carefully maneuvering in her two-inch pumps. She did a light and graceful jog down the hallway, past the entrance, in the direction of the catering department. She could hear the activity and the shouts and orders among the staff as they hurried to accommodate two events scheduled at the same time. She caught a glimpse of the folded tables for the buffet, a short stack of tablecloths, a box with other wares and supplies, and an easel, all stuffed into the little elevator. The two men Eden had already seen working on the second floor managed to squeeze in, the doors closed, and the elevator ascended.

She looked around and spotted several platters of food. "I'll take this up," she announced. And without waiting for a response, she lifted one of the plastic-wrapped trays and headed back to the staircase. Eden heard the main entrance door open behind her as she walked past. A cool wave of late-winter air wafted over her, but she didn't look to see who'd come in.

She checked her watch and frowned. Thirty minutes and counting before guests arrived. Eden started up the stairs. She hesitated, deciding against holding the banister. But trying to hold the tray with one hand was *not* a good idea. Instead, Eden balanced the tray in both hands, off to one side. She started up again, looking down to watch the placement of her feet on the steps.

Beck Dennison pulled open the entrance door of the Guild Society and entered the lobby. He momentarily stopped in his tracks as a young woman hurriedly marched by with a large, cumbersome tray in her hands. She was focused on the obviously unwieldy tray and didn't notice his presence at the door. He, on the other hand, was caught by her erect bearing and her slender figure confidently rushing to a destination. The lush dark curls of her natural hairdo, mostly at the top and back of her head, bounced gently with each step. He quickly noticed she was tastefully attired in slim black slacks, and a short bolero-length jacket in black-and-white tweed with a stand-up collar. It was sophisticated but simple attire, still feminine but unlike what many of the females in DC would choose to wear. Her silver hoop earrings reflected the hall lighting as she walked. Beck came out of his focused appreciation of the attractive, stylish picture she presented when he realized she was actually going to attempt to walk up a flight of stairs in heels, carrying a tray of food.

He rushed forward, taking the stairs two at a time until he reached her, almost halfway up. So as not to startle her, he reached out, placing his hand beneath the tray at the center. His left hand hovered at her back, but not touching her, in case she lost her balance.

"Let me take that," he said with quiet authority. He lifted the tray away from her.

Surprised by the sudden action, Eden glanced over her shoulder at him. She blinked, gave him a slight smile, and turned to continue up the steps.

Beck heard her murmur, "Thank you." He followed her. When they both reached the landing, she went striding off into the bright room straight ahead, where several men were busy covering buffet tables, setting up for an open bar, and strategically placing small stacks of cocktails napkins on several tables. He maneuvered off his cross-body mailbag and left it on the floor against the baseboard near the entrance. Beck could see that this was a setup for an event and walked the tray over to one of the catering staff, a young Black woman with an attractively arranged pile up of long dreadlocks.

"I've got it. We'll take care of the rest," she said, taking the tray.

"Thanks." Beck nodded, looking around for the young woman he'd helped. She was busy giving directions to other staff in a quiet but commanding voice and willingly lending a hand where needed. He went over to introduce himself. She turned and saw him but gave him no chance to speak.

"Oh, good," she said, signaling him over. "I need your help. Could you please shift this love seat forward and on a slight angle? I think that will make the space cozier."

"Yes, ma'am," Beck responded agreeably and went to do her bidding. He hid his amusement and fleeting annoyance that she was, unknowingly, abusing his services. She was clearly an employee of the catering company hired to provide for the occasion, in charge of making things happen. He positioned himself behind the sofa and began to push it. Beck glanced at her again, not yet willing to admit he admired her presence. She wasn't aloof and bullying, and her directives were more...thoughtful. Things were to be done *her* way, the right way. And thank you very much. He allowed himself a slight grin. It was hard to say no to someone so charming *and* pretty.

Beck followed her movements as she, in turn, watched what the staff was doing in the placement of the trays. One side of the room was finger food items. The opposite-side table was laid out with desserts.

She turned, giving her attention to the approach of a short middle-aged man in a business suit, speaking and gesturing in disapproval.

"Ms. Marsh, I have to insist..."

"I know, Mr. Madison. But we're almost finished, and your staff has been amazing. I'll make sure they're compensated."

Mr. Madison fell silent as she again adroitly avoided a face-off.

Beck finished repositioning the love seat while eavesdropping on the exchange. He had to grin. The woman probably didn't work directly for the club, but she was certainly in charge at the moment.

He reached into his pocket and withdrew a business card from his wallet. He approached her, ready to introduce himself. But the young woman's attention was again caught by something near the refreshment table. She walked away before he could speak, not realizing that he was behind her.

Beck waited patiently. She bent to pick up a folded easel from the floor, opened it, and placed it in a prominent spot facing toward the open room. When she bent again to lift a large, flat rectangular item wrapped in brown paper, he stepped forward.

"I've got it." He passed his business card to her as he took the flat package out of her hands. She barely glanced at the card before slipping it into the pocket of her jacket. She stood watching as he removed the brown paper. The board underneath was a mounted black-and-white photograph of a seventy-something white male. His image took up nearly all of the frame of reference. In the background was an out-of-focus crowded bookshelf with models and oversize catalogs and manuals, evidence of a workplace setting. The man was leaning back in his chair, his brawny arms up with his hands locked behind his shaved head. His open-necked shirt had the sleeves haphazardly pulled up. He was staring right into the camera, and he wasn't smiling.

Beck stared, caught off guard by the suddenness of seeing the larger-than-life face of Everett Nichols, whose memorial he'd been invited to attend. Beck was also caught off guard by the sadness that coursed quickly through him. For a moment he was transfixed, a rush of memories flashing in his head. So was the young woman next to him. Beck reached in front of her and placed the dramatic photo on the display easel. It was eye-catching and very revealing, but only to those who'd known Everett Nichols well. Beck suspected the number was relatively small. He heard a small, almost inaudible sound from the woman. He turned his head to look at her.

She was standing with her arms wrapped across her waist, hugging herself. Beck was trying to figure out what it meant, that she now seemed so self-protective. What was she feeling? And why? If this was a simple work engagement, where did her personal reaction come from? Abruptly, she turned and walked away. Beck watched her go, having no idea what to make of her reaction to the portrait of Everett Nichols.

What's up with that? he wondered.

"Beck! Hey, glad to see you."

Beck turned to the friendly voice and accepted the outstretched hand of the tall, stocky man with graying hair. "Hello, Matt. Why invite me if you didn't think I'd show up?"

"You writers are a strange breed," Matt said dryly. "You're like some people who get invited to everything and then weigh which is worth their time. I was hoping you'd make the memorial today."

"Sorry about the funeral…"

"You don't have to explain anything to me. I guessed it would have been hard for you. For sure I know Everett would have understood."

"I appreciate that."

"And we both know he didn't stand on ceremony," Matt remarked. Then, his demeanor sobered, and he watched Beck closely. "So, how are things?"

Beck grimaced, arching a brow, and tightening a muscle in his jaw. "I think I underestimated how much…"

"Yeah, I know. Me too. I'm still adjusting to the fact that…he's gone. Like you, I still get emotional. When people asked how come you were a no-show, I said you were in Brazil covering a story…"

Beck's expression cleared and he laughed quietly. "Thanks. It turned out you were almost right. I'd already accepted an assignment in Toronto. I couldn't beg off at the last minute."

"You know, writers can get away with excuses like that."

Beck pursed his mouth, thinking. "Ah…did…did my mother attend?"

Matt shrugged. "I can't say, Beck. I don't recall seeing her, but that doesn't mean she wasn't there. There were a lot of folks who came out." He chuckled. "I think even Everett would have been surprised. But he always underestimated what he meant to people."

Matt was suddenly distracted, looking over Beck's shoulder, turning to scan the room.

"Looking for someone? Besides me, that is."

"As a matter of fact, yes. Eden Marsh. One of Everett's lawyers, Katherine Perkins, asked me to arrange everything here at the society and get Eden to act as hostess. She knew Everett would like that. Katherine flew out to LA to be introduced to her latest grandchild."

Beck nodded. "A priority."

Matt gently slapped Beck on the shoulder. "This should get going soon. I see a few people I want to say hello to first."

"I'll hang here."

Matt nodded as he turned away. "No problem."

Beck moved, working his way to a spot where he could see the whole room and everyone in it. Other than Matt Sorkin, he didn't expect to see anyone he might know. That gave him the perfect opportunity to be an observer, to try to decide the angle he would take on the profile he would be writing about Everett for his publication. But in the meantime, he couldn't help but scout out the growing number of arriving guests, trying to find… What did Matt say her name was, again? Marsh, the club manager had called her. Marsh. *Eden* Marsh.

Eden touched up her blush, using her index finger to stroke the cream across her cheeks. She stared at herself in the mirror and sighed. She knew that the slight upward slope of her fine brows showed she was still a bit emotional. She *had* to pull herself together and stop dissolving into a teary mess. She quickly grabbed a tissue and dabbed at an errant tear on the ends of her lashes. She inhaled deeply.

Eden used the remnants of the cream on her fingers to brush over her lips, finishing with a quick roll of her lipstick. As she pressed her lips together and stared at herself, it suddenly came to her that she had not been alone in that moment of appraising Everett's photo and once again experiencing his loss. There was that man, a club staffer, standing right behind her, watching. Had he seen her crying? Yet if he was waitstaff, why should she care what he thought? Nevertheless, she was annoyed with herself for almost falling apart in front of a stranger.

When Eden left the ladies' room, she could hear conversation, light laughter, and the sound of ice falling into glasses coming from the reading room even before she'd walked back in. Guests had begun to arrive in her absence, and already the room was busy and noisy. She scanned the room, recognizing a few of the guests but not all.

It had been more than three years since she last worked for Everett Nichols, so Eden was surprised when she was asked to oversee this memorial service. Not that Matt, Everett's best friend, couldn't have handled it all and done a great job. But as she'd been told, and come to learn on her own, she had known Everett in a different way. She had talked her way into his employment as a brash undergraduate with a little bit of a chip on her shoulder, sure she knew more than she did, as Everett would quickly, in amusement, point out to her. But he never tried to crush her spirit. Instead, he'd sparked her curiosity and helped her develop better judgment and more careful and thoughtful decisions. He'd broadened her worldview.

Everett had helped her to grow up.

As she was finally leaving his employment at Everett's urging, Eden had asked him why he'd bothered taking so much time, often combative, to teach her so much. Eden smiled even now as she considered his response.

"I see myself in you, Eden, when I was determined to go out and build a life for myself. I was also just about your age. But without the long hair and lashes, big smile, and promising personality. I got into a lot of fights before I got it right. I hoped to save you from that."

Eden was glad that people were introducing themselves and forming little clusters of conversation. No one appeared to be a wallflower, compelling her to rescue them. Then she spotted the man who'd been so helpful.

Now that she could study him, he didn't seem at all the sort to be in the business of catering work. He was a tall, fair-skinned Black man who stood on the opposite side of the room near the windows. She found herself walking toward him, all the while assessing him, and quickly deciding that he stood out from most other men in the room. He displayed a masculinity and strength that she found attractive. Quiet, but very noticeable. Only as she was almost directly in front of him did it strike Eden that he was dressed kind of preppy. It didn't seem the right kind of attire for setting up buffet tables and serving finger food. His collarless long-sleeved shirt was pale gray. Pearl. Not so far off from the color of his eyes. She did recall that he had light eyes as well. Maybe he was Mr. Madison's assistant or held some other managerial position at the club?

Eden walked on the periphery of the gathering to approach him. She caught his attention, and he stood with his gaze fixed on her like a laser beam.

Eden felt a peculiar reaction in her chest. His steady stare was not haughty...or wolfish. Maybe just curious. She forced an apologetic smile.

"I'm sorry I went rushing off like that."

"No need to apologize," he started slowly. "I could see you were...busy." Eden shook her head. His voice was deep. Baritone. That had an effect on her as well. "You were helpful and I thank you for that. I'll let Mr. Madison know."

Beck's gaze suddenly became bright with amusement. He hid a smile. "You think I work here, don't you?"

The smile disappeared from Eden's face and she blinked. "You... don't work here?"

Beck slowly shook his head. "I don't work here. I'm here for the memorial for Everett." He made a slight gesture with his hand. "I'm a guest. But I didn't mind lending a hand when you were getting set up with your team."

Eden continued to stare and blinked again. Then she arched

a brow and amusement curved her mouth in a pretty, saucy grin. "And you think I work here as well. Right?"

He looked confused, considered the error, and chuckled in an apologetic manner. "Oops. I think I made the same mistake."

"Don't worry about it," Eden said, shaking her head dismissively. "Actually, I think we made a great team. Got it all done."

The corner of his mouth went up in a half grin. "Yeah. I agree."

Eden studied him for a moment and realized he was making light of the situation. She briefly averted her gaze, covering her embarrassment. "Well…"

"I'm Beck Dennison," he said, introducing himself.

"Eden Marsh."

They didn't shake hands but, for several long seconds, simply studied one another. She knew the moment completely changed the way they were seeing each other. Eden felt a bit shy suddenly, wondering what he was thinking, but she never shifted her gaze, meeting his straight on. And sensing a new connection.

The sound of conversation and laughter suddenly wafted into the room from the salon below. She saw the puzzled look in his eyes and shrugged. "Bridal shower."

"They must be having a good time," Beck commented with a grin. "So are the guests here."

She nodded, looking around. "Everett would like this. He'd want everyone to enjoy themselves. I don't actually know everyone here," Eden said. She stared at Beck. "You knew Everett?"

Beck hesitated, blinking. "I…did. It's been a long time since we'd seen each other before he died," he said carefully.

She nodded, accepting his explanation. Eden inhaled, glancing around the room. "One of Everett's best friends put together the guest list."

"Matt Sorkin?"

"Yes, Matt. Then I was asked to be the hostess. I'm not sure why me."

"You don't sound very enthusiastic."

Eden shook her head, her curls gently quivering. "I don't think Everett would have wanted anything like this, but I know he deserves it. There are a lot of folks here today. They liked him. Even loved him…" Her voice cracked and trailed off. She forced her gaze to meet Beck's. "It's just that…I'm sure other people knew him better. Like Matt, his best friend."

Eden thought Beck Dennison was watching her closely, calmly assessing her expression…her exposed emotions, no matter how hard she tried to try to keep them at bay.

"I'm sure Matt knew what he was doing when he came up with the idea for the service. He may have had the idea, but I think you're doing great."

Eden smiled weakly, blinking. She glanced around. It looked like everyone was here who was supposed to be here. The atmosphere was very relaxed. Almost jovial. It hardly seemed a sad occasion to mark a man's passing. The day was shaping up as more of a celebration. The afternoon, the memorial was about Everett's life, not his death.

"Eden!"

She turned to see Matt Sorkin motioning for her. She knew what was coming and moved toward Matt without any further comment to Beck.

"I think we can get started, don't you?" Matt said, taking her hand and leading her to the center of the room. She found herself standing right next to the portrait of Everett. "You know what to say. Welcome. Glad you could make it. Everett was a great guy. Enjoy yourselves. The end."

Eden laughed at Matt's summary.

And she was on.

Beck changed position, moving so that he could better see Eden, watch her as she prepared to speak. In truth she did *not* look very happy, but it was well disguised under a natural poise and presence. Passing the open bar, he grabbed a glass of tonic water and let the server drop a twist of lime into the drink. Taking several cocktail napkins to soak up the condensation, Beck took a sip as Eden smiled, looking around. Like magic, she didn't have to wait long. She drew attention. The room grew quiet.

At that very instant, raucous laughter and squeals burst out from the salon below, causing a little titter in the gathering. Beck's gaze was on Eden. Only for a split second did she seem flustered, then almost immediately become composed. He didn't hear her clear her throat, but he knew she did.

"What can I say? A bride-to-be, twelve bridesmaids, and a lot of champagne."

Light laughter broke out, but everyone relaxed and it was easy after that to mostly ignore the celebration one floor below.

"Hi, everyone. My name is Eden Marsh. Many of you have never heard of me. And I don't know most of you."

More light laughter.

Eden momentarily became pensive, blinking into space and then focusing on the people around her.

"The most important thing is that we're all here for Everett.

When he died last month after two heart attacks, one after another, I couldn't believe it, to be honest. I always thought of him as invincible, someone who could live forever."

"Yeah. He was the *man*," came a male voice from somewhere in the back of the room.

"A wonderful man," Eden added. "But a heart attack is a heart attack. Often there's not much you can do about it. Maybe he enjoyed life a little more than the rest of us, simple things…like eating too much red meat." Now there was a little laughter, here and there. "But Everett was also an incredibly focused, hard worker. And he showed so many of us where hard work could take you. All of that wonderful…amazing energy is lost to us, and to the world."

Beck watched her, sensing that Eden was venturing into territory that was painful for her. He couldn't help but wonder why.

"After his funeral, many people got in touch with Matt Sorkin to find out about a memorial service. Well, anyone who knew Everett knew he didn't want any of that. No funeral, no memorial. He'd say, 'I'll be gone, and that will be that.' But the reason we're here today is because, as Matt explained to me, memorials are not for the deceased, but for the living. People need a way to honor Everett and to say goodbye. As good an excuse as any to have beer and empanadas."

There was more gentle laughter, a smattering of applause. Eden turned her head from side to side, as if looking for something. A hand appeared holding out a beer to her. She accepted the bottle and held it out to all those gathered.

"Here's to Everett Nichols. An extraordinary businessman, boss to many, mentor, and very good friend to all. We'll miss you."

"Hear, hear," Matt said, his voice projecting through the room.

"Hear, hear," came back the loud and enthusiastic response.

"Thanks again for coming," Eden finished.

People began moving around. They fell into new groupings and conversation picked up. Beck lost sight of Eden and then realized she was chatting with Matt, as well as addressing people who stopped to either say hello to her or to introduce themselves. There were quick rounds of hugs and cheek kisses.

As much as Beck was enjoying just watching her, he finally moved. He slowly switched back and forth among the guests, randomly selecting some to ask how they knew Everett. He had to listen to several lengthy affectionate or bemused anecdotes. Not all the personal stories were complimentary, but the fact that people were present to drink to, honor, remember, or even curse Everett spoke for itself. He had gained a lot of people's respect.

Everett Nichols was pretty unforgettable.

Matt appeared at his side. "I'm going to get out of here. I need a quiet moment—and a stiff drink—to remember that I'm not going to see him anymore. I'll miss the guy."

"I understand," Beck said. Matt shook his hand.

"Glad you could make it today. I'll see you Tuesday."

Beck merely nodded as Matt strode away.

Thirty minutes later, the waitstaff was starting to break down the services. People were saying goodbye, exchanging cell phone numbers…or making dates. The room slowly emptied out. Beck looked around, but it seemed that Eden might have already left as well. He was hoping for another chance at a brief conversation with her—he had a lot of questions—but apparently that wasn't going to happen.

Beck had already started down the stairwell when he remembered he'd left his bag on the floor near the entrance of the room. In no hurry, he turned and started back up, his mind now occupied with the conversations he'd had, the evocative little speech Eden had so gracefully made…heartfelt and sincere…as well as considering a number of angles for the piece he wanted to write about the service.

He didn't actually walk back into the room but reached inside near the baseboard for his bag. He grabbed it, already turning to descend the stairs again. He heard something that sounded like… like someone crying. Beck turned, listening closely in case he'd made a mistake. But, no. Someone was crying. He stepped back into the room, again glancing around, but it appeared empty. The buffet tables had yet to be collapsed and removed, and the easel with the dramatic image of Everett Nichols was still prominently displayed.

He caught a movement out of the corner of his eye. Behind the easel, near the window on the opposite side of the room. He saw only slim black pant legs, but knew immediately it was Eden. Beck approached, walking on the enormous modern area rug until he reached the portrait. He stepped around it and found Eden quietly sobbing into a paper napkin. He saw her hunched shoulders shaking, her lustrous curls bobbing on her head, her crying muted in the napkin.

Beck considered that maybe the best thing to do, under the circumstance, was to leave Eden alone. Of course she didn't mean for anyone to witness her emotional display, but Beck couldn't move. He couldn't ignore her plaintive sobs. While he stood debating his next move, Eden straightened on a deep and quiet sigh. She dabbed at her tears, sniffed, blew her nose. Beck very carefully placed his fingers on her arm. She went still, but Eden neither was startled nor recoiled at his touch.

He leaned closer to the side of her head. He took a chance.

"Do you need a hug?" he whispered.

CHAPTER 2

Eden remained perfectly still for a second or two. Then, she nodded and turned to let a perfect stranger gather her against his chest. She was instantly in tears, quietly sobbing again without saying a word. Her body shook. Her arms were bent between their bodies, her hands curled into loose fists. The tears kept flowing from somewhere deep inside, and Eden didn't seem to have any control over it ending. All day she'd been trying to maintain some decorum. Not a single other soul during the afternoon seemed to have felt what she was feeling. There was no question that they mourned Everett's passing, but they were also going to mark the moment in a way that Everett himself would understand and appreciate. But none of them had known Everett the way she had. She'd once told him he'd saved her life. Everett had chuckled, not in amusement but in irony.

"*No,*" he'd murmured ruefully. "*You saved mine.*"

Beck was stunned. Not only because Eden had readily accepted his offer, but because now that she had, he felt an odd responsibility to respect what she was going through. He had another, totally irreverent thought. That in all the years since he was seventeen and had begun dating, he'd rarely had to comfort any woman. He could count on one hand the number of times he'd seen one cry.

He didn't have to remind himself that he didn't know anything about the woman Eden might be. Her forehead rested on his chest, her curls brushing softly under his chin and jaw. He didn't hold her tightly. Just enough so that she'd feel secure. But it was a powerful moment and, in its own way, very intimate. Beck felt protective of her. He remained silent. Maybe Eden didn't fully realize that she was in his arms. He let one hand ride up her back to her heaving shoulders and cupped her nape, fingers automatically lightly massaging the skin.

After a few minutes the sobs subsided, and she began to pull herself together, to withdraw from him. Without much thought Beck tightened his arms infinitesimally.

"Stay as long as you want. I don't mind," he murmured into her curls.

And with that Eden gave in again and accepted the shelter of his arms. Her crying now was far less emotive, and more tired little sighs. She sniffled. Awkwardly Beck reached into his trouser pocket and pulled out several cocktail napkins now crushed into a wad. He pressed them into her hand.

Eden accepted the napkins and flattened them to dry her cheeks. She drew back, staring at his shirt, now dotted with her tears.

"I'm embarrassed," she said, barely above a whisper.

The silence was suddenly broken with the approaching sound of someone jogging up the staircase. Beck pushed Eden away gently, looking into her face to see how composed she was. She hardly looked like she had been crying, blinking rapidly to clear her eyes.

"There you are! I thought you'd left already," Mr. Madison said. He took a swift glance around the room to see if it had been put back in order, making note of the folded tables and the easel still open and supporting the portrait of Everett. He approached them briskly.

After one final scrutiny of Eden's face, Beck stepped aside. She managed a smile and let Mr. Madison speak.

"I hope everything went well today." He glanced around again. "Glad to see there were no accidents or damage to the room," he hinted.

"It went very well," Eden said in a soft tone.

Beck could hear a little underlying tension in her voice.

"Your service people were really wonderful," she added.

"Excellent! Then I guess we're done. Correct?"

"There is the matter of a correction to my invoice for the inconvenience of having to switch rooms."

Mr. Madison smiled thinly. "We did make the switch, it was timely, the service went off without a problem…"

"None of which would have happened if I hadn't arrived early enough to catch the problem. Correct?"

Mr. Madison maintained his calm demeanor, pursed his lips, rocked back on his heels. "Can I see the contract?"

"Of course," Eden said, her voice stronger now. She walked to a corner of the room and withdrew the contract from her bag.

Beck began to back his way to the entrance. He raised his hand to catch Eden's attention.

"Thank you for everything," she called out simply, and continued her conversation with the club manager.

She was distracted, already separating from the ten minutes alone in the room together. Eden was fully present in her exchange with the manager. Beck grinned wryly to himself and left. But he didn't leave the club. He thought about it all the way down the stairs. How strange the afternoon had turned out to be. Next to an ornate credenza in the center of the lobby, directly opposite the main doors, Beck took up residence in one of the high-back chairs, pulled out his cell, and began scrolling through a pileup of texts and emails and voicemail messages…while he waited for Eden to come down from the reading room on the second floor.

"Thank you, Mr. Madison. I appreciate the extra discount."

Mr. Madison smiled benignly. "It's my pleasure."

"The ladies down in the salon sure sounded like they had a good time. I take it the shower was a success? Any problem with the change of rooms?"

"I threw in two more bottles of champagne, on the house. That helped a lot. They were having such a good time I don't think anyone noticed."

Eden smiled and nodded. "Yes. So lucky for both of us."

With the financial adjustment of her contract settled, Eden said goodbye to Mr. Madison and placed the contract in her purse. She made her way to the ladies' room, not to cry—she was well and truly finished with that for the day—but to check the damage of her teary deluge in the mirror. Her eyes were not as red as she'd feared. She used her fingertips to dig into her curls and fluff them up again, creating an attractive disorder. She stared wide-eyed at her image. And stared as she began to fully recognize the part that man, Beck something, had played in her melodrama.

Do you need a hug?

And she'd accepted.

Eden felt a warm appreciation for the gesture and for him. Unbelievable but so…kind. She washed her hands and gathered her things. She left and made her way to the main floor. She was almost near the entrance when she noticed the man sitting in the entrance chair. Eden slowed her steps. It was *him*. He looked up and saw her standing and staring at him with a combination of curiosity and bewilderment. He jumped to his feet.

They faced each other, not unlike when they were first introducing themselves before the memorial began.

"Finished?"

"You're still here?"

"I decided to hang around, make sure you're okay."

Eden came closer, noticing things about Beck that hadn't fully registered during the afternoon. The light, light brown of his skin and the light covering of facial hair that was trimmed and neat. He had a curly crop of hair that added to her first impression that he appeared biracial. Certainly handsome, with incredible presence.

He had a distinct baritone voice, low but not booming, with a very soothing quality to it.

"You didn't have to wait. I don't think I…"

"Look, it's been a really full day. Lots of details, lots of people… I think the club manager got on your nerves…"

Raising her eyes in surprise, she grinned.

"I suspect you're pretty wired at the moment."

"A little," she admitted, nodding.

She could see Beck hesitate, trying to read her expression

"Maybe you'd like to just get home. But I have a suggestion to make."

"What kind of suggestion?"

"I think you could use some time to decompress. So…how do you feel about going for…coffee?"

She shook her head showing regret. "I don't drink coffee."

"Tea?"

"You're persistent."

"Would you like me to leave?" he countered.

Eden sighed. "Got anything else?"

"Ice cream. It's not my final offer, but the other might force you to slap me."

She blinked. The comment went over her head. "What?"

"How about ice cream? Have dessert first? Life is short? Something sweet. Won't take long to consume. Goes down easy. Makes you smile."

She didn't smile. She looked skeptical.

"Or not." He peered into her face.

Eden became momentarily thoughtful, as if she were considering other options and not finding any of them appealing. She glanced at Beck, trying to judge his sincerity. Wondering if his invitation was very likely the most original come-on line she'd ever been handed.

Eden inclined her head. "Actually, ice cream sounds like a nice idea."

"Ice cream it is." Beck swung the strap of his cross-body bag over his shoulder. He opened the entrance door and let Eden exit before him.

Eden let Beck lead the way, their pace comfortable and unhurried. Until he settled into a specific direction and path, there wasn't much conversation of note between them. Eden abruptly filled the void.

"We're on Pennsylvania Ave, so let's head toward the White House," she pointed. "We're sure to find some place..."

Beck looked at her with a raised eyebrow. "Do you think I don't know where I'm going?"

"Well…I just thought…"

"I'm teasing. There used to be a small ice cream place near the Archives Metro Station." They quickly reached the corner but there was no small ice cream shop, only several souvenir kiosks starting to close up shop for the day. Dusk was settling over the area. "So much for that idea," Beck murmured, glancing around.

"Let's keep walking. I know there will be lots of food trucks on Independence. One of them has *got* to be selling ice cream. It won't be fancy, but…"

Beck laughed under his breath.

Eden picked up her pace and took the lead, hearing Beck's quiet chuckle as he caught up to her. "We're a block from the Mall. This is one of my favorite parts of DC," she commented as they glanced to their left to Independence, where a quick look showed that this most visible and heavily trafficked sector of the city, now emptied of tourists and visitors, was closing down for the night.

"Looks like we're striking out on ice cream…"

"No, not yet," Eden said with a shake of her head. "Now that you've gotten me all worked up over ice cream"—he laughed again—"we can't give up. I have one more idea before I'll admit defeat. This way."

Beck was happy to follow.

This was not turning out as he'd imagined. Not that he had an actual plan. The thing was, he was totally intrigued by Eden Marsh. She was bright and animated. She came across as unselfconscious and forthright. Or maybe she was fearless. Beck reminded himself to pay closer attention before he fine-tuned that thought. Eden had a beautiful, full mobile mouth. When he watched her as she spoke, he had to remind himself not to stare at her lips.

"I love the Mall. I'm positive it's the largest open space in all of DC. Sure, there are all these building and museums on either side of the Reflecting Pool but..."

Beck let her talk. He'd never paid much attention to the Mall, couldn't recall the last time he'd been even close to it or any of the national monuments.

"Are you a guide for the city?"

She frowned. "Am I...? Oh, sorry. I didn't mean to go all tour guide on you. When I first came to DC, I discovered that you could walk continuously right from the Lincoln Memorial to the Capitol in just under two miles."

"And that's important because?"

She didn't respond right away. Eden slowed her steps and looked north toward the Washington Monument. The twilight lights were on around the obelisk. She crossed her arms as they continued walking.

"It's a good place for me to be when I...when I need some space and time to think. And be alone. I'd come here after classes, or work, and just walk. I'd start anywhere along the path, set a direction. Lincoln Memorial. Washington Monument. The Capitol."

Beck casually looked around, trying to see the free space that she saw. He gave Eden his attention again. "What kind of classes?"

"Third-year law. Georgetown."

"Why not Howard?"

She swung another thoughtful glance his way, hesitating on how much she wanted to share. "I did my undergrad at Howard. But I had a chance to go to Georgetown and took it. Nothing against Howard. I would have gone there if it worked out that way."

"Law school can be pretty...tense," Beck suggested.

Eden humphed quietly. "You have no idea," she commented, but didn't clarify.

When they reached Fourteenth Street, she veered off to the right to a brightly lit shop called, appropriately, *Presidential Scoops*.

"I think we'll have to make do here. Is that okay? I mean, everyone is all into gelato, but I love good old fashioned *ice cream*. I think they have everything here."

Not that she waited for his answer.

She ordered a medium cup of vanilla ice cream...with sprinkles.

Beck settled on vanilla and chocolate scoops in a cone.

After he'd paid for everything, he indicated an empty wrought-iron table outside. He sat a little catty-corner to Eden so that he could continue to study her without appearing to do so. He became fascinated with her ritual of filling the spoon with ice cream but only slipping half of it into her mouth. Shifting it around until it was gone, and then finishing the remainder on the spoon in a similar fashion. Spoon. Taste. Savor. Repeat.

Eden ate her ice cream slowly, and she let her gaze wander and settle on whatever caught her attention around her. It began with a teenage boy walking his dog while flipping through text messages on his phone. Eden made a soft clicking sound and the dog made a beeline for her, pulling on the leash held by its owner. Holding her cup of ice cream and spoon in one hand, Eden held out the other to the dog, scratching it under the chin and stroking the top of its head. The dog suddenly sprang up, planting its paws on her legs. Eden was taken by surprise but laughed when the dog made a swift and targeted attack on her ice cream cup. Just like that, it plopped to the ground and the dog was on it!

The teen owner was understandably horrified. "Oh, man. I'm… so sorry. I can buy you…"

Eden shook her head. "Don't worry about it. I'm glad he's enjoying it."

"She," the boy corrected. "Sorry…" he mumbled before gently tugging the dog away. Eden, smiling, watched them walk away.

Beck was on his feet, heading for the door to the shop. "I'll get you another one."

"No, don't."

"Sure?"

She nodded. "Sure."

It seemed like a perfect moment to get her attention, to bring her back to the event earlier in the day and the reason that they'd even had the possibility of meeting. Beck very much wanted to try to get a handle on why she'd been so emotional at the end of the service.

"How do you know Everett?" he finally asked, rotating the cone and using his tongue to consume his ice cream.

Eden watched him with a distant gaze. Then she blinked, pulled a napkin from the dispenser to wipe her hands before responding. Beck had a feeling she was deciding what and how much she was going to share.

"I used to work for Everett."

"One of his designers?"

She shook her head, becoming thoughtful now that he'd brought up the subject. "No. Everett once told me I didn't have a particularly good spatial eye. He said I was much better at details."

"And you were his…?"

"I began as his gofer."

"Really?"

"Why do you sound so surprised?"

"I assume he hired you for your organizational skills. You seem to know how to take charge and get things done."

"I didn't come in knowing that. As a matter of fact, I was pretty resistant to even meeting him. I was in my sophomore year at Howard at the time. We did not hit it off."

Beck raised his brows. "You faced off with Everett?"

She nodded. "And lived to tell."

"Why a gofer? That's pretty low on the food chain."

She chuckled to herself and quickly sobered. "I was pretty cocky. Fresh, and thought I was so smart. I think it came from having a lot a responsibility at an early age. And resenting it. I was angry. I had a chip on my shoulder, but I kept it all inside. Everett saw right through me and would have none of it. He said to me, 'I like your confidence, but your ego is making demands you can't afford.' I didn't know what he meant, but I found out fast. Of course I didn't like it but I didn't want to give up. And I think...I think I didn't want to disappoint him. I learned that Everett was willing to give a lot, to teach you and...and whip you into shape. But he expected a lot, too."

"Sounds like a really interesting beginning, for both of you."

She nodded thoughtfully. "I'm glad. I can thank Everett for that. I think I was very, very lucky to have had Everett as my... everything."

My everything.

Beck was curious and alert. What did that mean?

"Is that why you were so...emotional at the service? He meant that much to you?"

She looked away, but he knew it wasn't because Eden didn't want to answer. It was because he'd hit close to home.

"Yes," she answered simply.

It was not forced out of her, but Beck recognized that it was a personal admission. He felt oddly honored that she'd admit that to him.

"I think making me a gofer was the start of Everett breaking down my bad attitude and helping me build a better one. Then I became an intern with him when I was still in school. I eventually complained that I couldn't work for free because I had bills and responsibilities. I was taking care of my baby sister. Are you going to finish that?"

Beck looked at his half-finished cone. He was done. He looked to Eden. "Want some?"

Eden leaned in a little and he extended the cone to her. He was both surprised and thrown off guard by her unexpected audacity. She placed her fingertips on his hand to hold it steady. Beck thought she would take a taste with her lips. But Eden took a very small provocative lick on the side of the softened cream. And then another.

"Hmm. That's good."

"More?"

"No, that was fine. I hope you don't mind…"

"My pleasure," Beck said, amused.

He didn't mind at all.

Beck had lost interest in the cone and hastened to finish it, well aware in the moment that his lips were following a trail her tongue had left. It gave him an odd sensation. It seemed very personal. To clear his head, he got back to the conversation about how Eden knew Everett.

"You were saying you started as an intern. What happened then?"

"Then, I was just about to graduate from Howard and realized I didn't have a clue what I was going to do afterward. I had no career goal, no job prospect. I was a little scared about going out into the world with a degree in marketing and communications. Suddenly, I saw my future looming in front of me…"

She stopped. Beck waited for her to continue, but Eden suddenly stood up. "Are you finished, now?"

Beck wasn't sure if she was talking about his questions or the ice cream. He stood, once again following her. They were silent for almost a full block, with the White House just ahead, a formal white block illuminated around its perimeter, stark against a dark sky.

"So, how did you end up in Everett's office in the first place?"

"Everett hosted an open house for one of my classes. I had no idea what kind of business he was in. My class got there and this bald-headed guy met us. He was tall and had a booming voice, but he was kind of funny and…well…he talked like a gangster!"

Eden couldn't see his expression but Beck smiled to himself, nodding.

"He said right away that he didn't go to college, but he expected us to finish. I loved his office. Big and open, like a warehouse. When the visit was over, everyone else left but Everett said he wanted to talk to me. The first thing I said to him was, 'How come there were no Black people in your company?' He started laughing! He said I could be the first, and the first female. He was looking for an assistant to help around the office. He asked if I'd be interested. I think I said something like 'You can't afford me.' Everett laughed at me again, and it made me feel like maybe I was passing up something that could work. He said to me, 'Probably not. But if you come and intern for me, what you learn might be priceless.'"

Beck said nothing, having become vested in the story Eden was telling and not wanting to interrupt.

"It was a dare. And I accepted. Everett was right. What I learned from him was as important as my time at Howard."

Beck suddenly realized a man was approaching them from the shadows of the buildings to his left. Eden was on his right and wasn't immediately aware. Beck reacted by putting an arm out to block the man from reaching them. He was mumbling.

"Got somethin' for me? I could use the help…"

"Watch it," Beck firmly advised the man, also taking Eden's arm to hold her back. They both stopped to study the man. "Please stand back…"

The man was poorly dressed, his hair wild and overgrown, sprouting from beneath a filthy cap perched at a rakish angle on his head. A derelict but not appearing dangerous, he stopped abruptly in front of them with his hand out. It was shaking.

Eden pulled her arm from Beck's protective hold and put her hand out to prevent him from taking further action with the stranger.

"It's okay," she said in a calm but firm voice.

Beck was still very much on the alert but sensed that Eden was not only unafraid, but fully in command. She reached into her purse, rummaged for a moment, and withdrew money.

"Are you sick? Hurt? What do you need?"

"Nothin' much. Just a little help, ma'am. He gestured slowly toward the money she held. "Thank you, ma'am. I 'preciate it."

"What are you going to use this for?" Eden asked, curious but not judgmental.

"No liquor. I swear. I'm hungry. I ain't eat nothin' t'day."

Surprising himself, Beck reached into his pocket and also pulled out some money, separating a few bills and holding them out to Eden. She took the offering from him and added it to what she held. Eden was fully engaged in talking to the stranger, giving him attention…and advice. The man appeared to be listening, nodding and mumbling in return, gesturing with his hands. But he didn't appear to be a threat, and neither did he become aggressive or hostile with Eden. She gave the money to him and he thanked her. Beck touched her arm again, urging Eden away.

"Take care of yourself," Eden said to the man as she and Beck finally walked past him.

"Yes, ma'am. Thank you."

They walked half a block before Beck spoke. "Look, I'm enjoying the walk and your company, but if we're planning on walking to Baltimore, I think I should know."

She looked horrified for a second, and then embarrassed. "I'm so sorry! You must think I'm a lunatic. I live just up this way, on Logan Circle."

"That's fine. I was just wondering if we should have packed food and water for the journey…" Beck commented.

Eden burst into a laugh that sounded almost like chimes. Her eyes were bright. He was glad that she'd found his suggestion funny. Beck was finding her personality remarkably upbeat.

"Come on. I'll walk you the rest of the way home," he offered.

They continued along streets becoming more and more residential, fewer and fewer government agencies and institutions, and much more crowded with local residents. Beck knew Logan Circle, knew that young people were drawn to the neighborhood for its cafés and bistros, the restaurants and watering holes. Its quirky little shops and liveliness.

"I think it's your turn. Tell me how you know Everett."

Beck said nothing for a long moment. Of course she'd want to know. "You haven't finished telling me your story. You can't leave me hanging."

"Not much more to say. Everett and I made a deal. I interned for the rest of my sophomore and junior years…with a stipend. He hired me full time when I was a senior. We fought like cats and dogs. He had his way of doing things, and I had mine. His was better. He had no problem telling me when I was wrong or didn't know something. But then he'd take the time to talk to me, explain things. In three years I knew his business almost as well as he did. He was rough around the edges, but really smart…and really kind. A bundle of contradictions. A good man. An honest, *very* good man…" Her voice trailed off.

Eden stopped in the middle of the sidewalk, forcing pedestrians to walk around them. She looked at him squarely.

"Alright. Go."

"Go?" Beck pursed his lips, thinking fast. "I–I'm writing an article about him."

"Are you a reporter?"

"Not really. I am a writer. This is a freelance assignment. I came up with the idea, and I have a place to get it published. The magazine that I work for."

"Why?"

"Why what?"

"Why are you the one writing the article? What do you know about Everett?"

"Well, he…er…he…lived in the same neighborhood as me."

"That must have been when he was married," Eden murmured, staring at him.

Beck made a noncommittal sound.

They began walking again, into the Logan Circle route around the central plaza. "What are you going to write?" Eden asked as they peeled off from the circle on the second street and into a row of residential buildings.

"I want to write about this man who doesn't fit into the mold of traditional businessman. He was very good at working with his hands and built a company from the ground up. He made his own rules, was respected. What I like most about what I'm learning about Everett Nichols—from people like yourself—is that he always reached out to teach and help others. What did he get for that?"

"Loyalty," Eden readily filled in. "Respect. From me, sainthood."

"Okay. That's what I want to get across. That's what I want the business community to see. His was a different but maybe not unique way of doing business. He paid everything forward."

Eden had stopped in front of a building. She turned to Beck, studying him. "That was a nice way to put it."

"Thank you," Beck said, oddly pleased that it met with Eden's approval.

"This is me."

Beck looked at the building, its entrance and general architecture. "Nice. This used to be a pretty rough neighborhood."

Eden smiled as she unlocked the outer door and pushed it open. "Gentrification."

The short entrance opened onto a larger lobby area. There was no doorman or concierge, but a small public sitting area for visitors, with two club chairs and a side table in between. They came to a stop and faced one another in the tiny space.

Beck was immediately struck with how, in all their one-day time together, they'd managed to keep the conversation flowing. Not inconsequential, but fairly light and comfortable. Suddenly now the air had changed a little. There was a certain warm intimacy that had not been defined. They now stood as acquaintances, but there were still questions, a distance and the unknown between them.

Eden shrugged with uncertainty. It was as if she was suddenly uncomfortable with the silence…and feeling a need to fill it.

"I know I've already said it…"

"And you don't have to say it again. The memorial went well. You wrestled the club manager into submission and got what you contracted for."

Eden started to laugh, that open, easy musical sound that Beck was coming to identify with her. She had a quick sense of humor. She averted her gaze now, shifted, pursed her lips and moistened them.

"Thanks again," she murmured.

"You're welcome, again," Beck said. "Thank you for the tour of downtown DC…"

She grinned, shifting. "I probably talked too much."

"It was interesting and informative," Beck said with formality.

She narrowed her gaze, "I think you're making fun of me."

"Not," he said firmly, learning toward her for emphasis. "I really enjoyed spending the rest of the day with you."

It was time for him to leave, but for a moment longer they gazed at each other. He smiled a little. Eden smiled even more. She blinked, seemed to hesitate, but then finally made a decision.

Eden stepped forward and quickly put her arms around Beck, embracing him.

More than the sudden feel of her arms around him, Beck immediately registered that the way their bodies pressed together now was not at all like earlier in the day when he stepped in to comfort her. He returned the embrace, feeling his chest flex as he held her in a different way as well. He squeezed her a little bit, but didn't worry if Eden might get the wrong idea. If that was going to happen, it would have before she'd reached out to him. This was her call. And he welcomed it. Eden turned her head, and once again, Beck experienced the soft cushion of her hair against his face.

The next move seemed to be a natural follow-up to that moment. They both pulled back, their lips a hairsbreadth apart. Not touching but close enough to feel one another's exhalations.

"Thank you…for a…really great ending to the day. I–I wanted you to know…" Eden said, her voice a little bit breathless and quiet.

"Eden, believe me. It was my pleasure. I'm glad I was part of it with you…" Beck said, swiftly debating his next move. If there was one. And there might have been, except…

There was a sound at the front door as it was being unlocked. The sound of the door closing again reminded Beck and Eden where they were. Not alone. And in a public place. They stepped away from each other, their gaze still holding as someone approached and appeared in the small open lobby. A young woman dressed in a navy-blue pencil skirt and blazer with insignias on the lapels. She was wearing low-heeled functional pumps, all part of a uniform. She was pulling a roller suitcase with an additional bag strapped on top and had a tote on her shoulder. In her hand she held keys and a cap that was part of her attire. She was quite attractive with an air of worldliness, but there was something also open and carefree about her. She stopped when she saw them. Her eyes brightened in surprise and quickly moved between Beck and Eden. She stood her luggage up to free her hand.

Eden recognized the new arrival, and the two women began laughing hellos and briefly embraced around exclamations and questions and talking over each other. Beck stood watching. For the moment he was forgotten as the reunion played out in front of him. While Eden was trying to engage with the young woman, the recent arrival was busy casting glances of open curiosity at him. He acknowledged her with a nod of his head but remained silent.

"Hi." She interrupted Eden's chatter.

Eden stopped midsentence, turning her attention from the other woman to Beck. She touched the woman's arm.

"This is my sister, Holly…"

Beck raised his brows, broadening his grin. "Beck Dennison."

"Beck. Unusual name."

"Like Holly," he said.

She grinned, appreciating his observation. "Touché."

Beck turned his gaze back to Eden. She was distracted, gazing at her sister with obvious affection, maybe even pride.

"Returning from a trip?" Beck asked.

"Holly is an international flight attendant," Eden answered and then regarded her sister. "I didn't remember you were flying back home tonight."

"I wasn't coming until tomorrow. I switched with someone who wanted to stay one more day in Milan. So. Here I am."

"Oh. Okay," Eden said, as if trying to work out in her head how Holly's change of plans would now impact her own.

Beck could almost see the wheels turning in her head.

"I'm going to go, give you two time to catch up, say hello. Unpack," he said indicating Holly's luggage.

Holly punched for the elevator. "Don't leave on my account! I'm going to head upstairs." She smiled at Beck as he slowly headed to the exit. "Nice meeting you!"

"Same here," he responded with a wave. He spared one final look at Eden, who watched him walk away. Her expression was unreadable. But he wondered if she was experiencing the same kind of soft punch to the gut that he was.

As Beck reached the front door, the chatter between the two women picked up again. He realized with some annoyance that he'd neglected to get a number or email from Eden. He hesitated a moment, considering a move back to them to correct his oversight. Instead, he pulled the door open and stepped out into the cool night.

The opportunity was lost.

CHAPTER 3

Eden felt her mattress give under the weight of something...or someone...climbing onto her bed with her.

"You awake?"

"Go away," Eden groused in a slur, trying to stay in her subconscious, her dream still unfinished.

The bed moved, rolled a tiny bit as Holly settled next to her, sitting back against the headboard and grabbing an extra pillow to hug against her chest. She stretched out her long legs, crossed her ankles, and wiggled her toes, admiring her recent pedi and the gold toe rings on both feet.

"My clock is off," Holly said calmly. "I can't sleep anymore."

"Not my problem. You've been flying long enough to know how to work out the difference. Why do you always do this to me?" Eden rolled over from her stomach to her side, her back to her sister. It was hopeless. She wasn't going back to sleep. Holly was going to wait her out, in any case, twitching around on the bed, sighing, and otherwise not leaving her in peace. "I swear, you're like a spoiled house pet who needs constant attention."

"Meow," Holly imitated in a silky voice.

Eden didn't laugh even though she found her sister's response funny.

"How was the recent trip?" Eden mumbled into her pillow.

"*È stato fantastico*," Holly said smoothly with a credible accent.

"How is Massimo?"

"Out."

"Out? What does that mean?"

"*Abbiamo finito*." Holly sighed, sliding down to a comfortable reclining position next to Eden.

Eden sighed dramatically and turned over to face her sister. "Holly, seriously?"

"Okay, okay. No more answers that require translation. I'm done with Massimo. I found he has another woman. Two. He let something slip on the drive to the airport, but I'd already suspected. We argued all the way."

"Why are you upset? And how is that so different than you having some main squeeze in every country on the continent? You fly in for a day or two and then fly out. Why should some European lothario be more faithful than you are?"

"They're not serious. They're…fun. Short-term amusement."

"Well, girl, turnabout is fair play," Eden said, finally sitting up and taking a similar position next to Holly, facing her with her knees drawn up so that they could talk.

"I never understood what that meant," Holly murmured, momentarily playing with Eden's curly hair, now sleep disarrayed.

"You should have stayed in school. Lots of things you might have learned."

Holly made a face at her, rolling her eyes.

Eden watched Holly closely. She unconsciously inventoried her sister's expression, her body language and movement. Holly had never been a complicated person. She was easygoing, gregarious… although there had been a frustrating wild-child period in her teens when Eden found herself expending far too much energy keeping her sister out of mischief. Holly had a black belt in charm and knew intuitively how to use it to great effect for her own purposes. Men naturally loved her, but Holly also had more true girlfriends than she did, Eden had to admit.

In lieu of the presence of parents—a deceased mother and a father who was content to find women willing to take care of him had left them orphans—Eden had long ago accepted care of both herself and Holly. At first she had accepted that responsibility with bravado and lots of secret fears. It wasn't like there were a lot of other choices at the time. And it only became challenging when Holly was no longer a young teen, but an emerging young adult.

"Everything okay?" Eden asked Holly. It was a standard question after they hadn't seen each other in several days. A simple question on the surface, but it was Eden's way of ferreting out information to make sure Holly was okay.

"Yeah. Pretty much."

"Okay, what's going on?"

"Nothing. I'm good. Well…I did meet this guy."

Eden sighed, patient and ready to listen. "You are the world's most prolific serial dater. Who is he and how did you meet him… and why are you sounding all funny about him?"

"Because he's different."

"Holly, that's so old. You say that about every man you meet. Don't you have anything more original to say about this one?"

"Okay," Holly said quietly. She looked squarely at her sister. "I met him at a club where the crew hangs out when we stop in the UK. He and I did the whole eye-meet thing across a crowded room. And then he sent over a drink to me. And it was *my* drink!"

"So, he was paying attention."

"Yeah. And then he came over to talk to me. He was tall, and he had a close-cut beard, and his hair is red, and his eyes are hazel, and he had perfect teeth and…and he made funny things happen in my stomach when he looked at me."

"That's unusual," Eden said with raised brows. "You never said Massimo did that for you."

"Yeah, but…Massimo had other talents."

Eden couldn't help the look of curiosity that raised her eyebrows.

"Anyway, I told him I was a flight attendant. I told him I didn't know when I'd be back on another UK tour. He said that's okay. He'll wait."

Eden looked at her sister, thoughtful and dreamy and smiling to herself. Now Holly was playing with her own hair. She wore it long, with help from expensive extensions.

"What else happened?" Eden asked.

"Nothing," Holly said. "Unfortunately, there was no time for us to, you know, *really* get together. I think a reunion is going to be… something else." Holly giggled, very uncharacteristically. "When the group finally left the club, he said he'd take me back to our hotel. I thought for sure he had a detour in mind, but he really did take me back to the hotel. We walked, talking the whole time," she said in wonder.

Eden chuckled. "I guess you're not used to talking with your beaus."

Holly glanced at her, blinking. She shook her head. "No. But he had a lot of questions about me, my family. You. His name is Connor, and…he kissed me good night on my forehead!"

"Disappointed?"

"Surprised. Anxious to see him again."

"Sounds interesting. By tomorrow morning whatever he had stimulated in your stomach will have cleared up. Are you finished? Can I get some privacy now? You come home and it's all about you."

"I can't help it if my life is more interesting than yours," Holly said good-naturedly, getting even more comfortable.

Eden openly studied her sister again, her pretty tan face with its features a cross between delicate and fine, and sensual. Holly's mouth was wide, and when she smiled, it was big and bright. Her brown eyes could cast glances that fell under the label of smoldering and inviting, which somewhat explained a lot of men, like Connor, being attracted to her instantly.

"How was your thing yesterday for Everett?"

"The memorial."

Suddenly, just like that, the details of the event weren't what replayed in Eden's head, but the time with Beck Dennison afterward, starting with those last moments in the empty reading room.

Do you need a hug?

And those enticing unfinished moments in the lobby of her building, before Holly inconveniently appeared. She'd fallen asleep wondering if Beck was going to kiss her...astonished that she wanted him to. They hardly knew each other. But did that really matter? It would have changed in a heartbeat if he'd been able to follow through.

Even now, remembering, Eden experienced the tightening cords of surprise that also had her accepting Beck's comforting embrace at the memorial. And then feeling safe enough with Beck to let her emotions run free. She wasn't ever going to forget that quiet offer, or the way he so carefully and tenderly held her. Or the way she relaxed against his chest.

The ice cream and walk through Capitol Hill had been easy. They'd already established a rapport. Then, there'd been that moment in the lobby of her building when they'd stood smiling at one another, neither knowing what to say next. And then Holly had fortuitously walked in behind them. Before they could say, or do, anything else. Had she imagined that he was about to kiss her good night? Nothing really personal, but maybe more comforting.

"It went very well."

"Did you cry?"

"Yes. I cried," Eden confessed. But that was all she shared.

"I'm not going to tease you for that," Holly said quietly. "I know how much Everett meant to you. But, who in the world is Beck Dennison? He's new. He's cute! Where did he come from?"

Eden blinked, fidgeting on the bed. "He was at the service. I thought he worked with the club catering staff," she said with wry recall. "He was one of the guests."

"What does he do?"

"He said he's a writer. As a matter of fact, he's writing an article about Everett."

"A writer. Hmm. Who does he write for?"

"I don't know."

"Did he tell you what he writes?"

"No. I think he freelances. But I did ask how he knew Everett."

"And?"

"He said he met Everett when he was a kid. I mean, when Beck was a kid."

Holly nodded. "I got that part. What else?"

"There isn't any *else*." She fidgeted on the bed.

Holly sighed in frustration. "Did you find out where he lives?"

"No."

"Are you going to see him again."

Eden frowned. "I don't know."

"Eden, you're impossible! It's not like you have a string of men salivating to date you."

"Thanks for that."

"I'm serious. I thought Beck whatever had potential. How did he end up in the lobby downstairs with you? I know he didn't just follow you. He *came* with you. You *let* him!" Holly popped straight up in the bed. "*Damn!* If I hadn't shown up when I did, you might have asked him up."

Eden stopped before responding. Would she have?

Would you like something to drink? Coffee? Ice cream?

Me?

The follow-through to Beck's question suddenly hit Eden, falling into place. She laughed that it had taken her so long to figure out what he'd meant. It would have made her laugh rather than be annoyed at the implication. "No, I wouldn't have. He walked me home. We were about to say goodbye when you came in."

"Well…sorry if I spoiled everything."

Eden sat up and swung her legs from the bed. "I'm getting up. Aren't you meeting someone for brunch? You're always meeting someone for brunch…or lunch, or dinner, or drinks…"

"Maybe later," Holly admitted, also rising. "I might call April to see if she's back from overseas yet."

Automatically, she lent a hand making Eden's bed, repositioning the six pillows carefully on top of the comforter for aesthetic decoration. Eden went to her closet to stand in the open door and decide what she was going to wear for the day. Holly walked behind her, heading for the bedroom door. She stopped and leaned back in.

"Did you at least get his phone number?"

Eden turned her gaze to her sister. "No."

Holly made a face that could have been interpreted a dozen different ways. But the most obvious was, *too bad.*

———————

Beck sat slouched in his chair, his long legs stretched out beneath the table at French Roast, the neighborhood café where he often took up space in order to work. It was Sunday morning, and there'd been a steady stream of people coming in for takeout. Although there were half a dozen places for people to stay and sit to have coffee, if they chose to, French Roast was pretty much a grab-and-go establishment. Beck had figured out the routine and timing of customer traffic pretty quickly a few years earlier when the café opened in his neighborhood. Now, he was a regular. Now, *this* table by the window was *his* table.

Except, this morning he wasn't getting any work done. He stared at the laptop screen, rereading the last sentence he'd typed, trying to pick up the thread of his thoughts and the direction of his article on Everett Nichols. Mostly, he was thinking about Eden Marsh and the indelible impression she'd left him with the evening before.

Beck suddenly sighed deeply, pushed back in his chair to sit up straight, and leaned into his screen. The good news was he was happy with the opening paragraph. The bad news was he'd gotten stuck trying to describe the man that Everett was, and what he meant to so many people...to himself. But Beck wanted to keep himself out of his narrative. He wanted to be objective. And so he'd turned to the revealing backstory and information that Eden had willingly shared with him. What she knew about Everett, what she'd experienced, was the crux of his piece. It was going to be about a seemingly ordinary man who was anything but, who had made a huge difference in the lives of a wide and varied group of people.

An Uncommon Man of Influence. That was his working title. But Beck also liked *How to Make Friends and Influence People.*

He placed his fingertips on the keyboard. He thought for a moment and then began writing.

Entrepreneur Everett Nichols functioned mostly under the radar, but he was one of DC's most successful builders and, according to people in the know, a force to be reckoned with. He was a brilliant contractor and a ruthless businessman, but he also was considered to be a thoughtful man, a caring mentor, an incredible teacher, and often a pain in the neck. To many, he was a father figure whose most redeeming quality was that he cared about those who wandered into his sphere of influence. Who was he really? How did Everett Nichols come to be Everett Nichols?

Beck squared his shoulders, now on track for what would come next. Everett's backstory: his upbringing in the Lower Ninth Ward of New Orleans where he was raised, incredibly, in a Black family as an errant foster child who had been difficult to place in a permanent home.

His thoughts thus engaged, Beck didn't immediately look up from his work when someone approached his table and sat down opposite him. When he finally lifted his gaze and focused on a woman smiling at him with knowledge and possessiveness, his mental and emotional immersion in his writing was broken.

"I knew I'd find you here," the woman said, her voice filled with quiet satisfaction.

Beck was caught off guard to see Alia Sutton but didn't show it. His own gaze was open and mildly curious, and he tried to let his body relax. He ignored the carefully coiffed hair, every single strand in place and artfully draped over one shoulder and trailing down her back. He gave no hint that he noticed the way her cowl-neck cashmere sweater drooped in front to display a slender neck and flawless skin, disappearing into the hidden valley between her breasts. The dangling earrings that just brushed the top of her shoulders were also meant to draw his gaze to her. And she was in full makeup. It was subtle and looked very natural, but Beck knew the amount of time and expertise it had taken to achieve the look. He knew full well that Alia was very good at convincing people that she did nothing special to appear as beautiful as everyone believed her to be.

"I hope I'm not interrupting something important."

"I have a deadline."

"You always have a deadline."

"At least you remember that."

"I remember a lot more. I…"

"Why are you here?" Beck asked, his tone flat, not exactly welcoming.

Beck could immediately see the effort Alia was making to appear humble and contrite. The color was high on her cheeks…but he couldn't tell if it was a natural response to the awkward moment and his cool challenge, or if it was her rouge.

"I wanted to apologize."

"Really?" he asked with clear skepticism.

"Yes, really."

"It's been more than a year, Alia. It's late for apologies."

"I've been under a lot of pressure from the studio. They want to change the format of my program. They want to bring in a sidekick to play off me with more humor."

"You're not happy."

"I don't need a sidekick or some other ingenue who's the girl-friend of one of the producers," Alia said with barely concealed impatience.

Beck studied the woman opposite him. He'd once thought her one of the most beautiful women he'd ever met. That they'd ever become a couple seemed, in hindsight, implausible. A fantasy of large-scale proportion that he'd fooled himself into believing had real potential for a future. He had even played around with the idea of asking her to marry him. But for the entire time they were a couple, her attitude had made that an on-again, off-again idea.

Alia had been attentive, playing into his male ego that he had a prominent place in her life, even as she cultivated her own career. Beck now knew that he'd underestimated the power of ambition, the stranglehold of dreams, and what the lure of fame and fortune could do with the heart and soul. He hadn't seen it coming that what Alia really wanted would totally consume her, overshadowing his hold on her and their relationship. Making him take up residence in second place in her life. No. Third.

"I don't understand what that has to do with me," Beck said. But it had no effect. She wanted something. This only cemented the realization it had taken him far too long to arrive at about his former lover.

Beck stared momentarily at his screen, at Everett's name, and recalled the image of Eden Marsh as she had transformed through the afternoon, the day before, allowing him to see her displaying real emotion, uncertainty, generosity. Unguarded and genuine. In pain. He looked at Alia again and only saw a perfectly crafted actress masquerading as a loving sweetheart and partner. It had cut him to the core that her love for him had been predicated on what she believed he could do for her career.

"Look, I know you think that whatever is happening is unfair…" Beck began, trying for reason and some small measure of compassion.

"It is."

"Sorry. That's the way TV works. That's life."

She studied him for a moment. "You're still angry."

"Not anymore," Beck said honestly, with a small shrug.

"I didn't mean to hurt you, Beck."

"Maybe not consciously. There was something you wanted for yourself, a golden opportunity, that came way ahead of our relationship. Got it."

"I know it's going to take some time, but I think that we can still…"

Beck sighed, leaned forward. Alia was scared. He could see it in her posture, the lowered fluttering of her lashes, the pretty pouting of her mouth. "Look. I know you want me to get in touch with the head of the production company for your show and talk you up. I'll do it…"

She closed her eyes briefly and visibly slumped. "Beck…"

"As long as you understand that doesn't mean you'll get what you want. I don't have any power over that decision."

"What you tell them will help. I'm sure of it. And if we give ourselves some time…"

Beck stared at her, stunned that she actually believed there was any possibility of them reuniting. "That's not going to happen," he said flatly. "*You* made the decision. You were very clear. There's no going back."

Alia slowly stood before him. Whatever humility she'd arrived with was being replaced with her mind rushing forward to what her next move had to be after he made that call…and the studio called her.

"I appreciate you making that call for me," she said formally.

"Sure. Good luck." Beck's tone was unemotional. It had been hard won. He gave his attention back to his laptop, pulling up his Gmail account to write the message to the production company contact, and his best friend from college, to ask for the favor that would help free him from the past.

————————

"See you later," Holly called out from the front of the apartment.

There was no need or time for Eden to respond. She heard the door close with a quiet thump behind Holly's departure.

Eden exhaled into the silence. She took her time getting dressed and combing her hair. As she fluffed the short loopy curls, she suddenly had a vision of leaning in to Beck's chest, his chin brushing her hair. Once again it came back in full detail to Eden, her meltdown and behavior at the club the day before. She thought she'd done an admirable job of self-control, right up until the moment she thought she was all alone in the reading room and free to let loose. She cringed with embarrassment at how that had actually played out. Including the near ten minutes in Beck's arms. She couldn't get that out of her head.

On the other hand, the circumstances had certainly changed for the better after they left the club. Maybe he really thought nothing of those few minutes. Whether he knew it or not at the time, Beck had helped to restore her balance. But Eden was concerned, especially after the third degree from her sister, that she knew nothing about who Beck Dennison was. After all, anyone could say they were a writer. And it would have been easy enough to crash the open-bar event since she knew only a handful of the guests. What was he really doing at the memorial? Had he really known Everett? She'd seen him speak with Matt Sorkin. Was that just a brief social exchange?

With a sudden thought, Eden hurried to her closet and searched for the jacket she'd worn the day before. She rifled through the pockets and withdrew a business card. It was plain and unadorned on silvery gray—like his eyes—metallic card stock.

DC DIALOGUE
BECK DENNISON
ASSOCIATE EDITOR AND COLUMNIST

At the bottom of the card were a cell number and email address. Eden wasn't a social media devotee, but she knew the icons for Twitter and LinkedIn. And she knew how to do an obvious Google search. She stared at the information on the card. Grabbing her cell phone, Eden went into the living room and sat at her laptop on the dining table. It was true that anyone could be located through a search engine, and in a nanosecond Beck Dennison's name—and images—produced a long menu of information. At the top was the publication name. Eden clicked it open to find it was a well-known and popular DC publication. She typed Beck's name in the search bar, and that opened to an article by him on the National Museum of Women in the Arts website. There was no accompanying photo of him, only the byline.

But the next item in the search menu was a website. It was very straightforward and all business, but nicely organized to show the breadth of his experience and background. She got the point, and the confirmation she wanted that he was a writer. Eden input his number in her smartphone. While she waited for the line to ring, she became distracted by the signs of Holly's return home from her recent trip. Eden was exasperated at seeing clothing, accessories, duty-free bags, and various papers and receipts left all over the living room. Holly's uniform jacket draped over the back of—

"This is Beck. Can I help you?"

Eden started. For a second she'd forgotten who she'd called.

"Ah…yes! Hi. Beck Dennison?"

There was a second of silence.

"Yes. Who's calling…? *Eden?*"

Eden chuckled nervously. "Yes. Hello. I–I hope I didn't call at a bad time."

"No, not at all. Sorry if I sound surprised. I didn't expect to hear from you."

"I found your card this morning in my jacket pocket. To be honest, I wasn't sure if… Well, I wondered…you know…"

He chortled, the quiet sound rumbling from somewhere in the back of his throat. "Checking me out?"

"Right," she admitted.

"No need to sound apologetic. There are lots of scammers and sociopaths out there. I promise I'm not one of them."

The amused calm tone did a lot to reassure Eden. Still. "So you really were at the memorial yesterday to write about Everett?"

Beck laughed. "Oh, *man!* I let you cry in my arms and now you doubt me?"

Eden gnawed her lip in shame. Was he making fun of her?

"I didn't mind at all. Seriously. I could tell that Everett's passing was a blow to you. Your distress was real."

She got up from the table and sat on the sofa, curling herself into a corner, settling into the conversation. "Thank you for your understanding."

"And the ice cream?"

Now he *was* making fun. "That too."

"Despite how we met, I thought the evening was pretty nice," Beck said.

"It was. I hope I don't sound ungrateful."

"You know I'm teasing, right?"

She chuckled, again nervously. She liked the way he sounded, the way he was teasing her. Eden settled further into the sofa, digging her toes in between the cushions.

"I made one mistake after I walked you home," he started.

"What?"

"I didn't ask for your number. An oversight."

"Well, I had yours."

"With no guarantee that you'd ever use it. The burden was mine," Beck said. "And there's one more thing. Your sister's sudden appearance was untimely. Don't you agree?"

She was silent for a moment, but Eden knew where this was

headed. Her stomach tightened, and she strained to make sure she heard everything Beck said, what he was implying.

"From what?" she asked quietly.

"From…what you started. Unless…unless I was completely off base."

She sighed. "It was very *pushy* of me. It was very spontaneous. I didn't give it a lot of thought. I…"

"You don't have to explain. And I'm not complaining. I'm sorry you…we…couldn't finish. Your sister distracted me."

"Yes. She has that effect."

"I'm glad to hear from you, Eden. I do expect a payback from you," Beck said.

Eden thought she could hear playfulness in the statement. "Like what?"

"I don't like leaving anything undone, if I can help it. I think—if *I* can be pushy—you and I have unfinished business. Agree?"

"Okay."

"Do you have paper and a pen or something? I want to give you my personal cell number. You reached me on my business line."

"Okay. I'm ready." Eden scribbled the number he recited. And a second email address.

"Second, what are you doing this afternoon?"

Eden hesitated, her mind momentarily blank because she had no plans…and she sensed that Beck might.

"Well, not much. I do have some schoolwork to finish, but other than that, nothing."

"How do you feel about getting together? We could do that walk you like along the Mall, but I'd like to do something more interesting that doesn't feel like exercise."

Eden smiled. "You'll have to be more specific. What do you have in mind?"

Beck sighed. "How about we meet at Scott Circle? I'll have more details, but I promise you won't be bored."

"Careful. Don't make promises you can't keep. Anyway, you don't know much about me."

"Part of my plan, Eden, is to change that. I'm finishing an article right now. But I'll be free after about one o'clock. Will that work for you?"

"Hmmm. I think it will. I'd better let you go…"

"Eden?"

"Yes?"

"I'm glad you called to find out if I'm for real," he teased quietly.

Eden sat for a long moment after the call, feeling a giddy sense of excitement. She was pleased that Beck had set forth an idea to get together with her. And it wasn't until he'd made the suggestion, spontaneous and carefree, that she realized how much it meant that he'd taken the initiative. On the other hand, Eden hadn't really thought through what she expected when she called Beck. As he'd suggested, a part of her had wanted to be sure that he, and what he said he was, were real.

She climbed from the sofa, still engaged in a "suppose" scenario of what might happen when she and Beck got together…in just a few hours. Eden absently gathered up her sister's possessions and put them in Holly's room to deal with. And then she quickly pulled out her latest classwork and sat to diligently write and edit a field report for her adviser.

It was not a particularly sunny day, but there was no wind and it wasn't very cold, so Eden decided she would walk the quarter of a mile south from where she lived on Logan Circle to Scott Circle. It wasn't her usual reflective walk on the Mall, but it served the same purpose in allowing her to imagine being able see Beck Dennison again. Eden smiled to herself as she set out, remembering Holly's derisive attitude that she'd made no attempt to show interest in Beck. She was looking forward to proving her sister wrong.

Beck was pacing at the Circle, in a prominent place where Eden was sure to see him. A little smile played around his mouth that he was unaware of, but there was no mistaking a certain buoyed spirit that wrapped around him, and he was grateful. After the surprise call from Eden, during which Beck found himself right back in the frame of mind of enjoying her company, he was able to concentrate on his article and whip it out in short order. Then he'd spent another hour editing the 1,500-word piece twice, knowing that his reward at the end was going to be time spent with Eden again. He was pleased and relieved that he felt meeting her held a lot of promise. Or was that wishful thinking and it was much too soon for predictions?

His speculation also took into account that he'd had an unplanned opportunity to make an instant comparison between Alia and Eden. It was not his intention to go tit for tat, pro and con, and that would have been unfair to both women. But Beck had known for the better part of the last year that, while emotionally difficult, the breakup with Alia had absolutely been the right move for him and for her. That left him free to openly and willingly explore possibilities with Eden.

She wasn't anything like Alia, whose only real flaw, in his mind, was that she seemed to be incapable of putting anyone but herself first. But things change all the time. Maybe Alia would grow out of her tunnel vision and stop taking love for granted.

Beck pivoted in a new direction to pace and saw Eden at a distance. She was just far enough away that he could take his time and watch her approach…the way she walked with an erect and purposeful stride but not hurried. She wore simple black jogging pants, a bulky-knit paprika-colored sweater that complemented her smooth brown features, and a richly patterned scarf…or shawl or wrap…around her neck and shoulders. And she was smiling.

Wow, Beck thought, stunned by the bright picture Eden made as she walked right up to him. He felt suddenly at a loss for what to say first as she stood waiting.

"Good to see you again," he finally got out, his voice steady and light.

"Same here," Eden followed her response with a smile that reflected in her eyes. "I didn't keep you waiting, did I?"

No way was he going to admit he'd been walking in a small circle of anticipation for almost twenty minutes. "Not at all."

"I walked."

Beck grinned and nodded. "I get that you like to walk."

She glanced around at the sky. "I hope it's not going to rain."

"Bite your tongue, woman." He held a hand up. "I declare that the weather will cooperate and stay dry and mildly seasonal for the day."

"I didn't realize you are also a sorcerer."

"I've been known to perform feats of magic."

Beck was pleased when they both laughed, the ice broken and a comfort level established. He felt that he and Eden were pretty much picking up where they'd been interrupted and left the day before. He turned to begin walking south, and she easily fell into step beside him. She didn't ask questions, which he took as a sign of trust. He glanced down at her, aware that she was not nearly as tall as Alia, who'd started as a print model when she was just fourteen, her beauty and presence commanding the attention of an industry that had propelled her forward and upward ever since. He liked that Eden didn't mind the uncertainty of plans for the day. Beck looked thoughtfully ahead as he chose a direction for the two of them to take. It was such a pleasure, a relief to be in the company of an attractive female who could stay so totally in the moment…without expectations or a plan.

"I thought we'd sort of wander down toward Lafayette Square."

"I know Lafayette Square."

"You really should sign on to be a resident tour guide for the tourist center."

"I like DC."

"That's obvious."

"What's going on in Lafayette Square?"

"There's a Sunday farmers market. I thought we'd explore that, if that's okay?"

"I'd love that! I never get to go to any of the markets. I'm always so busy, and the neighborhood grocer is only two blocks away."

"You really need to get out more."

She sighed. "I should. I will."

"I'll see to it," Beck found himself committing to it without a second thought. Eden readily agreed with a nod.

There weren't more than ten or so vendors still set up to sell piles of fresh-from-the-farm vegetables and seasonal fruit, jams, homemade bread, and doughnuts…even wine from a small vineyard in Virginia. Beck and Eden strolled slowly past stalls and tables, commenting on the options and sharing the foods that they liked, loved, or had never heard of. And soon, separated, they were making purchases, chatting with vendors, and leaving the market with hands full of bulging bags.

"I didn't expect to get so much…" Eden lamented, trying to consolidate her bags.

"Me either," Beck admitted and then brandished a bottle of wine. "But I did score this. It's a vineyard I like a lot."

"Is it good?" Eden asked, interested.

"I'll save it and we can have it together, and you tell me."

They left the market and continued south, and began to see signs for the upcoming Cherry Blossom Festival around the circumference on the Tidal Basin.

"Have you seen the cherry blossoms in their full glory?" Eden asked.

Beck didn't want to admit he had only once, when he'd taken Alia, sure she'd be bowled over by the majestic display of the trees in full bloom. He recalled that she'd gotten tired of walking fairly quickly…and her attention span had begun to wane.

"Not recently."

"Okay. Then I'll lead an expedition when it starts in another two weeks or so."

Beck silently accepted the invitation, again surprised and happy with the ready offer.

Unfortunately, Eden's sharp observation about a change in the weather came true, and it began to drizzle with no question that rain would follow. Thinking and looking around quickly, Beck spotted a noodle and sushi café a block and a half from the square. They rushed in, laughing at their attempt to dodge raindrops just as it became serious. Waiting to be seated, they shook off rain, removed damp articles of outer clothing, and fussed with their slightly wet hair.

Once they were seated, their conversation was filled with animated banter and laughs. They both decided that this wasn't a real meal, but a sort of late-afternoon snack. Beck was getting together with colleagues from work that night, and Eden admitted that her sister would be expecting them to have dinner together. Holly was only home for another two days before flying out again on her next tour.

Beck didn't mind when Eden began to talk about her sister, and he was taken with both the obvious love and exasperation with which Eden relayed their history. He only mentioned that his mother lived in the suburbs, was twice widowed, and no, he'd never been married…nor had kids.

Beck called for a cab rather than deal with the logistics of the Metro to get them home. He was aware that their very congenial afternoon was coming to an end. Once they were in the cab, he could feel his elation with the day and time spent with Eden dissipating…like he was coming back down to earth.

He asked the cab driver to wait as he and Eden dashed to the entrance of her building in the continuing light rain. They were a little breathless and faced each other with a different kind of curiosity and expectation. Beck didn't wait for a signal from her but leaned in to kiss her not on the lips but just off to the side at the corner of her mouth. He hoped that was a signal of his interest without being too intimate but demonstrating how he felt about the afternoon with her.

"I don't suppose there's any chance of seeing you again soon? For dinner."

Eden pursed her mouth and reluctantly shook her head. "I can't tomorrow. That's probably too soon anyway…"

"I wouldn't say so. I have an important meeting tomorrow, but why don't I call you? We'll check our calendars and dance cards"—he smiled broadly— "and see when there's an opening."

"Sounds like a…a date," she said quietly.

"It is," Beck said, squeezing her arm before turning away to jog back to the waiting cab.

CHAPTER 4

"Good morning. I'm Eden Marsh. I'm here to see Katherine Perkins."

Within seconds, Eden was buzzed through to an inner lobby where someone was already waiting to escort her to an office. She looked around as they walked a silent corridor, getting a glimpse inside the working offices of attorneys, associates, and other staff. As a law student about to graduate, she'd visited a slew of law offices in the last year and found it actually demoralizing how much they all looked alike.

"This way," the escort said, grabbing her attention.

Eden was ushered into the proverbial corner office. One wall was floor-to-ceiling windows overlooking a commercial sector of DC, this morning shrouded by a low ceiling of clouds and slow but steady rain.

Eden had not given a lot of thought to being asked to the law offices of Hartz Perkins and Dodd, the firm that had represented Everett Nichols and his developing business enterprises almost from its start.

Eden had never actually been to the law offices before. There'd never been a reason. Even now, Eden believed Katherine Perkins simply wanted a report on the memorial that she herself couldn't attend and probably needing to see the contract and accounting of the costs that the law firm would be picking up. Eden had welcomed the invitation to the office, hoping it would also give her a chance to ask what was going to happen with Steel Work, Everett's business.

As she entered and was greeted by the one female partner, Eden was surprised to see Matt Sorkin rise from a chair to greet her as well.

"Hi, Eden," Katherine said. "I believe this is one of the rare times we've actually seen one another. Thanks for coming in this morning. Have a seat. You know Matt."

"Yes." Eden smiled, hiding her confusion at finding Matt present. He nodded as she sat down.

She was suddenly not only puzzled but concerned about being called into the law offices. Eden only knew Matt as the CEO of a marketing firm and Everett's best friend. She was so busy trying to understand what this meeting was really about and why she needed to be here that Eden missed the light chatter between Katherine and Matt.

"We're just waiting for one more… Oh, here he is."

Elizabeth and Matt had turned their attention to the door, both smiling a greeting to the newest arrival.

"Am I late?"

Eden started at the voice. Her midriff tightened at the now familiar, unmistakable deep cadence. She craned her head over her shoulder as Beck Dennison entered the room. Her gaze met his instantly, and there was an infinitesimal spark of recognition before he greeted Matt with a handshake and exchanged polite hellos with the attorney. Eden hoped she gave no indication of being thrown by Beck's appearance. She was now acutely aware of him.

What is he doing here?

What's going on?

"I'm sorry I couldn't make the memorial last weekend. How did it go?" Katherine asked.

Eden blinked, her stomach somersaulting as she realized all eyes were on her. She was distracted.

Too many surprises.

Matt saved her.

"First, I want to say that Eden did a great job," he said. "Everything went perfectly, and her testimony was simple but heartfelt. And there were moments of humor. I loved the one about red meat." Matt chuckled.

Eden and Beck could not muster even a grin, but Matt didn't seem to notice.

"Okay, I won't ask," Katherine said, wisely not pursuing a moment from an occasion she had no part in.

Eden fixed a smile to her mouth. "Thank you, Matt. I think."

"It was well done," Beck confirmed.

Eden covertly gazed at him, surprised by his added support. But he nonetheless looked as questioning as she felt. And uncomfortable. They exchanged quick glances that expressed their confusion. She was also acutely aware that whatever was going on in that moment had somehow diminished the rapport she and Beck had established between themselves just the day before.

"Have you two met?" Katherine asked, addressing Eden and Beck.

"At the service," Eden said.

"We introduced ourselves. Eden was in charge and busy, so we didn't really have a chance to talk," Beck added.

Eden was relieved that Beck made no mention of how their knowledge of each other had grown rather quickly or their post-memorial adventures.

"And, of course, Matt and Beck know one another," Katherine added as if everyone would know that.

Eden didn't. She was beginning to feel a slow burn waft its way through her chest and up her throat, bringing with it suspicion. And disappointment.

"I know everyone is busy, and not to rush through this proceeding, but I have another meeting after this. Let's get started," Katherine said formally, now in attorney mode.

Then, in her professional guise, she briefly outlined her firm's commitment and responsibilities to Everett Nichols, his business Steel Work, and his estate. She recited Everett's holdings. Eden was stunned at the size of the enterprise he had built almost single-handedly. She was amazed he had remained a modest if forthright man, and had not been damaged or made cynical by the cutthroat business of contracting and working in and around the nation's capital.

She could see that Beck was also paying very close attention to what was being said. But his brow was deeply furrowed, and she could see the tensing of his jaw muscles.

"I can say this now. Everett knew he had a heart condition some time ago and kept it to himself. That was his choice. He discreetly managed to have treatment and even surgery, and only a handful of people knew. I will say he was great at keeping a secret. He didn't want to be coddled. He didn't want a lot of attention. As his lawyers, we were able to help Everett understand the wisdom of assigning an executor and power of attorney for his estate. Enter Matt Sorkin."

Matt merely pursed his lips and nodded in acknowledgment.

"And, of course, Everett did have a will."

Without thinking about it, Eden shifted her gaze yet again to Beck. And he turned his head to regard her in the same way. More than surprise, Eden was sure she could detect some level of anxiety. And sadness. It puzzled her, yet, in a way, she understood. All of this was a reminder of what had been lost with Everett's passing. But what significance could his holdings possibly have to her and Beck?

"Formally, it's the executor's responsibility to carry out Everett's wishes through his will. He was very clear about what he wanted to happen, and to whom. To that end the firm did advise Everett that at his passing his will would go through probate, and any bequest could take as long as a year for distribution. Everett, therefore, opted to form a trust from which he could direct gifts to specific people immediately. That would be you, Beck and Eden."

Eden was still, alert. She wasn't sure she had heard right. She wasn't sure she understood. Her mind ran through a number of insignificant things she had grown attached to in Everett's office and showroom, thinking maybe Everett had left her some of those items she'd always coveted. A detailed model of a private beach house he'd built for a client. Books on places he'd wanted to visit, but never had. Neither had she. They both had joked frequently about escaping to Tuscany, he to buy and run a vineyard. She to learn Italian. There was also a wonderful photo of Everett as a young fit-and-muscled man on his first construction job. It had paved the way for him to go independent and start his own small company. And Eden would have loved to have his first company hard hat. He had almost a dozen from the various companies that had hired him over three decades.

"And it makes sense that he chose you two in particular."

"Everett and I discussed this, and I agreed. There were few others that he had gotten as close to, who held such personal meaning to him," Matt added, glancing from one to the other. "That's quite a testimony from him."

Eden had missed some of what had been said. She wondered if it would seem strange or inappropriate to ask to have one of Everett's hard hats.

Katherine looked from her to Beck. She frowned at their mutual silence, at the blank expressions. She smiled and shook her head.

"Well, it's clear you both have no idea what's going on, so let me put it succinctly. You have inherited significant gifts from Everett's assets."

Beck leaned forward as if to make sure he was going to be able to hear and understand everything. "What do you mean by 'significant'?"

"I mean *a lot. Most* of them."

Matt placed a hand on Beck's shoulder, grinning like a Cheshire cat. But he glanced past Beck to Eden.

"By the terms of the will, Eden, you are *bequeathed*... I love that word... Everett left you $5 million. The sole stipulation is that you finish your JD and are employed using your...what Everett called 'considerable talents.'"

$5 million?

The number was large. Very large. Not chump change.

WHAT?

Eden realized that her heart was pounding. She looked to Matt, who continued to grin as if he'd just given her the greatest news of her life. She looked to Katherine, who was rifling through a binder of official-looking legal forms. She turned her gaze to Beck and saw he was stunned, sitting silent and still. Eden blinked at what she perceived as disbelief, but also something else...maybe disapproval?

A chill rolled through her, and she averted her gaze and sat straight in her chair. She was caught off guard by Beck's reactions, and Eden had a terrible, shattering suspicion of what he was thinking.

"There's a mistake. There has to be. Everett wouldn't leave me that much money. Why in the world would he?" Eden nearly stammered.

Katherine smiled kindly. "I understand. I've seen some remarkable responses from people who learn whether they're in or out of someone's will. Especially if it's family."

Eden shook her head. "I'm not family."

"You were pretty close." Matt said to her. "I think you underestimate Everett's regard for you. He was really glad when you stayed in touch after you left the company to start law school. He was glad when you called just to see how he was doing."

Listening to Matt try to explain made Eden even more uncomfortable, and more aware of Beck's posture.

"Congratulations," Beck said, sparing Eden a brief glance. "Your future is set."

Eden knew his comment wasn't sincere. His voice was hard. Aloof. He wasn't congratulating her at all. Her spirits sank.

"My future was set before this announcement. I know what my goal is, and I don't need $5 million to get there. That…that's a…a crazy amount of money."

She could tell that Matt and Katherine were taken aback by her comment, and Eden quickly adjusted. "I mean…I don't want to sound ungrateful but…I–I honestly don't think I can accept the money."

Katherine nodded and studied Eden closely. "Everett said that's exactly how you'd feel. You're the first person *ever* in all my years of practice who felt undeserving of a gift."

"I think I should tell you that…" Eden began, girding herself for even more censure from Beck. "He paid the tuition for my degree. All of it. Up front." She didn't bother adding that she'd fought Everett tooth and nail about the money.

"Yeah, we know about that, Eden. On the other hand, it was Everett's idea that you go to law school. I remember," Matt argued.

Beck settled back in his chair, and this time when he looked at her, Eden saw something else. And she instinctively responded. His gaze was less judgmental, more curious. She was suddenly completely aware of the sway of his thoughts, and she didn't like it. Eden was sure that Beck was making assumptions about the nature of the relationship between her and Everett. She was infuriated by his shortsightedness. It was so contradictory to what she'd already come to know about him...or so she thought. How could she have been so wrong?

"He made me mad, trying to tell me what to do. He said law school was perfect for me."

"Was he wrong?" Katherine asked, concern evident in her question.

Eden sighed. She shook her head. "No. I realized over the course of a year that I could get a lot out of law school. By then I knew what I was interested in. I wanted to help people. I wanted to be like Everett, in a way. He was so good at paying it forward. I have been on the receiving side of that. I did pay for the first semester of school by myself," she inserted defensively. "Then...he gave that back to me. Told me to use it to get a car to get back and forth to campus. I never did," Eden insisted as if that would make a difference.

"Which campus?" Beck asked.

"Georgetown. I had already filled out the applications for a student loan for the next semester. Everett went right to admissions and wrote a check."

Matt burst into loud laughter. "Sounds like something Everett would do."

Beck was sitting with his hands clasped and his index fingers tented under his lip.

"Third year?" he asked.

Eden felt very annoying relief that Beck was finally addressing her, and he was listening. And he remembered that she'd already told him that. "Last semester. I graduate in May."

"That's wonderful, Eden. Everett would be so proud," Katherine said. "Have you placed in a job yet for when you graduate?"

Eden shook her head. "Not yet. A lot of interviews. But I'm being as picky as the recruiters."

"Good for you. Why don't you submit one of your packets to my office? Send it directly to me. That is, if you think you might be interested in our firm."

Eden blinked at the totally unexpected invitation. "Thank you. I'll do that."

"Do you have a specialty? Probably not criminal law," Beck speculated to the amusement of Katherine and Matt.

Eden swallowed. His comment felt like an attack.

"No. I don't have the stomach for criminal law. I don't like to argue…"

Matt chuckled again. "Everett would disagree with you."

"Probably. If I think I'm right, I can be stubborn. I know that. But I'm looking at either family law…or civil rights." She shot Beck a telling look.

"Sounds like you'd also be very good at ethics." Katherine looked pointedly at Beck. "That leaves you."

It was only in that moment that Eden, observing Beck now that she was off the hook, could see he was a bundle of nerve ends. He had appeared very relaxed and attentive seated next to her. But perhaps she was the only one who noticed he continually shifted in his chair as if trying to find a more comfortable position for his body, his long legs.

"I'm afraid to even guess," he said with an attempt at humor.

And actually, Katherine and Matt both became more somber, more serious. Even Eden's stomach tightened with anticipation.

"Beck," Katherine began, almost as an announcement. "Matt and I, of course, know your history. Everett was crushed by the failure of his marriage to your mother…"

Eden's head shot around, her eyes wide, her mouth opened in a small O of shock.

"And although he never legally adopted you—"

"I don't think he considered the need." Matt interrupted.

"He's always considered you his son. He used to talk about you with great pride and concern. He cared about your future. And then…things happened."

Eden listened intently. She only knew that Everett had been married, but didn't know to who, or that there was a son. A stepson. She stared at Beck's profile as his history was revealed. If he didn't want it brought out before a stranger…her…he didn't and couldn't now object.

Katherine was right. Everett had been very good at keeping secrets.

Despite a brick of indignation that felt lodged in her chest, Eden felt for Beck's personal history. How must he be feeling right now as it was all laid bare?

"It was never Everett's intent that anyone but you, Beck, inherit his business holdings," Katherine stated. "He knew you had no knowledge of his company or clients, but he absolutely trusted that you would not only do the right thing, but consider every possible angle and make smart decisions. Congratulations on becoming the new owner of Steel Work Enterprises, LLC, and all its divisions. The buildings, the clients, the equipment, and the workers…"

"Everything and then some… You get the picture," Matt said, checking to see if Beck fully understood the enormity of the challenge.

"I can't replace him," Beck argued.

Eden caught the poignant truth in what he said about the responsibility that had just been dropped into his lap. But unlike her response to Everett's gift, Beck never suggested turning down Everett's wishes.

"Of course not," Katherine said. "That was not the plan. Even without his heart troubles, Everett was aging and he recognized that. Contracting is a tough business. Very physical and hard. He also knew that if Steel Work, his legacy, was to survive, it would need new ideas, upgrades in the technology, modernization all across the board. Fresh leadership."

The conversation from then on was about the business and how to introduce Beck to the company at large. Fortunately, the attorney and Matt didn't attempt the impossible. That was to indoctrinate Beck in under an hour. The meeting drew to a close.

"Before I let you both go, I have something for you." Katherine opened her official folder again and withdrew two legal envelopes. She handed one to Eden and the other to Beck.

"Should I…open it now?" Eden asked softly.

"If you want." Katherine nodded.

Beck was already peeling open the flap on his envelope and staring into the envelope without removing the contents. Then, he carefully closed the envelope and placed it into his mailbag.

Eden watched his actions, hoping for a clue as to what the envelope held. But Beck was stoic, giving nothing away. He continued to sit, contemplative, as Katherine and Matt continued to chat. Beck glanced at her, waiting, and Eden knew she was expected to do the same as he had. She was less careful, ripping off the opening and half withdrawing the single page inside. It was a bank check in the full amount of $5 million. She held her breath and kept reading the amount to herself, over and over again. She counted the zeros in case she'd made a mistake.

It's real!

At the end Katherine stood up, signaling that she was done and the meeting was over.

There was another round of congratulations for her and Matt. For her part, Eden was feeling more than a little dazed and numb. There was more coursing through her, but she did her best not to let any of her other reactions show to the others. She couldn't account for Beck's feelings as they left the office. He'd been pretty silent through much of the proceedings, keeping his emotions locked away, at least to Katherine and Matt. Eden hadn't missed any of it.

Katherine Perkins personally escorted them back to reception and the exit. A final remark from Matt to Beck suggested that they talk again, soon. Once in the outer corridor with the bank of elevators, Eden suddenly felt the oppressiveness of the silence between her and Beck. There was nothing she wanted to say to him.

They didn't speak and Eden had to admit it felt odd, especially after the friendly, teasing banter between them just the day before in what had been, in her mind, a wonderful afternoon and the early promise of something much more to come. In any case, there was no time for even light conversation as the elevator going down arrived almost immediately. It was filled with building occupants heading out to lunch, chatty and public with their conversation and laughter. Eden found herself squeezed somewhere in the middle, and Beck had maneuvered to the back. She was aware of him, as if he was staring at the back of her head that was overflowing with TMI. Eden felt almost claustrophobic with a desperate need for fresh air.

The elevator spewed out everyone on the main floor, and when Eden got out, she headed right for the building exit, her stride brisk and stiff. It was still raining so she dug her collapsible umbrella from her tote.

"Eden, wait up."

Beck's deep voice carried. She didn't acknowledge him and kept walking.

"*Eden…*"

She waited her turn at the revolving door, advancing and step-ping into the moving space. Someone stepped in behind her at the very last moment, forcing Eden to shorten her gait so the person behind her wouldn't step on her heels, or she wouldn't trip against the glass paneling.

"Excuse me!" she said over her shoulder with harsh indignation.

And when the space opened so that she could step out onto the street, the person behind her used a strong hand to hold her in place as the revolving door brought them right back to the lobby. She was gently pushed out, and she whirled around to face Beck.

"What do you think you're doing?"

"You heard me calling you," he said, annoyed.

"I have nothing to say to you." Eden glared at him.

His expression was not only frosty but the silver-gray of his eyes shone like steel. His mouth was firm and stern and a sexy pout as he glared right back. Eden wondered if Beck was doing that thing with his mouth deliberately to distract her.

"Do you want to have at it right here and cause a scene, or should we step aside and you tell me what is going on with you?"

His voice was very low, a growl that reached only Eden in that moment, although the two of them facing off near the exit did draw several curious stares from people walking past or around them. As if even strangers could detect the thick tension between them. Eden took up a silent and obstinate stance, fearlessly staring Beck down.

His brows wrinkled into a fierce frown. "Okay. What is it?"

"Don't take that tone with me," she growled back.

Beck was thrown by the storm clouds gathered in Eden's large and expressive dark eyes. She was in his face, her mouth pursed uncompromisingly as if she was preparing to slug him soundly. She was mad; he could see that. But what he saw more was the way Eden was holding in, behind her lips, what she wouldn't speak. He changed tactics. He had the distinct feeling that if he moved, got out of her way and let her storm off, he might never see her again. Beck was prepared to bear the consequences right then and there for whatever had gotten Eden riled up. He also suspected he was the basis for her chilly hostility. Of course she had read into his cold demeanor in Katherine Perkins's office. At the moment it wouldn't work to try to intimidate Eden. She wasn't afraid of him. Beck allowed his posture to change, becoming merely curious rather than threatening.

"Talk to me," he coaxed quietly.

He could see her continuing to fume. Her nostrils flared and her lashes fluttered briefly as she sought the words to explain.

"I know what you were thinking upstairs."

He remained quiet and didn't even move.

"Yeah, $5 million is ridiculous. It doesn't sound like a gift that any employer would leave an employee. How can I be worth *that* much, unless…" She stopped.

He got it. His stomach roiled because Eden had found her way to the truth.

As the lawyer laid out the details of Eden's gift, Beck's immediate reaction had been disbelief and suspicion. He hadn't acted quick enough to hide it, and it had stayed with him through the meeting upstairs.

Except there had been those moments together behind the portrait of Everett after the memorial service when he was glad he could comfort Eden as she cried in his arms. So, which was it? She was everything she appeared to be in that first encounter, or she was equally as good as Everett at keeping secrets? At the moment her dark eyes seemed almost black with emotion. Gone was that bright sparkle that he had identified as Eden's open spirit. Her anger as she stared at him was enough to tell Beck that maybe he should have believed his first instincts about her.

"Unless what?" He coaxed her to continue.

She glared again. "I'm not in the mood, Beck. You know exactly what I'm talking about, because I know exactly what you were thinking. That there must have been something going on between me and Everett." Her voice cracked. "You wondering…am I worth it?"

Beck watched Eden's struggle. He leaned in just a little toward her. She didn't flinch. Her gaze boldly met his.

"Don't try to read my mind. You don't know what I was thinking," he said, the only defense he had.

"I'm not wrong," she spewed at him. "You probably were asking yourself that since we first met."

"Are we having our first fight?" Beck challenged.

She gasped, blinking at his temerity to treat her lightly. "We're not fighting. I'm telling you what I believe."

"So, if I flip your accusation and say I could tell you were shocked and probably unhappy to learn that Everett left all of his business to me, would I be wrong? If I tell you I didn't expect to have my personal history recited in front of someone I'd only recently met, would you believe that I might be feeling the same as you do now? Annoyed. Embarrassed. Scared."

Eden gnawed the inside of her mouth, considering his point of view. The inner end of her brows rose, and Beck saw a touch of doubt and sympathy. It was a 180-degree turn from what she had showed him just minutes ago.

"Eden, we both got blindsided. I had no idea coming in this morning that I was going to walk out with Everett's assets, and that's a real big problem for me. Far bigger than you getting a lot of money to do with as you please."

"I'm not sure I should take the money. I said so."

Beck chortled deep in his chest. "Go on the mother of all shopping sprees. I thought it was in a woman's DNA to spend money."

He could see her getting riled again. She made a sudden move to skirt around him toward the exit. Beck grabbed her arms and forced her to face him again. "Eden… You're really ticked off at me. It's stupid and…and arrogant for me to joke about it."

"You're trying to pretend making a horrible assumption about me is no big deal. We don't know each other well enough for that."

Beck felt helpless. Now he understood that they had lost ground. *He'd* lost ground with her. Whatever knowledge they were beginning to build about each other was evaporating before his eyes.

"You need to take how I'm feeling very seriously. If you could so easily, so quickly believe the worst about me, I don't think we have anything more to say to each other, Beck. I don't think I can trust you."

Beck released Eden's arms but braced for her to try to leave again. She didn't.

"You know what I think? We're both in shock. Obviously, neither of us expected to have the lawyer deliver the news we heard. Neither of us expected that Everett would do something so wild as to leave his net worth to the two of us. You and I should *not* be trying to make any decisions right now. Or to second-guess his intentions, really. It can't be as simple as what the lawyer and Matt said. I don't have a clue what I'm going to do with Steel Work, and I don't have to decide this minute. But...I think we need to talk. We both need to calm down and take a deep breath and clear the air. And"—he sighed deeply, staring down at the floor for a thoughtful moment— "I owe you an apology."

She just stared at him, no hint of forgiveness in her eyes. She was still too angry to cry, but her eyes shimmered with rage.

"I'll understand if you want to haul off and let me have it."

Eden stood her ground for another few moments. Then she averted her gaze and shook her head.

"Can we go find some place to sit and talk?" he pleaded quietly.

Eden nodded her consent, still reluctant.

"Good." Beck sighed. He glanced around to peek out the door and turned back to her. "It's still raining. Let's see if we can find someplace nearby. Is that okay?"

"I don't want to eat anything," Eden confessed.

"I don't either. Maybe something hot to drink. You're trembling. Your hands are cold."

He didn't wait for an answer but led Eden to the exit. She prepared to pop open her umbrella as they pushed one at a time through the revolving door out to chilly air and rain. Beck didn't try to share, and Eden didn't offer. He didn't mind getting a little wet. They were in a commercial area with tons of businesses so there was a large selection of restaurants and cafés. They quickly found a small old-fashioned mom-and-pop place and seated themselves inside, crunched into a corner for privacy.

"Whattaya have, hon?" a woman called out from behind a counter as they settled into their seats.

Beck glanced at Eden, but he could see she was still processing not only the lobby one-on-one, but also her own feelings, and she remained silent and thoughtful.

"You don't drink coffee. How about hot chocolate?" Beck said. Eden brought her attention to him, and he could see a subtle shift in her eyes. But he wouldn't call it forgiveness.

"Fine," she answered quietly.

"One hot chocolate, one coffee. Thanks," Beck called back to the woman behind the counter.

Beck looked at Eden closely. She had withdrawn into herself, thoughtful and quiet. He desperately wanted to know what she was thinking but decided against asking outright. The silence settled in between them, and Beck knew that he had to wait it out. He could at least tell that Eden was processing all that was running through her head: what she was feeling, all that had been said. But the fact that she wasn't ranting and raving told him so much more about her.

They both barely noticed when the drinks were served and, wisely sensing the strain between them, the waitress glanced at them, didn't ask if they wanted anything else, and returned to her counter.

He watched as Eden took a careful sip of the steaming cocoa and sat with her hands wrapped around the mug. Beck could see that she'd calmed down considerably. It was apparent that she was not the kind of woman who held a grudge or held out. Otherwise she never would have agreed to accompany him. Beck held on to that, hoping to get beyond his foot-in-mouth moment.

"Look," he began, his voice very low and confessional as he frowned into his coffee. "Full disclosure. Everett also paid to put me through college. No different than what he's doing for you and law school."

"There is a difference," Eden said, her tone no longer laced with anger and indignation. "You are his son."

"Stepson."

"I don't believe for a moment he ever saw you as anything but his son. And I bet he treated you that way."

Beck looked at her, assessing her remarks and her insights. He nodded. "Yes, he did."

"Everett was one of the few people I've ever met who committed forever when he committed to something."

He kept his gaze on her. "I can't tell you how sorry I am that I was so wrong. The thing is, I knew better. I should have gone with my first instincts."

"Exactly," she said quietly, arching a brow but still managing to look at him with disappointment.

Just what he was hoping to avoid. Eden drank the cocoa. Slowly and unconsciously, she licked her upper lip to catch the foam. Beck watched, smiling to himself, taken with the action. He took in a deep breath and exhaled in defeat. He braced his elbows on the table, cupped his hands together, and rubbed his chin back and forth over a knuckle.

"This is not my finest hour," he said, chuckling nervously. "You're right about what I was thinking in the attorney's office, Eden. I didn't even give myself time to consider I could be completely wrong. I don't even have a good excuse. It was purely a guy thing, I guess. A total knee-jerk reaction."

Eden listened. Her expression never changed. She gave no quarter. The ball was still in his court.

"What did *you* feel for Everett? In your heart?"

The question came out of nowhere. Beck let his gaze narrow as he gazed at Eden. He knew exactly where she was headed.

"I loved him. My birth father was killed when I was three. Everett is the only father I've ever known. I loved him," he repeated for emphasis.

Eden nodded in understanding. Her trembling of nerves had stopped. "So did I. He was my mentor and teacher, my boss, my friend…my father figure." She stared pointedly at him. "There was never anything else."

Beck clenched his jaw tightly. "I believe you."

"I don't *need* you to believe me. I should have gotten the benefit of your doubt. What you believed is your problem." Eden finished her cocoa and began to gather her things. She hesitated on the edge of her seat and sat back again. "What was in your envelope?"

"A check for $100 million. There was a Post-it attached, *Pocket change for now. Full accounting to come.*"

Eden nodded. She didn't quite meet his gaze, appearing distracted and thoughtful. "I got a bank check, too. $5 million. No Post-it note.

"How do you feel about Everett leaving his business to you?"

Beck sighed deeply and furrowed his brow again. He shook his head. He swept both hands over his damp hair, and it settled into dark shiny waves. "I don't know. On one hand, I think it's probably an honor that he's trusting me. On the other hand, I don't know much about his business. I guess I'm hoping the attorney and Matt will give me the short version of how Steel Work operates."

His cell phone vibrated and he quickly stood up to step away and answer, glancing at Eden. "Give me a minute?" She nodded.

"What's up?" Beck asked. It was Alia. He glanced at Eden who seemed absorbed in looking for something in her tote. He turned his back.

"I'm in an important meeting. What is it?"

Beck listened as his former girlfriend, almost fiancée, once again tried to strong-arm him into helping her. Her audacity amazed Beck. The woman worked hard. If Alia one day found herself with an Emmy nomination for outstanding performance by an actress in a daytime series, she would have earned it.

"Look, I've done all I can. I've spoken to my connection. I had no part in your career building, and frankly, I think we're even… Yeah, well that's all I can do right now… I have to go. Good luck."

Beck took a moment to compose himself before returning to the table. Eden glanced at him, and he took a few seconds to absorb the sudden impact her presence, the bright questioning in her eyes, had on him. It was not lost on him that whatever fury Eden had brought with her into the little café, she was not going to continue to beat him over the head with it. There was no question that she'd made her point. She was right. And he was humbled. She was so unbelievably natural, and the realization only made him all the more ashamed. Her expression again showed she was giving the moment, her attention, to him.

"Sorry," Beck said, returning to stand behind his chair.

"I have to go." Eden abruptly stood.

Beck went to the counter to pay the bill.

"Where are you off to?" he asked her.

Eden didn't appear to want to answer, which Beck found strange.

"I have an errand to run. I'm going in the direction of the Metro."

"I'll walk you that far, and then I'm going to my office. It's close by."

They stepped back into the rainy afternoon. When Eden popped open her umbrella this time, Beck took it from her and held it to shield them both. He lifted his elbow, and after a moment of indecision, Eden took hold of his arm.

They walked without conversation at first. Beck knew the tension that had stood as a brick wall between them leaving the lawyer's office was still in place. Every step deepened his regret that he hadn't used the best judgment with Eden.

They stopped at the Metro entrance and faced each other. "Thanks for giving me a chance to redeem myself."

Eden merely nodded. Beck decided honesty was the best policy with her. He was quickly learning that anything else was sure to get him in trouble. She was quick and sharp. And she couldn't be played.

"I'm hoping I'll be given a second chance, maybe. Interested?" he asked, watching her closely.

Eden took her umbrella back, gazing at him beneath the rim. "Maybe." She turned to walk away.

Beck watched her, not satisfied with her response.

"Eden?" She slowed and turned to him. "Are we good?" he asked quietly.

"We'll see," she answered, again turning away.

Beck watched Eden disappear beneath a moving canopy of colorful umbrellas.

I think I just blew it, he thought.

And it mattered.

CHAPTER 5

Eden gnawed her lip and frowned over Jamal Harrison's account of how he lost the scholarship awarded him upon graduating from high school the previous year. He almost didn't even make graduation except for the scene his grandmother created in the principal's office a few days before. Eden was recording Jamal's deposition, but she was making notes as to how she would present a legal a case for him, a very righteous one in her opinion and from her legal viewpoint. She was going to make sure his scholarship was restored to him.

"Jamal, you say you weren't in school the day of the senior finals?"

"No. I didn't have to be there. My teacher told me so…"

"My grandson had straight A's for the whole three years," Grandmother Harrison bit out in huffy indignation, drawing back her shoulders and breathing deeply into her lungs. Grandmother Harrison, her head wagging, her rheumy eyes flashing, and her mouth poised to curse you out if you dared to challenge her was going to fight for her grandson. Woe be it to him or her who got in Grandmother's way.

"I have that in my notes, thank you," Eden said with a perfect professional demeanor, turning to the true subject of her query. "Jamal, do you happen to know the students involved in the cheating that day?"

The skinny teen slid his spine further down in his chair. "Two of them, I think."

"Let me have their names." Eden saw his reluctance.

Even at the risk of possible loss to himself, she could see him about to skirt the truth to protect his friends, a peculiar teen code of honor that was fairly pointless at a time like this. His future was at stake. It was an infuriating code of the streets, and this was not the first time Eden had to be brutally honest about a client's chances of winning their case if they couldn't be honest with their attorney. She sighed, briefly clicked off the recorder, and looked sternly at the teen.

"Jamal, I understand they're your buds and you don't want to do them dirt. But if I can't get to the truth, I can't defend you, and you won't stand a chance of getting your scholarship back and going to college. I'm on your side, like your grandmother. Your friends can't help you here."

"I know," he mumbled, staring unhappily at the floor.

"Don't let them throw you under the bus."

Mildred Harrison grunted, agreeing with Eden. "I'm tellin' you," she lamented with a shake of her head. "Some of these kids don't have the sense they were born with."

"It's obvious from your school records you're a smart kid," Eden continued. "Don't give it up now. If you really want to become a software developer, I think you know you need the math and computer science first. That means college, okay? You can do this."

Jamal nodded.

"Okay. So, what are the names?" Eden clicked the recorder back on and Jamal responded.

When the interview was over, she was confident about where the problem really lay. With inexperienced administrators who'd lost control of a situation and were trying to strong-arm a young man into giving up information they couldn't get on their own. Eden was outraged, and she promised—something lawyers were *never* supposed to do—that Jamal would not lose his chance at college.

When the boy and his grandmother left her cubicle of an office, Eden sat quiet, her elbows on her desk and her forehead braced into her hands. She was always aware of the terrible disparities in the life of a boy like Jamal, raised by a grandmother because his mother couldn't parent, and he had no knowledge of his father.

And it was always brought home to Eden that her own life might not have been so different but for her fierce responsibility to a younger sister and the fortuitous mentorship of Everett Nichols. She couldn't let Jamal down. She wasn't going to fail.

Somehow, in a weird, not very clear way, the day cycled back to Beck Dennison. Like a divining rod, Eden's mind drifted back to him, the meeting in the lawyer's office, and his admitting to his less-than-charitable thoughts about the money Everett had left her. She had been so mad. And so saddened. Almost from the first time they met, Eden had quickly put Beck into the category of *possibility,* a space empty of any of the male gender since her breakup with a beau at the end of her first year of law school. Everything from Beck stepping forward to help her at the Guild Society to asking for a date seemed to have been stamped with promise. What happened at the disclosures of Everett's will was a total crash and burn. Almost.

Eden knew it was an *almost,* a near miss because, to be blunt, she wasn't ready to give up on a chance for her and Beck. But she wasn't sure that the fledgling relationship between them could be saved. In all truth, it depended on what happened next. She replayed all of the pluses that Beck had managed to stack up in such a short time.

He was an astonishingly good listener. He was attentive without imposing his own belief systems. He was a good-looking Black man, with a possibly very interesting background. Every single time she recalled Beck's incredible bottom-of-the-well voice, the muscles in her stomach tensed. As if he was beckoning to her nonverbally. Eden, with great expectation, was willing to follow. There was no question that she wondered where her interest might lead her if given full rein. And there was another truth to be faced.

Even during her suspicions as to what Beck was thinking about her and Everett in the lawyer's office, Eden recalled very similar open accusations from her own sister. Beck was not the first person to suggest that she and Everett had more going on between them than just a mutually caring relationship.

Holly had boldly asked her, more than once, if she and Everett were having or had ever had an affair. Coming out of her sister's mouth, the question had stunned Eden for the obvious reason. It also had caused a great deal of worry and anger. No, there had *never* been anything like that between her and Everett, nor had there ever been a hint from him that his thinking lay in that direction. Now, Eden wondered how many others had drawn the same conclusion as her sister.

Beck suddenly wasn't looking like the devil incarnate. He'd tried to call her that evening after the face-off. Eden hadn't taken the call. She'd caught herself in time. She waited to see if he would leave a voicemail on her smartphone. He did…and she promptly deleted it without listening. Eden believed her anger was real and raw and justified. Yet, one sleepless night of mulling over what she knew and what she believed had begun to make a difference. Maybe they'd each misjudged the other?

Beck tried her again just that morning, by which time Eden's ire had softened to putty and was malleable. She could shape it into anything she chose. She had been standing in front of her closet slowly dressing in skinny black jeans and an off-white, nubby boat-neck sweater. Looks weren't going to matter any place she had to be today. She had stared at her smartphone, the LED screen blinking the incoming call, her ringtone like the old-fashioned ring of telephones of the past. Eventually it stopped…and the call went to voicemail. She had snatched up the device and sat on the side of her bed to play the message.

"It's Beck again, Eden. Okay, I get it. I made a false step, but maybe you can cut me some slack. Like I said, we don't know a lot about each other yet. Can I be allowed one mistake? I would really like that. I haven't given up. I know it sounds strange… I don't believe we're done yet." He hung up.

Eden sighed and began to gather her papers to leave the center. A young child went running by her shared desk (on Wednesdays and Fridays) with a younger sibling in hot pursuit. The voice of a harried and no-nonsense adult yelled out across the entire office, "Boy! Stop fooling around and get your butt back over here!" Not a single person in the still crowded office seemed to have heard, or cared. Eden actually liked the chaos, the noise and people talking to each other in loud neighborhoody voices. It was lively and like a large dysfunctional family that, in many ways, it was. That's why she was needed and welcomed. Eden recognized the rhythm, and she understood it. She actually looked forward each week to her pro bono work at one of DC's local advocacy centers for low-income families.

Eden had one stop to make and then she was headed home, thrilled that Holly wasn't due back until the next day. Good. The rest of the evening was her own. She needed time to write up a brief for Jamal's case, make a motion to the court for complete dismissal of the charge—a flimsy, poorly supported accusation by a teacher—and set a date for a hearing with an arbitrator.

She maneuvered through the narrow aisles, a bustling, too-busy convergence of volunteers, licensed practitioners and social workers, and desperate people with myriad troubles. She'd reached the front door of the center when she nearly collided with a tall white man trying to enter. She gasped and stopped short, as did he.

"Looks like I got here just in time." He grinned at her amicably and continued to step into the front office, forcing Eden to step back.

"Zach."

"Finished for the day?"

"Why are you here?"

"To see you, of course," Zach Milford grinned at her. "Great timing."

"No, it's not."

"Where are you headed?"

Eden hedged, so caught off guard by the appearance of one of her 3L classmates—and former boyfriend—that she couldn't think of a sound excuse to avoid him. "I…have another appointment. And I have a ton of work to do tonight," she quickly added before he could make any suggestions.

"I thought I'd surprise you. I have to use subterfuge to get any time with you."

"You mean *alone* time. You're right." Eden said. "We have a group clinic meeting tomorrow. You'll have to make do with that." She stepped around him and out the door.

Zach crossed his arms in front of his chest. "I have no problem with that, but seriously, I was in the neighborhood and I remembered you'd be here at the center. If you're about to leave, maybe we can grab a drink somewhere. I know a place."

He studied her closely without saying anything, and Eden realized her current state of confusion and anxiety was not Zach's fault. He obviously couldn't know about her and what she'd hoped would be a promising new man in her life.

"Sorry. I didn't mean to bite your head off."

"Bad day?" he asked with quiet concern.

"As a matter of fact, the past two days have been…difficult. And I'm not going to explain, Zach."

She considered him, his handsome and masculine, angular face with its look of perpetual cheerfulness and bonhomie. When they'd first met, Zach had her at *go,* with his killer smile and his lustful attention. Within a very short time, that first year of law school, Eden knew their flirty, fun, and physical relationship wasn't going to last. Zach never seemed to take anything seriously. That included the substantial work and focus required to get through law school and become a practicing attorney. Eden had already come to the conclusion that, *if* Zach actually made it to JD, and *if* he passed the bar exam, she couldn't in good conscience ever recommend him to anyone needing legal advice. If there was a place for him in law, she had yet to figure out where. She wasn't sure that Zach was overly concerned. And he didn't need to be, she considered in some annoyance.

"You don't have to explain anything, you know that. Besides, you'd never let me get away with stepping over the line, and you're right. I should have called. I just thought it would be a nice surprise to have drinks together. Tomorrow with the rest of the group will be different."

"Drinks were a nice thought but I'm just not up to it. And I have a ton of writing to do tonight…"

"Always." He nodded in complete understanding. "I don't know about you, but commencement can't come fast enough. Not that I haven't enjoyed every torturous moment…" he ended dryly.

Eden grinned and stepped around him. Zach held the door and they both exited to the street. She faced him with an apologetic gaze. "Thanks for wanting to take me out…"

He frowned and leaned closer to peer into her face. "Are you okay? What's going on?"

She affectionately patted his arm. "Nothing you can help me with. I have to go."

"Can I drop you off somewhere? I'm parked at the corner."

She shook her head ruefully. "You're the only person in all of DC who parks wherever he pleases and doesn't worry about being towed or getting a ticket."

He shrugged. "Yeah, I'm well connected, and yeah, I use it. What would be the point otherwise?"

"I wouldn't brag if I were you."

"I'm lucky that you like me anyway. Where're you headed?"

"You can drop me off at Seventh and Massachusetts."

"You got it," he nodded.

Which was exactly what Zach did, less than five minutes later. Eden thanked him with a sweet smile and a reminder that they'd see each other the next day. She let him assume she was headed for the original DC Carnegie Library building, now converted into one of the largest Apple stores in DC. Eden waited until the Range Rover had pulled back into traffic heading west. She walked right past the Apple store to New York Avenue where she made a left turn and approached Tiffany & Co. When Eden entered the quiet, brightly lit interior, the security guard and the first salesperson behind the counter both smiled and nodded. It made Eden feel like she was being welcomed home.

With her sure steps, the stress and anxiety of the day fell away. She was safe here, this was *her happy place,* and for the moment Eden had only one thought and destination in mind. She continued down the aisle of the famous luxury store as if she owned it. There was only one other customer shopping, a businessman examining a necklace at a far counter. *Birthday,* Eden thought. *Or anniversary.*

The male sales associate behind the display case on Eden's right saw her approaching and grinned a greeting.

"Welcome back. We missed you!" The associate chuckled playfully.

"Thank you," Eden responded.

"The usual?" the associate asked, already unlocking the display case with a carefully arranged variety of earrings. The settings were tasteful and simple, but the sparkle and shine of the diamonds that each pair gave off said real and very expensive.

Eden nodded. A slow smile of satisfaction shaped her mouth, producing dimpled grooves on either side. The salesman lifted a particular pair of earrings with a round, slightly scalloped edge of small diamonds, which was then lined with smaller diamonds. The setting was named Enchant Fleur in platinum. The salesman held the earrings out to Eden.

"Would you like to try them on again?"

"If you're sure it's okay." Eden spread her hands and wiggled her fingers. She pushed up the sleeves of her winter coat. "See? Nothing in my hands or up my sleeves."

"I'm not worried if you can be trusted. You visit these beauties so often you're almost like family, Ms. Marsh. We hope one day these will really be yours."

Once the earrings were on, it suddenly occurred to Eden that she could actually buy them several times over, if she wanted to, recalling the check she'd received a few days earlier. She'd been visiting the earrings for an unimaginable three years…when she felt the need for a pick-me-up, a spirit boost, and descent into a daydream. It didn't matter if that dream ever came true. That wasn't the point.

Her phone didn't ring particularly early the next morning, but having gone to bed very late the night before, Eden felt groggy as she tried to surface from a sound sleep. She extended an arm from the warmth of her comforter to grab the unit on her nightstand. The morning chill made the tiny hairs on her skin stand straight out. She tucked the phone between her ear and her pillow and quickly pulled her arm back beneath the warmth of the cover.

"Hello?" Eden asked, her voice wispy and faint.

There was only silence from the other end.

"Hello?" she tried again, her voice stronger with curiosity.

"It's Beck. Did I wake you?"

Eden struggled to free her head from beneath the covers.

"Don't hang up."

Eden swallowed the response that rose to her mouth, *I won't,* and remained quiet.

"Eden? Are you there?"

"Yes."

She could hear him sigh. Her heart was racing. She turned onto her back, drawing her knees up and holding the phone close to her ear.

"I've been calling…"

"I know."

"I wasn't sure I should keep trying."

"I won't hang up."

"Does that mean I get a reprieve?"

"It means the jury's still out. No pun intended."

Beck seem to hesitate just a second, and then he chuckled deep in his throat.

"I'm…glad you answered," he said, his tone sincere.

"I've been thinking… Maybe I overreacted."

"I wouldn't blame you if you're still angry, but I hope we're making progress."

Eden shifted under her bed linens. "You were wrong about me and Everett. But I know why you were wrong."

"Okay," he said, encouraging her to continue.

"It's because you don't really know anything about me."

"I don't know enough," Beck corrected.

"Yes."

"I want to change that, Eden. That's why I keep calling. I want to start by having that date we talked about that never happened. Can we?"

"Do you think that will make a difference?"

"I know it will."

"You seem very sure of yourself."

"I am. Know why? Because you don't know much about me, either."

All alone in her bed, she was bantering with Beck and waiting for him to say something outrageous to make her mad again, but he didn't.

"You're right."

"Are you…interested?"

"I am," Eden confessed, hoping she wasn't giving too much away.

"A date, right? Not a negotiation or interrogation. No trick questions or false accusations. Know what else I think? I think there could be something between us. Are you willing to find out?" Beck asked, his voice very low…and almost personal. Challenging.

Eden considered. "I'm willing to give you a second chance," she offered, willing to step up to the plate.

"Let's see what happens."

"Fair enough."

———————

Eden was standing just inside the entrance to her building two nights later when Beck pulled up in his metallic navy-blue Honda Accord sedan. He'd been teased any number of times by the hipsters in his office or his own peers that a Honda was not cool. It was sort of "your father's…or mother's…sedan." Recently, it had begun showing signs of an expiration date, and Beck hoped the transmission would hold out not only through the evening, but for a few more weeks. All of that was pushed to the back of his mind at being with Eden again.

There was no time to explore what the difference was, but he was suddenly viewing Eden with new eyes and changed feelings. Beck couldn't recall the last time he'd found himself begging for redemption from anyone. Well…maybe with his mother, but that was a very different story. He felt a momentary pulsing in his chest. More than just excitement, it was seeing Eden standing watch and waiting for his car to pull up in front of her building. She didn't acknowledge him in any other way, but Beck very much felt that she'd been on the lookout. Was she as anxious as he was?

He put the car in neutral, and although Eden had opened the door to step outside, he'd already exited his car to meet her near the passenger door. He reached into his inside jacket pocket. Eden was walking to meet him but suddenly slowed her progress and frowned at what he held in his hand. She began walking again, trying to figure out what he held. And then she broke into a wide grin. She stepped closer and reached to take the object—a slender wooden dowel tied with a white napkin at two corners—from Beck.

Her eyes were bright with suppressed humor as she held and turned the flag, examining it before giving her attention to him.

"Very cute," she murmured.

"I didn't want to take any more chances." Beck said, his gaze studying her. "They're becoming very rare around here."

Eden smiled as she continued to examine the flag. "I accept the truce."

"Thank you." He knew it had not been an easy concession, and he wasn't going to be arrogant and take it for granted. "Hi," Beck suddenly said in a whisper, realizing he was really glad to see her. Now that they'd arrived at a peace treaty, he wanted to greet her properly.

Eden turned her smiling face, her always bright and open gaze to him. "Hi."

Beck slowly held up his hands, fingers relaxed. "One more thing," he said carefully, as if to warn her. Eden blinked and waited. Beck closed his hands as he cupped her face, tilting it up. As he closed the distance, his last glimpse of her face was seeing her eyes drift shut. He kissed her. His mouth lingered for a few seconds before he released her. Eden's eyes popped open and stared at him. "I'm so sorry," Beck said softly, hoping that she could hear his sincerity.

He turned and opened the passenger door and held it for her as she climbed in. She'd fastened her seat belt and was carefully rolling the napkin about its pole when he got into the driver's seat.

"Can I keep this?"

Beck turned on the engine but studied her for a moment. "I might need it again," he said simply.

Eden tilted her head and displayed the vertical dimples in her cheeks. "I don't think you will."

Beck said nothing but gave her a small, satisfied smile. He pulled away from the curb and into traffic.

"Let me know if you're warm enough."

"I'm good," she said.

And then Eden fell silent. Beck glanced quickly at her profile, trying to read her mood. Now she seemed distracted. After a few blocks, they came to a red light, but they were already on the edge of U Street, as was evident from the increasing pedestrian crowds, the bright neon lights of businesses, and the volume of excited conversation audible even through their closed windows.

"You know, if you're not up to dinner, maybe we could skip it for…"

Eden shook her head. "I'm looking forward to tonight, Beck."

"I don't get the sense that you really want to…"

"I…think I'm a little nervous," Eden confessed.

He glanced at her again. "Let's start simple. How have you been?"

"Busy. And…*very* busy."

"Want to tell me about it?"

She grinned at him. "I don't want to bore you."

"I'd like to know what you did today to save the world or influence government."

He was totally sincere. Whatever Eden was going to talk about, he knew it wasn't going to be all about her.

Eden laughed quietly. "That's an overreach. I think I've figured out how to help one Black teenager go to college after all. He graduated from high school last year."

Beck was instantly interested. "Seriously. What happened?"

He could see Eden take her time to begin her story, and when she began, it was a concise tale of a shy boy from a low-income neighborhood who'd managed to get through high school on his own initiative and hard work. Then, finding himself in the middle of a school cheating scandal when he was not even in attendance, but for which school officials outrageously wanted to hold him accountable. Administrators came to him for facts and names of who were involved. But how would he know? He wasn't there. Frustrated at their efforts to ferret out the truth, they made him a scapegoat. They withdrew an awarded academic scholarship that would have paid for college.

"Is that legal? That they could just take away the boy's chances of college just because..,"

"Just because they could. I have to prove that what they did was not legal, and he can't be legally held responsible for the actions of his classmates. Or the inability of the administrators to properly handle their suspicions. I'm probably going to throw in the race card. I don't usually like doing that but..."

"Yes?"

"The administrators are, in this case, all white. Most had never worked in an urban school before where the student body is predominantly Black. I think those may be important factors. I took statements from some of the staff, and there's a strong suggestion of bias. I have to be careful about how I argue the point. We'll see."

Beck was silent, thinking through what Eden had told him. "You're still a law student. Are you allowed to take a case like that one?"

"That's exactly what I'm allowed to do as a student. It's pro bono work as part of my clinic. A clinic is set up to give JD candidates experience with actual cases. I wrote up a brief and made a motion for the court that the charges against my client be dismissed and the school forced to reinstate his scholarship. I'm thinking of throwing in some sort of monetary award. That would help with some of his nonacademic expenses. I scheduled a hearing for next week."

They both fell silent. For his part, Beck was thinking of the complexity of the case and the ease with which Eden had outlined the problem. And he suddenly knew that beyond Eden being very attractive...and comfortable to be with, she was sharp. He'd already experienced firsthand how sensitive she was and now how caring. And thoughtful and conscientious. And...

He chuckled to himself. She turned her attention to him.

"What?" Eden asked, a little uncertain at the quiet sound he'd made.

"I'm thinking about your case. I can tell from what you told me that one, you believe this kid has a righteous position, and two, you're going to not only fight for him, but bury the opposition. You're already sounding like one hell of an attorney."

Eden seemed relieved and began to laugh halfway through his comments. "I don't want to bury anyone. But I know I can prove they demonstrated poor judgment."

"You can take that as a compliment, Eden. Man, I'm telling you. If I'm ever accused of murder, or of trying to steal a car, I want you to defend me."

She burst out into sustained laughter that had Beck joining in, just for the pleasure of hearing her laugh. And he could feel the last of the uncomfortable tension ooze out from both of them. He lowered his window several inches, as if to definitively clear the air.

"I'm not there yet, Beck. And I still don't have a real job after graduation."

"You're going to get your JD. I have no doubts about that, Eden. And I further predict you'll pass the bar exam on the first try. You're going to be great."

Her humor slowly subsided and she glanced at him with speculation. Was she wondering if he was sincere? Beck smiled back and let his gaze show what he didn't say.

She blew him away with her simplicity and considerable charm. *Yes, Eden*, Beck considered to himself. *You are different.*

No.

Unique.

The restaurant was beyond noisy.

It was a too-high decibel level of human sounds that bordered on being a frenzy of conversation exchange to the max. But after a while Eden didn't mind. She felt swept up in the energy and the liveliness of all the groups and couples around her and Beck, packed into one of the popular U Street joints. It forced her and Beck to sit up tight to their table and lean in a little in order to have conversation. And the better to let the rumble of his deep voice and laughter roll over her spine in a most pleasurable way. After only a little while, they no longer felt the need to shout to be heard. All they had to do was to give their attention to each other and listen. Everything else seemed to fall away into the background. Like white noise.

That became easy and enjoyable during their long dinner, as they fell naturally into an agreeable habit of sharing their food. It began with Eden asking Beck if he'd like to try her short ribs and then lifting her plate to scrape a portion onto his. He seemed caught off guard but taken with her casual generosity. Beck did the same with his fettuccini bolognese. Dinner conversation did not go near what had blown up between them. Instead, they talked about college experiences and how he came to be a columnist and associate editor for *DC Dialogue*, a fairly new digital startup about people, places, and projects around the DC and Belt arena. And, of course, Eden's law school experience was finally going to end in just a few months. They quickly discovered their individual life decisions had both been heavily influenced by their ties to Everett Nichols and their mutual admiration for him.

Sitting back leisurely in his chair, Beck seemed to be listening with great interest and enjoyment. They'd finished dinner but still nursed drinks. Eden was in no hurry to get home, and let their conversation come free and easy while they waited for dessert to be served.

"Most students pretty much have a job lined up by third year, and all they want to do is get through commencement so they can start working and…"

"Earning a *lot* of money."

She grinned and nodded. "Funny, when I started, I never really thought about the money. I only wanted to work in something I believed in. I'm not trying to make a killing, you know?"

"Yes," Beck said, his tone showing understanding. "And now, because of Everett, you won't have to."

"That's true. It's still hard to believe. Anyway, I'm a little older than the typical law student. I don't feel the same hurry to become famous or file a case that goes all the way to the Supreme Court. My fellow students call me an Owl."

Beck looked puzzled.

"Older and wiser," Eden informed him.

He laughed again. "Eden, I can tell you from my limited perspective you are not *older*, even by law school standards. But…there is some evidence already that you show signs of wisdom."

She averted her gaze, blushing under her skin and taken aback by Beck's compliment. She didn't know how to respond.

Beck straightened and placed his folded arms on the table so he could look right at her.

"What are you planning to do with the windfall that Everett left you?"

She blinked. "I don't know. To be honest, I've barely thought about it since I found out I was instantly rich. I guess I'm in shock." She glanced off into space, now starting to consider some of the possibilities. Eden shook her head. "There really isn't anything… Well…maybe *one* thing I've been lusting over for a while now."

Beck raised his brows, amused. "*Lusting* over? I don't suppose that has anything to do with…"

"*No.*" Eden quickly cut him off, emphatically, before he could say what she thought he was going to suggest. Then she looked at him and saw he was once again baiting her. "There's a pair of earrings I would love to have. I know that doesn't sound like such an impossible wish, but they're very expensive."

"What? Five hundred dollars? A thousand?"

Eden was almost embarrassed to say it out loud, but he was waiting, giving her time to get it out. She knew he was going to be surprised, and she watched for the response she was already expecting.

"Twelve thousand dollars."

His brows rose even higher, but he didn't say anything right away.

Eden began to smile, mostly to herself as she began to consider the single wish she'd maintained since starting to earn a real salary working for Everett. That she might actually, one day, be able to afford the one thing she most wanted to buy herself.

"Okay. I admit that is a lot of money just for earrings."

"They're Tiffany's Enchant Fleur, round diamonds set in platinum."

"They have a name?" Beck questioned.

"Well, it's Tiffany," Eden said as if that explained everything.

"Okay," he murmured for want of anything else to say, hiding a grin.

"I've been visiting them at the store for three years now. I'm finally at a point where I can ask to try them on. The first time," Eden said with some reverence, "it was really a magical moment for me."

"And how did they look on you?"

"Perfect. I felt...royal. Thrilled. Beautiful."

Eden sighed, the memory brightening her eyes, her smile quiet and content. She felt a little embarrassed saying it out loud, but Beck didn't appear to find her remark silly or juvenile. She shifted in her chair and drank the last of her wine.

"Well, I guess it does seem like a pretty big and expensive deal but...start small. Get something for yourself that's not so expensive. Work your way up to the earrings. How about...a weekend away somewhere, first class? Or all-day spa treatments? Do you like champagne? You can't go wrong with Perrier-Jouët 1966 for about $6,500. Cheap compared to the earrings."

Eden laughed, delighted with the suggestion. "I *love* champagne. But that's still expensive…and I'd probably never drink it."

"Ummm. I see I'm going to have to give you lessons in living large."

"Really? What do you know about it?"

"Experience and opportunity. One of the benefits of being a writer. I get to try a lot of things I don't have to pay for. You'll have to hang out with me more often," he said in a quiet, sly tone. Beck could see that Eden was taking that part of his suggestion seriously.

"What about you? What do you have your heart set on?"

Beck sighed, raised his brows, shook his head a little and made a dismissal gesture with his hand. "I don't have a clue how to spend the kind of money Everett left me. I could get a new car…and I need one. But that's not a wish-list kind of item. That's not…big enough. I don't know how to be foolish and buy whatever I want. Like a pair of sparkling diamond earrings." He grinned at her. "I don't know what I want."

Eden nodded. "Maybe we need to sit down and make a list. I'd call it 'Foolish Wishes and Impossible Dreams.'"

He nodded. "Great title. What's first on the list? Besides the earrings."

Eden shrugged with an impish twist of her mouth. "I don't know. Same as you. The truth is, I've never had a lot of money to spend. And I got used to always making sure that my sister had what she needed."

"Big-sister duty?"

"More like a surrogate mom."

"That's even harder."

"It is. But she was too young to take care of herself when our mother died, so…I had to."

Beck studied her closely. "Who takes care of you?"

Eden was surprised by the question. "No one. I take care of myself."

Beck thoughtfully studied her, but Eden couldn't decipher his expression or this thoughts. He became momentarily pensive, looking down at the table.

"What?" she asked tentatively.

"I was just thinking… I probably should seriously look into hiring some sort of financial adviser. I mean, I know there are going to be huge tax implications with what Everett left us. It's something you should probably consider, too."

"I hadn't even thought of that," Eden said, sounding somewhat overwhelmed at the thought. "I guess I can't just expect to deposit $5 million into my savings account…and then spend like crazy."

Beck burst out laughing, and Eden smiled not only at the way it transformed his face, but also the way his whole body responded.

"No, that is not a good idea." He had been leaning back, open and enjoying himself. Suddenly Beck sat forward, again resting his arms on the table, looking at her with careful speculation in his narrowed gaze. "But I do have another thought. A couple of years ago, I interviewed a former baseball player who began a new career in sports broadcasting. He was making a lot of money, really popular… great guy. And then as if it wasn't enough that his cup runneth over, he wins the New York Mega Millions lottery…for $75 million."

"Wow. That's a lot of money."

"Yeah. That's one way of putting it. The thing is, it was so much money that he actually took some of the winnings to seed his own charitable foundation. I think it's called *The Millionaires Club*. I think I'll give him a call, find out what the foundation is all about. And I think I'll ask him what he buys for fun."

The waiter finally reappeared and placed desserts before each of them. And then Beck's cell vibrated. He thought about ignoring it but pulled it from his trouser pocket and glanced at the screen. He immediately pressed a button that silenced the humming sound and put the device back in his pocket.

Eden waited him out but was happy when he didn't take the call.

"Sorry about that," he said.

Eden waited as he raised his fork with the sliced-off pointy end of his triple-layer mud pie. When Beck looked up, mouth open, Eden was poised holding her spoon already filled with her panna cotta with strawberries. She reached toward Beck with the offering. She couldn't interpret the look he gave her as he craned his neck to accept the spoon into his mouth. She held firm as Beck drew the creamy custard between his lips, slowly. Then he returned the favor by extending his fork to feed Eden the first bite of the pie.

Eden felt a little transfixed, some unexpected emotion roiling through her quickly that totally shifted her awareness of Beck. She realized that there was something very erotic about their exchange, and she belatedly wondered if Beck was having the same reaction. What she'd done now seemed very provocative, although she didn't consciously intend it to be. But there was no denying that the really innocent action had elevated their game to a different level.

"How about we share? We'll each eat half and then switch." Beck suggested.

"That's so…neat," Eden said. "We can share like it is. No waiting. Just dig in."

"Okay. Let's go for it."

Their forks and spoons went back and forth between the two desserts until they were finished. When they stepped outside, the streets were still crowded, still loud and lively, with music faintly wafting through the air from several different venues. Beck kept his hand on the small of her back to steer her through the slow pedestrian traffic, and Eden was very conscious of the pressure and the sense of protectiveness.

There had been no conversation about what to do next, and if Beck was heading back to his car to drive her home, she was content with that. But they passed a small club where people were moving inside for a soon-to-start 9:00 p.m. set. She slowed to try to read the marquee announcing the performer.

"I didn't think to ask if you'd want to listen to some music."

"Well, I didn't, either, but it might be fun."

She turned to Beck to see if he approved, but he was staring at the entrance to the club, and it was obvious to Eden that he didn't seem drawn to the idea. She found his reaction puzzling.

"We don't have to…"

"Tell you what. Will you take a rain check for another time?" Beck said, his voice suddenly somewhat flat and aloof.

Eden could tell right away that it wouldn't do for her to insist, and she wasn't going to. She agreed with a light shrug. "Sure. Another deadline?"

Beck chuckled and seemed embarrassed. "Always. I haven't started the piece yet."

"I understand. But I want you to know I was willing to sacrifice editing a class paper tonight that's due tomorrow." She glanced at the awning for the building. "Let's come here. The Gaslight Salon."

"I know it," he said as he touched her arm to lead her away.

Only once they were in Beck's sedan and on the road for the very short drive to her house, less than half a mile away, did Eden sense Beck more or less relaxing again. She slouched down in her seat, her head against the headrest. She was feeling pretty content. Everything about the evening had been wonderful. Being with Beck had been...wonderful. Better than she could have imagined. Friendly banter, lots of flirtation, and laughter. It had been one of the best first dates she'd had in years. That was a sad commentary on the state of her love life. Eden sighed, closing her eyes, imagining something more with Beck. From Beck.

That would be nice, she mused to herself.

She stole a glance at his profile, but he was concentrating on his driving and the heavy traffic out of the U Street corridor.

When they reached the front of her building, Eden wasn't prepared for Beck to turn off his car. But there was a space near the corner that he pulled into.

"You don't have to park. I'll be fine on my own."

"I'll walk you in," he said firmly.

Eden was secretly pleased at his gallantry, raising her estimation of Beck another ten points. If this kept up, she was going to start dreaming about him at night. And although she was ahead of Beck, getting out of his car without assistance, she loved his extra effort.

She'd already begun walking toward her building when Eden glanced around to see Beck retrieving something, a large envelope, from his back seat. He jogged to catch up with her. As they waited for the elevator inside the narrow lobby, they exchanged looks, and suddenly both began laughing.

"You're thinking what I'm thinking," Beck said.

Eden nodded. "That my sister is going to come through the door again, just like last time, sucking out all the oxygen."

"You said it, I didn't."

"She's not due back until day after tomorrow, I think. I'm never really sure."

"Must be difficult to plan having company," Beck said quietly, watching her, his expression speculative.

Eden arched a brow, her gaze candid and bright. "It's never been a problem."

At her apartment door, however, she was uncertain. She unlocked it and turned to him, the door partially ajar.

"I have something for you," Beck said, handing the manila envelope to her.

She took it, handling it gingerly, turning it over as if searching for some clue to the content. "What is it?"

"A surprise."

"Okay." Eden studied him, blinking, looking for a sign. "Would you like to come in?"

Almost immediately she wondered if the invitation seemed too forward, too suggestive. What did she have in mind if he accepted?

Beck carefully returned her scrutiny. She was sure there was a curious smile beneath the mobile pursing of his mouth.

"Yes," he said, his voice low and gravelly. "But not tonight."

The way Beck said it, on a deep, slow drawl, the innuendo sent a shiver down Eden's spine. He took a step toward her until there were only inches between them. Beck reached to curl his large hand around the back of her neck, his fingers teasing the soft hair at her nape. He coaxed her to tilt her face up, making it much easier for him to bend and softly capture her mouth for a kiss. There was more to this kiss than the one they shared when he'd picked her up for their date.

Eden had been hoping. She was ashamed to admit it to herself until it was actually happening. She let her eyes close, the better to concentrate on what Beck was doing so deliciously with his full, mobile mouth…and tongue.

Eden expected his touch to be a brief good night thing, that it would quickly end. Thank goodness Beck had other ideas in mind. All she had to do was welcome it and enjoy it. She let Beck's lips guide her, lengthening the kiss and the complete melding of their lips, the exploration of their tongues. She could just feel the soft, flat layer of his facial hair that tickled around her mouth and cheek. Their fused mouths got acquainted. He staked a claim. Stirring her senses until she felt all soft and docile. Eden was starting to slip into a gentle euphoria of mindless pleasure, her mind emptying of any other consideration but the pleasure of this moment. She felt Beck's other hand on her waist pulling her toward him to close the distance until they touched chest to chest. The suggestion of anything more, the possibility was enough.

Eden wasn't ready for the kiss to end, but knew it had to. She stood for a long second, her breathing a little hurried. She opened her eyes and Beck had stepped back. Eden couldn't think what to say. She couldn't seem to *think*.

"If we hadn't had that dustup, it would have taken us longer to get to this point. It was worth everything to get to where we are right now. This feels good. *This* was good," he said, his breath warm against her skin.

She swallowed, inhaled deeply to slow her breathing back to normal. Beck's admission was heady, surreal, and she absorbed it, feeling a sudden flutter in her heart. She nodded. "Yes. It was."

"Okay?"

"Okay," Eden confirmed.

Beck was about to kiss her again. Eden was waiting, but he decided the point had been made.

He now knew he was right. There was something starting between them.

The elevator had waited for him. He pressed the indicator button and the door slid open. Beck stepped inside, pressed for the main floor, and stood watching her as the door closed between them.

During the elevator ride up to his apartment, Beck indulged in some hard truths. He liked Eden Marsh a lot. More than he'd imagined even a few days ago. He liked spending time with her. The conversations were never about her, or what she wanted, or what she had done. He had to ask the right questions to even get Eden on that line of thought. He couldn't recall Eden complaining about anything…except when she was really pissed at him for not admitting his relationship to Everett. Beck now understood that was not in an effort to know his innermost secrets or life history. It was simply Eden expecting the same level of honesty that she'd so willingly given him, even when they'd known each other for mere hours.

Eden confounded him. Eden made him sit up and pay attention, but in far more exciting ways than most women he'd known since he began dating. She wasn't predictable or obvious. Beck had to admit he had still been waiting for her to show her hand, her true self. But everything he'd seen and experienced with Eden so far *was* her true self. He was pretty sure now that the proverbial other shoe was not going to drop.

He was still wondering if he could have given Eden a better excuse for not wanting to end the evening listening to a female jazz singer. And truthfully, he was not surprised when she readily accepted his excuse. It was a very weak one, to be sure. But she never showed impatience or disappointment. Another first for him as Alia came unavoidably to mind.

Beck entered his apartment and didn't bother turning on the hall light. He hung his jacket in the closet by the front door and headed to his bedroom. He stopped in his tracks, a few feet beyond the kitchen entrance, where he caught a glimpse of the blinking red light on his landline. It was ancient technology, but having more than one form of access was important for a number of reasons. Not the least of which it was the one way his mother used when trying to reach him. That had been sporadic. Until recently. Since Everett died, she'd reached out to him more than usual.

Beck pressed the lit button, headed to the refrigerator for a bottle of spring water, and heard the buzz that began the playback.

"Hi. It's Eden…"

Beck had the bottle opened and almost to his mouth when he stopped abruptly. He could tell immediately that Eden was or had been crying. He put the bottle down and was already headed out of the kitchen, back to get his coat and car keys.

"I had to call right away and thank you, Beck."

The voice was soft, quavering, and broken with her effort to speak clearly. Beck stopped again and turned back to the kitchen. This was not an emergency.

"I just finished reading your article about…about Everett. Beck, it's…it's so *good.*"

He stood in his kitchen doorway, staring at the cordless on its cradle, and listened. He heard her sniffles, the quiet blowing of her nose. The image actually relaxed his shoulders. He could imagine every changing emotion on her face. Eden was not good at hiding her feelings.

"You really captured who he was, Beck. It's such a true portrait and filled with respect…and love. Now I understand why. I know Everett was your stepfather, but…I–I could read the admiration, the love you had for him, in your written words." She blew her nose again, almost inaudibly. "I think you should get a Pulitzer," Eden murmured with a watery chuckle.

Beck leaned against the doorframe, Eden's words reaching deep, *very* deep, into his psyche, her affirmation an unexpected balm on his senses. Everett's death had hit him hard, but he was relieved and pleased that Eden had heard all of what he wanted to say.

It had been a challenge to be the objective journalist when his heart wanted to say so much.

"Then I found the little box inside. Thank you for the jigsaw puzzle. I've never done one before. This one looks like fun…and hard. I hope you're planning to work with me on putting it together. Would you like to come over this weekend?"

"I guess you're not home yet. Well, maybe you are and… Anyway, I had a great time tonight. It was fun spending it with you. I–I'm glad I said yes. And thank you for giving me the article and the puzzle. I promise I will definitely read more of your work. Bye."

CHAPTER 6

"Beck, do me a favor and put that in the kitchen on the counter. Put the bottles right in the fridge."

Beck lifted the flat of water bottles and did his mother's bidding. Nora Dennison Nichols passed behind him, headed for an overhead cabinet, and pressed her hand on his back. Beck's jaw involuntarily flexed at the action, but it wasn't a rejection of his mother's touch. It was a longing. It came from an honest adolescent place of trauma that had stood its ground for more than two decades.

"Thanks for helping with the shopping. You know, you don't have to come all the way out to Arlington to help me with that," his mother said. "I could have everything delivered. But then I'd miss the fun of filling my wagon with things I don't really need."

"Well, there you go," Beck said. "I'm all for you having more fun," he added generously.

This was also that time in his visits when, chores and routines out of the way, he began to search for easy conversation. Their lives had been different for years. For many reasons, it seemed to take a lot of work to have a relationship. At least for him. He regretted that.

"You performing tonight?" he asked, as she filled a mug with coffee prepared earlier in the day.

Nora shook her head. "Not tonight." She pulled a bottle of beer from the refrigerator and handed it to him as she continued through the dining room and into a small space that was used as an *every-thing* room. There was a haphazard pile of magazines and Sunday news sections waiting to be read. There was a laptop surrounded by opened letters, bills and statements, sheets of music, and used mugs that hadn't made it back to the kitchen yet. Nora sat in an old-fashioned Queen Anne chair and settled in.

Beck no longer bothered to look around his childhood home when he came to see his mother, unless she asked him to take care of something. A repair or moving something that she could not. Not a lot had changed in years. Well…there was one thing. Long ago his mother had moved or gotten rid of the dozen or so photographs that had crowded the top of a credenza. A few years ago, here, in her *everything* space he did notice two photographs placed on her crowded desk, but the images were mostly obscured by the papers and books. Beck had approached closer to see who or what they were of. And he'd gotten an emotional shock. One was of his mother cuddling him lovingly when he was a toddler. They were both smiling beatifically. He didn't know if it was taken before or after his birth father had died. His mother was beautiful, cheerful, and he did recall that early love and safety and well-being. The other framed photo was, again, of his mother and another toddler, Mason, his younger brother, the child his mother had with Everett.

The first time Beck discovered the photographs, what struck him most was that he was the product of a mixed relationship. His mother's pale skin and auburn hair was in sharp contrast to his abundant curly dark hair and light-brown skin. With Mason, there was obviously a more natural fit. The little boy had his mother's pale skin but dark eyes. There was no question they were mother and child. Beck recalled feeling such a sudden wrenching in his throat, such a wave of heat that deposited doubt over whether his mother loved him less than Mason. What happened when he was twelve and Mason seven had cemented Beck's doubts.

He also tried never to have to venture upstairs to the second floor. The only room in use now was his mother's master suite…the room she'd once shared with Everett. He'd had no interest in visiting his childhood room once he'd finally managed to escape it when he left for college. There was a third bedroom, but it had been closed off since Mason's death, before his mother and Everett had finally divorced.

Beck reached for the cushioned desk chair and placed it so that he faced his mother. He handily twisted off the bottle cap and took a swig of the beer. "I can leave if you have things to do."

Nora sighed, idly using a hand to smooth loose strands of her once natural auburn hair, now aided with dye, back into the loose knot at the back of her head. "No, stay. Keep me company for a while. No need to rush off…unless… Do you have plans?"

Beck hesitated, taking another deep drink of the beer, and blinked at his mother's invitation. He nodded slowly. "I do, but not for a few more hours. And I have something to finish at my office."

His mother stared openly at him.

"Not Alia, is it?"

He arched a brow. "Alia and I broke up more than a year ago, Mom. There's not going to be a reconciliation."

Nora stared into her cup. "I shouldn't have mentioned her. I know that must have been hard."

"Not really. I was starting to see the light. It always shone on her. There wasn't much room for me."

"I'm sorry."

Beck stared at his mother, at her show of sympathy. She was sincere. "The breakup was better for both of us. She can pursue her single-minded agenda for fame and fortune, and I can stop wondering why I wasn't very happy."

"Then I'm glad, too. And to be honest, honey, I didn't think she was right for you."

"You never let on," Beck murmured, again surprised.

She shrugged. "It wasn't my place to pass judgment. You probably thought you were in love with her. It didn't look like love to me."

He chortled. "When did you become such an expert?"

She stared at him, her blue eyes looking both startled and a bit glassy, like there were tears hovering. She blinked and averted her gaze. "You will find this very strange but…when Everett and I broke up, when he decided to leave…I knew almost immediately I'd made a terrible mistake. And…I knew there was no turning back. But I still knew I'd been fortunate in love. First with your father, and then with Everett. It was my fault when Everett felt he had to leave. My loss. Our loss."

Beck couldn't move. He drew a sharp breath in and then held it in the center of his chest. He didn't want to indicate how stunned he was at his mother's revelation. He waited for her to say more, to explain why his stepfather went away. He'd wondered if that had been his fault as well.

"I never knew you felt that way. You were so…angry."

Nora nodded. "I was," she whispered. "He never wanted a divorce. He tried so hard to help me…to help…but I was crazed at the time."

"I…don't know what to say. I didn't know…"

"Of course you didn't, honey. It's taken me years to sort it out in my own head. You were a child. How could you know? Why should you?" Nora sat up abruptly, putting down her mug. "Anyway…" she murmured, as a way to end the discussion and change the subject. Beck let her. "Shortly before Everett died, I learned he was leaving me money. A great deal of it. He didn't put it in his will. He gave me the money before he died. He…he knew he didn't have much time."

"I was going to tell you he left me his company. All of his business holdings and the rest of his assets."

"I'm not surprised. He always treated you as his own son. And I was always grateful, always impressed that he didn't care that I had first married a Black man and had you before he and I came together. When Mason came along, Everett said from the start that the business would be left for you two boys to share."

She suddenly looked very small, very sad in her floral chair. Beck suddenly did not see her as his mother, but as a still-attractive sixtyish woman who had a sensual presence that disguised a core of uncertainty and old tragedy. And there had been many.

"You don't have to talk about."

"I do. I do. More than you know. And it should have begun so many years ago. Where to start?" she whispered as if to herself. Nora pulled herself together, sat up straight, and looked squarely at him. "Why don't you ever come back to see me after the show?"

"What?"

"You come to my show every now and then. I see you sitting in back of the audience by yourself. I always expected you'd come backstage to say hello. Why don't you?"

Beck shifted in his chair, finished the beer, and rolled the empty, wet bottle between his two palms. "I didn't want to…bother you. There was always a lineup of fans…"

"Bother me? I'm sorry you never felt you could let me know. I would like that, Beck. Very much. You come first."

"I wasn't sure, Mom. I didn't…"

"I know. I know," Nora said, her voice very soft and very… maternal. "That is also my fault."

Beck felt strange. There was instantly a sense of that was then and this is now. Was his mother trying to tell him something? Was she offering something? He'd been waiting since he was twelve to have her speak to him about her feelings…or to listen to his. He stood up. He was suddenly feeling the way he felt the night Eden wanted to go into the club that was showcasing his mother as the evening's performer. She couldn't know that, of course, and the why was too long, complicated and painful to try to explain in twenty-five words or less. And now his mother was telling him *right out* it would have meant something to her if he'd let her know of his presence—all those visits, all those months, years—while she sang ballads and love songs to an audience of strangers. She'd wanted to know he was there, too.

"Next time, I promise. I'll come back to say hello. I gotta go," he said, walking out of the room and into the kitchen to dispose of the beer bottle. Alone, Beck took a moment to brace his hands against the edge of the sink and lean his body into them. He bowed his head and let more than twenty years of grief and loss and awful pain roll over him. His mother's words had just spun his entire world around. For a moment it had been possible to smooth over the fact that she'd once blamed him, in horrible heartbreaking words, for the death of his younger brother, the white child she'd had with Everett.

His heart was racing, and he felt overheated. He'd spent all of his adult life with guilt and shame, and a desperate need not to lose his mother's love, holding on by his fingernails to the edge of her life so that he could still be a part of it. Of her. Was it possible that in fifteen minutes his mother had intimated that she didn't hate him for what had happened when he was a little boy? Was she really suggesting, after all this time, that they needed to talk?

Nora returned to the kitchen behind him. Again, there was that almost tender touch on his back. He slowly straightened and exhaled. He faced her, his gaze confused and questioning, searching deep into her eyes for answers.

"Thanks again for your help."

"Sure. You know you can call me anytime."

She smiled at him, but it was sad. "Thank you, Beck."

He embraced his mother, loosely and briefly, and headed for the front door. Nora was right behind him. He grabbed his jacket where he'd hung it on the doorknob.

"I know you're not interested in running Everett's company. What are you going to do?"

"I have no idea," he said honestly, and then added, "I'm going to meet with Matt Sorkin…"

"That's a good idea," she said. "And what about all the money? The company is one thing. Millions of dollars of disposable income Is something else. You could go hog wild. Just be careful not to let Alia know."

Beck couldn't help laughing cynically at the idea. "I can't think of anything I really want."

"Well, honey…maybe what you really want isn't a *thing*. Find a way to have some fun. You deserve a little fun."

Beck suspected his mother was right.

"Man, I've seen you more in the past month than in the past several years," Matt said, taking the chair from the empty desk next to Beck's in the open, non-modular office. He glanced around quickly to see how close they were in earshot to anyone else. There were fewer than a dozen young men and women in the enormous space, all focused on their computer screens. "I appreciate you suggesting we meet here. I know I own my company but there's absolutely *no* privacy," he finished with a chuckle and a wry shake of his head.

"The benefits of remote work," Beck agreed, swiveling in his chair to face Matt. "One of the unexpected benefits of the coronavirus pandemic, I guess it's fair to say. Lots of folks decided they liked the option of working from home."

"Sounds great in theory. How many people actually are disciplined enough to stay home, in their pj's or sweats, and actually get work done for six or seven hours? And how much weight do they gain each week?"

They both laughed at the possible answer.

"So. I just want to make clear that I don't know all the ins and outs of Everett's business," Matt said. "I know he was very organized, trusted all his contractors and subcontractors, and was brutal about letting people go who crossed him, messed with his money or his business, or didn't do their job. I put together some information about the structure, top to bottom. Everett, of course, was at the top."

"Okay," Beck said, accepting a folder of information and immediately opening it to the first page. He scanned it quickly, went to the second page and did the same, and then closed the folder. "Weekend homework," he murmured without much enthusiasm.

"Look, I know this is overwhelming. It doesn't sound like Everett prepared you at all."

"He didn't. It was by accident that I found out from my mother that he actually always intended for me and my brother to take over one day."

Matt nodded thoughtfully, his brows furrowing. "Yeah, well. No one expected Mason to die so young. But there is you."

Beck focused, not allowing his mind to drift back into history and loss. He remained silent.

"That was an awful time," Matt murmured. "My wife and I felt completely helpless. We didn't know what to do, what to say. When Everett and Nora and you got back from Myrtle Beach without Mason… It was unbearable for them."

Beck crossed an ankle over his knee. His jaw tightened. He remembered very well. No one had asked him how he felt. From the time they got back home to DC until pretty much a year later, Beck had no recollection of anything, not in the family, not in his life. Another year before Everett left home. Beck was about to enter high school.

"Anyway…here we are," Matt said, pulling them both back from the past.

For a moment neither of them knew what more to say about that terrible time.

"I was actually thinking…maybe I should talk with Eden. She was in Everett's business for many years."

Matt brightened. "That's a great idea! Of course you should talk to her. She'll know far more than I do." He leaned forward in his chair. "Have you spoken to her at all? That day in Katherine's office, she left in a hurry. I think maybe she was upset about something."

Beck thought carefully. A lot had gone on between him and Eden since that day, and he was not inclined to share or explain any of it.

"Yeah, she was upset. It was a lot to take in. Neither of us knew we were coming in to hear the contents of a will, and we both left with more than we could have dreamed of in a lifetime. She's okay. We...talked."

"Good, good," Matt nodded. He leaned forward even more. "I have to confess something, Beck. I made a big mistake some years ago. I actually asked Everett if there was anything going on with him and Eden." Matt's voice dropped low with embarrassment.

"What did he say?" Beck questioned quietly.

Matt chuckled without any humor. "He nearly ripped me a new one, if you get my drift."

"I do."

"Man, he really was furious. I apologized. I wasn't sure we were going to get over that. The thing is, Everett had enormous respect for Eden. In her own way she was a little like him. Found herself with a lot of responsibility at an early age, and there was nothing for it but to do what she had to do. Take care of herself and her sister. Everett said she was willing to work hard, but she didn't have a focus, a plan. She really had no idea what she wanted to do with her life. She was just putting one foot in front of the other, trying to keep her and her sister together. That impressed your father. And he was willing to give time to teaching her what he could." He shook his head and chuckled. "And now she's about to finish law school. Incredible. Unusual young woman."

Beck had already learned he'd made the same misreading of Eden, but he was more than happy to have his own conclusion confirmed.

"I agree," he said.

"Anyway, you have what I know. Look it over. Make a list of questions and then talk with Eden. I think we're done. Anything else I can help you with?"

"There was an item in one of the trade papers about Everett's company being passed on to me. Within a week, I started getting notices and threats of lawsuits. Some from Everett's clients, but some…kind of mysterious with unclear connection. Unhappy folks who'd found reason to sue him."

"Oh, oh. Here we go," Matt said sarcastically. "The scent of money."

"You mean, because I've come into this inheritance?"

"Of course. Talk to Katherine. She can certainly advise you."

"For real?"

"Yep. For real," Matt said. "I guess the good news is you don't need to do anything all by yourself. There's plenty of professional help available. But don't go around talking about this, okay? I mean, about acquiring the business or a lot of money. Once people know who you are and what you have, the more they'll find reasons to make themselves known to you."

"What about Eden?"

"She got a personal inheritance. Yours is part of a much bigger obligation. Eden doesn't have anything to worry about."

"Zach, this is actually very good," Eden said, turning over the several pages of the brief Zach Milford had asked her to review. It was all about his own clinic, his pro bono work in a courtroom setting where he'd be expected to aid in an actual civil trial.

They were sitting next to each other in one of the small study cubicles in the music division of the rare-book collection at the Library of Congress, where Eden worked a few hours a week. Zach had his long legs stretched out, frowning over pages of his work that she had finished editing.

As Eden sat back and sighed after concentration on Zach's paper, she had only one thought that kept repeating itself in her head like a metronome. Beck's writing was far superior.

She knew it wasn't a fair comparison. Beck was a professional writer, as was more than evident in the few samples of his work she'd read. It was moving. It was descriptive. It evoked a scenario and a real person at its center. And the beauty and sincerity in the article about Everett had made her cry. Nothing that Zach Milford would ever write was likely to draw the same response.

"What should I do next?" He abruptly sat up and leaned forward to talk quietly to her.

Eden looked patiently at Zach, who in turn regarded her with a combination of affection, trust, and reverence, and the belief that he could always expect her to tell him what he most wanted and needed to hear. It still astonished her that Zach put that much faith in her.

Maybe he really did love her?

No.

Absolutely not.

"I suggest you read this over and over until you have it practically memorized. You don't have to argue the case, but your partners are going to expect you to lead them, okay? This response is their road map."

Zach was listening very closely, watching her eyes and her mouth as she spoke. And he nodded so that she knew he was listening.

She'd trained him well.

"Thanks, E. You have no idea how much I appreciate that you haven't kicked me to the curb and told me to fend for myself."

"It crossed my mind more than once," Eden said seriously. "And I'm not even being paid for this. You know, Zach, as a Black woman, I shouldn't let you take advantage of me this way."

He laughed. "As a very *smart* Black woman. I know that about you very well. I'm even more grateful."

"If I already had my degree and my license, you would not be able to afford my billable hours."

"I hear you, and you'd be more than worth it."

"Thank you."

"Okay." He sighed richly, satisfied that he'd gotten all he needed to know from her. He took all the other pages from Eden and began to carefully place them in a very expensive brown leather portfolio with his initials stamped in gold leaf on the outer flap. He glanced at her, studied her with a look that shifted smoothly from fellow student to former lover. "Can I take you for a drink? How about dinner?"

"No."

"That was fast. You didn't even hesitate."

"We're not going into that again," Eden responded quietly, not meeting his persuasive gaze. "I'm trying to maintain a friendship with you, Zach. I like you. I really do. But that's *all*."

"Can't blame a guy for trying," he said dryly.

He rubbed her arm briefly as he stood to leave. He affectionately ran his hand over her thick, looping curls, smiling as they sprang back into place.

"Zach?" Eden called out as he began to walk away. He turned. "Let me know how it goes, okay?"

"I will. Thanks."

Eden had to admit he had a rock-solid ego. Nothing scratched the surface of it or left marks. He shrugged good-naturedly and knew when to give up. Mostly. And he was genuinely a good man. Just not one she could be in love with. There were character traits she felt were missing. The ones that Beck had already demonstrated. Eden sighed, feeling herself slipping into the depths of wishful thinking. Not for the first time she wished he'd stayed that night after their U Street dinner.

Dare she hope?

With her smartphone silenced she almost missed the flashing LED screen signaling an incoming call. Eden reached for her cell, simultaneously turning the key for the rare-bookroom lights to Off as she shouldered her backpack and closed the door behind her.

"Hello?"

"It's Beck."

"Hi. What a surprise."

He laughed quietly. "It shouldn't be. I'll have to up my game so you will expect to hear from me more often."

"I'm glad to hear from you. Can't you see me smiling?" Eden asked brightly. He laughed in her ear.

"Is this a good time?"

"I'm just finishing a shift at LC, and I'm about to leave."

"Any plans for the rest of the day?"

"Why do you want to know?"

"Why do you think? Any chance of getting together? I know it's last minute."

"Oh…I–I can work something out."

He laughed again. "Are you sure?"

"Why don't you plan on coming to my place. In about two hours?"

"Sounds great. Want to do dinner?"

"We will. At my place. And then I have something fun we can do. At least I hope it'll be fun."

"That sounds like an offer I can't refuse."

"Ummm. You might regret it if you do," her tone teased him.

"Sold. I'm on it."

———————

Beck sat back against the edge of the sofa from his position on the floor and flexed his back. He drained the last of his wine and set the glass aside. It was the wine he had purchased on the Sunday they'd made their way to the farmers market near Lafayette Square. He watched Eden as she studied the pile of odd-shaped but colorful pieces scattered over the coffee table, frowning over what piece would go where in the sixteen-by-twelve-inch partially finished puzzle. He was enjoying watching her serious consideration of her choices. Beck scanned over the board and the pile of small pieces and picked up one, passing it to her.

"Oh. Thanks," Eden said absently. Quickly, she inserted the piece into its proper place for a perfect snug fit. She sat back on the opposite side of the table from Beck and grinned, pleased with herself. She glanced at him, her eyes bright and inquisitive.

"If this was a contest between us, you could have won easily about an hour ago," she said, sighing. "Why did you give up?"

"I don't see this as a contest. Besides, if we actually finished the puzzle really fast, what would be the fun in that? What would we do for the rest of the evening?"

Eden grinned ruefully, giving him a sly glance. "I bet something would have come to mind. But I wasn't sure putting together a puzzle was exactly how you expected to spend the evening."

He leaned forward. "I really didn't give it a lot of deep thought, Eden. As long as I had a chance to spend it with you, I really didn't care what we did."

"Seriously?"

"Seriously," he nodded.

"Well, for a second date, it was certainly different."

"Then that's good enough for me. For a second date."

"Why did you give me the puzzle in the first place?"

Beck tried to stretch out his legs beneath the table, and when he did so, Eden was positioned between his feet on the other side. It seemed like he was cradling her, but she wasn't close enough for that. She didn't appear to notice, and he was careful not to touch her, not to be too familiar. He wasn't about to blow any opportunity to stay in Eden's good graces.

"The digest was doing a two-part piece on young startup businesses in the district. By young, I mean based on ideas that came from high school through undergrad students. One project that caught my writer's attention was a freshman class from Hopkins that took special occasion slogans, paired them with illustrations or photographs, and made them into puzzles. Some were fanciful and pretty. You know…flowers and sunsets, that kind of thing. Some were science-based, like the solar system or constellations. They left their samples with my staff."

Eden picked up the box top and reexamined the cover art. "This one says *You're T-rrific!* with a dinosaur—"

"T-Rex."

"—running through a field of flowers?" She chuckled, shaking her head. "I don't think that's scientific or accurate."

"Okay, so it's corny."

"I love it." She put the top down and leaned her forearms on the table to regard him.

Beck loved the warmth and affection he saw in her eyes. He was feeling very comfortable with her. And he believed she was once again trusting him. Surprisingly, he *was* having a good time.

"And you were thinking of me when you picked this particular puzzle?" She got thoughtful for a moment, looking away. "If I had a dollar for every guy who'd *ever* surprised me with something simple and thoughtful, I still couldn't afford a cup of coffee."

"And you don't even drink coffee."

"Right," Eden said, rolling her eyes.

He looked over the table, the puzzle not even half-finished. It had been a relaxing, very easy time with Eden, not having to be on or entertaining, or to pretend anything. He glanced at her again. She was yawning, her slender hand held politely in front of her mouth.

"We're not going to finish it tonight," Beck said.

"No. I think I'm done. And I don't know if I can stand. My butt…"

Beck stood up from the floor without jostling the table or accidentally kicking Eden. He came around to her side and helped her up from the floor, chuckling as she moaned and groaned in exaggeration of stiff muscles and sitting too long in one spot.

They turned and faced each other, and Beck knew immediately that the casual, easy part of the evening was over. When he'd arrived at Eden's apartment earlier, he didn't have a single expectation, except that they have the evening together. He just wanted to be with her. The puzzle was mindless entertainment. And she had surprised him by making dinner. He'd been prepared to take them out but was actually very happy it didn't work out that way.

There was no mention whatsoever of the standoff between them, but they talked about their recent U Street date. They didn't mention the incredibly stirring and sensual good-night kiss when he returned her home. What was there to say about a kiss that had left him wanting more? Had Eden felt the same way? It could have led to something but now, thinking about it, Beck was glad that it didn't. Too fast. Too predictable. He didn't want *anything* about his relationship with Eden to be predictable. He was ready for big surprises. Something to look forward to.

Eden yawned again, arched her back, stretching. He didn't know if she realized how suggestive her movements were. She reminded him of a dancer, moving to loosen joint kinks, not aware of or concerned with how they might look to someone observing them. Beck swallowed and tried to get a rein on his imagination, thinking of her twisting sensually like this against him, in his arms. He averted his gaze and corralled his thoughts. He *knew* Eden wasn't being deliberately provocative but, *man*, it was messing with his libido.

"Well…" Beck began. He realized he sounded a little nervous. "I better get going. It's close to midnight." He pointed to the puzzle. "We'll knock it out the next time."

"Do you…have to go?"

Beck's stomach roiled. The question was quiet. But serious and…hopeful. He swallowed, so unprepared. He looked at Eden, studied her expression, her stance. She stood with her arms wrapped around her torso, gracefully balanced on one bare foot, the other foot atop it. And she looked at him, openly questioning his decision.

What did she want? What would she have him do?

"I thought you'd be ready to kick me out. It's late. I actually have some reading to do tonight. And you? You typically have a pretty impossible daily to-do list."

"Always. The question is…would you like to stay the night? With me?"

The last words were barely a whisper.

How could he possibly refuse?

He took a step closer to her, forcing her to look up into his face. Her eyes were wide open as she tried to read what was reflected in his gaze. He put his arms on her waist, and she wrapped her hands around his arms as if to hold him there, and they stared with mutual uncertainty.

"Eden, I would love to stay. Isn't it obvious?"

She shrugged and lightly slid her hands up and down his arms. Beck unconsciously tightened and flexed his biceps, her very touch stimulating. "I was afraid maybe you'd think…I was…I was throwing myself at you."

He slowly put his arms completely around her, drawing her to him, rubbing his chin against her cheek, stroking her back. "And you're not used to doing that. I know. I suspect you don't want a lot of macho bullshit in your space from some dude trying to jump your bones."

Beck winced. Not delicate, he considered. But Eden chuckled, the sound muffled against his chest.

"That's about right."

"So, how do you know I'm any different?"

She drew back and looked into his face. "I'm known since the day of the memorial for Everett."

"That simple?"

"For me, yes."

He let the back of his fingers brush down the smoothness of her cheek. "When is Holly due back?"

"Tomorrow afternoon."

"I'll leave in the morning," Beck decided. He held his breath at the gaze of pleasure she bestowed upon him. He hoped he deserved it. He gently pushed her away. "I'll move the puzzle so it doesn't accidentally get pulled apart."

"If you can, move it to the dining table."

It was settled.

Eden disappeared down the short hallway, and Beck heard a room door quietly close.

CHAPTER 7

Beck shifted the board holding the puzzle as Eden had directed, all the time thinking of the spontaneous sleepover he was about to have with her. The level of his nervousness was matched only by the other possibilities and promise. He moved their wineglasses and a half-consumed bowl of popcorn to the kitchen.

After several more minutes, Beck heard the door at the end of the corridor open, and Eden came out just to the living room entrance. She'd taken a shower. He caught a whiff of scented body oil. She was dressed in a cute pajama set of short shorts and a matching tank top. As she approached, he was momentarily distracted with how incredibly lovely and natural Eden appeared, and seemingly unselfconscious of being mostly undressed before him. It was a becoming dichotomy of innocence and erotic sensuality, bashfulness and boldness.

"I'm ready," she said.

He walked toward her, and Eden turned back down the hall to her room, going to her bed and immediately climbing in under the duvet.

He took off his front-zippered sweater and tossed it on top of a wicker trunk beneath the window. He was wearing a black T-shirt beneath that he left on. Eden was clothed, and he took his signals from her. She watched him, and he watched her as he stripped out of his slacks and socks…and nothing more.

How far to go?

One step at a time.

Beck carefully got into the bed next to her and settled close so that they faced each other. Eden turned out the bedside lamp. The bed linens rustled and shifted until Eden had moved closer to him and rested her hand against his chest. Testing.

He felt the need to say something into the dark void of the room.

"You'll have to let me know what you want. I'm game."

She was quiet and still for a long moment. "I don't know," she finally said softly. "I don't mean to be coy or flaky. A tease. I only know I didn't want you to leave. I don't think I wanted to be alone. I've never felt like that before."

He placed his hand on her waist and just rested it there. "That's a good enough reason for me."

"You don't mind if…"

"I don't mind, *whatever*. Relax. It's okay."

She sighed deeply, and Beck could feel her body go limp beneath his hand, her waist rising and depressing with her breathing.

His body urges were signaling the need for more from Eden than hugs and cuddling. Beck made the first move, accepting the open invitation. His hand began to stroke the length of her smooth thigh, the skin warm and soft. She shifted, her thigh almost pressed to his groin. Beck hissed in a breath, and his body pulsed against her. He let his hand glide back up to her waist, to the hem of the tank top, and beneath to tease his fingers over her stomach, and around her belly button. The muscles quivered under his touch and Eden released a breathy sigh on a high note.

"I guess we're not going to sleep yet?" she asked softly.

He laughed deep in his chest and the back of his throat. "I don't think that's what either of us have in mind." Her slender hand was brushing over the tiny point of his nipple beneath the black T-shirt.

"I have a better idea," he suggested, beginning to nuzzle the side of her neck.

Her hand suddenly went irrelevantly to her hair to finger and fuss through a crown of small puffs of all over dark, natural curls. He grabbed her hand, pulling it down to her side. Beck dove his hand into her hair, cradling her head as he bent over her and gave Eden a deep, passionate kiss. "You are incredibly beautiful."

He kissed her again before she could respond, letting his tongue invade the warm cavern of her mouth. Their tongues did a wet erotic dance that further heightened his desire. Eden undulated her pelvis against him, feeling the full, hard length of him, making Beck moan and return the favor.

He suddenly pulled away, pivoting his body to get out of the bed. He could just make out Eden, lying curled on her side, watching as he shed the black T-shirt and stepped out of his briefs. He wasted no time, empowered to let his desire for her run free. He'd come prepared for this moment, waiting for the signal from Eden that she was ready for what might come next. He'd pulled away long enough to take precautions to protect both of them before returning to her arms, kissing her with a growing need that made Beck feel like he was on fire and about to explode. He felt his passion mounting and returned to the bed and to her.

I want you to stay, she'd said.

That meant more to him than Eden could possibly know or he could ever explain.

Beck climbed back onto the bed and settled his mouth on hers, their tongues dueling slowly in a tango that could only have one ending. She pulled her mouth free long enough to inhale and exhale on a soft moan. He slipped his hand beneath the band of her sleep shorts, briefly stroking her to help bring Eden to the same degree of readiness that she could clearly detect in him. She awkwardly lifted her hips to wiggle out of the shorts. He stripped off the top. Waiting until the very last moment to expose her entire body only heightened his expectations. She lifted only one knee almost to her chest as he maneuvered over her hips and aimed true to thrust slowly into her. She breathed out a long, shuddering sigh, her eyes closed tightly, her fingers kneading into his back as the exquisite motion made her hold her breath.

Their mouths separated as they gasped for air, panting and holding tightly to each other, Beck skillfully controlling the speed of his movements and guiding her with a cadence that had them both panting in time to his plunging and her advancing to meet it. The undulation of her hips, her hot breath against his neck signaled the moment when the ultimate pulsing shattered within her. He syncopated his slow thrusting with Eden's counter-withdrawal, and they suddenly shared a shattering release almost together. He held on to her tightly, knowing it had been a miraculous moment. Instantly, the coupling cemented what he'd already come to believe, to want. They lay limp, his body on top, Eden's body imprinted beneath his. He didn't want to move. She accepted him and he felt like he was still sinking into her. Melding. She began planting little kisses on his neck, his throat. It was so gentle and loving that Beck felt a deep wave of emotion. It signaled how much he needed that kind of touch that he hadn't realized he needed, or wanted...until this moment with her.

Beck eased her leg down and moved onto his side, the better to hold Eden against him. He lifted his leg, bent at the knee to give her room to lie partially on him.

"You...okay?" he barely whispered close to her ear.

Beck stayed still, to try to hear what she was saying, burrowed as she was against his chest. Her voice was muffled, but he understood. He sighed with relief, continuing to comfort her, smiling at his good fortune. What Eden said to him wasn't at all what he was expecting. Beck had a response, and he agreed with her. Except...

Together they had been much more than "so good."

"You have to leave soon, don't you?" Eden asked, her head pillowed on Beck's smooth chest and stomach. It rose and fell with his breathing. Her finger was drawing a lazy circle around the nipple of his left breast. He drew his breath in and the peak hardened between her fingers. She did it deliberately, playfully trying to get a rise out of him. It was working.

"Yeah. Soon." His voice was a drawl, low and lazy.

Beck lay supine, not wanting to move or go anywhere. But he still felt a tickle of apprehension because where he was seemed too easy, so perfect, and he was afraid that after he got up and left, he and Eden might be in different places when they came back together. What if it wasn't the same? This moment felt so intense and natural. He closed his eyes and let his body, all his senses, absorb whatever Eden was offering. He didn't want to let go of it.

Her hand moved to caress across his abdomen. He was trying to adjust to the discovery of how sensual she was. How tactile and fearless in touching him wherever she thought it would give him pleasure. *That's a novelty*, he thought wryly. It was an incredible, wonderful surprise. He'd thought he would have to be far more careful with Eden before they got *here*, together most of the night and early morning enveloped in each other's arms. But she'd not been afraid to make the first move. That was more than just confidence. That was trust...and hope. He wasn't about to disappoint her.

As Eden had already done since they'd awakened from a post coital nap, she let her fingers trace the blue-ink-scripted tattoo that circled the bicep of his left arm. Easily visible now in daylight and intriguing. She seemed surprised to find he had a tattoo. She hadn't exactly scoped out every inch of his body, but this was the only one she going to find. Eden didn't ask what it was for, but she did ask what it said. Beck had quoted for her, in a solemn, quiet voice.

"If love could have saved you, you would have lived forever."

He knew it seemed profound, and it was, but Eden apparently decided not to question it. Maybe she understood instinctively, something she was very good at, that to do so would be invading something very private to him.

Beck didn't want to encourage any more questions.

His hand began to explore, stroking along her hip, curving around her bottom and pressing her pelvis to his. Eden closed her eyes, letting Beck's intentions, his arousal growing between their bodies, and the sensations and the mutual need take over. It was as if they suddenly realized they would have to get up and dressed soon. She rubbed her hand over his chin and cheek, finding the slight abrasion of his five-o'clock shadow masculine, very sexy. He turned his head and managed a brushing of his lips on her palm. Her fingers felt the tensing of his jaw as Beck clamped down to meter his quickly rising desire.

"Do we have time?" Eden asked in a whisper, already accommodating his weight over her.

He began pulling kisses from her mouth, teasing with his tongue. Changed tactics just long enough to answer. "No. Want to stop?"

Eden exhaled with a shuddering breath and a quiet moan as he maneuvered her hips and thighs to enter her. She shook her head, no longer able to say anything.

Beck made sure there was no need to.

———————

Eden was riddled with guilt, feeling the tension twisting at her stomach. She kept repeating to herself that she had no business frivolously walking into Tiffany's to treat herself to…*something*. But it was not just *anything*. It was the *thing* that had brought her into Tiffany's in the first place. That had been when she'd successfully completed the brutal first year of law school. And it had not been her now-beloved diamond earrings.

She felt she deserved a treat, a small one. She was close to commencement, cause enough for a celebration. But she'd also allowed herself a certain delirium of happiness after the spectacular, sensual, and loving night—and morning—she and Beck had spent together. Now, Eden stood outside the venerable shop ready to take the plunge and actually buy herself a gift, to spend money without worrying that she was neglecting some other essential expense. Like the rent.

The store had just opened. She was there when the doors were unlocked, and she was the very first customer to enter. She'd have to hurry because of an appointment at Central City, her advocacy pro bono office. She knew the sales associates who were familiar with her would not yet be on duty, so there would be no need to stop and greet and chat with anyone. Eden continued on to the section marked Elsa Perretti Diamonds and browsed the cases until she found what she was looking for: the diamonds-by-the-yard pendants and necklaces that were the designer's trademark.

She knew exactly what she wanted and quickly made two selections from the display. Eden waited until the sales clerk reappeared with her purchases in the traditional baby-blue boxes tied with inch-wide white grosgrain ribbon. She left the store smiling, and her guilt miraculously disappeared. Eden silently thanked Everett Nichols for making it possible for small dreams to come true.

"What did you say? Did you just tell me Everett gave you money?"

"He *left* me some money in his will."

Holly stared wide-eyed at her sister, her mouth partially open in total disbelief. "How much?"

"That's not really any of your business."

"It can't be all that much if you won't tell me." Impatient, Holly pushed their shopping cart down the aisle, heading for checkout. "$50,000? $100,000?" Holly asked, starting to unload the cart at the register.

"I'm not going to say, Holly."

"What are we doing here?" Holly fussed, waving an arm around. "We could have called in an order and had it delivered."

"An hour ago you wouldn't have complained. And I do most of the shopping anyway. You're the one who wanted to tag along." Holly pouted. "What are you so worked up about?"

"There's so much we could do with more money."

"What do you mean *we*?"

"We share everything."

Eden looked steadily at her sister, causing Holly to avert her gaze as if she hadn't noticed. "Want to give me an example of the last time you shared something with me? Besides gossip."

"We share the apartment."

"That doesn't count. It's a cost-saving measure. Two can live cheaper than one."

Holly didn't respond and Eden knew she was mulling over the truth.

They were through the checkout, each grabbing two bags and leaving the store. The morning had begun sunny but was now clouding over and threatening an early spring rain.

"We better hurry," Eden said, walking briskly the three blocks to their building.

"Did you get enough to pay for a car?"

"Yes, I can afford to buy a car. But I'm not going to. I don't need one."

"Okay, buy one for me."

Eden grinned at her sister with the amusement of listening to someone with a childish wish list. "You're gone out of the country four days out of seven. When do you expect to drive one? Did you ever renew your license? Where would you go when you're not catching up on sleep or clubbing with your local buds? You don't need a car, either."

They reached the building just as the first fat splats of rain hit the sidewalk. They hurried inside and up to the apartment. In the middle of unpacking and storing items, Holly stopped and turned to Eden again, staring pointedly at her.

"How about doing it just because I asked you to. It only seems fair."

"Why would that be fair?" Eden questioned, truly puzzled.

"Because," Holly said as if that explained everything. "Because now you could buy anything you want."

Eden thought immediately of the earrings. But also something more recent.

"I do work hard, you know. If my school tuition wasn't covered, I don't know how we'd manage this apartment on your salary and my part-time jobs."

"If you'd played Zach the right way… You said he wanted to marry you. You'd be set. I still don't understand why you threw him over. He's rich!"

"First of all, Zach didn't really want to marry me. He only wanted to aggravate his family. Second, he shouldn't get married. He doesn't know what it means. Last and most important, Zach is too young for me…and I wasn't in love with him. That's a biggie."

Holly shook her head. "Well, *I* would have married him."

Eden stole a glance at her sister. She believed Holly would have, had the relationships been different. But that would have been a mistake as well, and a mess.

"What time are you leaving tomorrow?" Eden asked.

"Eleven. I think I'm working with a different crew and a new pilot. There's an orientation."

Holly grabbed a freshly purchased apple and washed it under the running tap water. She methodically cut it up and placed the wedges on a small plate. She sat at the dining table next to Eden and began sorting the mail they'd picked up coming in from their shopping. Mostly bills and announcements. And one card that Eden slowly opened.

"Who's that from?" Holly asked.

"It's from Daddy." She opened the card and read. "*Hey, Eden and Holly…*"

"*How are my two beautiful girls…*" Holly picked up by rote.

"*Sorry I haven't been in touch in a while but…*" Eden read in a flat tone.

"*You know Daddy's thinking about you…*" Holly followed.

"*All the time,*" they quoted simultaneously.

"*Things have been a little tough here,*" Eden continued on her own. "*We had some extra expenses this month. You know how much I hate to ask…*" Eden and Holly exchanged amused and skeptical glances over the top of the card. "*But I'll appreciate it if you could send a few bucks my way.*"

"Well, you know he doesn't mean two dollars, or twenty," Holly murmured sarcastically.

Eden sighed, putting the card back in its envelope. "No. He means at least two hundred."

"We can't keep doing that," Holly said, annoyed. "We never even get birthday cards from him."

"That's not the point. He's not a great father, but he's not a terrible person. He's just…just…"

"Go ahead and say it. Weak, selfish, thoughtless. Okay, maybe he can be charming sometimes," Holly concluded grudgingly.

"He is our father. You only get one in a lifetime," Eden murmured. And then thought, no. Sometimes you get two, like Beck having Everett for a stepdad.

"I know that tone. You're going to send him the money, aren't you?"

"It's not a lot of money. He might need it for something important." Eden thought seriously for a moment. She was already thinking of sending much more. "I hope it's not something like a medical bill. I should call him and find out what's going on."

"How come you won't do as much for me?"

Eden didn't respond right away. She looked at her younger sister, with her light, animated features and wide, full mouth capable of a breathtaking smile. Her ability to charm guilelessly and leave a trail of broken hearts. Whether she knew it or not, Holly definitely had more than her share of her father's genes.

Holly suddenly got up from the table and headed to her room. "How are you doing with your student loan payment?" Eden asked as she walked away.

"I'm doing it, but it's killing me. It's never going to be done. The number only gets bigger each month with interest and other fees."

Eden quickly reappeared, sliding back into her chair next to her sister.

"I'll pay it off for you," Eden said.

Holly at first didn't seem to understand, and then she stared at Eden in the same way as when Eden first told her Everett had left her money in his will.

"Are you kidding me?"

"I'm serious. At the rate you're going, you'll be paying it off when you have grandkids. It would have been better if you'd finished your degree."

"I know, I know. If you really mean it…"

"I really mean it," Eden said sincerely. "I'm not going to buy you a car, but paying off that loan makes more sense right now." She brought her hands to the tabletop and slowly pushed a small blue box with white ribbon across the space to Holly.

Holly blinked at her sister, then down to the blue box, her mouth dropping open. She looked at Eden again with a questioning gaze that was bright with expectation. Eden merely smiled. Holly unwrapped the box, gasping when she saw the Perretti necklace with two small diamonds, one at the end of a short descending length of gold chain. Holly suddenly got up, rushing around the table to gracelessly hug Eden and squealing in surprise.

"Thankyouthankyouthankyou. Oh, Eden! This is so fantastic. And about the student loan, too."

"It would have been a better surprise if you weren't whining so much. I was going to take us to dinner and give you the necklace then. You can thank Everett," Eden said, arching her brow. "I got a necklace for myself, too. Not like yours, but..."

Holly nodded, releasing Eden and staring at her with renewed interest. "He really did leave you a lot of money?"

"That's what I said."

"How much, exactly?" Holly tried again.

"$5 million," Eden replied in a quiet voice.

Holly's eyes grew huge. "Holy shit."

"This way," Beck instructed as he placed his hand at the back of Eden's shoulders to guide her.

They were leaving the campus of the Georgetown Law Center and found themselves on the pedestrian street not far from Union Station. Eden glanced at him, curiosity in her gaze, but he could see it was mingled with a quiet joy that he had shown up with little advance notice to see her. And, of course, Beck was hoping that Eden was feeling and thinking the same as he was. That after what he could only term a mind-blowing night together she would want to see him as well. Simply seeing her now made him recall the warm and stimulating intimacy they'd shared.

"How did you find me?" she asked.

Beck grinned and turned them down Massachusetts Avenue. "I was paying attention the other morning when I asked about your schedule for the next couple of days. Work, school, volunteer, school, interviews, court hearing. And school. Did I get that right?"

"Pretty much. But...why did you want to know?"

Beck suddenly stopped and turned to her. He was perfectly happy for the moment, just looking at her. It was an overcast day, the sun ducking in and out of a mesh of clouds, but it wasn't going to rain. Still, it was late March and spring had finally arrived and there were little gusts of wind. Eden's soft hair was whipping about but she didn't seem to care. She wore a black knee-length cardigan that provided more than enough warmth for the spring day. There was a cashmere scarf wound twice around her neck, the colors picked up in her berry lip rouge. He wanted to kiss her but a thousand and one students and faculty swarming on and off the campus didn't allow for that kind of display.

"Why do you think? I was looking for a chance to get together again. I'm on deadline for the next issue of the magazine, I have interviews tomorrow..."

"I have a final to turn in, and a hearing to prepare for..."

"And Holly is probably due back the day after."

Eden sighed and gave him a half smile of regret. "Right."

His brows furrowed over the top of his sunglasses. "The hell with it," he muttered and bent to kiss her. It was quick but still filled with feeling and longing before he pulled back.

Beck clicked the automatic opener on a full-size silver-gray SUV they were standing next to. He held the passenger door for her as Eden slid the backpack off her shoulder and he took it from her. He put it on the floor behind her seat and came around to the driver side and climbed in.

"I forgot to tell you about the new wheels."

She was looking around the interior features of the car and inhaling the smell of new leather.

"Is this with your inheritance from Everett?"

"He made it possible for me to buy a brand new car sooner than I'd planned."

"It's nice. Congratulations," she said, not knowing what else to say about a new car. It was just a car as far as she was concerned. "I don't really need a car, but I did treat myself to an open account with Lyft. It's such a trip pushing a few buttons on my cell and ordering a car at any time, any place. I do feel a bit spoiled."

Beck grinned at her.

"It's incredible that we now have the means and the money, and so far neither one of us can think of anything more exciting to spend money on than transportation to get around DC."

"So sad," Eden lamented with a shake of her head.

"You have those diamond earrings on your wish list," Beck said, pulling into traffic. "Have you bought them yet?"

"No," Eden said simply.

"Why not?"

She thought for a moment. "I'm still enjoying the fantasy of them. I like having something to look forward to down the road. I still love the anticipation of going into Tiffany's and how all the sales people are glad to see me. I'm sure they're all saying, 'Here comes that crazy woman who just wants to stare at these diamond earrings that she'll *never* be able to afford.' I actually did buy myself a gift. I also got something for Holly."

Beck laughed. "That's guilt. But you're getting there. Listen, it's your jam. Play it out the way you want."

"I will." She glanced out the window. "Where are we going?"

"On a picnic."

She studied him through her dark glasses. "A picnic? You mean…a picnic?"

"Surprised?"

"Well…yeah."

"That's the idea."

Beck didn't take them very far. Only a mile plus down to Main Avenue and the pathway around the Tidal Basin. But on the approach, he heard Eden's soft inhalation as she saw the clusters of pink blossoms on the hundreds of cherry trees surrounding the Basin. The blooming had just begun, but Beck had a coworker check with the botanic garden staff to confirm it would be several more days before all of the trees were at their full glory. They arrived and parked at a spot that placed them between the Lincoln and Jefferson Memorials. And directly across the width of the Basin was the newest addition to the grounds, the majestic Martin Luther King Jr. Memorial.

Getting out of the SUV, Beck removed a small shopping bag from behind his driver's seat. Eden watched in silent curiosity as Beck headed into the park, reaching out to take her hand. He wanted her to feel that they belonged together. That she was his girlfriend. That she was being courted.

Under the canopy of blossoms they reached an area of benches and a small grouping of stone tables where they stopped and Beck put the shopping bag down. Eden looked at him.

"Do you think it's too windy?" he asked, not having considered that.

"No. It's a nice spring day."

"Good. I wanted it to be easy and relaxed. Nothing formal or too fussy. I don't think that's your style."

"You seem to have learned a lot about me."

"I'm paying attention."

"So? Anything…maybe…I should know about?" she asked.

He chuckled deep in his chest. "I'll only say, not a thing you need to worry about."

She'd been too long out of the game to know what attracted a man, what to do to hold his interest. How to be striking and sexy and let him know she was willing. And ready. It seemed like so much work. What if she failed? What if she was being compared to all the bodacious and well-endowed Black women who seemed to be the current examples of what Black men wanted their women to be? Eden wondered if Beck might have a different perspective, but did that really make any difference in what he liked in a woman?

How many of the women in his life would be delighted with a picnic in late March in the park?

To Eden, it was an original idea. She liked that. Did Beck already know that it didn't take a lot to please her?

Beck began unpacking the bag and placing food containers on their impromptu dining table. Also plastic service ware…and even wine! Pretty soon they were sitting and serving themselves from the plentiful dishes…Italian pasta salads, subs stuffed with red peppers, salami, and shredded lettuce drenched in olive oil. Eden loved it.

They caught the attention of any number of passersby who boldly asked if they could join in. Eden loved that Beck was very good-natured about the friendly interruptions but made it clear it was a private lunch.

They ate leisurely, wrapped up in their own conversation…and each other, enjoying the incredible beautiful setting surrounding them. But Eden was very aware that just a day or so ago, when they were last together, they had spent a great deal of time discovering one another in a way that still had her distracted and daydreaming. The best part was that it had been largely unplanned. The evening ending on a spontaneous moment of Eden suddenly knowing what she wanted.

Now, around their casual talk, she was studying him, his handsome face with its shadow of trimmed hair, his mobile mouth as he talked, and ate, and smiled. His well-shaped hands that served the food and gestured in the air for emphasis…and had performed such thrilling magic on her body. Eden shifted, momentarily imagining them together like that, again.

"It occurred to me too late that you might have had plans to walk after your meeting with your faculty adviser this morning. You're down to the wire, right? About a month before commencement?"

"Pretty much." Eden shook her head, adjusted her sunglasses, and grabbed an olive from the antipasto. "No walking today. I have to go back to the campus when we're done to use the library."

Beck listened, nodded. "How are things between you and your sister?"

She shrugged. "We're very different women. It's sometimes hard to navigate that and respect our personalities. I don't want to be the mommy figure always telling her what she should and should not be doing. It's tiring, and it makes me out to be the wicked bitch who's trying to control her."

Beck reached across the table and unexpectedly stroked her cheek and then took her hand to squeeze and hold it.

"We don't fight all the time anymore, and I've learned to be patient. One of us has to be the grown-up in the room."

He chuckled.

"Are there any leftovers?" Eden suddenly asked, peeking into the now repacked bag.

"Two of the salads. Half a sandwich. Some of the rainbow cookies. Want to take the rest home?"

"No. But if it's okay with you, I'd like to give what's left to the two men over there."

She pointed and Beck turned to look over his shoulder at two men who were down on their luck, from the looks of what they were wearing, their shaggy beards and unkempt hair under worn baseball caps.

"I'll take it over," Beck said, starting to rise from his stone seat.

"No, I'll do it," Eden said, and already she had lifted the bag and was making her way to the two men.

She slowed her pace until they were aware of her approach, and she asked if they would like to have some leftover food she had from lunch. They listened warily, not appearing terribly interested and wanting to first look into the bag to see what she offered. Finally, one the men nodded and took the bag. Eden began making her way back to Beck, who stood watching her approach very closely. It gave Eden pleasant satisfaction to see that he was prepared to step forward quickly if he thought she needed help. She smiled as she came close, and sensing Beck's intentions to safeguard her, Eden placed her hand on his chest.

"It's all right," she said simply. He nodded, took her hand, and they began to retrace the pathway back to the park entrance and where he'd left his car.

"If you like, if you're not wildly busy this weekend…"

She laughed quietly, shaking her head.

"Maybe we can come back. By then the trees should be in full spectacular bloom."

"You're just trying to persuade me to come out and play with you."

"Yep. But I'll understand if you say no."

Eden shot him a sly, questioning glance. "I'd really like to, but let's see how the rest of the week works out. My experience is anything that can go wrong…"

"Will go wrong."

"Exactly." But she smiled.

Eden was a bit sorry when they pulled up on campus. She would rather they had more time together. Beck said nothing but she was sure he must be thinking the same thing.

"Well…you made my day," she said simply.

"Ditto."

But before she got out of the car, Beck stayed Eden with his hand on her shoulder. She turned back to him, could sense his regret that they had to go their separate ways for…who knew how long? Spontaneously, with her own regretful smile, she took his face gently in her hands and held it until she could lean in to kiss him. It was a sweet and light thank-you. She liked taking the initiative. She liked being bold and comfortable enough to let Beck know she welcomed their time together, his making his interest obvious. He lifted his hand, wrapping it around her wrist as if holding her in an awkward embrace. It might have ended there except they then looked intensely into each other's eyes, looking for signs, looking for answers.

Beck took the lead and came in close to fully capture Eden's mouth, and she opened her lips ready to accept the warm and insistent mobility of his lips, the aggressive but slow plundering of his tongue. The kiss had an immediate effect on her, perhaps on them both, and they had to make do with what they could share in that moment. It was exciting and frustrating at the same time.

Beck got out of the car to walk to her side, removing her backpack and handing it off.

"Thanks for the picnic. It was so sweet."

"Sweet, huh?" He kissed her briefly once more. "I promise to do better next time. How about a night at one of the music clubs on U Street?"

"Yes!"

"I'll make a reservation. But…I do need to ask you for a favor."

Eden stared at him, tilting her head in curiosity, trying not to prejudge what kind of favor. "Okay."

He grinned, reading her mind. "It's nothing illegal. I'd like you to meet me at Everett's office and show me around. Tell me what you know about the company, brainstorm with me about what I should do. Can you arrange that?"

Eden relaxed. "Of course I'll help."

CHAPTER 8

Beck followed Eden back to the open conference space just outside Everett's former office. They were in the company of Steel Work's general manager, Ken Duncan. Even after readily agreeing to be a guide for Beck through the company headquarters, Eden recognized that it wouldn't be appropriate, or even legal, for her to be the person in charge. When she'd reached out to Ken with Beck's request, he was more than happy to agree.

The three of them took seats at the table outside Everett's office that was normally used for group or staff meetings and for orientation with visitors and prospective clients.

"I know your head is spinning…" Ken said. "I understand it's a lot to take in in just a few hours. If I'd added another hour, we'd be taking you out on a stretcher."

Eden grinned, watching Beck and noting that he was on TMI overload. Ken could only guess at that, of course, but she knew Beck was very concerned about what he didn't know about his stepfather's business…his legacy.

Beck confirmed with a rueful grin. "Thanks for recognizing that I was reaching maximum saturation."

"Well, it was more like your eyes had gone glassy…and were starting to roll back into your head."

Beck burst out laughing at Ken's very accurate observation.

"Don't worry. No one else noticed," Eden said smoothly.

"You did," he said without rancor.

"I'm in training to notice. Lawyers have to pay attention to body language."

Beck turned to Ken and reached out to shake his hand.

"I can't thank you enough…"

"No problem at all," Ken replied. "To be honest, I was impressed that you wanted to come in and have a look around. Meet some of the staff and ask questions. This was a great opportunity to meet the new owner without too much formality."

Eden remained silent but watched Beck closely for reaction. She understood perfectly what Ken was hinting at when it came to businesses being passed along to family members who knew nothing about the business.

"No formality at all," Beck said honestly. "I readily admit I'm out of my depth. I appreciate you…and Eden offering to show me the ropes."

"It'll get easier. It's a lot to take in all at once. But if Everett fully trusted you could handle keeping the company going, then I have no problem whatsoever."

Beck reached out his hand over some of the papers and notebooks that Ken Duncan had put together for him about the business, far more detailed than what Matt Sorkin had provided. He spread his fingers, tapping the tips lightly on the topmost report.

"I have my homework cut out for me. But…when I see what my father has built, what he's accomplished…" Then he was stuck for the right words. "There's no question I have to do everything I can to make sure the company keeps going."

"I knew you'd feel that way. Everett would be very happy," Eden said.

"Well…" Ken said, standing, and they all did. "I'm going to head home. Building security knows you're here, Eden, so you can hang out for another thirty minutes or so…" He checked the time on his watch. "They'll be around to lock the doors."

"We'll be leaving soon. Thanks, Ken, for accommodating us. I hope we didn't put you out by coming so late in the day."

"Not at all. It was perfect." He turned to Beck, putting out his hand. "Welcome aboard. Please call me any time you have questions or want to come by. It's spring and this is a very busy season, so forgive me in advance…"

"…that you'll have to put me off again, and again."

Ken laughed sheepishly. "Glad you understand. But the invitation is open."

With that, he waved briefly, grabbed a jacket from a coat closet just inside the entrance, and nodded a farewell as he left.

Beck and Eden's gazes suddenly met and held for a long moment. Eden could see so many expressions cross his face in that time, not the least of which was a kind of warm personal regard that resonated with her.

"Thank you," Beck said with real sincerity.

She found herself blushing, happy that she could be of help to him, knowing that Beck felt very much out of his league and concerned that he might not be able to live up to the faith Everett had placed in him. "You don't have to thank me. I'm glad that I could help."

"Follow Ken's directions. If new business comes in, I think you should be in on the discussions so you'll learn. Talk with Ken. It's just another good way to get acclimated. Think you can handle that?" Eden ended with a bright smile laced with amusement.

Beck chuckled. "As long as I have you on my side, I'm good."

She blinked at him, not wanting to show exactly how much his faith and high regard meant to her. Respect and regard were one thing, but with more—affection and warmth—tacked on, it was different. Eden had a clear and present sense that she was ready for the *more* part.

"I'm concerned about something else," Beck began, looking at her earnestly.

Eden tilted her head and waited.

"I can't be the face of the company. I can't head it up."

"What do you mean?"

"Beyond the fact that I know zip about building construction and city planning, I don't think we're in a place where I can expect Everett's wide circle of business associates to accept me as his replacement. They might know that I'm his son, I'm large and in charge. But I'm his *Black* son. And only a stepson at that. That might hurt more than help the business."

His eyes bored into hers, and it was a moment of recognition that they had not dealt with yet. He was putting it out there, and Eden knew she had to respond honestly.

She'd briefly questioned his ethnicity as they were getting to know each other. Natural curiosity. But Eden never thought that Beck was white. There were too many physical indicators to disprove that. His way of speaking sometimes, not so much the words as the intonation, the emphasis. The rest was just in the way he responded to her. Eden knew she'd find the cultural similarities between her and Beck.

"I think you're right." She reached out to take his hand. He absentmindedly squeezed hers. Eden didn't flinch, understanding he took her hand like a lifeline. "I'm used to being judged by my looks. I walk into any room and it's clear what I am. Maybe you've had to handle stuff like that in a different way."

"I know you see the dynamics of what I'm up against. I don't want to fail Everett. But I don't want to be a sacrificial lamb, or the poster boy for cultural awareness, either. And I do have my own life, my own career. Besides, I think with the right side of my brain," he said dryly, making Eden chuckle.

She nodded. With another gentle squeeze of his hand, she let go. "It's all going to come down to what you want your place to be. You don't have to be the CEO. You could name yourself as director…or the owner. That makes it clear that you own the business, but you're not the day-to-day head. It helps ward off any backdoor complaints. I'm sure you know what I mean."

"I do."

Beck stared at her…and suddenly started laughing. "*Man!* I knew I did the smart thing in asking for your help."

He leaned forward to talk more intimately. "How come no one has claimed you?" he asked quietly, seriously.

The question caught Eden completely by surprise. "First of all, *no* one gets to 'claim' me. I'm not public property. And I'm not a prize anybody can win. Anyway, it's not a very interesting story. I could ask you the same, you know."

Beck acknowledged that with an arched brow. "I'd answer the same. Thank you for being honest."

"I haven't told you very much."

"More than you know."

Beck suggested dinner at another of the U Street hot spots, but Eden didn't want that. She wanted something simple and unpretentious, maybe with comfort food that actually made her feel comfortable. Beck decided on Ben's Chili Bowl, famous even before one of the nation's presidents decided to visit and test out the menu, which made the place even more famous afterward.

It was the kind of place with the kind of food that required a lot of napkins and that had not very comfortable seating. No ambiance, but the atmosphere was very "local," low-key. They each ordered different menu items that opened the way for Eden to presumptively want to sample Beck's dish. He seemed to get a huge kick out of her familiarity, Eden was aware, and he never behaved like it was rude, or nasty, or impudent. Eden was more than willing to return the favor. It was one of *their* rituals that she really enjoyed…and apparently so did Beck.

Now that some of Beck's concerns and questions about Steel Work had been dealt with their conversation was relaxed and random, running from college war stories to their upbringing, although Eden did become aware that Beck actually said very little about his growing up. Eden confessed that she was looking forward to commencement. And she'd be just as happy if she never had to litigate in an actual courtroom *ever*. Beck told her he'd decided on writing, reporting, journalism, and composing future novels, in high school after his composition notebook was confiscated while he was writing in it during math class. He was stunned the next day when the teacher told him he showed a real talent for writing.

"The usual route followed after that. I sent my stuff to the school magazine. Became editor in my senior year. Published my first work professionally when I was a sophomore at Duke. And I liked it. I liked thinking about a lot of different things and then writing about them. When I started getting great feedback and encouragement, I was hooked."

"Fed into your ego?" Eden asked as they left Ben's.

"Told me I was actually good at something."

"I have a feeling you're good at a lot of things you don't recognize," Eden offered.

The only response Beck made was to place his hand on her back, sliding it slowly, possessively, up to the back of her neck, and gently squeezing and massaging. She glanced up at his face to try to read his expression. But Beck's countenance showed nothing but a man who was relaxed and having a nice evening. And showing his feelings for her by keeping Eden close to his side.

"There it is," Eden pointed out when she spotted the lit marquee for the Gaslight Salon.

Beck followed her inside to a very small podium desk where their reservation was confirmed. They were then navigated through the tight placement of small bistro tables and chairs. When the staffer was about to seat them at a spot much too close to the door and too far from the miniscule stage, Beck quickly whispered something to her. She acknowledged his comment and took them farther into the room, seating them three tables from the stage and to the left of the microphone.

Once they were seated, Eden eagerly looked around, a smile of interest accompanying her roaming gaze. "What did you bribe her with to score this table? It's perfect."

"I told her that I wanted to impress my date."

Eden laughed, delighted with his clever and simple response. She liked that Beck confirmed this was a date, not a quid pro quo for their afternoon together in Everett's office.

"If anyone sneezes in here, the whole place is going to catch a cold," Eden whispered sarcastically to Beck.

He signaled a passing waiter to order drinks. The space filled up fast, and the buzz of conversation and anticipation flowed through the room. Eden was paying attention. She again leaned in to whisper to Beck. "I think every table is taken. The singer must be well known. I hope she's good."

Beck nodded. "We'll see." He drew his chair closer to Eden's and placed his arm along the back of her chair.

It wasn't much longer before the lights began to dim and the last orders were hurriedly served by the waitstaff with sure-footed confidence, able to walk the narrow pathways with speed. A trio of musicians took their places behind their instruments and tested them quietly. Someone checked the mic to make sure it was on. Someone else placed bottles of water near each of the musicians and a glass of something on a small stand near the performer's stool.

"Do you think that's water or whiskey?" Eden joked.

"I doubt if it's liquor. The house wouldn't want to risk a tipsy performer," Beck whispered, his thumb casually stroking along her arm. Eden leaned back into the movement.

The drummer did a little paradiddle on his bass and then tapped on the cymbal with his drumstick. The room went black. The disembodied voice of an announcer loudly boomed across the room.

"Ladies and gentlemen, good evening. Welcome to the Gaslight Salon and tonight's entertainment with local favorite and frequent guest Nora Michaels…"

There was a smattering of applause and whistles. The announcer quickly and efficiently listed the usual safety regulations, exit and awareness notices before concluding…

"And now, for your entertainment pleasure, please welcome to the stage *Nora Michaels!*"

The applause began again, louder, with a few cheers thrown in. When the spotlight came on it was focused near the mic, quickly widening to show the face of a woman already seated on the stool, her body relaxed and already gently moving in rhythm with the opening chords of the first number.

Eden was riveted. The white female singer was not a young woman, but she was attractive and vivacious, giving off the vibes of a woman with experience performing. Her backswept hair was auburn in color and cut just above her neckline. It was fastened in place on one side with hair combs adorned with silk pink and peach blossoms. She wore a black wide-necked silk top that just hugged her shoulder, a tunic over black pants. Her short dangling earrings appeared to be turquoise, a stunning contrast to her pale skin and black outfit…but not distracting. And she was wearing dark glasses, solidly black so that there was no hint of her eyes or their movement. She was obviously comfortable with her surroundings, with an audience, with the music opening for her. She smiled and made a small carefree wave of her hand to the audience and then adjusted the height of her mic.

"Good evening," she said cheerfully but quietly.

The answering response was more applause and more whistles. Eden joined in the applause with her own excitement and expectation. She wiggled more comfortably into her chair, her shoulder and side resting partially against Beck's chest. She gave her complete and undivided attention to the woman on the stage.

Beck didn't begin to relax until well into the first number. And he wasn't really listening to the music. He'd heard it before. He was deliberately seated in such a way, at such an angle, that he could easily watch Eden's reaction to the performance. At the moment it was with complete engagement with the singer. Assured that Eden was enjoying the set, he gave his attention to the woman on stage. There was no way to know where her eyes were focused, or where they roamed, or what she could actually see behind her protective shades. But he knew the music was very good. He knew the singing was first rate, professional, and thoroughly enjoyable. The performer's voice was strong and well trained, but even beyond all of that, it demonstrated a deep understanding and feel for the light jazz movements and switches, allowing her to improvise smoothly and with confidence. And therein lay her appeal to her audience. Nora Michaels was totally in tune with her music and the musicians, trusting them not to lead her into improvisation she couldn't follow or riff on.

The first number ended, applause again signaling appreciation. Eden enthusiastically joined in. The trio was already segueing into the second. Eden leaned forward on her elbows, the better to listen to and appreciate the performance.

Beck exhaled and took a swallow of his mixed drink. He sat back more comfortably in his chair and finally gave his full attention to the attractive performer in front of him. Now watching her closely, he admired her style, her performance chops and comfort with what she was doing. After a while his foot began to keep pace with some of the numbers. But he kept checking on Eden to gauge her reactions. She was absorbed in the music and the singer, and the love songs playfully cloaked in jazz movements.

He leaned forward at one point. "How you doing?"

She didn't turn to look at him, merely nodded rapidly. "Good. Good."

"Ready for another drink?"

"Ummm. Just ginger ale," Eden said. He could hear a kind of thoughtful consideration to her request, but Beck ignored it, signaling for the waiter.

The set was about seventy-five minutes long, allowing for the songstress to interact briefly once or twice with the audience between numbers. She also handily showed self-deprecating humor while looking out over the audience, taking a sip of water, and giving her musicians time to make changes in their instrumentation or to confer among themselves about the program and music.

"How's the voice holding up tonight?"

Shouts and disclaimers from the audience that she needn't worry.

"You're just being nice so I'll do an encore..."

Light laughter. She appeared to squint out into the dark. "But I really don't see that well anymore..."

"Take off the glasses..." someone shouted to more laughter.

"No way. I'm too shy," she mewed to more delighted laughter. "But I think...I think I see Lamar and Kitty..." A returned acknowledging shout. "Smith and Carolyn..."

"Yo!"

"...Mickey and Pam. Thanks so much to everyone for coming out tonight. Love you all."

There was applause again. Beck watched Eden swiveling her chair as she attempted to catch a glimpse of each special pair. He was busy processing how Eden was enjoying the performance, since she was not leaning on their table, *into* the music and the singer, but relaxing back against his arm, while she hugged herself.

"Do you think that was staged?" she quietly asked Beck.

"Probably not. I would guess she called out to a fan base of folks who come to a lot of her shows, who maybe send her love notes and flowers, that kind of thing."

"That's so nice," Eden cooed.

Beck grinned, charmed by her response, and rubbed her shoulder briefly. "It's also good business."

Eden tsked air through her teeth in mock annoyance. "Cynic."

The performance continued, and then the music slowed down and moved into a cadence that suggested a more thoughtful song. Maybe one of heartache and loss. Beck was listening and knew what was coming. With low, soulful feeling, Nora Michaels launched into an old Judy Garland favorite, "The Man That Got Away".

The audience loved it, applauding appreciatively for a time. Nora *killed it*, and Beck gave her credit for understanding the inherent pain and disappointment in the lyrics as well as the music. For a moment at the beginning of the song, he had an image of Alia, with her stunning beauty, who had jacked him up for more than a year. He did not see her as the one who got away, but the one he'd dodged who could have ruined his life.

Eden had not moved. But he suddenly felt a strong need to touch her and placed his hand on her lower back. Beck gently massaged in a small circle. She undulated her back against his hand before he removed it. The song came to its wrenching end and the audience gave loud and sustained applause. Nora Michaels smiled and pressed a hand to her heart, thanking everyone for their warm and enthusiastic response. She stood up and left the stage as the applause continued. The musicians never moved. In half a minute Nora returned and took her seat again. The audience, expecting her return, quieted down.

Eden eased herself back into her chair, her shoulder coming to rest again on a narrow part of Beck's chest and his arm. He enjoyed the little ways she showed her affection for him, her trust.

The encore song began, and Beck realized Eden had inhaled sharply and held the breath for several beats. She tilted her head up to him.

"I know this song. It's one of Everett's favorites."

Beck nodded. He knew this song, too. You Don't Remember Me.

It was a straightforward song about an old affair and time and separation and loss. The song ended, the lights faded out, and the audience enthusiastically demonstrated its approval. Nora Michaels stood to incline her head in thanks, to introduce, over the continuing applause, her accompanying trio, to blow a kiss to the audience, wave briefly, and leave the platform.

The lights went up, and people were already making their way to the small, narrow exit.

"What do you think?"

Eden nodded. "It was fantastic," she said quietly.

Beck touched her arm to get her full attention. She gazed at him and, for a split second, he thought he detected some sort of distress. He didn't question it. "Would you be interested in meeting the singer?"

She looked skeptical, frowning. "Are you serious? Do you know her?"

"Actually, I do."

She nodded. "Of course. You've probably interviewed her."

"Nope. Never. Come this way."

With that, Beck got in front of Eden and began heading even farther into the depths of the club, back along a narrow passageway where it was necessary to walk single file. They encountered someone from the club about to stop them when, again, Beck said something quietly and was immediately passed through. He came to stop in front of a door that was partially open and rapped on the doorframe.

"Yes?"

"Can I come in?" he said.

There was just a moment of silence, and then the door was pulled opened, and there stood Nora Michaels, dark glasses removed, her face and blue eyes bright with surprise.

"Beck! Come in, come in. Why didn't you let me know you were coming? I saw you out there."

She reached to give him a hug and Beck stooped to accommodate her petite height. He quickly stepped back and stood aside to reveal Eden standing uncertain just behind him. He used a hand to usher her into what remained of the space in the tiny closet of a dressing room. Nora sat at what passed for a dressing table in front of a framed mirror propped against the wall. It gave them all a little more maneuvering room.

"This is Eden Marsh." Beck began the introductions.

Nora turned her attention to Eden, studying her with an open but curious smile.

"Welcome."

"It's so nice to meet you," Eden said with warm sincerity. "This is an extra great surprise." She glanced briefly at Beck.

"I hope you enjoyed the show."

"Yes, I did. Beck promised to bring me. I never imagined that I'd have a chance to meet you," Eden said, looking to Beck for some guidance, but he was focused on the singer.

Beck looked at Eden. "This is my mother...Nora Michaels Dennison Nichols."

Eden was stunned into silence for a moment by the revelation. She quickly recovered to paste a smile to her lips, her eyes widened in complete surprise.

"I...didn't know. I'm sorry I'm so clueless. Beck never said... He didn't warn..."

Nora shook her head, chuckling in understanding. "No harm done. I don't quite understand why he keeps me a secret."

"Probably for the shock value," Eden said.

She didn't want to make either Beck or his mother uncomfortable. She had to stay focused, not make a big deal of the oversight... ignore that the surprise announcement had, nonetheless, begun adding to a dawning distress she was experiencing. Eden was flashing through her mental hard drive trying to figure out what had happened in the evening to suddenly cause her to feel a little sick to her stomach. She blinked and looked down at the floor, trying to find a point to stare at in hopes of settling her queasiness.

"Are you okay?" Nora asked.

Eden took a deep breath, held it, and gave a brave smile to Nora...and to Beck who had zeroed in on her, perhaps sensing that something was wrong. He didn't ask if she was okay, he merely took her hand, trying to communicate through touch.

"Fine. I think I got a little overheated in the club. It's...very tight seating in there. Maybe it's just the shock of meeting you," Eden said graciously to Nora, rewarded with a kind, warm smile. "It's been a real pleasure for me."

Her mouth was suddenly very dry. Her stomach roiled. She could feel perspiration starting to break out on her upper lip, her forehead. Eden discreetly brushed her hand above her brow. She didn't want Beck or his mother to notice.

Nora turned and casually poured a small tumbler of water from a liter bottle on her dressing table. She passed the glass to Eden and looked at Beck.

"I'm delighted Beck brought you back to meet me, Eden. This is rare. Usually he's a bit of a ghost! He comes to the show, he sits through the whole performance. I have a secret signal to let him know I know he's in the audience, and then he quietly leaves at the end. *And*…he's always alone. Except for tonight."

Eden gave Beck a quick glance that he'd made her feel very special, and she could see that he was now clued in to the fact that she was suddenly not feeling very well. She gave him a small smile, her eyes signaling a big thank-you on both counts.

"I'm glad he changed his routine for me," Eden said.

"Me too," Nora said kindly. She suddenly reached out and patted Eden's shoulder as if she also sensed that something was up.

"I think we'll be heading out. You just finished a show, and I know you'll need some time to wind down."

"Honey, I'm really glad you came by after the show."

This time when Nora motioned to hug him, Beck was prepared, and their embrace was much warmer, much more sustained, as Eden watched closely.

She finished the water and passed the glass back to Nora. "Thank you," she said quietly.

"Come back," Nora invited.

Beck had the door open and was ushering Eden out into the dark narrow corridor.

"Will do," Beck said with a brief wave before closing the dressing room door.

He took hold of Eden's hand again, carefully guiding them out of the club and out into the bright energy of U Street. But suddenly, to Eden, it was a bit too loud and too bright. Beck stopped in front of the club and turned to stare into her face with furrowed brow.

"What's wrong?"

"I...don't know. I'm just... I'm not feeling very well."

"Are you in pain? Do you feel dizzy?"

Eden closed her eyes briefly. "I have sharp cramps...in my stomach."

"Let's get you home," Beck decided succinctly, heading toward a nearby municipal garage where he'd left his SUV.

They were in his car and out of the garage, and she sat with her head against the headrest and her eyes closed, relieved that he was taking her home and she could crawl into bed. Maybe all she needed was sleep. Maybe it was something she'd eaten or a late winter flu. When Beck reached for her as he drove Eden took hold of his hand, grateful that he seemed to understand her need.

When it became clear that they'd slowed down and he was parking, Eden opened her eyes...and didn't recognize the street. Puzzled, she looked around and turned to Beck, but he was already out of the car and coming around to her door.

"Where are we?" she asked when he opened the door, but making no move to get out.

"At my place," Beck announced, and then held out a hand to help her from the vehicle.

She didn't resist and let him lead her, an arm around her as they walked to the elevator, and he hugged her to his side during the ride that seemed to take a long time, and quickly got a door unlocked and got her inside. Beck turned on a lamp on the accent table just inside the door. And then he turned her into his arms and just held her. And finally Eden thought it would all be all right. She was where she wanted to be. She hugged him loosely, feeling a little like she was floating because the room felt like it was slowly spinning. And her insides seemed to be twisting, causing a cramp-like pain that made her clench her teeth.

"Why didn't you take me home?"

"You're staying with me tonight. If you feel better in the morning...we'll talk about it."

"Tomorrow I'm working at the library. And I have a hearing in the afternoon. My clinic team has a special thing..."

"I know you think all of that is very important, but none of it is life or death, is it? No. So it's all up for review." Beck began by taking her bag from her, then ordering her to take off her jacket and step out of her shoes. "This way," he said, leading her around a corner and right into a darkened room. He flipped a switch and a ceiling light came on. He used the dimmer to lower the brightness of the room. Eden stood, feeling her stomach roiling, the cramps coming hard and then slowly subsiding. She sensed Beck moving quickly around her in the room from the bed to a closet, to a bureau, and searching for something, rifling through folded things finding one he wanted and then coming back to her. He turned her by the shoulders and gently forced her to sit on the side of his bed. Beck handed her a garment.

"The bathroom is right outside in the hall. Change into this for the night. And then I want you to get into bed." He lifted her chin to make her look at him and focus. "Want me to help?"

She shook her head. "I can do it."

He squeezed her shoulder. "I'll be right back."

When she was alone, Eden just sat, listless and annoyed that she couldn't make herself do what she needed to do. To get up and pull herself together and move. To convince herself that there was nothing wrong and she just had to force herself to keep going and eventually she would feel better. But she wasn't home, she was with Beck, and maybe it was best to let someone else…him…tell her what to do. Then she could rest and get some sleep because he was going to take care of her.

Why would he do that?

Eden did as she was told, removing her clothing and pulling on a large men's T-shirt with something printed on the front. She slowly made her way to the bathroom, closing herself in, not even turning on the light. She felt cocooned there, leaning her forehead on the cold edge of the enamel sink. When she could, she stood to wash her face in cold water, repeatedly bringing cupped handfuls to splash against her skin. She reached for a towel and held it against her face. She heard a tap on the door.

"Eden? You okay?"

"Yes. I'll be right out."

When she finally opened the door, Beck was standing right in front, hands on his hips, watching her closely. He took her arm and guided her back to the bedroom. Eden gave him an apologetic grimace of a smile.

"I'm so sorry… I feel…"

"Get in bed. I made you tea."

"Oh…Beck," she murmured, unable to say anything more, completely overwhelmed by his thoughtfulness, his tenderness. She wasn't used to this kind of attention. She wasn't used to being weak and helpless. She finally let herself succumb to not being in control and, for now, not wanting to be. She just wanted to feel better.

Eden got into the bed, relieved that the sheets were cool against her skin, a soothing, gentle balm to her nerves. She slouched against the headboard, and Beck sat next to her handing her a mug of aromatic peppermint tea. "Hmmm," Eden sighed. She carefully took several sips and gave the mug back to Beck, and surrendered to the inevitable. She slid down into the bed, and Beck tucked her in.

Eden closed her eyes, feeling the cramping only taking little jabs at her insides now. The twisting of her stomach felt half-hearted, as if it was finally dying out. She heard Beck quietly moving around her, going into the bathroom, the kitchen again, and returning to join her in bed. She sighed deeply, suddenly knowing a kind of peace that made her feel safe…and cherished. Beck settled next to her, turned out the light. He didn't attempt to hold her, but merely got close enough to comfort her with his hand on her waist.

Eden felt herself sinking into a kind of hinterland of comfort, safety, and dreaminess. A peace she couldn't remember ever having felt before. Like she could let go because someone else was in charge. And if she fell, Beck would catch her.

"Want anything else?" Beck asked, his deep voice a low rumble above her ear.

"Uh-uh," she uttered.

"Had enough tea?"

"Ummm."

"Want me to read a bedtime story?"

She was still for a moment, and then she began to shake with suppressed amusement. "Not now."

"Anything I can do?"

Eden sighed. "You already have."

CHAPTER 9

Eden typed in a finishing sentence on the last case brief in her final semester in law school and sighed with relief at being done with it. It was an easy case, poignant, but unusual. It involved one Emilio Miguel Bravo accused of illegally acquiring a controlled substance… marijuana…for personal use. The simple details of the case were not in error or question, but the state failed to take into consideration the what, why, and how of Emilio's need to break the law. English as a second language aside, he'd confessed that he knew exactly what he was doing was wrong but had no choice. After reading his deposition and checking on the District's current laws involving the legality of marijuana, Eden had to agree with Emilio's reasoning. Now she only had to find the loopholes in the law and argue the penalties.

Was it worth the risk of jail to provide relief for his wife of fifty years for her sometimes debilitating migraines? A storefront pharmacy, often used by immigrants ignorant and fearful of the established medical field, had told Emilio that marijuana was very good for migraines. Hence, his willingness to break the law and pay shady neighborhood dealers to provide the remedy in gummy form for his wife. And it worked. Emilio was swept up in the drug bust that jailed his supplier. To make his story even more interesting, it was a Latino police officer who steered him to Center City where

Eden and a few of her fellow classmates handled the kind of cases that normally got swept under the rug.

It was challenging, but she found she enjoyed questioning the logic of established systems that kept doing things the way they'd always done things. And an *if ain't broke, don't fix it* attitude didn't work with human beings.

"Eden, I'm *never* going to forget what you're doing for us."

Nacine, a stunning beauty originally from Iran, stood in front of Eden looking like she was going to burst with excitement. "I want to thank you not only for thinking of this amazing treat for everyone, but for actually volunteering to pay for it. Why would you do that?"

Eden shrugged. "When you all get fabulous jobs making tons of money and I'm slogging away at a not-for-profit, you can treat me to something. For now, a thank you is enough."

"I heard that," Brianna shouted from across the lounge area. She had taken over not just a corner of the long, overstuffed sofa, but the entire sofa, her papers and books spread around her. "Don't mind me if I don't get up to grovel at your feet but, *grrrl*, this is the *bomb*! If you have a sugar daddy no one knew about, thank him for me."

Eden and Nacine joined in the laughter with Brianna. And Eden was glad that she'd thought of this way to get the team focused. They were all on an eleventh-hour push to the finish line before graduation. Even Zach. As Brianna and Nacine settled back into their separate private corners of the lounge, Eden turned her head to find Zach and the last member of the group, Regina, relaxing with no open book or study materials in sight. They were gossiping, no doubt, about all the people in their social and economic strata, who had chosen the grind of law school to prove they could do something useful with their lives even though they didn't have to. They enjoyed monthly allotments, trusts, passive income from rich family. Regina's family owned a nationally known brand of athletic sportswear for which she was the sole heir apparent. And Zach's father was the CEO of one of the big tech companies in Silicon Valley. Eden smiled ruefully to herself. Only she, Nacine, and Brianna apparently had to work for a living.

Well…maybe not her so much anymore. But piles of money were no excuse for being a slacker.

Everyone had returned to their respective study space, able to summon whatever they wanted from food service…or the bar. Given the way they all seemed inclined to move around and chat among themselves, everyone had hopefully finished the work they'd set out to do that afternoon when they'd arrived at the Four Seasons with their overnight bags and big smiles of excitement, ready to knuckle down and work so that the fun could begin.

Eden rested her head on the back of the lounge chair and considered what she might otherwise be doing tonight. As a matter of fact, she might not even have made it to this carefully planned night if Beck hadn't stepped in to see her through a twenty-four-hour stomach flu. Inconvenient and very uncomfortable. Not to mention maybe embarrassing herself in front of his mother. Eden still worried that she'd left an unfortunate first impression.

Currently, for a few days, she couldn't ask Beck to the apartment because her sister was back in residence. And she couldn't very well tell her sister to go elsewhere for the evening because she was expecting company. The fact of the matter was, she and Beck had made no plans for the next time they'd meet. Two days ago that didn't matter as much as it did now.

When she'd awakened in Beck's bed after the club performance and getting sick, Eden finally admitted to herself that there had been something missing in her life. She'd never particularly felt that way before. She smiled just remembering the moment Beck had happened on the scene with the implausible come-on line of *Do you need a hug?* He had come through with that and more.

A warmth, and now sensual longing, accompanied the memory. He was the biggest and nicest surprise in a very long while.

She was testing the waters, wanting to see if there was any sign that Beck was as anxious as she was to push the envelope further, to…*hurry*…to get them to the next level. To grow the relationship, because Eden already knew she was ready. Beck was the object of her desire.

She started out of her pleasant and thoughtful reflections when Zach sat down next to her. She moved her laptop to make room for him.

"Of course you finished first. Just what is it you eat for breakfast every morning? I've never known anyone with your kind of discipline."

Eden rearranged herself, making sure her hotel robe covered her legs. Zach placed his hand on her robe-covered thigh and playfully squeezed before removing it. Eden grinned at him, not taking the gesture for anything more than genuine affection.

"I have to. You know me. I take on the work and responsibility, I have to make sure I get it all done."

He slouched, letting his head rest on the sofa back but not so close that Eden needed to nudge him away.

"You put the rest of us to shame," he said smoothly without the least rancor. He glanced briefly around at the other three members of the team. The other women were in casual conversation, not so much working as sorting through their many papers, folders, reports, briefs, and pulling everything together, but often diverting into plain old gossip. Zach glanced warmly at Eden again. "You didn't have to do this, you know. A stern word of caution from you would have snapped us into shape."

"I wanted to do it. I thought it was a great idea and would be a great way for all of us to work together with a fun wrap-up and way cool prize at the end. A night at the Four Seasons."

"It's expensive, E," he said with some quiet concern.

"So?"

"Let me pay for the night. It is a great idea…and I can afford it."

Eden arched a brow. "Thanks for not saying I can't. I had it in my plans all along to do something like this at the end of the semester. And I budgeted for it."

He stared thoughtfully at her for a long moment. "I don't know if I can trust you. I did the math, and this is going to cost a couple of K's."

"It will, and I've got it covered. Let it go, Zach. I'm really happy to do this."

He sighed heavily, linking his fingers and placing his palms flat on his chest. "Well,,,all I can say is I can't tell you how glad I am that you included me with you 'girls.'"

Eden laughed. "I couldn't leave you out. You're one of us…from the first week of school. I know you and I…things happened fast… and…"

He took her hand, briefly holding it between his own with a warm, gentle squeeze before, in essence, giving it back to her. "I know the history, E. No matter how it eventually worked out it was an amazing time for me. Believe it or not, hanging with you probably made me a better man. The woman who eventually gets me will have to thank you for that." He considered her seriously, and Eden waited to hear what else he was going to say. "And the man who gets you better deserve you."

"Zach," Eden said, raising her brows and grinning. "That's one of the nicest things you've said to me…"

Eden smiled at Zach with genuine warmth. Yes, there was a history, and what might have been between them had never actually worked out. It couldn't, and she couldn't help the now and then comparison to Beck.

Both men were very attractive. Both were obviously educated, and not full of themselves. Maybe Zach had self-work and growing up to do, but most women would not consider his shortcomings to be a deal breaker. Their initial meeting, the first day of class in the first year of law school had been memorable. Zach proved to be charming and Eden had been immediately caught off guard and gobsmacked by the attraction between them. He had set off sexual alarm bells that had made it hard for her to concentrate on her work…at least, for a few months when she'd let Zach pursue her right into his bed. He had been physical, and tender, and playful, affectionate, and loving.

Zach had been a vast improvement over the men Eden had known as an undergraduate, a young adult. What men were being taught growing up about relationships, or women, had been abysmal and disappointing. But there was no chance that their kind of relationship could be sustained.

And then Beck had come along. Game changer.

Eden was still smiling vaguely at her reminiscence as she regarded

Zach next to her, and what he had to say about her offering to treat their study team for a special night in a special place.

"Maybe. But I really mean it, Eden. Anyway, I've never stayed at a Four Seasons…in the U.S."—she laughed again, shaking her head in resignation as if he was incorrigible—"so I'm glad to have this opportunity. I know the invitation said sleepwear, robes will be provided, but I don't do sleepwear as you very well should remember."

"I do," she conceded, glancing down at his attire. An attractive man's lounge set, casual but not pajamas. "I like your outfit. It's… cute."

Zach snorted in response, standing up. "When's dinner?"

Eden gasped, checking the time on her smartphone. "The reservation is for seven. Okay, everyone. Time's up. If you haven't finished the drafts of your paper today, tough. Next up, spa treatments. *Let's go!*"

"I want them to do *everything* to me," Nacine said rapturously.

"I'm ticklish but I want them to massage and pound the stress right out of my body," Brianna said, wiggling her plus-size hips and breasts.

"You ladies have fun at the spa. I'm using the pool for some laps. What about you, E? Want to join me?"

Eden didn't take the bait and narrowed her gaze at him. "And you were doing so well."

He laughed out loud, heading for the elevator.

"Where do we go after the spa?" Regina asked.

"Back here," Eden advised. "They'll set up one of the side function rooms for dinner."

"Oh my God, Eden. I'm going to put you in my will. That's the only way I can ever repay you."

"Remember what I said about a simple thank-you. And you've all already done that, so 'nough said. I hope I don't have to tell you not to dress in jeans, leggings, flip-flops, or other inappropriate clothing. It will kill the mood, and then I'll have to kill you. I really want tonight to be a special break from all the work we had this year, so treat it as special…"

"It sure is," Brianna said as she, Regina, and Nacine left the room and also headed for the elevators.

Everyone dispersed to their individual rooms to dress or prepare for whatever their spa choice was to be. Eden's cell was vibrating in her robe pocket when she unlocked her room door and entered to the soft lighting provided on a round table near the window. The drapes had not been pulled for the night, and she could see the last of the sunset in the west and over the Potomac.

"Hello?"

"Hey. You're a hard lady to keep track of. I should have asked for an itinerary," Beck said by way of greeting.

Eden broke into a private smile, dropping her tote and papers on the table. She settled on the queen-size bed, leaning against the padded headboard.

"Well, you found me. When did your search begin?"

"Not that long after I dropped you at your place yesterday and we went our separate ways. Seems like forever ago."

Beck drawled in a way that sent a warm shock through her body at the memory. Eden momentarily closed her eyes and sighed with pleasure at how wonderful the morning had been. "That's so nice to hear."

"How are you feeling?"

"Much better, thanks. I'm glad I was only down and out for the night. You were really wonderful to me," she whispered.

"My pleasure. Did you make your appointments?"

"Yes, I did. I'll be glad when the semester is over. Good news, I think. I got a job offer from Katherine Perkins, Everett's attorney. Her firm wants me to come on board as an ethics attorney."

"Get out! That's great. Interested?"

"I think I am. I now know the attorneys and the office. I think I could be productive there."

"I'm happy for you."

"I haven't said yes, but I'm thinking about it. What about you?"

"The usual. Last-minute staff meeting to discuss some major changes. It only ended about an hour ago, and then the staff broke out into chat groups. I felt the need for a break. And to talk to you. If I haven't already said so…"—his voice dropped low and quiet—"yesterday morning was incredible."

"I thought so, too. I'm glad I was up to it," she said slyly.

"Amen."

There was a moment's silence between them, and Eden had a feeling she knew what Beck also wanted to find out.

"You remember that my sister flew home today."

"I remember," he said.

"I'm actually not home at all tonight. I'm at the Four Seasons with my class team."

"The Four Seasons?"

"I know what you're thinking. Two month's salary…maybe three… I'm treating all of us to one night. The thing is, I don't have to worry about how I'm going to pay for this. The idea was to get together and polish our papers due in a few weeks. I thought offering a night at the hotel as a bribe would be incentive enough to get the work done, and then we could enjoy our stay."

"That's pretty cool."

"I've been thinking about doing something ever since I came into all that money. We've all been working really hard, we can see the light at the end of the tunnel…and we're all feeling burned out. I know you understand."

"I do. So what does one night at the Four Seasons include?"

"We arrived in time to have high tea. Very English." Eden chuckled softly. "I've never even been to England. And then we had about three hours to review each other's papers or offer advice on any clinic issues. We just broke a few minutes ago to go for spa treatments."

"Ummm. I don't suppose any of this is in the curriculum at Georgetown Law?"

"I've never seen it listed in the catalog."

"And you're treating. That's really generous of you. But I'm not surprised."

"Really?"

"Really. One of these days…or nights…I'll tell you why."

"I am curious, you know."

"What happens after the spa?"

"We have a private dinner planned. It'll give us more time to decompress and chat, and gripe, and gossip. We'll get a good night's sleep and tomorrow go about our business."

There was another silence and, again, Eden knew exactly what had prompted no response from Beck.

"I wish I could invite you to come and…and spend the night with me, but I can't."

"I hope there's a reason why that's not going to make me feel palmed off."

"The deal was it's just the team."

"Your team should appreciate what you're doing," Beck murmured.

"They do. They've said so, over and over. And you know what?" Eden whispered conspiratorially. "I can afford it. I just came into a *lot* of money."

Beck laughed, like she'd just made the discovery and he found that charming and funny.

"Okay. So my calculations say your sister is still in town?"

"She is."

"Does that mean you'll be home, or do you have something else planned for tomorrow?"

Eden sighed, grew a little serious. She knew Beck meant *tomorrow night*. "I was actually thinking of staying here at the hotel one more night alone...until Holly leaves again."

"That is not a great living arrangement," he commented.

"No, it's not. And it is sometimes...inconvenient."

"Can I suggest something else? Why not come to my place, if the problem is Holly's distraction. I'm actually going to be out of town tomorrow on assignment."

"Where?"

"I'm driving down to the Eastern Shore to do research for a piece on the gentrification taking place that's, of course, displacing generations of African Americans who've lived and farmed on the Delmarva Peninsula for more than a hundred years. It's just a one-day turnaround trip, but I don't expect to get back until late. That will give you the entire day and evening to work on whatever, in peace. No strings attached," Beck added in his deep voice.

Eden sighed. "I'm really tempted. But I have to check my schedule. I'm still working on a marijuana case."

"You don't have to decide this minute, Eden. It's an open invitation."

"Can I let you know in the morning? I'll call before you start on your trip."

"That's fine. I better let you go. I know you have things to do, people to see."

She chuckled quietly.

"Have fun."

Her goodbye was filled with genuine regret. It had only been one day since they were last together. But under the right circumstances a day could be an eternity.

It didn't really matter to Eden what spa treatment she'd selected. She just wanted to let herself be pampered, a very rare occurrence. Beck had done an outstanding job of it two nights before.

Everyone was adhering to the pseudo schedule so that she did not have to get ugly and scold them like errant children. And the hotel had done a spectacular job of setting up the Smithson room with low lights and candles on the table and a formal setting including three different kinds of wineglasses. Her group aside, Eden was thoroughly enjoying the first-class treatment, a sad commentary on her ordinary daily life. Holly liked teasing her about being really smart but a social misfit.

How come you don't date? What about that cute guy, Beck? What's up with him?

Yes. What about Beck? Eden wondered, as she made her way to the elevator to descend to the private dining room. She was pleased to hear the disappointment in his voice when she'd told him the whole story about why there was no chance of seeing each other. She was disappointed as well. As the elevator stopped on a floor and Brianna and Regina got on, Eden smiled at the thought that *"Absence makes the heart..."* and so forth and so on.

———————

Beck accepted the ticket from the valet and took the elevator from the parking entrance up to the lobby of the hotel. It wasn't very late, but the lobby was empty, except for a handsome couple having drinks and flirtatious conversation in a small lounge area near Bourbon Steak, the hotel restaurant. Eden had mentioned the room where her dinner was being held, making it unnecessary to ask at the front desk for directions. But that wasn't his destination. Beck stopped by the desk anyway, ready to hand over the cellophane-wrapped bouquet he'd purchased after leaving his office. He wanted to surprise her, knowing there was no chance of them being together for the evening.

"Can I help you?" the front desk agent asked him as Beck sat his package on the counter.

"Yes. I'd like to have this delivered to the room of a guest, Eden Marsh. I believe she checked in this afternoon."

The agent proceeded to check the information in his computer and nodded. "Yes, sir. I can take care of that for you. May I have your name?"

Beck complied, also handing over a small, white florist gift card envelope. It was lumpy with something other than a card; it also held keys to his apartment. Just in case. So an evening with Eden wasn't in the stars. He'd accepted her plans for the night as something other than the pleasure of his company. He also had to admit being much more than impressed with Eden's plans and thoughts for her classmates. It was extraordinary, really.

He recalled Eden's minor emergency after the show at the Gaslight Salon and introducing her to his mother, but also the unexpected pleasure he got out of taking care of her, having her with him for the night at his place. Now Beck fully realized how much being with Eden meant to him. She was starting to have a profound impact on his life...making him feel more content and hopeful.

He thanked the hotel desk clerk for his help and headed back to the garage level to retrieve his car.

CHAPTER 10

Eden spotted Holly as soon as she entered the café just a few blocks from where they lived. She wound her way through the late lunch crowd feeling slightly harried and as if, all day so far, she was moving in a circle. When she left home that morning there was a plan. She had a court appearance and then was working a few hours at the Library of Congress, where she hoped she would have enough free time to review her case for Emilio Bravo.

She'd packed another overnight bag, this time for using Beck's apartment to squirrel away, hopefully uninterrupted, to work the rest of the day and evening. She'd returned home from the Four Seasons with her overnight bag, working tote, and a beautiful bouquet that had been waiting for her the night before, after she'd returned to her room from the group dinner. Eden mentally gave Beck ten additional points for *character*. The vase with the flowers now took up nearly all of the dresser top's surface in her bedroom.

Although Beck had said he'd return home late, Eden hoped they might have some part of the evening together. She had begun to anticipate being with him, even privately terming it a kind of *domestic bliss*. Cooking was off the table. She didn't feel it appropriate to rummage through his kitchen looking for food and equipment to prepare a meal. It seemed intimate in a way that was totally different from the moments they'd shared at her place. And certainly different than that night she'd spent with Beck, sick to her stomach. They'd had nights and mornings fulfilling strong physical needs, cementing an attraction, and slowly opening the path to a real relationship.

Were they there yet? Eden had begun to hope so. She recognized a certain giddiness to her daydreams, a levitation of her spirits that had her smiling secretly to herself often, as she wove the dream into whole fabric in her mind. Solid and real. Eden thought about Beck quite a lot. She looked forward to hearing from him and, so far, his interest in her certainly seemed genuine. Three times he'd surprised her in the most unusual, charming, and thoughtful manner. Beck was a standout…and a strong potential keeper. Or was that only her wishful thinking?

And then Holly had called.

Eden maneuvered through the restaurant, seeing her sister was now on her cell phone, texting away and not appearing in need of seeing her, as her urgent call had indicated. Eden had hastily changed her plans for Holly. She wasn't happy about it.

"Hi," Eden said, a bit breathlessly. "Are you okay? What's going on?"

She put her bag, tote, and lightweight jacket on a vacant chair, all the while watching her sister for signs of stress or anxiety, a problem, trouble, whatever Holly was going through that had made her seem on the verge of hysteria two hours ago.

"Just a minute. I have to finish this text," Holly murmured, distracted.

Eden sat…and waited. Her annoyance began forming as soon as it became apparent to her that there was no urgency. She took a deep breath, recovering from having rushed. She caught a waiter's attention and asked for tonic water with a twist of lemon. She openly stared at Holly, assessing her as she had been wont to do since her sister was sixteen and they'd just lost their mother. Holly was very vulnerable then. They had both been scared witless. Eden knew she had to be the one to step up so that Holly had someone she could depend on. Someone who wasn't going to leave her. Eden's fear now was that they'd both become too accustomed to, too safe in their roles.

Holly was bright, tall, and pretty, an experienced world traveler and yet still inclined to fall back into her old role of the insecure young girl. Eden tapped her nails on the table in front of her sister to get her attention, to let her not forget that she was waiting to talk to her.

"Okay, I'm finished," Holly said, texting for another few seconds before putting her phone down. She sat staring at her sister, waiting for Eden to talk first.

Eden raised her brows, spread her hands. "Well?" she asked, her annoyance building.

Holly shrugged. "I…don't know what you mean."

"*Holly!* Tell me you don't remember calling me a few hours ago, upset because you're leaving tomorrow, and I wasn't going to be home tonight…maybe. Why were you upset? You had me worried that something had happened, or you'd been furloughed…or fired. Or there was trouble with Connor…"

Holly was shaking her head. "No, no. It's nothing like that. None of what you think."

"Then what? Look…I've had a crazy busy morning, and I planned on getting some work done tonight…"

"Well, why couldn't you do it at home?"

"I need a quiet place to work. There's a lot at stake right now with the end of the term approaching and, to be honest, sometimes when you're home it…it's…not really quiet," Eden began, trying to temper her complaint. How could she be impatient with her sister for being gregarious, a little loud, and irreverent? How come Holly didn't seem to recognize all the work needed for law school, a part-time job, volunteering, writing briefs and reports? Still catering to her? Eden gnawed her lip and stared at her sister.

"Why did you call me?"

"I thought we'd be together at home tonight. I leave tomorrow, and if you stayed away tonight, we wouldn't see each other again for almost a week."

"But Holly, that's the way it's been since you became an attendant for the airlines. And you've been doing great. Without me."

"I just felt like…we don't see each other as much anymore."

Eden frowned, truly bewildered. "Where did that come from? I mean, you come home from a tour, and immediately you're making calls and arrangements with your local posse to hang out. Maybe you and I will go out for dinner, or lunch, or brunch. But it's not like you want to spend more time with me. Until now. I know I haven't been home much lately but…I don't really go anywhere or do anything, and you've never even noticed before. Why now?"

"Is it that guy you met?"

"What?"

"Beck. That's his name, right?"

Eden was silent and blinked at Holly. "You don't know him. You met him once and you exchanged exactly a sentence."

"Do you like him?"

Eden hesitated and continued to blink at her sister. "Yes, I do."

"A lot?"

Eden sighed, briefly closing her eyes. "Holly, seriously…"

"Do you?"

"Yes, I do. And I think he really likes me. But it's early yet, and I can't and won't predict anything."

"But what if it's serious? What if you get together with him…"

"And you're left alone?" Eden couldn't help but chuckle. "You know, I used to think that would happen with you. You were serial dating all over the continent, and I thought that after one of your trips, you'd tell me you met the man of your dreams and you're moving to Milan! Or Morocco, or Madrid! I'm told that Italians love African American women. I started losing count after number seven. And what about Connor? The man you met in Dublin? Tell me that's dead and buried."

Holly shook her head, almost blushing. "It's not. I saw him on the last trip. I'll likely see him this coming trip. He wants me to take some time off and visit with him in Dublin. Meet his family."

"That's never happened before," Eden said, looking at Holly with new eyes. To see her baby sister as a woman a man would fall in love with. Absolutely. "Sounds like he really likes you. Hard to believe," she teased.

Holly grinned. "I like him, too. He's really serious, and funny and very smart. And…he's always happy to see me. He's very kind to me."

"That's great, Holly. And so…how do you feel about him?"

"I think about him all the time. You know me. I don't take any of the guys I meet overseas seriously. Out of sight, out of mind. This definitely feels different."

"So instead of worrying about me leaving you, it could be the other way around. Right?"

"I guess."

Eden reached across the table and took her sister's hand. "It's going to happen, you know. Personally, I always believed you would find someone and leave home before me. Maybe it's too early to tell with your guy from Dublin, but it could."

"What about Beck?"

Eden shook her head. "I can't say."

"Were you planning on seeing him tonight?"

"I was hoping. He's actually out of town today on a work assignment. He probably won't get back until very late."

"So you might not even get to see him at all. Can't you stay home tonight? We should spend the time together."

Eden studied the plaintive look in Holly's eyes, knowing that she was probably being played. "Oh, Holly..." she began, doubtful about how to handle her sister. And her own heart and needs.

"Please?" Holly whined.

Eden grimaced in resignation. "Do you really need me to?"

"I do. This thing with Connor...it could be something. But I'm a little scared, and I need to talk to you about him. Him and me."

Eden felt ambivalent, and trapped...and resentful. "Okay," she said quietly, nodding. But she wasn't happy about making the concession and could feel a slow burn creeping up her neck and face. What would Beck's reaction be when he finally arrived home and she wasn't there? Would he understand? Would he be annoyed?

Holly had been instantly rejuvenated after getting her way, already chatting about her own concerns. Eden tuned out, feeling herself sink into disappointment that she had given in to Holly's plea. It was ever that way. Old habits die hard.

Mentally, Eden began composing the text she would send to Beck, hoping to explain.

———————

Beck's relief at arriving home was a little over the top, and he knew it.

It was close to eleven…late. It had been a very long day of driving and occasionally getting lost on the smaller roads off Route 13 South, keeping appointments or having a few canceled. A lot of time had been spent scouting out the area, determining where the Black community was actually situated and what businesses they owned, seeing where gentrification already had a substantial foothold. But in the back of Beck's mind had always been the prospect of eventually getting home and finding Eden there.

Beck was a little surprised at the level of his expectations, first when he invited Eden to use his place to study or work, and second when she'd called that morning to accept.

"Are you sure this is okay?" she'd asked.

It was very okay. Eden was so easy to be with. He looked forward to that more and more, as if testing to see if that would suddenly begin to change. When he unlocked his door and quietly entered, he still was expecting what he and Eden had planned. It was dead silent. Maybe she'd fallen asleep. He crept toward the kitchen and turned on the light. Then he approached the living room entrance from the hall and peered in. Eden wasn't there. There was no evidence that she'd ever been at all.

———————

For the third time, Beck went back to reread his opening paragraph. He wanted to give it the tone of the start of an adventure, heading off into unknown territory that was really not so far away from DC but where he'd never visited, or even thought to. He pushed back impatiently in his chair, intuitively knowing that what he'd written didn't ring true. He exhaled deeply in frustration. Almost immediately he sprang forward, leaning in to his laptop. He deleted the first paragraph entirely and started again.

It was his third false start. He was annoyed to realize that he was totally distracted by his disappointment that the almost rendezvous with Eden never actually happened.

Beck was annoyed that he was annoyed. Irrationally, he blamed the ruined plans on Holly, Eden's sister. Whether it was deliberate manipulation or a real personal crisis didn't much matter. In a childish way, Holly had been the puppet master and Eden had done her bidding…and he'd been left out altogether.

He'd gotten Eden's text. It was the last thing he'd checked on his smartphone before climbing into bed, feeling not only dispirited but lonely. He really missed her not being there.

> Beck,
> Sorry I didn't leave the lights on. I never made it to your place. Frantic call from my sister to meet with her. No emergency, but… I'm still disappointed.
> Eden
> P.S. I won my court case this morning! Jamal will start college in the fall.
> P.P.S. Another time?

He was annoyed that her note didn't help. And Beck wondered if there would come a time when *he…they*…would come first in Eden's life.

The driving distance from the middle of DC to Salisbury, Maryland, is about two and a half hours without stops. You start on Route 50 heading east through Annapolis, losing the urban landscape. Then, to continue to the Delmarva Peninsula, you pick up Route 13 going south on the eastern side of the Chesapeake. That's when the trip really starts as you're technically leaving the mainland...

"Beck, there's someone at the front desk for you."

"Who?" he asked bluntly, not wanting to be distracted now that he sensed a good beginning to his piece. He continued to type to finish his thought before it was lost.

"A lawyer is all I know for sure," the man said casually, walking past Beck's desk to his own work terminal. "I was on my way back here when Jill shouted out."

"Thanks," Beck said, already reaching for his phone to call the front desk receptionist for more information. Then he changed his mind. He was a little stiff from sitting and forcing himself to focus so he could maybe make some headway on his article, which seemed inordinately difficult. Beck knew the reason why. He just didn't know what to do about it.

He got up and rotated his upper back and shoulders. He walked between the uniformly placed worktables and the dozen or so writers and other staff staring into their computer screens. He rounded a corner and headed toward the open reception area, his gaze settling on the receptionist who watched him approach.

"Kevin said there's someone..." was as far as Beck got.

The receptionist casually pointed to his extreme right as she answered an incoming call on her console. When Beck followed her direction, he was met with the steady, wide-eyed regard of Eden. He stopped in his tracks and returned her uncertain, even troubled gaze. Immediately everything he'd been thinking and assuming since their missed connection vanished as Eden stood and reached into her tote to extract a round dowel to which was attached a white flag. She held it up, gently waving it back and forth in a small, tight movement of surrender.

Beck felt all his apprehension, all his questions and doubts, his fear slough from his body. He turned back to the receptionist.

"I need to take over the break room for a while. Tell anyone headed there it's in use."

"Can't. Someone else is already holding a meeting there. You can use Sarah's office. She's gone for the day. She won't mind."

Beck nodded. He gave his attention back to Eden with a barely perceptible, bemused grin. He gestured for her and watched with instant recognition all her physical traits that had so grown on him, that made her presence something he now wanted and actively sought. When she was close enough, Beck took the truce flag from her hand, rolled it up, and indicated she was to come with him. Eden kept her gaze on him, as if trying to judge his mood. Her uncertainty answered some of his own concerns, but he placed his hand on her lower back to guide her along. Beck led her into the executive editor's vacant office, but left the door a little ajar. That was HR office protocol. He and Eden faced off but it wasn't at all confrontational, just unsure…and emotionally charged.

"Why this?" Beck asked quietly, indicating the flag.

Eden squared her shoulders and raised her chin. "It seems to be our go-to thing when there's a problem. I'm glad we kept it. I felt I owed you an apology. For what happened the other night. For what *didn't* happen the other night. I was…so…so…"

Beck lowered the flag and took several steps toward Eden. He shook his head. "You don't owe me anything. But it means everything that you thought you might, Eden."

She took a step forward and had to tilt her face upward to talk to him. "I do owe both of us. I thought…the best way for me to let you know how much…"

Beck glanced into her face. "Like I said, you didn't have to apologize. I was sure I knew from the tone of your message. You had to do what you had to do. Yeah, I was disappointed."

"Me too," she said, regret laced in her voice.

"And…I was a little angry. I believed you were letting your sister control the situation."

Eden nodded. "I know. I don't disagree. I just didn't know what to do. She sounded so urgent…"

"And you took the bait."

They sat in two nearby chairs.

Beck studied her, seeing that she was anxious about coming to see him with her brave mea culpa. He arched a brow at her. "Nice ploy, telling the receptionist you're an attorney."

"I was sure you'd figure it out."

"That it was you? I didn't. I've been a bit…distracted lately," he said with meaning.

"I'm sorry."

"But you won your court case."

She smiled and nodded. "It was a great moment. Jamal's grandmother invited me to dinner to thank me. I couldn't. What I do pro bono is part of my degree requirement. I'm not supposed to take any kind of payment. Even a home-cooked meal."

Beck laughed quietly, soaking in Eden's smile, the way she seemed so completely devoid of pretense, unafraid of being wrong... or vulnerable. He recognized that from the very beginning Eden had been consistently herself and, therefore, real. In Beck's experience, that was rare. It made Eden even more desirable. He was very happy to see her, under *any* circumstance.

"Congratulations."

"Thanks."

"We should celebrate. What would you like to do?" he asked purposely.

"I wasn't thinking about a celebration. I was wondering..."

"Want to try again?" Beck asked quietly, watching her. She nodded.

He glanced toward the door and back to her. "I have to get back, but...my place?"

"Yes," Eden said. "Holly's away and I know she's not coming right back after her current tour. She's been invited to stay a few extra days in Ireland. There's a guy there..."

"Okay, that's great. For Holly and for us. Am I right?"

"You are."

"This is going to be a replay of the other night. I might be a little late."

"Alright. I have to report to LC for a few hours. And I have another arbitration to prepare for. My last for the semester."

Beck stood up and Eden did the same. "You still have the keys, right?"

"Yes. In here," she said, patting her purse.

He, at least, felt that they were now on a different plane. They'd moved past a *beginning* to another level. Moving forward. "I need to finish up a new project on that trip I made to the Eastern Shore. One more thing. There's a gala on Friday for the National Association of Black Journalists. I want you to come with me."

"I'd really like that," Eden said and then quickly became pensive. "Oh…I think I have to go shopping. I don't have anything to wear."

Beck erupted into an honest bark of laughter. "Right. I've heard that before." He said, moving to the door. Eden followed him from the office.

As they headed back to the front desk, they briefly clasped hands, and Eden beamed at him with her dark, bright eyes. Nothing lifted his spirits faster or higher than the way she looked at him in that moment. Beck's hopes jumped and soared. Everything felt right. On point.

In front of the company doors, they said their goodbyes.

"I'll wait up for you," Eden whispered.

Beck was caught off guard by that simple promise and the unspoken message behind it.

———

Beck was later than he thought he'd be.

He wondered if Eden was going to be pissed because their plans, although not very carefully laid out, were about to crash and burn. Again.

He had been about to leave when one of his writers rushed in to say she just needed about ten minutes of his time. She *really* needed his input on her column that should have been turned in the day before. As an associate editor, Beck couldn't very well say no. So, ten minutes had turned into almost an hour…and he texted Eden to let her know he might be later than planned. And he prayed that she'd be there, at his apartment, waiting.

When he carefully unlocked his door and stepped into the apartment, there were two lamps on in the living room. He could hear the TV at very low volume. Beck was relieved by the sound. He stepped into the room and spotted Eden curled into a corner of his leather sofa, asleep. He slowly approached to gaze down on her, to detect her even breathing and her parted lips. Instantly, he was taken back to that morning after his mother's show at the Gaslight Salon when he'd taken Eden home and tucked her into his bed. Taking care of her and being needed by her. To awaken in the morning to make love and to cuddle and to talk quietly about Nora and her show, and how Eden was feeling…and to make love again.

It had been a fantastic time that Beck knew for certain he wanted to build on.

Her laptop was closed, with a short stack of forms and papers haphazardly piled on top, along with two law books and a legal pad with Post-its, arrows, asterisks, and highlights. There was a mug with half-finished tea, and a handful of almonds on a paper towel. She'd almost made herself at home, but Eden had been careful. As if she recognized she was a visitor in someone else's home. Beck sighed as he quietly removed the mug and headed into the kitchen where he found another surprise. A bowl covered by a plate with a note lying on top.

I ordered in. I tried to wait but got hungry. I thought we could share, but I saved you some. Microwave 90 seconds. And there's wine. Dinner was supposed to be very French.

Beck smiled to himself, entertained by Eden's creative efforts and loving her amusing little notes and messages. He couldn't for the life of him recall Alia ever making such a thoughtful gesture for him. He couldn't recall her ever really caring. Eden's efforts were a huge alert to what he had been missing. Someone who genuinely cared and thought about him first.

He put the covered bowl in the refrigerator, the mug in the sink, and returned to the living room. Eden had not moved. Beck turned off the TV and both lamps. And then he bent over Eden, slipping an arm under her legs and the other around her back, lifting her easily from the sofa. She stirred, sighed, dropped her head to his shoulder.

"Hey," Eden said in a sleep-slurred voice. "I can walk," she said, starting to wiggle out of his arms.

"Keep still," Beck commanded. She obeyed and totally relaxed in his arms.

He carried her into the bedroom and placed her on the bed. She had wrapped herself like a burrito in an afghan his mother had given him that had lain over the back of a chair. Beck had never used it. He managed to untangle her from the throw. She had on only underwear, and Beck felt himself get mildly aroused at how little effort it would take to get Eden naked. He did remove her bra, enjoying reaching around her back to handily release the clasp, watching her face in repose, trusting and half-asleep. Beck found her compliant...and sexy, her exposed breasts making his mind and body reel with desire. He got her under the bed linens and got pleasure from this sensual undressing and touching her. Eden shifted until she was comfortable and lay quietly.

"I always wanted to be carried like that. You know, like in the movies," she said in a quiet, dreamy voice.

"How was it?" Beck asked, beginning to undress, stripping to his briefs. He watched Eden as she lay with her eyes half-closed, watching him.

"Perfect. Was I too heavy?"

"Like a cow," Beck said wryly.

Eden smothered her laughter, her shoulders shaking as she pressed the cover against her mouth. "Embarrassing," she murmured.

"Ask a stupid question…" Beck said, sliding into the bed to join her.

"Get a stupid answer." She sidled closer, lifting a thigh to place over his. Beck raised his arm so that she could lie against his chest, her arm stretching over his midriff. For a maddening, enticing moment Eden let her fingers trail through the curly hair above the band of his briefs and followed where it ended at his navel. He waited, wondering where her curiosity would take her. He loved her light exploratory playfulness, but wasn't disappointed when her aim seemed to be just to touch.

He let out a tired but content sigh. Beck felt his body sink into the mattress and lean into Eden. He let go of his disquiet and accepted the peace he found in her presence. He turned his head and more or less buried his mouth and chin in her hair. Beck sighed again. All of that moment felt so good and restful. So right.

"I know I said I'd wait up for you, but I fell asleep," Eden confessed.

"It's okay. You're here," he responded.

"It feels strange. Being here…"

"You'll get used to it."

She was silent and thoughtful for a while. "You want me to?"

"Yes, Eden. I want you to."

"I'm glad, because…because…"

Beck stroked her silky smooth back down to her panties and, like Eden, it was just a promising tease. "I think we both feel the same way."

There didn't seem to be anything else that needed to be said, and so they didn't. It was understood that the moment could lead to foreplay and then making love. And it was understood that they both would want that. Instead, by mutual silent agreement, they didn't. Something else seemed to be more important, very simple… just being together as they figured out what that something was. There were gentle little kisses and caresses, and their warm bodies entwined together in bed…like lovers with all the time in the world.

There was always tomorrow morning, or awakening in the middle of the night with a need that had to be satisfied. Whichever came first.

———————————

The middle of the night came first when Eden began to awaken. She was still nestled into Beck's side and chest, although their limbs had gone slack in sleep. But her dawning awareness of where she was, and Beck's strong, warm body making her feel safe, also had the effect of making her want *him*. It occurred to Eden that although she and Zach had begun an affair that quickly proved to be mostly physical, they had never connected on any other level. She was awake now because of an overwhelming desire to show Beck how much she cared. How much it was obvious to her now that she was falling in love with him.

His own capacity for love was shown in small but significant ways. She sighed, rolling toward him, stretching her arm across his body. Almost instantly, there was a response from him. Beck shifted, also rolling until they faced each other. His hand reached out to her in the dark to lie against her cheek, his thumb caressing across her mouth.

"Eden?"

"I didn't mean to wake you," she whispered.

"You okay? Bad dream?" Beck suggested.

"No. I suddenly woke up. And I felt so... I don't know. I..."

He came up on his elbow, but she couldn't actually make out his features, certainly not the expression in his eyes as he leaned over her. He pressed a kiss on her lips.

"Don't try to explain." He gave her another light, briefly deeper kiss. "Does that help?"

The deep, solid resonance of his voice rocked Eden, made her shiver. She nodded. "Yes." Her hand slid up his arm to his shoulder, to his neck and nape. And he got it.

Beck lowered across Eden's bare chest, her breast pressed against him as his upper body settled on her. He found her mouth with his, and the kiss this time was intensely personal—slow, erotic, much more than a meeting of minds or of their bodies. It was kind of lazy and filled with longing and ache that seemingly had gone untapped in both of them for too long. They didn't want to rush the spiraling buildup of their need. There was a delicious passion growing between them that could only be satiated with unhurried foreplay, letting their hearts race and beat together. The melding of their mouths, lips, tongues, the lazy exploration of their hands, undulation of their hips, Beck's hardened penis lodged between them signaled a powerful craving. He let Eden's hand caress him until his breathing signaled approaching uncontrollable need.

They continued to kiss, languidly. Beck let his hand stray to Eden's waist, finding his way to the curve of her hip, where it met her thigh, and unerringly fingering through curls to her center, eliciting a breathy moan from Eden when his fingers made contact. She moaned his name, positioned her body to let him have his way, which had her feeling as if her head was slowly spinning, making her mindless and dizzy and suddenly desperate.

Beck shifted to bring them there. Eden moaned again, lifting her knees, contracting her pelvis as Beck danced and shifted on and into her body. She clasped him to her, hugged with her legs, tried to remember to breathe in and out along with Beck's movements, until she felt she might faint. That wonderful, mind-boggling *thing* tightened within her, twisting into a sudden throb that wrenched a mew of both delight and near pain from her. That Beck could do that to her was a wonder. Eden took time absorbing all the shifting sensations. And it was as she lay drained and sated that Beck drove himself to his own climax. He squeezed her tightly in the final throes of orgasm and let his body rest limp on top of her.

They lay that way for so long Eden began to wonder if they'd fallen asleep again. Or was it just dreamy repose. Beck finally shifted his body from Eden's, and they more or less positioned themselves together the way they had been the night before, settling down to go to sleep.

"Better?" Beck croaked.

"Can't you tell?" Eden said, kissing his chest.

"I want to hear you say it."

Eden hugged him. "You made my toes curl. That's never happened before."

Beck was quiet for a moment, and then he turned his head to

kiss her forehead. "I think we should try to break our own record next time. In the morning."

"Promise?" She could feel his cheek curve into a smile against hers.

"Promise."

But now that they were spent and peaceful, Eden felt it was the right time to broach something that needed to be talked about. They were calm and languid, and she thought that would help to buffer whatever difficult memory Beck harbored.

"I want to ask you something."

"Okay."

"It's about the tattoo on your arm." She raised a hand to run her fingers along the line of prose. "Who's it for?"

He didn't answer for a long moment, but he exhaled deeply. She waited for him to deny the request.

"It's for my brother, Mason. My mother and Everett had a kid together. He died in an accident when I was twelve. He drowned."

"I'm so sorry," she whispered. There was no turning back now.

Beck sighed and turned to face her, was quiet for another long moment. "We were very close. I didn't think we would be when he was born, but he was a great little guy."

Eden stroked his chest, stopping to rest against his heart.

"Once, when Mason was still a baby, there was a picture taken of the four of us. And when I saw it, I…looked like I didn't belong. My mom, my stepfather, and my half brother were white. I didn't look like them. I was different. I think that was the first time I realized I wasn't white. I'd never thought about it before that."

"But they never treated you like you were different, right?"

"No, of course not. School was different. I was just insecure, I guess. But Mason…man…he got such a kick out of telling people I was his big brother. I got such a kick out of being his big brother. We were tight. When he died…I was crushed. I thought it was my fault."

"Maybe it was just a bad accident like you said."

He was quiet for a very long time. Eden felt herself getting languid and sleepy when Beck began speaking quietly again.

"My mother blamed me for Mason's death…"

She drew in her breath, stunned by his disclosure. "Oh…Beck…"

"I was supposed to be watching him. I was the older one. I was a better swimmer. It happened so fast."

"Beck…" She hugged herself close to him so he wouldn't feel alone.

"I thought I was responsible. Everett tried to convince me that wasn't true. But I only remember my mother screaming and yelling that it was my fault. Everything changed after that. It took a very long time to get over Mason's death. And I could never forget what my mother said to me. For a long time, I felt like I'd lost her love."

"That's not what I saw when you introduced me to her. She was so happy to see you. She hugged and kissed you. It looked very much like love to me."

"Your mother must have been in terrible pain when Mason died. She and Everett lost a child. You lost a brother. It takes a long time to get over that kind of loss. Losing my mom was different. But it was still a loss. I hope you and your mother find a way to heal."

He signed. "I don't know."

"The tattoo is a beautiful epitaph, Beck. And such a wonderful way to remember your brother."

Eden didn't know if Beck believed her. In that moment, she wondered if she'd caused him to resurrect a past that was still largely unresolved. She laid her cheek against Beck's chest. He tightened his hold on her. That's how they finally fell asleep.

CHAPTER 11

"Welcome. Come on in. I'm so glad you could come today," Nora said, holding open the front door of her Arlington house to let Eden enter.

"Thank you. It was so nice to get your invitation. I was surprised," Eden said as she stepped into the entrance.

"Let me hang this up for you," Nora said, indicating Eden's long cardigan sweater.

Eden momentarily put down her tote and a gaily printed gift bag as she removed the sweater. "I'm overdressed. It's a great spring day outside," she observed in chatty nervousness.

"Let's go sit in the back."

Eden followed Nora, assessing the layout and ground-floor rooms of the split-level house. The back room was a large space, an add-on that seemed to be a combination den/library and sunroom.

"What a great space," Eden said as they both took seats in comfortable padded chairs with tufted cushions. "This is for you," she said, passing the gift bag to Nora, who seemed genuinely surprised by the gesture.

"You didn't have to bring anything. Thank you."

"I wasn't sure. My sister said that prosecco and chocolates always work."

Nora laughed. "Your sister has good taste."

"Not really. But she's in Europe a lot and finds out about all these esoteric habits that most Americans don't have. I liked this one."

"Well, I thank you both." Nora sat the bag aside.

This was the part that Eden had been so uncertain of when Beck's mother, incredibly, reached out to invite her to lunch. She accepted eagerly, realizing a golden opportunity to not only get to know Nora but, also, hopefully to glean insight into Beck and even Everett.

"First things first," Nora said as if starting an agenda for the afternoon. "How are you feeling?"

Eden frowned. "How am I feeling?"

"You seemed…distressed the night we met. I actually thought about you with some concern after you and Beck left."

"Oh…" Eden shook her head. "I had some sort of stomach thing. I was fine by the next morning." She thought for a moment. "Beck took care of me. He was great."

Nora smiled knowingly. "I'm not surprised. Turns out he's a great nurse. He moved in with me for almost a month a few years ago, when I came down with COVID-19."

"Really?" Eden said, expressing her own concern and surprise.

"I was fortunate. I was able to ride it out at home without having to be hospitalized. And I was doubly fortunate that Beck so willingly came to help me."

"Of course," Eden responded with certainty. "You're his mom. He's going to be very protective." But she noticed that Nora had a different expression that could be interpreted as doubt.

"Yes," she said slowly. "Believe me, I was very happy Beck stayed."

Eden suddenly sensed that perhaps Nora was also scoping her out for information about Beck, although she wasn't sure what she might know that Beck's mother wouldn't. Or was Nora really more curious about the relationship between her and Beck? There were no secrets between them, but that didn't mean she wanted to discuss what was developing between them with his mother.

Eden was also aware that, in a very odd way, she and Nora might have bonded that night in her dressing room. While she had no idea how or why, she was curious enough to readily accept getting together. And Eden was sure that Beck, somehow, was the cornerstone of that night and this moment.

"I want you to know that I–I was surprised when you suggested we get together. We'd only just met."

Nora shrugged. "Well, how long is it supposed to take? And that does bring me to the second point about you coming today. When you came in with Beck, there were so many things I noticed. First of all, I looked at you and thought, *Wow.* You're so pretty. But more than that, I just felt you were open and friendly and seemed really pleased to be meeting me."

"Well, I was. Your show was great. I couldn't believe Beck was taking me to meet you. When I found out you're related, I was… pleased."

"Me too. I mean, about meeting you. I could tell right away that whoever you were, you were important to him. Beck has never been in the habit of introducing me to his girlfriends."

Eden felt herself demurring. "We…are…I mean…just…"

Nora chuckled. "Stop. You don't have to explain anything. But it's true about my son. And I felt like I understood right away what drew him to you."

"We first met at the memorial service for Everett Nichols. I learned that Everett was Beck's stepfather. And then I met you. I used to work for Everett when I was an undergraduate."

Nora sighed. "The world is getting smaller. You and I are meeting like six degrees of separation. Maybe less. I hope you don't mind if I say it sounds a little like fate."

"Yes, it does," Eden agreed. But to what purpose? What was the outcome going to be?

When she considered her own revelations about her feelings for Beck, she also felt a mild wrenching of expectations in her chest. She didn't want to put much meaning to it, except she knew what she felt was her instincts signaling her. *Pay attention. Go for it. This is real.*

For a moment Eden found herself babbling, sharing information that explained the connections between her and Beck, her and Everett, how she learned about Beck and Everett. It was like a very small-scale circle of life. Eden could see that Nora was riveted, focused on her every word, as if to do anything would break a spell in which holes in the fabric of their histories with Everett…and Beck…were about to be filled in.

"Beck and I started seeing each other right away. We just sort of…fell in step with each other and kept moving. And now"—Eden looked directly at Beck's mother—"I think it's fair to say there's an attraction," she said quietly. "I like him. A lot." Her voice was almost a whisper. She was nervously twisting her hands together. She hadn't expected to admit so much. Once spoken, all her reveals became cemented in truth.

"I'm glad to hear that, Eden." Nora became thoughtful for a moment. "What has Beck told you about his family? Anything?"

Eden was alert. Of course, she suspected that the question, so simple and straightforward, was part of Nora's agenda. She was very aware of the confidences Beck had shared. Eden knew now that Beck's family history had a lot of sadness and loss attached.

"Of course I now know that Everett was his stepfather. I…know about your divorce from Everett, but that happened before I worked for him. He never talked about his marriage, or you." She knew she'd have to mention Mason, sooner or later, but Eden wasn't willing to do so if it was going to make Nora uncomfortable…or indict Beck.

Nora stared at her.

Eden shifted, wondering if she'd gone too far.

Nora looked pointedly at Eden. "My first husband was African American. We were both teaching music when we met. He had a trio, and it was Pete who suggested I sing for them. It was a lot of fun. I didn't expect it to go anywhere. I found that out when we sometimes got to play in other cities. We toured as far north as New York, Atlantic City…Philly. But we quickly realized we couldn't go much further south than DC."

"I get it," Eden said.

"Pete was attending a music festival without me…and was killed on his way to a club date. He died with another member of his original group."

"I'm sorry. That must have been pretty awful for you and Beck."

Nora smiled, shrugged. "Beck was much too young to remember his father. Pete was a wonderful man. He was kind and talented. We had a rough time. Peter's mother, at least, loved me. Her family name was Beckford. That's how Beck got his name."

Eden decided not to follow up with other questions about Nora's first marriage. "So, Beck grew up here?" Eden asked. The veil of memories lifted from Nora, and she smiled.

"Yes, he did. Until he graduated high school and went away to Duke. He only stayed a year. He transferred to Morehouse. He said he needed a college where he *could be in his own truth*...live his real identity and be Black. After college he never really returned home."

Another topic Eden decided not to question. She simply wasn't going to learn everything during a few hours with Beck's mother, although her curiosity was rampant.

"Can I ask for a tour of the house? This is exactly the kind of house I wish I'd grown up in."

Nora immediately stood up. "Happy to."

Eden followed slowly behind Nora through the first floor, stopping now and then for Nora to point out and talk about certain items or accessories that had a story attached. Eden loved that part because it made the life Beck, Nora, and Everett had here come to life. Eden vaguely made note that there didn't seem to be photographs anywhere on the first floor of the house, and none on the stairwell wall as they headed up to the second level.

The first bedroom at the top of the landing on the left was Nora's suite. The door was open, and she stood in the doorway and let Eden glimpse the inside. Eden got excited when she spotted several framed images on the bureau, but she was not in a position to see who they were of before Nora was backing them out of the doorway. There were two closed doors on the right. Nora walked right by them to the end of the hall where there was a fourth room that Nora used for guests. It was a neat, comfortable small room. Eden speculated to herself that she certainly wouldn't ever mind being a guest using that room.

But as they retraced their steps back to the staircase, Eden stopped strategically between the two closed doors.

"Nora? Please forgive me but, would it seem really strange or rude to ask to see Beck's room?"

Nora did seem surprised at the request, but she didn't display any particular emotion. "You want to see his room?"

"I'm getting a very good idea of the kind of man Beck is. He's incredibly observant. He has a quick sense of humor, and...he's thoughtful. But I'd love to see the kinds of things that the little boy he used to be was interested in. Of course I'll understand if you think that's too personal. Or if you think he wouldn't like anyone going into his old room."

"I'm not sure how he'd feel about someone going into the room. Beck certainly has never talked about his room as a sacred space. As a teenager, he never put signs on the door like *EXPLOSIVES, KEEP OUT.* Or *Beware of Dog.* I think my favorite sign he said his best friend at the time had was *Quiet! Levitating! DO NOT ENTER.*"

Eden was laughing by the time Nora was done. In an odd way the laughter served to temper the awkwardness of the request. Nora approached the door and pushed it open for Eden. But she did not go in herself. In fact, she only gave the interior a cursory glance before walking away.

"I made a light lunch for us to have in the sunroom. Come down when you're done."

Nora began to slowly descend the staircase, leaving Eden outside the bedroom. She slowly entered, stepping back into Beck's childhood.

The room was definitely a boy's room. The walls were painted blue. The space was big enough to accommodate a full-size bed, very unusual and generous for a teen. And it was neatly made up, as if he was expected back at any time. There were just two posters on the walls, one of Reggie Bush, NFL running back, and the other of Kobe Bryant, Lakers basketball player, early in his career. There was a bookcase, and Eden was surprised to read that most of the titles were not fiction, but biographies, Black history, and just about everything James Baldwin had published.

She took the liberty of sitting at Beck's desk where there was a single row of athletic trophies lined up at the back. They were for football, mostly, and a few for swimming. Eden swiveled in the chair to see the rest of the room and noticed that on the lower shelf of the nightstand next to the bed, there were several framed photographs. She stood up, approaching the table, and squatted on her haunches to get a better look at the photos.

The largest framed photo was of Everett with Beck at maybe age seven or eight. Eden drew in a sharp breath, realizing that she'd come across a treasure of real history. In another were Nora and Beck, he about fifteen and looking stern and unhappy, his youthful face a scowling frown of discontent. In this picture, Beck's parentage was obvious, his skin tan next to his mother's porcelain white. It was so apparent that he was developing into a handsome young man. It was impossible for Eden to tell if his expression was just a typical teenage *I-don't-care* attitude, or if he was actually expressing sincere feelings about something, or someone.

Knowing that Nora was waiting for her, Eden browsed the photos as quickly as she could. There was an image of Beck at high school graduation, but only of him and his mother. Again, he wasn't smiling, although Nora seemed to be trying for both of them. Eden mentally did the math and knew Nora and Everett would have long divorced by then. Pictures of Everett with Beck as a young boy, an adolescent, showed a palpable connection between the two. In one photo, Beck stood in front of the towering Everett who had his arms crossed in front of Beck's chest, affection obvious in their broad smiles. But then, almost at the back of the shelf, Eden found a photo that had her staring, both perplexed and fascinated. Beck at age ten or so slouched on a sofa with a toddler cuddled up next to him. Beck was looking down on the younger boy with affection, and patience, and protectiveness. The small boy was grinning like a Cheshire cat, playing to the camera.

The little boy was white with a thatch of dark hair, and blue eyes like Nora's. Eden stared long and hard at the younger boy. He had to be Mason.

"I'm a horrible guest," Eden said, returning to the first floor and finding her way into the kitchen. "What can I do to help?"

"Nothing, It's all done," Nora said, in the middle of plating food for them but indicating two glasses of wine for Eden to carry.

Together they made their way back to the sunroom and a small, round table set for two. Eden smiled at the arrangement, happy that Nora had invited her, happy for the chance to get to know her. They sat and spread lovely floral cotton napkins over their laps. Nora lifted her glass and Eden did the same.

"Here's to having met. I hope we become good friends…with or without sharing my son."

Eden laughed because the image was funny, but she also considered that the comment seemed both wistful and profound. Was Beck's mother, in some way, indicating a preference for her to be in Beck's life? Did Nora somehow see Eden as a pathway to her son, maybe in a way that had been lost as he grew into a man? Eden thanked Nora for letting her explore Beck's bedroom, but Nora made no responding comments about Eden venturing into her son's childhood room. The lunch conversation was taken up with two topics: Eden's anecdotes about law school and Everett encouraging her to apply, and Nora's experiences as a singer. Occasionally Beck came up in conversation, but Eden was pleased that neither he nor Everett took up space or time.

When they were close to finishing, Nora suddenly stood. "I want to show you something," she said, walking across the wide space to a desk in the far corner of the room. She picked up two items from the desktop and returned to the table. She handed two framed photos to Eden and sat down again.

Eden looked at the first photo. It was another image of Everett and Beck. But the second photo was of Everett and the little boy she'd seen with Beck in the photo in his room. Eden stared, and slowly she began to see similarities between the little boy and Everett. She raised her gaze, questioning, to Nora.

"That's Mason. He's my son with Everett. Beck was five when Mason was born." Nora took a deep breath, but she was composed. "Mason was almost seven, there with his father. He drowned a few months after that picture was taken. We were at Myrtle Beach for a long weekend vacation…"

Eden made a sound, but she later would not be able to say if it was a mew of horror, disbelief, or anguish for Nora's loss. "Oh… Nora," she managed, her voice breaking.

Nora reached out to take her hand, as if to thank her for her understanding, her smile sad and accepting.

"Beck was twelve at the time of the accident. When I think

about it now, what he went through, I can see he was in shock when it happened. Helpless and terrified. But I did something unforgiveable. I blamed him for not watching out for his brother. I blamed Beck for Mason's death." Nora squeezed Eden's hand tightly.

Eden stared wide-eyed at Nora, who stared back with a different kind of reaction. One of them absorbed the pain. And the other sought the peace of that empathy.

When Eden stepped out of the town car, she already had a tip ready for the driver to thank him.

"You have a good evening, miss. You look really nice," he said, waving as he pulled away from the front of the National Museum of African American History and Culture.

She'd always thought of the name of the Mall's newest national institution to be a mouthful, as if the designers and founders wanted to make sure *all* of the ground was covered: African American, history, culture, museum…monumental. She had visited the museum when it first opened, privileged to have been invited with hundreds of DC high school and college students. And she'd been awe-inspired by the grandness and scope of the collection, and the four hundred years of history that was its province. It was so vast, but so methodically displayed that she'd only been able to see about a third of the collection on her first visit. She had yet to return to see the rest. It was on the list.

Eden turned to the entrance, at quite a distance from the curb where she'd been dropped off. She spotted Beck standing watching her arrival. She could tell he was smiling to himself, and that made her efforts for the evening well worth it. He was dressed in a business suit, looking impossibly handsome. Not for the first time she wondered how come he hadn't been snagged by some equally gorgeous woman and, possibly, had a child by now. She started toward him, breathing out a little nervous sigh of satisfaction and self-doubt that Beck might see in her someone he found special, and gorgeous.

He began walking as well, to meet her halfway along the path.

"Hi. Made it." Eden grinned.

"I wanted us to arrive together. I would have come for you."

"Then I couldn't have made this grand appearance. Like Cinderella getting out of the carriage."

"I wouldn't exactly call a town car a pumpkin," he said dryly.

Beck was taking his time to study her, his mouth curved into a lopsided smile. In the early evening dusk, she could still read the appreciation in his gaze. He took her hand. Held it up and out to the side, and released it. Eden took the cue and pivoted gracefully, 360 degrees, so Beck could get the full effect of her attire.

When she came full circle to face him again, he still had a look that made Eden feel, for the first time in she didn't recall how long, that she was being regarded as a desirable woman. She smiled up at his bemused expression. Beck shook his head, raised his brows.

"You look…amazing," he drawled, his pleasure obvious.

"Really?" Eden asked, pleased by his reaction.

"You are all that. And a bag of chips," he said.

She giggled, definitely girlish. She *never* did that.

He gave a tug on her hand and held it as they approached the museum entrance, where there was a short backup of other arriving guests waiting to get in.

"So you obviously found a perfect dress in just a few hours of shopping," he said, still gawking over her appearance.

"Not just this one, but two others. And these shoes…" She held out one foot and shook the toe of her tapestry-fashioned shoe. "And my hair." She turned her head left and right to make sure Beck saw it all. "I did it myself." It was combed upward in the back, secured by two combs covered in different-sized pearls. The bulk of Eden's hair was in those same fat, loose looping curls, now bunched at the top of her head and in a gently off-center cascade over her forehead.

"Was this all for me?" he asked.

Eden smiled at his naivete and squeezed his hand. "You're fishing. It was for *me*, Beck. But I'm loving your reaction. I wanted to knock your socks off…"

He laughed. "I'll check later and let you know."

"Your invite was a wonderful excuse to go shopping…and I had so much fun!"

"Sounds like you don't do that too often."

"Honestly? No. Until recently I never had the time. And I certainly never had the money. Today it hit me, as I was riffling through dozens of very expensive dresses. I could buy anything I wanted."

"Great moment?"

"Scary. For about two minutes…" She chuckled. "Then I got over it."

"So, everything is brand new."

"Are the earrings new, too?"

"Yes…"

"The ones from Tiffany?"

She looked at Beck in surprise. "You remembered that? No, they're not Tiffany's. Not yet."

"I wish I was taking you to some event that deserves how beautiful you look."

"This will do fine, thank you." She beamed at him, leaning into his arm affectionately.

"Still, you get a rain check for something bigger and better, to be determined later."

"Okay." She nodded happily. "I'll wait for that."

And Eden relaxed because of the conversation they'd had the morning after she'd gotten sick, after making love together, about the tragic loss of his younger brother.

Together they entered the cavernous lobby of the museum. There were a few hundred men and women standing around greeting each other, chatting, laughing. All were dressed semiformally for the occasion. It was only when Beck was greeted now and then as they meandered through the clusters of guests that Eden felt a wave of awkwardness. She was not going to know anyone here. But she noticed that people were giving her polite smiles, eyeing her with curiosity, not knowing who she was. Beck quickly remedied that by introducing her to as many people as each moment allowed. She even received a compliment here and there, on her fuchsia dress with its fitted bodice and just-off-the-shoulder top, the skirt slightly gathered at the waist.

"Beck! Man, it's good to see you."

Beck stopped to greet the man holding out his hand for him to shake. "Reese! Same here. My bad. Long time since we saw each other."

"As I recall, that was a tough time for you," Reese responded.

Eden knew at once, by the careful wording, that it was a significant comment, but Beck only pursed his mouth and nodded.

"I guess I did fall off the edge of the earth. I've been busy. You too."

"Yeah, that's what happens when you have deadlines and 1,500 words to write on a last-minute assignment. Know what I'm saying?"

The shorter Black man was a little overweight, with shaved head and chin-strap goatee. He joked, his gaze going back and forth between Eden and Beck in curiosity. "I guess you didn't get the memo that the earth isn't flat?"

"At least not this week. Depends on what conspiracy theory makes the news, right?"

Beck and the man laughed together at what Eden could only guess was a kind of routine that spoke to the nature of their work and their lives. Beck put his hand at Eden's waist, coaxing her a little closer to his side.

"Reese, this is Eden Marsh. Eden… Reese Talbot. He writes for the *Post.*"

"Hello, Reese," Eden said, giving him her attention and a smile.

"Not a writer, I take it?"

"Not journalism writing," Eden responded, watching a blank look come into Reese's eyes.

"Eden's an attorney," Beck supplied, looking down at her.

"I do write…a lot of briefs, reports, motions, complaints…"

Reese seemed impressed. "Sounds like a lot more work than what we do, right Beck?"

"Yeah, but maybe a toss-up about whose work is more important."

Reese studied Eden and finally said, "I can't see you as a lawyer."

"Why?" she asked, surprised.

He held up a hand. "Take this as a compliment, okay? But you look too…innocent to hold up against cutthroat prosecutors or cynical judges."

Eden grinned. "I accept the compliment part. But don't

misjudge me. The kind of opponents you describe make it very easy for me to get over because they're not expecting someone like me. Black and a woman. Their assumption…like yours…is predictable, leaving me to attack with grace and poise…" Beck chuckled. "And with unexpected arguments and logic that leave them gasping for air, wondering what happened."

Beck burst out laughing. "Oh, *snap*," he said, chuckling. His friend had the grace to look like he'd been caught flatfooted, and then he grinned.

"I deserved that. Clearly you have skin in the game," he said.

"Actually," Eden added. "I don't much like courtroom litigation. Too risky. Too many people to deal with. I like arbitration. Only one, maybe two people I have to persuade. I write a very convincing argument."

"I believe you. Tell you what. If I ever need a lawyer…and I'm going to make sure that I never do…" Eden laughed. Beck squeezed her waist. "I'm going to ask for you."

"I'm honored."

A loud bell could be heard throughout the gathering, a signal that everyone was to head into the auditorium for the evening's event. Reese and Beck said their goodbyes, and Reese walked away, joining another set of acquaintances.

Eden continued to look over the crowd, curious. She was enjoying being among mostly Black professionals who were not in law in any way, shape, or form. Tonight with Beck made her realize how much of her life had been consumed for three years with a specific challenge and a very small circle of friends and associates…and her sister, of course. Eden felt like the people in attendance tonight could be her peers, that within their association she could form new alliances and friendships. She fantasized about how meaningful and fun having a wider world view among other business people would be for her. Eden glanced up at Beck as he accepted programs for them from an usher standing inside the auditorium door. She had a new awareness that being with him made her feel grown up beyond the realm of a student or being a surrogate mother to her sister. Eden smiled peacefully to herself.

Yes. She loved the way Beck made her feel.

They stopped again for a moment to allow people ahead of them to clear the doorway into the auditorium. Suddenly, Beck abruptly let go of her hand and was stepping away from her as if he was distracted and summarily pulled aside.

Eden looked to see what had diverted his attention and saw Beck standing out of the way on the far side of the door as a tall, stunning young woman captured his gaze…and held it. Eden also stepped back out of the way of the door on her side, but she couldn't hear anything that was being said. The one thing Eden could detect was the woman's pose and purposefully flirtatious posture with Beck. He regarded her politely, with a vague smile and without engaging in chitchat. But the twisting in Eden's stomach warned her instinctively and instantly that there was a history between the two of them. The young stunner was obvious in her attempts to make it known that she knew Beck…and she knew him well.

It was only as another man appeared, a tall stocky white man in glasses, looking a little uncomfortable behind his bow tie, that the tension eased. Beck broke into a broad grin and shook the man's hand. They exchanged a brief bro hug. Only then did Beck look around, trying to locate her. But Eden didn't move. Beck was forced to cross to her, searching her countenance, and Eden was suddenly very careful not to give anything away. He looked both apologetic... and sheepish.

"We need to get inside, but...I want you to meet someone else."

Suddenly Eden, oddly, felt exposed in her new dress, her shoulders bare, opposite the beautiful woman who was reed thin and light-skinned...like Beck...with a luxurious weave of hair falling halfway down her back. She was wearing a midi-length sheath dress in navy that was a perfect contrast to her complexion. Her make-up, hair, *everything*, was perfect and eye-catching. And she knew it. The woman wore her considerable assets with supreme confidence. Eden stood tall...taller in her new heels and piled hair, her chin lifted and her back straight. She was still a good three or four inches shorter.

"Max. Alia. This is Eden Marsh."

To Eden the greeting exchange was awkward. Max enthusiastically said hello, and although Alia smiled and looked Eden over with a critical eye, she didn't seem impressed or interested. It rattled Eden, but she kept her composure and smile in place.

"Max and I were at Duke together," Beck said. "We were roommates the first year."

Eden was about to add that she knew that Beck had transferred to Morehouse after that first year, but hastily swallowed her comment, recalling in time that she wasn't supposed to know that. Nora had shared that history with her.

Instead she addressed Max. "Are you a writer, too? Everyone here seems to be a writer of one kind or another."

"I'm a show runner," Max said. "In my profession I get invited to a lot of happenings like this one around DC."

"He works for Capitol TV Entertainment," Beck interjected.

"DC home of reality TV. As a matter of fact, I recently brought

Alia on board for a new show premiering in a few months. Beck recommended her."

Eden's stomach grew a little queasy. She looked at Alia with as genuine a smile as she could manage. "Congratulations. You must be very happy about that."

Alia made a theatrical gesture with her head...as if she were royalty standing before her subjects. "Yes, I'm pleased. But I'm also considering several film options."

Eden let her gaze briefly slide to Max, ostensibly Alia's boss, to see how he was taking the news. It didn't appear to strike him as arrogant or presumptuous, and Eden let it go. When she looked at Beck, he was suddenly studying the carpet where he stood, a muscle working furiously in his jaw. She continued to stare, waiting for him to look up and meet her gaze. He didn't.

"Listen, we really need to get inside," Beck said to Max, his hand on Eden's arm to lead her away. "You and I need to catch up. Seriously," he added.

"I agree. Let's talk soon."

With that Beck hustled them through the door that was about to close, and the usher quickly walked them down the nearest aisle to an open row on their right. They had to shuffle sideways to their seats, just as the lights were going down, and the emcee walked onto the stage to the recognition and enthusiastic applause of the audience. Eden recognized her! A nationally known Black writer who was frequently interviewed on TV and was a guest on talk shows.

After a minute or two of the introduction and opening remarks, however, Eden found her mind drifting, her insecurities suddenly surfacing and pressing heavily down on her usual balance, self-possession, and confidence. She had no doubt about a past relationship between Beck and Alia, but seeing the beautiful young woman made her feel that there was *no* competition. For the moment her emotions didn't allow her to see there was no need for her to feel competitive. In Eden's mind, Alia was already the winner, no matter what had happened in her relationship with Beck. She could see why they had once been a couple. Eden had counterarguments to her pessimism but she managed to talk herself out of most of them. She did know her own strengths, and she had to call on all of them now so that she could enjoy the evening with Beck. When all was said and done, *she* was the one who had been invited, who accompanied him as his date to his industry gala. *She* was the one who sat next to him.

She fought not to let her momentary self-doubt spoil the evening.

Then, an unexpected announcement turned everything around for Eden, and she again took the reins of her relationship to Beck. There were awards and announcements of recognition for outstanding industry reporting, stories, profiles for the year. Beck's name was called. Eden gasped, turning to him. She could see immediately that even he was caught totally off guard as he continued to sit for several disbelieving seconds before getting up. Maneuvering his way to the aisle, he briefly turned to bestow upon her a smile of surprise, pleasure, and gratitude. Beck made a very brief thank-you to his association, colleagues, and guests in the audience. It was a while before he could make his way back to his seat for the rest of the program.

When the program ended, they were converged upon as the auditorium emptied and Beck was approached by well-wishers with handshakes, hugs and kisses, and any number of instant selfies with friends. Eden wouldn't allow herself to be included in any of the pictures, even at Beck's insistence. This was his moment. But she thoroughly enjoyed it with and for him. She wished Nora could have shared in the recognition. Eden had no idea why Beck wouldn't have asked his mother, instead of her, to attend the evening's plan.

At one point she happened to catch a glimpse of Alia and Max very near to where she and Beck stood as he continued to accept congratulations, holding a mounted ten-inch sculpted silver scroll that was engraved with the nature of the award, Beck's name, the year, and the title of the article he'd written that had earned him the recognition of his peers and the industry.

Eden was gratified when Beck, realizing that he couldn't walk away and leave yet, looked for her in the crowd. Eden raised her hand and he saw the gesture. His gaze apologized. Her gaze indicated she was in no rush. He was about to be swept away with other winners for the official photo op when Beck got the photographer's attention and insisted that he take a quick photo of him with her. Eden allowed herself to be pulled out of the crowd to stand next to him for a quick flash round of shots. Beck then joined the other award recipients for more photos.

She patiently waited, having miraculously regained her equilibrium, her self-assurance, after meeting Alia and Max. But then Eden caught the drift of chatter and conversation over her right shoulder.

"I saw him come in with her."

It was Alia. Eden was sure she recognized her voice, her bored way of referring to people, places, and things.

"Who is she?" another woman asked in great whispering curiosity.

"I don't recall her name. Probably his date for the evening."

"Maybe not just the evening. Maybe Beck's dating her."

Eden heard Alia utter something dismissive. "I seriously doubt it. She's not his type. She's attractive, I guess, but nothing special. Not sure what he sees in her."

There was light laughter, and Eden felt her skin tighten as a chill rushed through her.

"She must have some redeeming qualities. Beck is a smart, talented man…"

"Maybe she's good at…"

Eden lost the last few words in the louder surrounding conversations. But then she heard a sudden burst of laughter from the gossiping group with Alia. Her cheeks flushed but she remained stalwart, not moving, wondering if it was more talk about her. Pretending not to have heard any of the talk.

"I love the dress she's wearing. Gorgeous color. It's very becoming," someone else offered a salve.

"You heifers are cruel. I think she's cute." A male voice threw in his opinion, and more laughter erupted.

"Puppies are cute," Alia corrected. The group laughed again.

After a moment, the group dispersed and the gossip ended. In another minute Eden turned in time to see the tall beauty head to the ladies' room. She stared, her heart beginning to race, but knowing what she had to do. *She had to.*

She followed Alia.

A few women were exiting, and Eden waited a few seconds before entering. Alia wasn't in a stall, but seated at the vanity fussing with her hair, gently shaking and flipping the locks to settle more becomingly behind her shoulders. She carefully checked her face in the giant wall mirror, under complimentary lighting, for any need of makeup repairs.

Eden entered slowly, but Alia detected her presence quickly. She barely spared Eden a glance before returning her attention to the mirror.

"Wasn't it great that Beck got an award?"

She surprised Eden with her remark. Eden sat next to her on the second stool. Alia glanced at her out of the corner of her eye but otherwise continuing her toiletry.

"It was," Eden said, belatedly looking for her lip rouge to give herself something to do that warranted a trip to the restroom. "I think he was really surprised to get something." By now other women were entering who stopped momentarily behind them to check their own appearances and make social comments to each other before leaving.

"Why are you staring at me?" Alia asked suspiciously when they were alone again.

"I'm not staring. But…I did want to ask you something," Eden said, while Alia continued with her makeup ritual, seemingly uninterested. "I…heard you talking with your friends a few minutes about. It was about me."

Alia half smiled, arching a brow at Eden's reflection in the mirror. "Were you eavesdropping? That's not nice."

"What you and your friends were saying about me wasn't very nice. You don't know me. You and I only just met."

Alia sighed, a little impatient. "You're right. None of us know you. It was silly conversation. I'm sorry if your feelings were hurt."

"It was such a middle-school mean-girl thing to do. Are you annoyed that Beck is dating again? I figured you two used to be an item. He got over it."

Alia turned to face her, not using the mirror as a shield. "Maybe. Maybe not. You know he was going to ask me to marry him."

Eden pressed her hand against her stomach. "But he didn't."

Alia shrugged. "I got offered a key role in a popular TV series. I made a half-dozen episodes before I was written off. But it led to two other appearances on other shows. I'm in demand, and my career is taking off."

"So you sacrificed your love for Beck for a TV career?"

"I wouldn't put it that way. In any case, Beck always knew I had career plans. Suddenly it was all happening. I couldn't pretend none of it mattered. I think Beck understood. We parted friends." Alia eyed her up and down again. "And then he turned to you."

"Your reaction sounds like jealousy to me," Eden said with quiet but firm confidence.

Alia rolled her eyes and glared coolly at Eden. "You know, I really don't care about you."

"He got you into the studio with his friend Max. He was being very decent to you."

"He only had to make a phone call."

Eden turned to study Alia. "Did you thank him?"

Alia turned to pointedly stare. "I'd say we're even. We were a very good-looking couple around DC. It didn't matter to him, but he knew it was important to me. Beck is a great guy. He's...wherever he is, with you now. Good luck with that. He's never going to be more than a writer. He'll never be famous."

"Maybe."

"Or rich," Alia added airily.

Eden chuckled in genuine amusement. "Actually, he might have that over you." She slowly stood up. "I was curious about you. I see how Beck was taken with you."

"I think he liked what he saw."

"But…you're not even real."

"*What?* What did you say?" Alia abruptly stood up to confront her.

Eden turned to her, maintaining her poise, allowing a smile of satisfaction to shape her mouth despite the pounding of her heart, her hidden agitation.

"You are a very beautiful woman. I bet you're told that all the time. But, you're a fake beautiful woman. That's not your hair. The eyelashes are obviously not real. *No one* has lashes that long. Your fingernails are plastic and so comically long that I don't know how you're able to dress yourself. Where does a man find the real *you*? What else is store-bought?"

Alia blinked in disbelief, then quickly narrowed her gaze, like something predatory trying to decide if they can take down their prey. She slowly gathered her things, put them back into her purse, and gave Eden one final long look of indifference before heading for the exit. "Good night," she said sweetly, calmly, and was gone.

Eden swallowed hard. For a second she'd thought Alia was going to hit her with her purse or push her aside.

It was very quiet…and then Eden heard a toilet flush. Three women came in and gave Eden curious stares, letting her know they'd listened to at least part of what had been said between her and Alia. They all entered available stalls as, unexpectedly, one in the far corner slowly opened and a woman hesitantly came out.

Eden sat down again, taking a moment to compose herself. She was trembling just a little but it was subsiding. She stared at herself in the mirror, blinking in disbelief that the encounter had even happened. But her heart rate was slowing. She took a deep breath and slowly smiled at herself. Someone sat down next to her. Eden looked at her. The woman was laughing under her breath, shaking her head.

"Honey, that was the best entertainment all night."

"Did you hear everything?"

"Well, I sure didn't mean to, but once you and that other lady started in, I couldn't just walk out. It would have been too embarrassing. Like I was deliberately eavesdropping."

Eden chuckled. "You were."

"Yeah, that's true. But...it was worth it. *Girl*, you got her good. Telling her she wasn't real." She cackled loudly in hilarity. The woman stood up, still grinning. "Sounded to me like you're with the man who used to be hers. She wasn't too happy about that no matter what she said. It was like telling her she's replaceable. No woman wants to hear that. She was probably hoping that the bastard was suffering without her. Crying in his beer. Wanting her back." She laughed, turning to head for the exit and giving Eden a parting smile. "Sounds to me like it ain't happening. You did fine. Have a good night."

Eden finally stood once more. She was poised, her hair...*her own*...was still nicely in place. And Beck had said she looked amazing. Despite the obvious differences between her and the gorgeous Alia, a woman who Beck had once loved. And all Eden knew she wanted was a chance to love him herself.

Rejuvenated, Eden left the ladies room to find him.

CHAPTER 12

Beck wasn't used to Eden being so quiet.

She was never overly gregarious, but neither was she inclined to brood or turn inward in silence. Beck had a very strong sense of what was on Eden's mind but was still trying to find a way to approach the subject. He knew about the encounter in the ladies room with Alia. They'd been surrounded all night by reporters, columnists, essayists, bloggers. These were people who knew how to listen and look for stories and to sniff out gossip and scandal. Not that all the assembled guests that night knew about the bathroom episode, but enough had—all women, of course—and hints made their way to him even before he'd caught up with Eden after the photo shoot.

Beck was relieved to see her smile as he met her, no sign that anything was out of the ordinary. That was all he cared about. That Eden's evening had not been spoiled, that she didn't feel he'd been ignoring her since the award presentation, or that other guests... *anyone*...had done anything to her.

"Sorry about this," Beck had said when they'd reconnected. She shook her head, gazing at him with what he couldn't help but interpret as a great deal of warmth and affection. Maybe even love, although the thought, the possibility, startled him.

"What are you apologizing for?" she asked, taking his arm as they walked to the exit. "You're Crown Prince for the night…" He laughed at that, his deep voice reverberating around them. "And I'm Cinderella, remember?"

"The chocolate one?" Beck dared and was rewarded with a bright smile and a chortle of appreciative laughter.

It had been a natural, unspoken segue, after the evening at the museum, that she was staying with him that night. Despite declaring to Eden that she would get used to it, Beck was unable to avoid a flashback to the period when he and Alia actually lived together. Her presence had been everywhere in his life, in the apartment. For him it was the expectation that they were eventually headed toward marriage. It stunned Beck now to struggle to recall if Alia had ever said that was what she wanted as well. His chest actually tightened at the realization that Alia finally revealing her true expectations had saved Beck worse nightmares…and heartache.

He and Eden were where they both wanted to be, but there were moments of undressing and donning lounge/sleepwear that felt strange because it was still so new. They began by watching the local news at eleven because Beck knew there would be a brief report from a news feed about the event at the museum.

But Eden had lapsed into reflection, now and then, for the rest of the evening. They'd talked about the gala, sitting on the black leather sofa together, with Eden nestled against his side, her legs drawn up under her. Beck filled in more information about his long-standing friendship with his former college roommate, Max, never once bringing up Alia's name. Eden did that.

"How long did you and Alia date?"

It was out there, and Beck didn't see any benefit to lying. "Almost three years. It ended a little over a year ago."

"Not well, I take it."

Beck tried to see Eden's face, her expression, but she lay against him in such a way that he couldn't. Instead, he placed his hand on the side of her head and tilted it toward him so he could kiss above her left ear. He wanted Eden to know the past with Alia didn't matter.

"No."

He knew Eden was still processing the evening, her encounter. He waited, hoping she would trust him with the rest of her thoughts, maybe…her fears. He more or less had a strong sense of the basis of her reflections.

"She's really stunning."

"Yes, she is. I would say Alia was gifted with an abundance of incredible family genes. But I don't think there's any doubt that she's put in a fair amount of extra work on herself. Max tells me the cameras at the studio *love* her."

Eden sighed. "Well…she's got it all over me. I…"

"Don't…" Beck whispered. "Don't compare yourself to her. It's obvious that her complexion gets her extra points. She had no hand in that. Alia simply figured out how to make it work for her. The bare truth for me, Eden, is that you're based more in reality that I can relate to. That…" Beck swallowed, stopping short of confessing, *that I want.*

"But…you got her a position at your friend's network?"

"I didn't. I made a call and introduced Max and Alia. The rest was up to her, whether she could impress him, and if she could fit into the programming." He hesitated. "You two spoke." Beck felt Eden sigh against him.

"How did you find out?"

"Word got around. Quickly. Someone said something to some-one, who was overhead by someone else, and it got to Reese…"

"He told you?"

"He wanted to make sure I knew. He was being a little protec-tive of you, when I think about it."

"I don't need protecting."

"It's clear that you don't. I'm just sorry that…"

"My fault. I overheard Alia say something and I couldn't let it go. Tell me it didn't spoil your evening," she said, real worry making the question a plea.

"It was a great evening, Eden. You were there with me."

"You should have taken your mom."

It was an observation that took Beck by surprise. He'd only ever thought to take Eden with him to the gala.

"I'll tell her all about it," he promised. "And I have a program for her. She'll be okay with that."

Eden stretched and yawned, dropped her head to his shoulder. "She'll be so proud to know you got an award." She giggled quietly "It was fun seeing you head for the stage, all serious as you buttoned your jacket. I watched to see if you were going to trip going up the stairs…"

Beck laughed, putting his arm around her. "Thanks a lot. I thought I was very cool and on point."

She tilted her head back on his shoulder and regarded him. "You were," she whispered. Beck kissed her.

When they were in bed together a little while later and every-thing became much more natural, Beck was also noticing how quickly they were adapting to a domestic intimacy part of life. He knew he went to bed peaceful at night and woke up happy to have

Eden there…the only word that fit the emotion coursing through him as they got up. But it was also scary, intimidating, to have a new routine fall into place around them. They managed the morning around one another with conversation, and teasing, and often just coming together to touch affectionately and kiss. And he was ever mindful that much of the beginning of his relationship with Alia shared similarities.

But he still could not let what was happening form itself into a simple compact idea that, Beck admitted, he was afraid to believe in. Instead, he concentrated on the reality that Eden had to return home. There was another part of her life that had little to do with him, and everything to do with the fact that Holly was a significant part of it. He and Eden had been together for four too-short days, and it had to end. With Holly returning very soon, they squeezed in one more day together.

"Are you ready to go home?" he'd asked when they were spooned together in bed in the dark.

"Don't ask," Eden had murmured. "Anything I say is going to be a half-truth."

"Are you going to miss me?" he asked, but his tone was light.

She turned over so they could be face-to-face. "The question is, will you miss me?"

"Cute dodge. You know the answer to that."

"Then, we both know that-which-shall-not-be-spoken."

Beck chuckled and began to kiss her in earnest, his amusement quickly morphing into something indicative of desire and passion, of a yearning he felt the need to make the most of in what time remained. They'd learned that the slow dancing of their lips and tongues was a delightful buildup to burgeoning arousal and a slackening of their limbs, their defenses, an opening up of their bodies, souls, and hearts. His arousal showed the evidence of his need. His touching and exploring Eden intimately gave the evidence of hers. The sheer joy of finally coming together, joining their bodies, was a destination they came to with anticipation and hunger mutually shared in each other's arms.

They both played hooky the next day, and that was another way Beck realized how his life was changing. He adjusted quickly, knowing that it all came with each hour, each day spent with Eden. He had a lengthy article to finish, but it would have to wait. Right now, there were better uses of their time.

Beck decided, in a moment of quiet reflection while Eden was in the shower, that his time with her was so good that he felt the need to somehow balance his hope with the inevitability that things change. All good things can and do come to an end. He didn't want that. But he also hadn't wanted it to happen with Alia. The big difference was that Alia had shown he had only been a convenience. Beck's insides quaked at the thought of Eden being so devious. He didn't see it. He hadn't felt it. And now he was too far gone in another way to want to believe it.

But what if...

———

Eden left the bathroom, the waft of scented body oils and moisturizers escaping with her in the steam from her shower. She had a bath sheet fetchingly wrapped around her but knew that it might not last for long once Beck saw her. Eden loved playing the game of *will he or won't he* strip away the towel and replace it with his strong arms and solid body. Other things would follow delaying getting dressed.

But he was not in the bedroom. She heard his voice coming from the living room and realized he was on the phone.

"That's a bit tight," Beck was saying, while he paced around the room. He spotted her and blew her a kiss.

Eden grinned and returned to the bedroom. She had just finished patting herself dry when Beck returned, half reclining on the bed next to her, supporting himself on his elbows.

"Okay. What?" she asked.

"We're going to New York."

Her head turned sharply to regard him. "What? New York? But…that's so far away. Why?"

"Remember when I said that I…*we*…really need to give some thought about how to manage all the money Everett left us? Well…I just made arrangements for us to meet with Patrick Bennett who's just started a foundation. It's called *The Millionaires Club*. It's a way for people with a lot of money they don't know what to do with to think about being more…giving."

"I like the idea," Eden said, stroking his shoulder. "Are you serious about going to New York? When?"

Beck reached for her cell phone on the nightstand and pressed the home button so that the clock would appear. "In…just over two hours. I reserved seats on the next Acela."

Eden gasped, staring at him. "Are you serious? Two hours? I–I don't know if I can be ready. Beck, I have so much work, and…"

"We weren't going to get any work done today, anyhow. Remember? Look, this is only overnight. Believe me, I'm aware of work that has to be done by both of us. But we're not slackers. I've heard about your commitments, and I know you're on deadline twenty-four seven…and you're close to commencement. But

I think getting to meet with Patrick is important. And you and I get an exotic twenty-four hours away from DC." He turned on his side to regard her closely, and Eden liked what she saw in his persuasive gaze. Bottom line, they would be together. Alone. With a very limited agenda.

"What else do you have in mind?" she asked, surrendering.

Beck grinned, arching a brow. "I think you're going to love it… but I'm not telling you everything. I like surprising you. I don't think you get enough of that. Neither do I. I just want you to nod your head and say yes…and leave the details up to me."

Eden blinked at him, and slowly an accompanying smile curved her mouth. She nodded. "Yes."

She couldn't remember the last time she had so much unadulterated fun. The not knowing everything, but knowing and trusting that Beck had covered everything. They dressed, and it was great to realize she didn't need more than her large tote to pack everything for an overnighter. Beck said they would have dinner when they arrived in the city, but it wasn't going to require getting dressed up. That helped a lot and kept Eden's travel items down. She knew that she and Beck would be meeting Patrick the next day, maybe for lunch, and then they'd head to Penn Station for their train back to DC. Eden understood there would be no time for touristy sightseeing, and Beck promised they'd have another longer weekend in New York at another time.

They both instinctively packed their laptops and enough work to occupy the round-trip time on the Acela. And then Beck called for a town car to take them to Union Station. They purchased very light snacks and drinks for the journey, and once settled in their seats, Eden sighed with what could be described as happiness. Quiet and content. As the train began a slow and soundless easing along the tracks, not picking up any speed until they'd cleared the tunnel a few miles out of the station, Beck turned to her, catching her attention. He grinned at her and gave Eden a soft, gentle kiss.

"See you on the other end," he said with humor.

Eden laughed as they both opened their laptops, prepared to get some serious work done. A very small price to pay for the time they'd have together.

Beck had done his research and had never been at any of the hotels on his short list of where he and Eden would stay for their too-brief overnight in the city that never sleeps. He'd arranged for another car to meet them in New York and transport them uptown. He enjoyed watching Eden's attention to the passing big-city landscape outside her window. Beck had been to New York a number of times, even since he'd interviewed Patrick Bennett a few years earlier. But being there on business—train to the city to the hotel to a meeting to the station, and back to DC—did not count as a visit to the city. He'd never seen much of the city, either.

When the car pulled up in front of The Ritz-Carlton on Central Park West, he heard a quiet inhalation from Eden. She turned to him.

"Are we staying here?"

"Of course," Beck said smoothly, aware of her surprise. "Is this okay with you? Want to go someplace else?"

Eden merely shook her head as her door was opened by a valet and she was helped out of the back seat. Beck quickly came around, and they were both relieved of their overnight travel cases and escorted inside to the front desk. The level of friendly attention and quick check in processing added to the sense of luxury that he was certainly not accustomed to, so he knew exactly what Eden was experiencing. They were given their room keys and directed to the elevators. Beck let Eden do all the gawking and craning of her neck to look around the old-world extravagance of the hotel interior. They rode the elevator alone.

"I'm not going to ask what this is costing. I think you arranged this on purpose, just to show off," she said, her eyes bright with pleasure.

"You're right. And I'm going to enjoy every minute of it."

Eden slipped her hand into his and Beck grabbed it tightly. "Me too."

The room was not just a room but a suite.

"My entire apartment could probably fit into this space," he murmured.

He watched as Eden silently wandered over to the panoramic windows overlooking all of Central Park. It was green and floral, lush with the evidence of a new spring. Eden stood staring out and Beck joined her, standing behind her with his arms circling her waist. It was an easy and very natural thing to do now. He didn't have to wonder if Eden, like Alia, might object because she was worried about her hair being mussed and out of place because of the three-hour train ride. Eden settled back against his chest.

"We won't be able to do much in the time we have, but it's still light enough for a walk through the park. Or would you rather walk along Fifth Avenue for a little bit? And then we'll head out to dinner."

"Are we eating here?"

"No. I thought we'd do something fun and head downtown." She turned her face up to him. "Sorry. You'll have to wait until we get there."

They freshened up a bit and started out. And they headed south. Beck knew enough about the city to cut east from Seventh Avenue over to Fifth. They immediately came upon Tiffany's on the corner, and Beck slowed his steps silently to see if she was interested in going in.

"No," Eden said simply and they continued. But it had started out as an early day, and by the time they finally reached Forty-Second Street near Bryant Park, they were both feeling a little weary. Eden, apparently happy to be able to offer something to their little adventure, summoned a Lyft to the address Beck gave her. Once the car arrived and they were comfortably seated, Beck finally announced they were headed to Chinatown, to Golden Unicorn. He knew it meant absolutely nothing to Eden, but she'd stopped questioning any of his decisions, and he knew she was just enjoying being along for the ride. That in and of itself was enough to satisfy him.

The restaurant, famed for its cavernous space and dim sum and Cantonese cuisine, was very busy, already crowded with well over a hundred diners and dozens of dim sum carts moving up and down aisles, stopping at tables so that customers could make selections. Eden had never had dim sum before. Beck was not surprised when Eden questioned everything on the cart, but willingly let the waiter make suggestions of foods she'd never seen before. Her favorite became the sticky rice wrapped in lotus leaves.

Dim sum dishes were like Spanish tapas...just small plates of different foods, and eating enough of them made a full meal.

They took another Lyft back to the hotel and were ready and content to climb into bed to chat about the day and plan the next day. Beck told Eden as much as he knew about Patrick, but also more fully explained how Patrick had suddenly come into his wealth, and both the horror-filled and poignant stories that had moved him to establish his foundation, the idea given him by his now wife, Jean Travis Bennett.

Beck continued to speak quietly, his voice low and gravelly, Eden cradled in his arms. But she seemed suddenly very still, and when he stopped to glance down at her, she was asleep, her breathing even, her breath warm against his skin. With a deep sigh, Beck lay for long moments just reflecting on the trajectory of his relationship with Eden, how it had come about, the changes that knowing her had so far made in him.

He liked all of it very much. And now it seemed simple and obvious.

He loved her.

Eden listened very closely to what Patrick Bennett was explaining to her and Beck about the mission plan and goals for his new foundation. But Patrick first explained why he didn't want to have the offices in Midtown but had chosen a whole floor in a newly built complex on 125th Street in Central Harlem. The format of the business and the space would allow for current and future staff to work remotely if they so desired.

The location made perfect sense to both Eden and Beck, as Patrick explained that their clientele, in terms of who would most likely need philanthropic help, were likely to be low-income, women, people of color, and immigrant populations. The highly diverse population of the historic and iconic community in Harlem really spoke to where the city was and what it could be in the near future.

"So says my wife," Patrick said smoothly, "and I don't disagree with her. And Jean would know."

"Does she work for your foundation?" Beck asked.

"Oh no," Patrick said with a shake of his head. "Jean has incredible experience in city government. She works for the mayor, but maybe not for much longer. She'll graduate in May with a master's in urban planning."

Beck cast a quick glance at Eden. "Eden will earn her JD in May also."

Patrick regarded her with interest. "Really? Congratulations. What kind of law do you want to practice?"

"I think the broad heading is ethics. But I want to continue as an advocate for low-income issues."

"Maybe I should hire you," Patrick said seriously.

Eden laughed. "That's very flattering, but I'm happy in DC for now."

"That's okay. But hold the thought," Patrick said.

"Eden and I are very interested in your foundation, and we seriously would like to know if there's a place for us."

"If you have a *lot* of money and a willingness to share, I think we can find a place for you."

Patrick stopped, and Eden could tell he was carefully considering his next words.

"I don't want to be too personal or say the wrong thing, but is your interest a joint consideration?"

There was no mistaking the implication, and Eden was at a loss for words. She didn't look to Beck for guidance but sensed he was equally caught off guard by the question. He shifted in his chair, but his expression and his response was measured and calm.

"I think Eden will agree with me that our contributions have to be separate. As you know from the documents I emailed to you, my late stepfather, Everett Nichols, left me all the holdings of his business. He was a very successful contractor in the mid-Atlantic area. And he left monetary assets to me, personally."

"And," Eden added, "Everett left me a gift of $5 million. I'd worked for him as an undergraduate, and he was a very important mentor in my life."

Patrick silently and swiftly let his gaze travel back and forth between them and nodded his understanding. But, again, Eden knew there were unspoken questions, and she was relieved that Patrick realized the present meeting was not the place for deeper inquiries.

"I want you to understand I haven't yet worked out all the categories of giving *The Millionaires Club* will have, how anyone can apply, *who* can apply, etc." He arched a brow and unconsciously ran a hand through his hair. "You know, I came from sports and then sports broadcasting. I never thought I'd include CEO of a humanitarian project on my résumé."

"Your wife Jean's influence?" Eden asked conversationally.

"Most definitely," Patrick readily admitted. "She keeps me on a path to true north."

"Lucky you," Beck responded, grinning.

Patrick nodded. "Oh, yeah. *Very* lucky me."

Eden swung the conversation back to the foundation, asking the kinds of questions she and Beck had prepared themselves for, and deciding she would be the one to field them with Patrick.

"I'd like to know if you have a minimum for qualifying to belong to your club. Will you require references or other financial statements from us? What are the tax rules I need to be aware of. And…is my $5 million enough to make real use of?"

"Most of your questions can and will be answered by the financial team here. I do not want to add accountant and math wiz to my skill set," Patrick groused, making them laugh. "But I can say, Eden, that you have enough, if you're still interested at the end of the meeting, to perhaps set up a special scholarship fund…or two. It won't require a large startup, and the money will be invested so that the scholarship money comes from interest and other benefits. That much I understand," he said ruefully, again making them laugh.

Patrick wanted to take them to lunch afterward. Jean was coming and he wanted them to meet his wife. They declined.

"We're headed to Penn for our train back to DC. Eden has a curfew, and I have to get her home at a decent hour." Patrick chuckled. "I appreciate that you could see us on such short notice," Beck said as Patrick walked them out of his office.

"Listen…you made me sound like I walk on water in that article a few years ago. And it appears I will be getting money from you. Not a bad deal all around."

Laughing still, Eden stood by as the two men shook hands and promised to make plans for another get-together. Maybe after the commencements of Jean and Eden…and the second-anniversary celebration for Jean's parents.

Eden's silent speculation went wild.

"Now *that's* an interesting story for an article. You'll have to return to New York for the details, but it's a very twenty-first-century tale," Patrick hinted.

Patrick surprised Eden when he gave her a very brief hug and then waved her and Beck off.

In the elevator down, she knew they were both thinking over the meeting, the utter charm and openness of Patrick, and all the information he'd shared. He'd promised to keep them in the loop of all developments. The foundation was only administratively up and running, their real purpose and business not quite ready for prime time.

They were standing outside the building waiting for their ride. Beck turned to her.

"So…what do you think?"

"Sounds to me like Patrick is crazy about his wife."

Beck was clearly surprised by her answer and grinned. "Yeah, that was obvious."

"Oh! You mean, about *The Millionaires Club*? I love the concept. I even love where the offices are located. I'm in. I really am impressed with what the club stands for, what Patrick believes in."

"I agree," Beck said, signaling to the Lyft that had just pulled up to the curb. They headed to the car. "I knew he was trying to ferret out what our relationship is."

"I think he wanted confirmation."

"Ummm. You're probably right."

"Do you think it's obvious that you and I might be an item?" Eden asked.

Beck smiled at her as he held the passenger door open. "It is to me. You and I are the only ones who matter."

CHAPTER 13

"Hi, Holly..."

Eden looked at Beck's profile. They were headed back to his apartment from Union Station and there was traffic. Eden knew he must be listening.

"Where are you? You're home already? Okay...okay... I guess I lost track of when you were flying home... No, I have plans. I'll be home tomorrow... If you must know, yes."

A smile played around Beck's mouth, and Eden knew he'd figured out the other side of the conversation and the questions Holly was asking. He glanced at her in approval.

"Oh, that's nice, Holly... How was Ireland?... Really?... I want to hear all about it, Holly, but not now. Well...it's a little complicated and I can't go into details, but we went up to New York yesterday. It was really business, and we've just gotten back into DC... No, we really didn't go to sightsee, I told you. Beck promises he'll take me again... No, you're not invited...You want to what?... Tonight?... But you just got home... Holly, you know I don't mind you having company, but don't you ever feel like just sitting quietly some evenings?... Fine. Whatever... I'm glad you got back safely. We'll talk tomorrow. And please don't unpack in the living room again. You do have your own room... Okay, 'bye."

There was silence for a moment, Eden feeling that she'd

somehow stepped over the line and assumed too much about Beck. But committing to him for the night did seem to come effortlessly. She didn't even hesitate. She glanced at him again.

"I should have asked you first. I'm sorry."

"I'm glad you were up front with your sister about tonight. You know I would have gotten you home, if you wanted to."

"I didn't want to."

"Remember that. And sometimes saying no doesn't take anything away from her."

"I know. I'm getting much better at setting boundaries with Holly."

"Practice," he advised quietly. "Thanks for giving us one more night together."

Eden sighed. "It sounds so…final. Like one of us is leaving the country for months."

He reached for her, clasping and resting their joined hands on his thigh.

"Don't you think it says something that we both feel the same way?"

"Yes…" she dragged out.

"But?"

"I don't want to spoil things, Beck. I don't want to have Holly rush us into something we haven't discussed or decided on our own."

"I understand and I agree. So let's not talk about what we have or where we're going. Let's see what happens…organically."

She grinned at him in the dark of the car. "Organically? Only a writer would use a word like that."

"Well, what would you call it?"

"Let's see what comes from our hearts. Isn't that the best judge?"

It was proof to Beck that they were not only on the right track, the same page, but also arriving at the same depth of feelings, although they'd never really talked about it. There was just this incredible comfort level, the warmth and sense of safety of being together. He guessed that maybe the reason they'd never had lengthy conversations about their feelings was precisely what Eden had suggested. *Don't talk about it. Let it happen.* But in not talking about it, a certain amount of insecurity was bound to creep in. For now, he kept his own counsel, only recognizing that he didn't want to lose Eden. He wanted her in his life. That did sound pretty permanent.

Being together for one more night was different because it was the last night. Hopefully just for now. Neither felt the urgency of copulation and losing themselves in the physical needs of their bodies. It was already beyond perfect…and they hadn't talked about that, either. Tonight they simply wanted to be together in mind and thoughts, good company and conversation.

Eden began quietly packing her things in preparation for Beck taking her home in the morning. He covertly watched her, not saying anything more about how they both felt about that. Now familiar with what was in his refrigerator and the pantry, she put together a quick and tasty charcuterie of cheese, olives, salami and summer sausage, crackers, and white wine to snack on during the rest of the evening. He turned on his sound system mounted to small speakers, with Alexa responding to their individual music choices to serve as a background. They both agreed that, in an odd way, it was almost like sitting at a bistro somewhere in the District…without noise, traffic, other people, or distractions.

At one point, Eden disappeared quietly. Beck became curious about where she'd gone, but on his way to the bedroom, he could hear the shower running in the bathroom. He stood listening to the hissing water spray and suddenly grew hot and excited imagining Eden naked and wet, glistening under the showerhead, soaping herself, bathing her limbs…

Beck quickly stripped, tossing his clothing onto the bed. He knocked on the door but got no response. So he slowly opened it to a light mist of steam escaping around him.

"I'm coming in," he said, reaching for the end of the shower curtain. She gasped.

"You're coming…*what?*"

Too late.

He swept back the curtain and quickly stepped into the tub, crowding her against the wall in the narrow stall. He was instantly soaked, water running down his face, chest, the tip of his penis, and running off the end in a thin stream. His hair flattened and then drew into its natural wavy pattern. He swept his hands through it, forcing the locks from his face and forehead. Beck looked at Eden, her own hair soaked and bunched to the back of her head. She hadn't had a chance to finish the shampoo. She had her arms crossed over her breasts, trying to see him through shower water obscuring her vision.

Beck laughed at the absurdity of her show of modesty.

Too late…

Without saying anything he took the loofah from the shower storage caddy and began to soap it. And then he began soaping and stroking her all over. Globs of white soapsuds dotting all over her smooth brown body. Eden gave in and let Beck bathe her, letting him meticulously do each arm, her neck and back, turning her around to circle slowly each breast, down her torso to her thighs.

And then it got interesting…and very intimate. It was pretty obvious that he was getting turned on by the chore, as was Eden, if her parted lips and taut nipples and his stiff erection were any indication. Beck thoroughly soaped his hands. He stepped close to Eden until her breasts met his. He gave her a deep, slow, erotic kiss while he put his soapy hands to her back, caressing in unhurried strokes up and down, curving around her buttocks all the way to where her thighs joined.

"Beck," she sighed, her eyes closed, most of the soap rinsed away under the spray. He brought his hands to the front and continued the bathing and stroking between her thighs until Eden was breathing in and out in little pants. She lifted a knee and braced a foot on the tub ledge, giving Beck access to the very center of her that made Eden release a whimper of utter pleasure.

He stopped, knowing they were going to have an accident in the slippery tub if they didn't rinse off, get out, and take their desperation to a safer surface. He hastily scrubbed his hands through Eden's hair, then his own, to release soap residue. He helped her out of the tub and thrust a towel into her hand. He took a second one, and then left the bathroom and went to the bedroom to finish drying off.

By the time Eden came out, her gait unsteady because she was in such a heightened state of excitement, Beck went to her, swept her up, and pivoted to deposit her on the bed. They were both barely dry, and the bed linens became a little damp under their bodies as they tumbled together, clasped and kissed and caressed each other, as they rolled and heaved and thrust toward satisfaction. After, they lay utterly limp and satiated, exhausted. It had been a long day.

Eden caressed his lower back, gliding her hands up toward his shoulder and feeling the way his muscles and sinew moved under her hands.

"Hmmm. That was pretty great," she cooed.

"That's all you get tonight," Beck teased in a sensual drawl.

"I can wait."

Me too, Beck observed, but he didn't have the nerve to voice it yet. He wasn't even sure if Eden, so free and open with her feelings, understood the implications of her confession.

But it was Eden who brought them both back to their real immediate future by saying, "Tomorrow we go back to our own lives, don't we?"

Beck stroked his hand up her back, pulled Eden a little closer so he could plant a light kiss on her forehead.

"For now," he said.

"Let me go up by myself," Eden said to Beck as he put down the shopping bag that held all her fun-day shopping, and the dress she wore to the gala, and her tote.

They were standing in her building lobby, in front of the elevators. "I don't like doing this. Let me help you get upstairs."

Eden shook her head. "I don't want to feel like I'm using you as a shield. And I have no idea what state I'll find my sister in. Asleep. In the shower. With someone."

"You know, you can always come back home," he said archly, causing Eden to laugh and to favor him with a sweet look of warm regard. It was a spontaneous, audacious thing for Beck to say.

"I'm just going to drop everything. I have to get to the law center, check in with my faculty supervisor…"

"And you'll bake an apple pie before noon, walk around the Mall again, check in with your classmates, finish the day at LC, and probably stop and chat with some homeless person or a street performer who needs a handout."

"Not a handout. A helping hand. There's a difference."

Beck stood studying her, seeming to absorb everything about her as if they were about to go into a drought of not seeing each other until they didn't know when. Eden felt such a twist in her chest of longing, of already missing Beck. She knew she was in far deeper in her feelings for Beck than she'd imagined or experienced just five days earlier. She knew she was so in love with him that it hurt just thinking about it, trying to process it, trying to divine a future. She swallowed back her emotions, her daydreams.

Beck rang for the elevator. They hugged and kissed with daring duration in the public space until Beck pulled away, walked back to the exit, and left her.

By the time Eden reached her floor, she'd already switched mental gears to focus on her day ahead. She worried that not until evening would she get to see and spend time with Holly. She got the door unlocked, not at all concerned about the dead quiet from within. Her sister was just as likely to sleep most of the day away her first day home. Eden pushed the door open with her shoulder, swinging her tote and her shopping bag into the entrance. She left everything near the door for a moment and straightened, moving into the living room. Eden got no further than a step or two and stopped dead in her tracks. Her mouth dropped open as her look swept around the room and she took in its condition.

There were dirty glasses and beer bottles on several surfaces, used napkins and paper plates stacked on the end of the coffee table, and two empty pizza boxes under the table on the floor. Eden was stunned at the mess, at the smell of tomato sauce that wafted in the air. She came farther into the room, and out of the corner of her eye, she caught something on one of the club chairs. Looking closer, Eden found a piece of pizza crust on the seat. She looked up toward the hallway leading to the kitchen…past the kitchen entrance to her bedroom door. It was partially open.

Eden rushed forward, feeling her annoyance grow into anger. By the time she reached her bedroom, she was furious. There was an almost-empty wineglass on her bureau. There was clear evidence by the rumpled bed linens and pillows that someone had been on her bed…if not in it.

She stood breathing heavily in sheer frustration and disbelief. Something came over Eden, something she was not used to experiencing that grew dark storm clouds inside her head with blood pulsing at her temples. She pivoted and in two strides was at her sister's door. She opened it, finding Holly peacefully sleeping. For just an instant, Eden felt some satisfaction that Holly had not left her travel bags in the front of the apartment as was her habit, but here in her room on the floor under the window. They lay open but still unpacked. She gazed at her sister, her practice of first checking to make sure her sister was okay thrown aside and replaced by weariness and disappointment.

"*Holly!* Holly, wake up!"

In the bed, Holly began to respond. Shifting around as her shouted name penetrated her sleep. She turned slowly onto her back.

"What?" Holly dragged out in a sleep-induced groan of irritation.

"Wake up."

"Can't you see I'm sleeping? I'll get up soon," she muttered, turning her head into her pillow.

Eden moved to the side of the bed, stood over her sister. "No. Right now. I need to talk to you."

The sound of her sister's voice finally got through. Holly lifted her head and pried open her eyes to blink at Eden towering over her.

"You're mad at me."

"*You think?*" Eden bit out through clenched teeth.

"I know I didn't clean up last night. I was so tired. I was going to do it before you got home," Holly justified, pushing herself into a seated position. She drew her knees up under the covers and hugged the top under her chin.

"I never said when I'd be home. You should have cleaned up last night no matter what. Who was in my room? *Who was sleeping in my bed?*"

Holly shot her a sideways glance and, unbelievably, began to giggle. "That's so funny. Like *Goldilocks and the Three Bears*,"

Eden stared down at her sister, whom she'd looked after, protected, worried about since they were still teenagers. But she wasn't a kid anymore who was scared when their mother died and they couldn't depend on their father to parent them. Eden could sense her anger threatening to turn to tears, but she wouldn't allow it.

"This isn't funny. Why can't you be more considerate? What's so hard about remembering we share this apartment? You don't get to trash it and then clean up when you feel like it. *Who was in my bedroom? What went on in there!*" Eden spewed, unable to control herself.

Eden's intensity, the strength of her feelings, finally seemed to get through to Holly. She fully sat up in her bed and turned her attention to her sister.

"It was only April. She had two glasses of wine and got sleepy. She took a nap, for God's sake. It's not like...like...she was in your bed with anyone else."

"Why didn't you let her nap in your bed?"

Holly shrugged. "I had stuff all over my bed. I was showing off some things I picked up at the airport in Amsterdam. They have great shops."

Eden blinked in disbelief at her sister's cavalier, very disrespectful attitude about the situation. It wasn't new. It never changed. She shook her head, bewildered. "I'm done." Eden turned and headed back to the front door to retrieve her bags. She snatched them up and went marching back to her own room. "Did you hear me? *I'm done!* I don't want to do this anymore. I'm tired of having the same conversation with you. I'm tired of you thinking you can do whatever you want and not taking what I ask seriously."

She went into her room, dumped the bags on her bed, and went into a frenzy of activity looking for a change of clothing out of her closet, finding her laptop and rifling through papers stacked on one of the end tables to repack her tote bag for her appointments for the day.

Holly came to stand in the doorway, her arms folded belligerently over her chest. Her hair...*not her own*...a tangled fall of locks around her shoulders, but she still managed to look particularly pretty and very young. And all Eden could think in that moment was that it wasn't fair. Holly was not mean. She wasn't spiteful. Her misdeeds, in Eden's mind, were not harmful, only thoughtless and exasperating. It had always been easy to forgive her. Eden wasn't feeling it right then.

"I'm sorry, okay? I promise I'll clean it up."

"I don't care. Do whatever you want. You will anyway. I have a lot of work to get through today."

"We'll talk when you get home later."

"I don't want to talk, Holly. I'm done. I'm serious. Nothing gets through to you," Eden said, sending her sister a cold look that succeeded in getting her attention as Holly stood looking nervous and quickly hid it behind indignation…as if she were the injured party.

"You're really overreacting. I said I'll take care of everything, and I will."

"Fine," Eden said, disrobing from what she'd worn home from Beck's and quickly pulling on black slim-legged slacks and a taupe sweater with dolman sleeves and a wide boatneck. She used her fingers to frantically grab and pull at tufts of her hair, magically fashioning it around her face into her own style. She got down on her knees to search for and pull out a pair of black low-heeled booties from the closet, then stood up and shoved her feet in. Already she was reaching for her tote and pushing past Holly to leave her room.

"You went shopping?" Holly asked irreverently. "What did you buy? Anything for me?" she dared to tease.

Eden stopped to stare at her in disbelief for a second.

If looks could kill…

Holly shrugged. "I'm only trying to lighten things up." She yawned. "I have to go into the union office today. What time will you be home?"

"I don't know. Maybe I won't come home. It smells like warm beer in here."

"Well…maybe I won't come home, either. It's obvious you're so mad you don't even want me here."

"I never said that."

"I'm going to take a shower," Holly said, flouncing away.

"I'm going. I have a long day."

"Fine. See you later."

"Fine," Eden responded, mostly to herself as she headed to the front of the apartment, juggling a jacket, her tote, and a purse. She heard the bathroom door slam.

All day, Eden lived in a state of anxiety, her stomach tied in knots as she anticipated a continuation at home that evening of what had happened between her and Holly earlier. She managed to meet with her two clients at Center City to ask intelligent questions and gather the information she needed to write up briefs for their cases. She called her classmates instead of suggesting their monthly get together to catch up. And she wasn't in the mood to deal with Zach in any case.

She wanted desperately to call Beck and cry on his shoulder but if she was feeling a little overwhelmed by all she had to catch up with, now that the time they'd stolen from work and obligations had ended, she had to respect that he was experiencing something close to what she was going through. Eden was pretty sure that if she did call Beck, he might immediately want to drop everything he was doing to come and join in her worry about her sister. And that simply wasn't fair. Holly was her burden, her worry. Not his.

Eden still had a few hours to put in at her part-time job at the Library of Congress and wouldn't think of canceling, having already done that a few days ago to spend time with Beck. But the afternoon did begin to feel like a slog. She couldn't think of eating anything for lunch, afraid food would taste like nothing besides further upsetting her stomach, which was already churning with stress. Instead, Eden used what would have been a break in the day to go to Tiffany's and roam around the store, distracted, replaying the whole wretched conversation with her sister. She didn't even say hello to the doorman or the sales associates who she always saw as caregivers to the cherished...but not yet hers...earrings she so coveted. She wasn't ready to make that big purchase, yet. What was the point? Eden didn't feel she'd earned them.

"Hi," someone said at her shoulder.

Eden stopped her meandering to look at the young woman greeting her with a smile of familiarity.

"Oh. Hi."

The woman frowned. "Are you alright? You didn't say hello when you walked by a moment ago. Is something wrong?"

Eden managed a smile, shaking her head. "I'm fine. I have a lot on my mind today."

"Came by to visit your earrings to cheer up?"

Eden sighed. "No, I–I was just looking for a quiet place to hide out...and think."

"Well, it's very quiet today," the young associate said, looking around. "You practically have the whole store to yourself."

Eden glanced around. "You're right." She pulled her smartphone from her bag and checked the time. "I really should get going, though. I have someplace else to be..."

"If you hurry, you'll have just enough time to try on the Enchant Fleur again. You know you want to. Maybe it will help to clear your mind, cheer you up," she said brightly. "We've missed you. You don't seem to come in as often."

"I know. It's been crazy. A lot going on."

"Follow me," the woman said, walking away. "We'll send you on your way with a smile…with or without one of our little blue boxes."

Beck did not try to get in touch with Eden the entire day. And he didn't expect to hear from her. Since they'd first met, it was clear that her life, her day-to-day routine, was a tightly orchestrated round of meetings, school, pro bono clients and depositions, part-time work…and of everything else she was doing that wasn't work…and maintaining energy, poise, and patience. Certainly where her sister was concerned.

Beck had developed tremendous admiration for Eden and her discipline. He'd quickly come to see it wouldn't be fair to draw any comparisons to Alia because the two women were polar opposites in every way. In his mind, however, there was no question that Eden was a gold standard. But there was another concern for Beck, and that was his own insecurity questioning if he was even in her league. He'd never questioned himself before, his ability, his strengths, what he brought to the table. Or even in a purely male way, other women's attraction to him. But she was so far and away above the women in his life B.E. Before Eden.

In truth, Beck's day kept him busy as well, with no time to dwell on his romantic life or happiness. The day turned into a wild round of editorial meetings, unexpected drop-in visitors he couldn't ignore, and learning that he was chosen to attend an industry summit in San Francisco. There hadn't been one the year before as the country continued to exercise caution and distancing after the scourge of

COVID-19. He generally enjoyed the conferences as an excuse to get away from the office for two or three days, to meet colleagues he only got to see at the yearly meetings, and to engage in interesting conversation and the exchange of ideas. So Beck's preoccupation allowed him to think the day was a lot shorter than it actually was. It was only after getting home, having declined an invitation to hang with some of the office staff for drinks, that it hit him hard that he wasn't going to see or be with Eden for the evening.

He'd never realized before just how loud silence could be.

He was lazily reviewing and editing several spec articles by staffers, the TV on a foreign soccer game that he wasn't paying much attention to, when his lobby buzzer sounded. He sat still, alert, wondering if he'd actually heard it when it sounded again, this time a little persistently. Beck put the papers aside, used the remote to mute the TV, and swung his long legs from the coffee table top. Next to his apartment door, he pressed the intercom and asked who was there.

"It's Holly Marsh."

"Who?"

"Holly. Eden's sister."

He was taken aback but immediately pushed the button to unlock the lobby door. Then Beck, bewildered and curious…and concerned, stood and waited for his doorbell to ring. When it did, he pulled the door open, staring in disbelief at Holly in the hallway. He had not seen her since the first day he'd met Eden, but he had surmised a lot about her based on Eden's anecdotes and a few one-sided phone conversations.

Holly was a few inches taller than her sister, lighter in complexion. Very pretty, but in a different way than Eden's attractiveness.

Kind of girlish. Young. Eden's persona was more mature and grown-up. Holly smiled at him and it seemed a little flirtatious, but then Beck decided that she smiled that way at everyone. It was like an attempt to put everyone at ease, and it came across a bit shy and uncertain. For the life of him, he didn't know if it was an act or just Holly being Holly…whatever that actually was.

"Hi," she said, friendly enough.

Given that they'd only met once, Beck felt she was assuming more of a connection than he felt.

"Hi. What are you doing here? How did you know where I live?"

"Your business card. The one you gave my sister. It was written on the back. Can I come in?" she asked, this time sounding genuinely uncertain.

Beck hesitated. He was uncomfortable with Holly's sudden appearance. And then he noticed that she had her crew luggage with her. There were a ton of questions to be answered, not the least of which was where was Eden? Did she know her sister had arrived at his door? For what? Asylum? Was there a problem?

Slowly, Beck stepped back and let her in. Holly walked slowly into the hallway, glancing into the living room, and then turned to regard him. He honestly did not know what to make of her. One minute she presented a forthright open pleasantness, and the next…now…she seemed confused and even nervous.

"Okay. What's going on? Where's Eden?"

She shrugged. "I don't know. She said she had a long day. Was going to be busy. I have no idea when she'll be home. But…I had to leave."

"Leave? As in…"

"I couldn't stay. We had a fight this morning, and she's really pissed off at me. I thought I really don't need to be there when she gets home. She'll probably still be mad and…"

"But why come here? What is it you want?"

"Can I stay the night?" Holly blurted out, watching him wide-eyed.

Probably another ploy she used to get her way, Beck suspected. But there was no question, in his mind, that she was upset. But, *what about Eden*? He was much more concerned about Eden.

"I'm not sure that's a good idea. I take it Eden doesn't know you're here, or that you would even think of coming here. I don't understand, either. She didn't throw you out, did she?"

Holly shook her head. She sat down heavily in a nearby chair, looking a little lost. "She'd never do that. But…I did something… or rather I *didn't* do something before she got home this morning. I'd never seen her so angry at me. I can't go back tonight. I thought maybe things might change in the morning, and she'll get over what happened."

Beck sighed deeply. It was going to be a long evening. He sat on the arm of the sofa opposite Holly, crossed his arms, and regarded her. "Why don't you tell me about what happened when your sister got back home."

Beck listened, not letting it be known by gesture, expression, sound, or movement what he thought of Holly's tale of woe that, of course, made her the victim…with extenuating circumstances. But watching her as she talked, he could see how Eden was inclined to forgive and make allowances for her sister. She'd been placed in a role she'd long outgrown, and her patience, the way Beck read the story, was slim to none these days.

"I mean, she carried on as if the apartment was a wreck. Okay, so I didn't clean up after my friends left, but I was going to," she excused herself.

"How often does that happen? She gets on your case because of cleaning up…or whatever?"

Holly shrugged, gnawed on her lip, appeared…touchy. "Sometimes."

"Maybe Eden just got tired of having to tell you what to do. Maybe she thought that by now you didn't have to be told to uphold your end of the living arrangements."

"I don't know. I've just never seen her as mad as she was this morning. I wasn't sure what she would do."

"She wasn't going to kill you, okay? Look, I don't know you. But you're Eden's sister…her *baby* sister, and she's used to watching out for you, right?" Holly nodded. "Maybe you have to stop making it so hard for her. She's not your mother. You're not a teenager."

Holly narrowed her gaze. "She treats me like I am. I have a responsible career. I'm a grown-up."

"Seems to me that Eden might not be clear on that, based on the things you do…or don't do. Why make it so hard for her to see the difference?"

"I guess," she muttered.

Like a teenager.

"What was your game plan when you packed and left?"

"I have a girlfriend, April. I can always crash with her. Except tonight. She has a steady boyfriend and…"

"I get it. She's a flight attendant like you? So when she's home she spends time with him."

"Right. But she said I can come tomorrow. The two of us fly out again the day after. We don't work for the same airline, but we have very similar schedules in and out of DC. I thought, maybe you wouldn't mind if I stayed just one night…"

"I do mind," Beck said firmly, honestly. "I don't want to be used by you to deflect your sister's anger. Frankly, I think she has good reason to be annoyed with you. But you two have to work it out. I don't want to be in the middle." He got up to pace for a moment, Holly sitting and watching him…waiting for his decision. "You can stay *tonight*. That's it. But the deal is you have to call Eden and let her know where you are. I'm not going to do that for you. As it is, I'm not sure I'm doing the right thing."

"I don't know if that's such a…"

"Do it, otherwise I'm calling a hotel and booking a room for you."

She vigorously shook her head. "Not a hotel. I sleep in hotels all the time, all over Europe."

"Alright, so we'll do it my way. Or you'll have to come up with another plan." Beck regarded her with a thoughtful frown. "Did you have dinner?"

"No."

"Let's go get something to eat. I have to kick you out in the morning to get to work. I can drop you off somewhere."

"I can hang out at the airline's DC headquarters and kill time until I can meet up with April."

"Fine. Let me get my wallet." He pointed at her. "Call your sister."

Holly slowly pulled her cell phone from her pocket, went through the motions of unlocking it, expertly using her thumb. Satisfied, Beck turned away and headed to his room.

Holly looked at the phone, considered it for a long moment. And then returned it unused to her pocket.

CHAPTER 14

Eden only began to gain some perspective on her anger with Holly when she got home that evening and Holly wasn't there. Not only that, but all of her crew luggage was gone. Had she taken an earlier assignment? Had she returned to what's-his-name, her Irish prince? Eden felt such a profound sense of guilt and regret that she was almost nauseous.

Where was her sister?

Eden began an agitated mental assessment of the situation and hoped that wherever Holly was, she was safe. For the first time the entire day Eden tried calling her. It went right to voicemail. Holly had her phone turned off. Was that deliberate? But Eden had not received a call from her, either.

A little concerned, Eden paced the living room, her mind a blender of mixed-up possibilities as she persuaded herself that nothing was wrong. Holly was probably just as annoyed or upset by their encounter. It would all blow over because it always did. Finally, late, there was a text message, and Eden's hands shook as she opened the text and quickly read it through. It was from her sister.

I left early. Don't worry about me. We need a break.

Eden dropped to the edge of the sofa and experienced a rush

of heat through her body. *We need a break.* What did that mean? How long a break? She quickly forced herself back into control mode, letting reason sink in. Holly was an adult. She was a reliable employee in a major industry with an excellent reputation. She had friends. She traveled all over the world… She knew a smattering of other languages! Her sister was not helpless, and she would *not* do anything stupid or put herself in danger.

But, where was she?

Eden knew several of her sister's local friends, but she didn't have phone numbers or email for any of them. She sat for a very long time trying to figure out what to do and finally decided there wasn't anything to do. She had to let it be. Infuriatingly, Holly was in control. The next move or message had to be from her. But Eden had a miserable night, sleeping fitfully and willing Holly to call or text again.

By the next morning Eden was calm and composed by virtue of being utterly exhausted. She had to be on point and ready for her morning appearance. Her marijuana case was returning to court. She'd lost the petition to have the case dismissed. She'd argued that the charges were punitive but the arbitrator, of course, saw it differently. There was the matter of a very clear and precise law that had been broken. Eden sighed heavily, knowing it was all on her to ask for leniency for the client, under the guise of medical emergency in which the use of the controlled, illegal substance was a proven treatment for the recorded problem. Given her emotional state, her worry, Eden was also afraid she might blow it.

By noon it was over, her client reprimanded and given a token fine that he couldn't afford to pay. Eden covered it for him, making up a fictitious fund from which the money had come.

Zach reached out to her as she was on her way to the Georgetown

Law campus, and she quickly and maybe too abruptly told him she didn't have time to chat or help with any assignment issues or whatever. Eden continued to LC, grateful for her position that pretty much left her all to herself in a department that was never heavily used. And it was there that Beck reached her in the early afternoon.

"Hey. How are things?"

"Okay."

"Caught you at a bad time?"

"I'm at work." She knew she was being short with Beck. She knew it was so unlike her to be that way with anyone.

There was a pause.

"Are you okay?" he asked, a hint of worry in the question. "You sound..."

"It's been...a tough morning."

"That has Holly written all over it."

Eden was alert, surprised. "Why did you say that?"

"Have you two finally talked?"

"Talk?"

"About what happened when you got home from my place."

"How do you know about that?"

"Holly told me. I said I shouldn't be involved and told her she had to call you and let you know where she was."

Eden was pummeled with a conflicting and confusing range of emotions. Some of it was more anger, as she began to sense an involvement from Beck that bothered her.

"How do you know where she was?" She heard him let out a deep sigh.

"She didn't call you."

"What happened? What did Holly say to you? *When!*"

Beck's tone also changed, picking up on an uncharacteristic edginess to Eden's questioning of him. Almost accusatory. A little... hysterical.

"Where are you?"

"What does it matter?"

"Eden..." Beck said, bringing a cautionary tone into his voice. "*Where are you?*"

His tone was clear and brooked no pushback from her.

"At work. I'm at LC."

"When can I see you?"

"I don't know. I mean...I finish in about an hour."

"Can I come over? Pick you up? We'll find a place where we can talk."

"Can't you just tell me now? What is there to talk about?"

"Apparently, a lot. This can't be done over the phone. The situation sounds a lot more complicated than I thought it would be. Have you talked with Holly?"

"No." She couldn't help it, but her voice was flat and cold. Eden was angry. And she was scared.

"I'm coming over. Wait for me." And he hung up.

Oddly enough, Eden felt a little relief relax her shoulders. If nothing else, she was now aware that Beck knew more about what had happened between her and Holly than he should have. All Eden wanted were answers. She could try to figure out later why it mattered that Beck had somehow gotten in the middle.

When she left the library, it was still light out, one of the wonderful benefits of the spring. On any other day, she would suck in fresh air and maybe head over to the Mall for a shortened version of her walk, one that would allow her to walk home afterward to make up for the distance she wasn't going to complete on her route. Instead, she stood on the top step of the main entrance, looking down and searching for Beck's arrival. Still, she never saw him approaching from a different direction.

"Have you been standing here long?"

She started. Inexplicably, she was annoyed he'd caught her off guard. Even as Eden looked into Beck's eyes and saw only great confusion, questions, and concern. And then he quickly stepped forward to put his arms around her, the embrace careful and gentle, but brief. When he stepped back, his brows were furrowed, his mouth compressed with tension. Eden recognized that Beck had absorbed that from her.

She lowered her gaze, disturbed by her own inability to greet him more warmly. Actually, what she really wanted to do was to bury herself against his chest and let Beck comfort her because she knew he would. She needed that. But all of that fought with Eden's emotional thinking at the moment.

"A few minutes."

Beck was studying her. He took her hand. "Where do you want to go?"

She blinked and looked around. "I don't know."

"Let's walk," Beck said.

He took two steps down, forcing Eden to stay with him because he held her hand. They reached street level and randomly followed a pathway in front of the building with benches placed along it, empty at that time of the day. As if suddenly exhausted and not wanting to go any further she sat, and Beck sat next to her. Close enough to talk but giving her space. He released her hand. Eden glanced briefly at him.

"Do you know where Holly is?" she asked. She offered Beck no greeting.

"Did she call you last night? I told her to."

Eden shifted positions so that she can face Beck from a slight angle. He did the same. "What happened last night?"

"Holly showed up at my place…"

"She *what*?"

"…With her luggage."

"Why in the world would she come to you?"

Beck frowned, searching her expression. "She told me all about the dustup you two had over…I don't know…some mess she made while you were away. Seems like she felt it got ugly."

"It didn't get ugly," Eden countered. "I got angry. I got fed up. I threw a major hissy fit. That doesn't explain why…"

"Eden. Look. Calm down. Maybe your sister thought…I'd be sympathetic to her. Like, it wasn't all her fault, what happened. Maybe she thought…because you and I are seeing each other, I could, maybe, talk you down."

Eden fumed, feeling righteous all over again. "You shouldn't have gotten involved. And…*I don't need to calm down!* This is serious!"

"You just admitted you blew up. I didn't want to have anything to do with whatever went on with you and your sister. I tried not to. I told Holly I have to stay out of it. But I knew what happened between you and her was not the first time. It seemed to me that it's a scenario that's been played out since…since you were teenagers and your mother died. And…"

Eden was shaking her head. "That's not it. Holly is just…"

"She's playing a role. The same way, I think, you are."

"What does that mean?"

Beck sighed. He shifted his position a few inches closer to her. "You told me yourself that when your mother died, you stepped in to be head of family. Maybe at the time it looked like it was just you and Holly against the world. You were pretty young to have to take over being a substitute mother. I believe Holly got used to depending on you to take care of her and overlook her…her poor decisions. And you did."

Eden glared at him. "You did the same thing. She talked you into feeling sorry for her."

Now Beck's gaze narrowed. "I didn't. Listen to me. I found myself trying to figure out how to deal with her. I think Holly was thrown off by your anger at her. I think she knew she somehow went too far with whatever it was she'd done. But to her, your reactions scorched the earth. When she came to my place, I figured she was looking for a safe harbor. I might be a way back…a conduit…to you getting over whatever had happened. I thought for a nanosecond maybe I should call you. But that would have put me in the middle as well. I thought it was *her* responsibility to reach out to you."

"I was suspicious of her motives. But I do get a sense that she's used to getting her way, that you're used to letting her charm forgiveness out of you. I offered to put her up at a hotel. In the end I let her stay, under the condition that she call you and let you know where she was."

Eden stared at Beck, and he met her scrutiny without hesitation. She believed him. She knew her sister was totally capable of the kind of setup he described. Holly was definitely a drama queen…without the malicious intent, but without taking any consequence seriously.

"I got a text from her really late this morning," Eden said quietly, exhausted by the entire episode. "She's at her friend's home. April. But I was crazed."

Beck had his forearm along the back of the bench and suddenly reached with just his fingers to briefly stroke her arm. "I know."

"I was angry when I thought…"

"I couldn't very well kick her out. She's your sister, and I thought I made the best decision I could."

"But don't you see? She played you just as she's always played me."

"If you know that, Eden, why haven't you done anything about it? Don't use the excuse she's your little sister. That's old. Holly is not a teenager. She's not helpless. She doesn't need you to manage her life. If you just let her go, she will find her way. Let her fail. Let her figure it out. You did. She'll be fine."

Eden blinked at Beck, knowing in her heart that he was right. It wasn't as if she hadn't given some thought to what to do about Holly. But old habits can be difficult to change or discard. It was interesting to have someone else so clearly understand and state the situation. She was still resentful, even if she had fallen in love with Beck. It was hard to accept the truths she knew about her sister… or even herself. At the moment Beck was the adult in the room, trying to offer insight. But he'd also, in the end, willingly spent the night with Holly, and Eden had known nothing about it. There was something about the resulting scenario that still made Eden's stomach churn. Was her sister really capable of that kind of duplicity?

Was Beck?

"I'd hoped to hear from you sooner. About what you knew concerning Holly, but…"

Eden could see his gaze getting slowly stormy.

"I recall that you had a killer schedule coming up yesterday. I think I mentioned that I'd postponed a lot of work as well…so that we could have more time together. Are you saying you're angry with me for *not* somehow knowing that you were upset about the fight with your sister?"

"No. For not realizing how spending the night with Holly would appear. To me."

Beck stared hard at her, and the sudden silence was deafening to Eden. Except for the rushing of blood in her head so forceful she could feel the pulsing of sheer anxiety.

"Right now I choose to believe you're not implying what I think I heard. Okay? Do you really think Holly is capable of doing something so…so…incredible like that to you? Are you saying that I might be capable of seriously being that kind of jerk?"

Beck had raised his voice. His brows were furrowed together, his teeth clenched. He closed his eyes, sighed deeply from his chest, as if struggling for control.

Eden swallowed hard. Had she let her insecurity take everything too far? Had she just pushed Beck over the edge with her stubborn and still hurtful unwillingness to see that truth? That Holly's really insignificant behavior had been the endgame for her, for years of trying to keep her sister in line. To *always* be the one with common sense and *always* see Holly as the thoughtless child. When was it supposed to end? Maybe Beck was right, and the choice was hers.

What Eden also saw now was another opportunity. Her heart lurched as she knew she was about to do something, say something, that would risk everything. But she and Beck were already standing on the edge of a precipice.

"So will you?" she asked him, in a quiet whisper.

He appeared completely confused. "So will I…what?"

Her mouth was dry. She tried to swallow. Suddenly Eden knew that what was happening between her and Holly would work itself out, one way or another. They were *always* going to be sisters. Tight. But everything with Beck was a work in progress. "I wasn't sure I should say anything, when you take time to look at the hurt and wound in your heart about what happened to Mason. Maybe we're in the same place."

He pulled back, and there was no mistaking the caution and suspicion that overcame Beck's countenance. "I don't think we are, Eden. My brother's death is not a fair example."

"You're right that my problem is I feel I have to have Holly's back no matter what. But I think…I feel that…what you've been going through is believing you didn't do enough to save your brother. I've been thinking it about it a lot, Beck. My heart aches for what you went through. Not only you, but Everett and…and your mother."

In just moments their situations had reversed, and Eden could see the shock darken the beautiful gray of Beck's eyes. And then darken them even more with an onset of anger and resentment, just like her own. She had overreacted with Holly. But right now she was about to enter family affairs that were not her own, long-standing unresolved issues from when Beck was a child. And he didn't know what she knew, what Nora had shared and trusted her with.

"I don't think it's a good idea to mix up the clear and present issues between you and Holly, and what you *think* you understand about me…or the death of my brother. How would you know anything about what happened, other than me telling you Mason drowned when I was twelve?"

Eden stared at him, a little intimidated by the cold and hard, cavernous resonance of his voice. He was right, but her heart began to beat faster with the awareness that she was also, in a way, invading sacred ground. If she couldn't get Beck to listen to her as she had listened to him, it might put irrevocable distance between them.

Be careful, Eden thought to herself.

"I don't have the whole picture. But…it feels unfinished in a way. I heard a lot of pain when you told me the story. Is that so much different than you weighing in on me and Holly and knowing how much I love her, but that I've been hurt by her?"

Beck pulled back even further from her, but Eden wasn't sure he was aware of the action. He was alert. He was trying to read her mind, second-guess her. No different than her reactions moments ago.

"There's a great deal of difference. I'm not prepared to go into it."

"Okay. I understand. I just hope you find a way to make things better. I'm a little afraid that Mason's death has been eating at you for…years." He was still regarding her with thoughtful consideration. "I know what I need to do about my sister. The money Everett left me is going to be a big help."

"To do what?"

She shook her head. "I'm not going to say, yet." Eden searched his countenance, seeing his furrowed brow that gave away quite a lot about his emotions at that terrible time when his brother drowned. She followed the tensing of his jaw. "Do you think you're still grieving?"

He chortled. "It's more than that."

"What?" Eden asked quietly. For the first time since they'd met up, she reached out to Beck, tugging gently on the opening of his jacket.

He stood up, pulling free from her hold. He buried his hands in his pockets and began to pace away from her. Eden stood. Beck stopped and turned to face her again, staring and retracing his steps until he stood looking into her steady gaze.

"There's still a lot about me, my past, you don't know or understand," Beck said. "But that's getting off topic and beside the point right now."

Eden nodded, but the censuring in Beck's tone worked completely against what she was trying to do…for both of them. He was absolutely right. And he'd withdrawn any warmth or concern he'd had when he arrived to meet her.

"Then I think we both need to stop talking about this…"

"What *this*, Eden?" Beck interrupted, suddenly angry.

Eden was caught off guard by his reaction…and now she was equally angry.

Beck looked like he would have added more, but he reconsidered and didn't. "I'm sorry you think I interfered where I shouldn't have. You're right. But what happens between you and your sister is as much your fault as it is hers. She's high maintenance."

"Holly is not a terrible person—" Eden said defensively.

"I never said that—" Beck responded defensively.

"We need to have a serious talk about the relationship between us," Eden blurted out.

Beck stopped shifting and moving and stared at her. It was hard now for Eden to interpret what she saw on his face, in his cold gray eyes.

"Whose relationship? Yours with Holly? Or…ours?" His voice was flat.

Eden swallowed, her insides twisting as her focus kept moving, and she wasn't sure what she meant. And she shook her head, confused.

"I can only manage one crisis at a time," she said, agitated, her voice beginning to quaver with emotion.

"Only one needs to be a crisis, Eden. Which one is the most important to you?"

She let out a deep, wrenching sigh. She blinked back tears, swallowed. She wasn't going to let crying replace her reason…her decision. The only one she could possibly make under the circumstances.

"She's my sister," she said more forcibly than was necessary. Was she trying to convince Beck or herself? "I get angry with Holly. But, she's my sister, and I have to do what I can to…not to lose her."

Beck never moved, but continued to stare, and it crushed Eden that she saw something leave his eyes, the way he gazed at her. Her heart skipped a beat with anxiety, pain.

"Okay, then," Beck assured her. "I can say, with certainty, you won't lose her, ever."

But, he also looked defeated.

Eden approached him but stopped a few feet from Beck. He didn't take his hands out of his pocket. He wasn't going to touch her. Her heart sank.

Had she lost *him*?

Them?

Eden's stomach twisted in an agony of regret and responsibility.

"We should be consoling each other," she offered.

Beck shook his head with a wry curve to his mouth. He stepped away from her.

"Not a good idea right now…and it's not possible. Family comes first."

"Beck…I… Was I wrong in bringing up Mason?"

"The timing is bad."

"I'm sorry."

"Are you?"

"What about you? What about you…and…me?"

His jaw tensed, his eyes darker than charcoal, almost black and unfathomable. "I'm clear on where we stand."

Eden was stunned when Beck turned abruptly and walked away from her. She gasped, opened her mouth to shout after him, but stopped. She couldn't even move.

Was Beck saying goodbye?

Eden had the horrible, *horrible* gut-churning feeling she was never going to see him again. This she couldn't blame on Holly.

This was all on her.

CHAPTER 15

"Here, please."

Beck pointed to his empty cup to show the passing waitress that he would like a refill on his coffee. And every time he did, he was reminded that Eden didn't drink coffee. It was an irrelevant memory, but very specific to her, and it was always going to be a connection. It was a reminder of a slew of other characteristics that left Beck feeling her loss. Another refill of coffee would be his fourth, but his images and recall of Eden had been constant…and torturous. With or without drinking coffee. Beck couldn't believe how much their last encounter, the last time he'd seen her, had derailed him, left him bereft. He had called himself all kinds of a fool since for letting his ego get in the way of his heart.

He slouched back in his chair and pulled out the notice he'd received the day before about appearing for a deposition. It concerned one Raphael Martin who was about to go up before the parole board. Beck was being called, at Raphael's request, as a character witness. He had interviewed Raphael more than a year earlier and found a young man who'd made a poor decision and was in the wrong place at the wrong time. Raphael had never struck Beck as an innate criminal, but just as a young guy who reasonably deserved a second chance.

Beck wondered if Eden might be able to advise him how to

respond. It was not lost on him that he was grabbing at straws, look-ing for anything that would give him a way back to Eden and end their stalemate. The truth was, he was still experiencing not only anger at what Eden had suggested at their last encounter, but also an awareness that she'd definitely set off a hot-button alarm in him.

The fresh cup of coffee was set next to his open laptop…where the screen was still on page two of a presentation he'd been working on since the day before for a conference. It was to have taken place in San Francisco, but had been rescheduled as a virtual webinar. Good. He wasn't up to traveling. And he didn't want to be so far away from DC, as if something critical might happen in his absence that he could not respond to. Eden might call, suggest they get together. Or…he could do the same.

Beck should have been able to knock out a bullet-point agenda in an hour, with revisions. Instead he'd been distracted by the recent glitch in his love life. It was one of the things he'd taken away from that tense and emotional meeting between him and Eden. He'd never anticipated how it would end that afternoon. Not in anger or screaming and yelling…à la Alia…but walking away in profound silence. It was tearing him up inside because the moment he made the decision and was the first to walk away was the moment Beck knew that he loved her.

What he was going through was infinitely worse than break-ing up with Alia had been, and he had to remember that. That was a cakewalk compared with the excruciating pain and confusion he'd experienced with Eden in front of the Library of Congress. He didn't blame her for her decision to champion her sister. But they'd parted with no clear understanding about what that decision meant to their relationship. Beck didn't blame Eden for that, either. What had actually gotten to him was the comparison Eden had drawn between her and her sister's situation, and the never-resolved, larger-than-life one between himself and his mother. Somehow Eden had tapped into the deepest-felt trauma of his life, and Beck was stunned to suddenly realize how much that had cost him.

He shifted in his chair, not exactly panicked that he couldn't concentrate on his work, but that his life had become intolerably messy. He really could use some sleep. Some peace and grounding. He could really use the comfort of Eden's positivity and her personal belief that everything would always work out.

How could she know that? How come he didn't?

When his cell vibrated, Beck felt relief at the interruption of emotionally flagellating himself. A quick glance at the LED screen showed it wasn't Eden calling. He answered with little enthusiasm.

"Hey! Dude. How you doing?"

"Max. Hey, buddy. Good to hear from you, man."

"Yeah. I'm sitting here waiting for a stage reset, caught sight of Alia chatting up the executive director...smart lady..."

Beck snorted but said nothing. He would have used a different term himself, but...

"...And I remembered we talked about getting together. So when are you free? My dime. I have an expense account," Max said.

"So do I. But I'm more than happy to let you pay. I'll probably have to arm-wrestle you for the check. You did me a huge favor by bringing Alia on board your latest project."

"Not a big deal. She's right for the team. She's got that whole It's-all-about-me thing going on. That's what we want for the show. Creates very strong competition among all the participants."

"Well, I'm glad you're happy with her."

"She's gorgeous, of course. I take it you two were not a match made in heaven."

"That's one way to put it."

"No matter. Looked to me like there's a much better fit with… Eden? Is that her name?"

Beck's insides roiled, and he shifted in his chair. "Yeah. Eden."

"Know how I know? She never once tried to grab attention or become instantly familiar with me or Alia. Like she'd known either of us forever. But I liked her with you. Very attractive. Very alert. Sexy. If you don't mind me saying so."

"I didn't know you were paying that much attention."

"It was a quick assessment. I could be wrong."

Beck sighed, closed his eyes, and rubbed his fingertips across his forehead. "You're not. Eden is definitely special. So, look, I want to get together with you but right now I'm hip deep in preparing for a conference presentation. There are sales meetings coming up at the magazine, and we're down a couple of writers, so everyone is sort of doing double duty…"

"Yeah, yeah I hear you. Okay, give me a call when you surface. Oh, wait! There is something else I wanted to run by you. Does your mother still perform?"

Beck frowned at the sudden swing in the conversation. "What?"

"Your mom. She's a singer, right? Jazz."

"That's right. What about it?"

"I have contacts that are organizing a mini jazz festival in Memphis this summer. It's being plugged as a female jazz-singer event. Female anything, like Black Lives Matter, is suddenly a hot deal. Everybody wants to show how woke they are," Max chuckled. "The organizers already have the venue, sponsors, money to bring in performers and take care of them properly. Do you think your mother would be interested in being part of that?"

Beck sat up straight. His brow cleared as if he'd just solved a difficult math equation. Or figured out the cure for some common malady. In his case it was a small but significant one.

"Man. That would be great. She's still performing. I go to sit in the audience a lot. She's gotten more confident over the years," Beck remarked. "She's got a following and loyal fans."

"Great. So this is what you do. Get me some tapes. Or MP3 recordings of her work. I'll make sure they get into the right hands."

"You mean you'll push her to the front of the line?"

"Hell yeah! No point in having juice if you don't use it. I can't promise she'll be chosen, but I'm going to do my best to talk her up. You know, even if you and I only roomed at Duke for a year, I think of your friendship as one of the best things that came out of school that year. And when I really came out…wow. You were the first guy who had my back, willing to take on anyone who dissed me. I can never repay that."

"You don't have to, Max. You've thanked me often enough in other ways, man. Like right now. What you're willing to do for my mother…"

"Just send me the music and some current promo stuff on her. Let me know if she has an agent or is under contract. That will speak for her."

"This is great, Max. Thanks."

"Glad I can do it. Don't worry about lunch. I'll run you to ground some other time."

"Bet," Beck responded.

When he got off the phone, Beck did a number of things. He

was able to miraculously shake some of the fog from his brain and complete his presentation agenda in the next hour. He polished it and then emailed it to the presentation coordinator. The second thing he did was pull up the interview he'd done with Raphael Martin and review the details of the case and his impressions of Raphael. If he were to appear as a character witness, he wanted to make sure he knew what he was talking about.

That decision led to a third thing that came to Beck as he closed his computer and finished his coffee…besides trying to figure out how to reconnect to Eden. He called his mother.

He could hear in Nora's voice that she was surprised. Their routine get-togethers had recently been built around errands and chores that Nora needed help with around her house. It made Beck feel like he'd been neglectful that she was so speechless to hear from him now, out of the blue as it were. Even if his mother didn't realize it, Beck knew that his call was long overdue.

He asked her out to lunch.

———————

Eden was sitting at the round dining table reading through several papers, forms, and documents when her phone rang. She was a little distracted when she picked up the device, a play of her pushing down anxiety with fierce determination, wondering if it might be Beck.

"Hello," Eden answered.

"Hi. It's me. Beck."

She let her eyes drift close. She exhaled.

"Oh… Hi." She couldn't deny her relief, and Eden knew that must have come through in her voice.

"How are you?"

Her anxiety began to creep up again. He sounded so formal.

"I'm okay. And…and you?"

"Terrible."

There was an awkward silence, and she strained to listen, to hear any change from him. She had her phone pressed tightly to her ear.

"Oh," she said inanely. "I'm sorry to hear that."

"Have you and Holly worked things out?"

"Not really. I mean…not yet. She returned home late yesterday. I haven't even seen her. I think she's hiding from me in her room," she said.

"I know how anxious you were to reach out to her."

Eden sighed. This was not the kind of conversation she'd hoped for with Beck, when and if he called. It wasn't encouraging.

"I am but…it will be okay. Holly never holds a grudge. I'm the one who bites my nails and agonizes that…you know…I've hurt her feelings."

She could hear Beck sigh.

"I bet you Holly is also feeling a little bummed out. I'm betting you'll both get over this recent face-off."

"I hope so. How are you doing? Really." she asked.

"I don't… There's a lot going on right now."

Eden went on alert. "It's nothing terrible, is it?"

"No, no," he hastened to assure her. "I should have called you, and—"

"You're angry with me. I shouldn't have—"

"I was angry, Eden. You reminded me of some things I need to take care of. It came out of the blue and…smacked me upside the head."

Eden made a soft, quiet sound of sympathy.

"I had a lot to think about after we last saw each other. A lot of unfinished business. It's not much of an excuse, but I got sidetracked—"

"I can understand that."

"—Thanks to you."

"Oh."

"It's all good," Beck hastened to add. "I promise."

"Then, I believe you."

"Before I forget, I do have another reason for calling. I got this notice from a law firm about an inmate I interviewed a while ago who's up for parole. I've been called as a character witness."

"Really?"

"I have to appear for some sort of hearing."

"A hearing," Eden repeated thoughtfully. "It doesn't sound like it's anything serious."

"What should I do?"

"You should go. Unless you don't believe the inmate has a righteous case."

"I think he's a very good candidate for parole."

She sighed. "Well, I could be there with you, if you want me to. I'm not all that familiar with criminal justice procedures, but Zach Milton, one of my classmates, would be. That's what he took on for his clinic this last year."

"Eden, I didn't call you because I need you or anyone else to speak for me."

"Okay."

"It's great that you're willing to, but…to be honest, I was taking the easy way out. I used the notice as an excuse to call you. I wasn't sure if you were still annoyed about me getting in between you and Holly."

"I was at first, but when I took the time to calm down and think about what you did, I should have thanked you."

"I'm glad to hear that."

"Beck, I'm really… I'm so glad you called," Eden said earnestly.

"I'm glad you're glad. I was worried that maybe…"

She was sure she could detect relief and humor in his voice. Eden heard the key in the apartment door, and it slowly began to open. She watched as her sister's head appeared through the space.

"Listen, Holly just walked in. Can we…"

"Sure. Good luck, but I don't think you'll need it."

"I'll come to the hearing anyway and act as an impartial counsel, or something."

Beck chuckled. "I'll take all the help I can get. Bye."

Eden turned her attention to her sister as Holly stepped into the apartment and closed the door. Holly's expression was one of caution and uncertainty. They made eye contact.

"Good morning," Eden said pleasantly.

"You're up," Holly murmured. She kicked off her sneakers, carefully holding a small Starbucks bag so as not to jiggle the contents.

She came right to the table, and Eden shifted her scattered papers to make room as Holly sat opposite her. There was no familiar chatter or sisterly banter, and Eden couldn't fill the awkward silence with meaningless small talk and pretend that everything was back to normal. It wasn't.

"I'm glad to see you," Eden began in a quiet voice. Holly looked quickly at her, her gaze filled with suspicion. "You disappeared so quickly into your room when you got home yesterday that I thought maybe you weren't feeling well or…maybe…didn't want to talk to me."

Holly opened the bag and began to pull out containers of hot drinks, and wrapped pastries, setting everything in the middle of the table.

"I didn't think you wanted to talk to *me*," she said. "We didn't exactly part ways feeling warm and fuzzy. To be honest, I really wondered if you'd ever talk to me again."

Eden was shaking her head. "That wasn't going to happen."

"I didn't know that." Holly looked around the apartment. "See? I hope you noticed I didn't leave any of my stuff all over the place this time."

Eden smiled kindly. "Thank you. Was this a test run, or do you think you could make it a habit?"

Holly sighed, pulling off the lid of her cup as the scent of steaming hot coffee wafted up. She pushed the other cup toward her sister. When Eden opened her cup, it was to smell the strong peppermint from herbal tea.

"I was acting like a little kid, maybe expecting you to pick up everything, like you used to do, and dump it on my bed."

"I'm not doing that anymore," Eden said, watching her sister for a reaction. Holly averted her gaze.

"I understand." She distributed the pastries, slices of nut bread and mini vanilla scones. "Funny. When I stay with April, or I'm overseas at a hotel…or even the week I spent with Connor, I never leave my things all around. It…it's like…"

"—You don't want people to think you're a slob," Eden said smoothly.

Holly chuckled and nodded. "Right. I want everyone to think I was raised well, and I'm a grown woman."

Eden stared at Holly. She was only mildly surprised that her sister offered any self-appraisal of her behavior… She'd heard similar attempts in the past. But hearing Holly add Connor to the mix, and what he might think of her, spelled a big shift. Maybe Holly always knew she could get over on her, Eden considered, but a boyfriend-lover-potentially-more-than-that was a different thing.

"Okay, then. What happened?"

Holly sipped thoughtfully from her coffee, broke off a corner of one of the slices of nut bread, and popped it into her mouth. She looked Eden. "Everyone else in my life has been temporary. You're the only person who's known me my entire life. Every single day. Even Dad doesn't know me the way you do. You're the only one who's loved me…and taken care of me, no matter what."

Eden blinked, realizing her sister was on the verge of tears. It was usually the other way around. "I'm sorry I got so mad at you."

"I'm sorry I made you so mad."

Eden shrugged, breaking off another piece of the bread. "As long as you're okay. We're different people and we're not always on the same page. And it's hard living with another person, even family."

"That's true. But I'll try to do better."

Eden arched a brow and gave her sister a crooked grin. "I'm not holding my breath."

Holly laughed. "Yeah. Don't do that." She played with her hair, cast another covet glance at Eden. "Did…did Beck tell you about me showing up at his place?"

"Not voluntarily. He thought you'd called me to tell me where you were like he asked you to. I told him you never did."

"Eden, I…"

"So, Beck had to tell me everything. Unfortunately, at the time I was still so angry with you that I blamed him for helping you, like he was taking your side against me."

"He wasn't. He really let me have it, telling me that I act like a kid. And that you shouldn't have to continue to be my second mother. Beck told me in no uncertain terms I need to grow up."

"Really?" Eden asked, unable to keep the need for reassurance from her tone.

"Absolutely. I was the one who dragged him into the middle. I *did* want him to take my side…poor little me…but he wasn't having it."

Eden was thoughtful, relieved that the exchange between Beck and Holly had gone exactly as he'd try to explain. "We argued over it. I didn't know where you'd disappeared to and I was scared. I was sorry I'd lost my temper. And I didn't want you to hate me…"

"I wasn't ever going to hate you."

"And Beck ended up on the receiving end of my…my anger and fear."

"Well, I hope you got over it. He was amazing. He told me you would never split the blankets so we'd go our separate ways.."

Eden couldn't respond. She felt that too familiar swelling in her throat and had to concentrate on not letting her emotions get the best of her. She hadn't shed any tears since she'd last seen Beck or her sister. And now that she and Holly could talk everything out, that only left the void that might still exist between her and Beck. Eden wondered if he even cared anymore. He didn't know how she felt about him. They'd had no time to talk about their feelings for each other. That thought had left a huge lump in the center of Eden's chest.

"I haven't seen Beck. I got so busy finishing up some cases, and with commencement…"

"Excuses, excuses, excuses," Holly said unsympathetically. "Figure it out. That's what you'd tell me, right?"

"Right."

"I like Beck. He's really awesome. He really likes you. Like… like I think Connor really likes me. He wants to meet you, you know."

The change in subject saved Eden. She swallowed, blinked, drank tea. "Does he?"

"Yeah…" Holly drawled in a dreamy voice. "He's such a…a grown-up. Like Beck. He thinks I'm the greatest thing since chocolate milk." Holly laughed. "I don't think he intended to make a joke, but…"

"Are you in love with him?"

Holly shrugged. "I don't want to jinx it. Feels like it. We tell each other we do but it's easy to say, isn't it, when we're 3,000 miles apart."

Eden listened, nodding. "If he starts coming to the States to visit you, it's going to get very crowded in the apartment."

"Yeah, I know," Holly agreed slowly. "And even less privacy for both of us."

"I think I have a solution. How about you and I go shopping before you leave again on your next duty tour. We could even start this afternoon."

"Shopping? Really? For what? And how is that going to solve the problem of privacy and Connor visiting?" Holly gasped and stared at her. "You're going to buy those earrings, aren't you? If you have so much money, why don't you? I haven't heard of a single thing you've bought yourself. That would not be my problem." Holly grinned.

Eden frowned and slowly shook her head. "No, I'm not buying the earrings, yet."

Holly sighed, exasperated. "Well, I don't know what you're waiting for."

"Remember when you got annoyed because I wouldn't buy you a car when you found out Everett left me money?"

Holly merely nodded, staring in a puzzled way at her.

"I have something else in mind that's more useful. How would you feel if I got you your own apartment?"

Holly's mouth dropped open and her eyes grew large. "Are you kidding me?"

"No."

"You would do that for me?"

"Yes."

"*Why?* Are you that anxious to be rid of me?"

Eden knew there was no hurt feeling in the question, but an underlying growing excitement. "I think it's time we live our own lives and have our own space, separate but always in touch. You need more room to do your own thing. So do I."

"You…you can afford to buy me an apartment?"

"Yes."

Holly put her cup down so hard the liquid sloshed over the side onto the table. She pushed back her chair to stand, the feet scrapping over the tiled floor. She yelped, rushed around to Eden's side, and threw herself into her sister's arms and onto her lap.

"*Oh, Eden!* I don't know what to say!"

Eden hugged her sister, experiencing a sense of relief, and satisfaction.

"That's a first." Eden grinned.

"How was it?" Beck asked Nora, watching his mother across the table where they'd just finished lunch and were spending additional leisurely time just talking.

"That was the most sumptuous lunch I've had since…since…"

"Dad would take us out for a birthday or other special occasion?"

Nora smiled in surprise at his comment, and Beck saw his mother's gaze soften with her own memories.

"Yes. That's right. Thanks for mentioning that."

Beck leaned back in his chair. He turned at an angle with his legs to the side of the table so he could cross them at the knee. It had been a good lunch. The conversation had been smooth, easy. There were unexpected moments of humor that came naturally. He was glad his mother was completely comfortable, although she had asked if taking her to lunch was a special occasion.

"I just thought it would be nice," he'd said carefully. "I had the time this week, and we don't get to see each other so much."

"That's true." Nora had chuckled quietly, a little awkward with the truth.

"I think we should do this more often."

Nora's eyes had widened again, bright crystal blue filled with a poignant longing that twisted at Beck's heart. It also served to demonstrate that he was probably on to something surprising and important when he considered the history between him and his mother that had grown up out of a tragic accident and had affected his life since he was twelve. He now reasoned that it must have affected her as well, in a much more profound way.

"Beck, I–I would really love that."

"Okay. Done. We will."

Nora was staring at him steadily. He didn't ask why. He knew his mother was assessing him anew, in much the same way as he had begun to do with her. Broadening his vision of his mother to include more than met the eye.

"You know, you seem so...so..."

"So *what?*"

She blinked and lowered her gaze, placed her used napkin beside her plate, fiddled with her unused dessert fork. Nora glanced at him again, and smiled a little. "You seem much happier than I've seen you in a long time."

Beck returned her smile but offered no explanation.

"Is it Eden? You haven't said a word about her all through lunch. But I saw how you reacted when she got sick after my show."

"How did I act?" Beck questioned, genuinely curious.

"*Very* protective. Very concerned."

"But you were the one who became all Mama Bear."

Nora laughed. "Oh, honey. I'm sorry I got in the way and just jumped in between you two. Eden has made a difference, hasn't she?"

Beck hadn't expected this turn in the conversation. He had something else in mind, far more to the point of both their lives. But that was okay. He looked at his mother and saw her interest... and a warmth, as if she could guess the truth about his feelings for Eden, in any case.

"She makes me laugh," he said simply, aimlessly rubbing his hand over the white damask tablecloth. "She's really smart, and she notices things. She's juggling, like, a dozen projects and work and school and has time left over to be...just...kind. She cares about people. Everyday ordinary people that most of us would never notice or would walk by on the street." Beck became thoughtful, bemused, as he shook his head at the ways Eden showed her true spirit. "I've never met anyone like her. I never even saw her coming."

"Sounds like she might be one in a million."

Beck arched a brow, and a corner of his mouth lifted in reflection. "A million to one. Sounds clichéd, doesn't it?"

Nora reached across the table and took his hand. "Honey, not at all. Sounds pretty genuine, and surprising to me. We don't often get to meet someone like her. I mean, I liked her immediately after, what? Ten seconds? I'm glad she happened to you."

Beck shook his head as he accepted the bill from their waiter and maneuvered to dig his wallet from his pocket. "You saw all of that in ten seconds?"

Nora shrugged. "When you know, you know."

They fell silent as they headed to Beck's car. He was thinking not only about his mother's comments and observations about Eden, but also his own. What he'd admitted to his mother had, in effect, summarized exactly what his relationship with Eden felt like. And when he put it all together, it spelled *l-o-v-e*. That was a confirmation of what he'd come to realize.

It was after Beck had taken his mother home, after their enjoyable, peaceful, and comfortable lunch, that he knew it was time to raise the other issue between them. His stomach began to knot. It wasn't fear that grabbed him. It was an expectation that maybe they'd finally end the impasse that had kept them at arm's length for so many years. They walked into the house, and with each step he felt the weight, the burden, of what he needed to do next. His mother turned to him, spread her arms wide, and approached to wrap them around Beck. He met the loving gesture, embracing Nora.

"Oh, Beck. What a lovely day! Thank you for thinking of doing it."

"I'm glad you enjoyed yourself. Me too." He kissed her cheek and very gently pulled away. Her smile was still in place, but her gaze became puzzled when he ended their hug. "Mom. I need to talk to you."

"Okay," she responded softly and hesitantly, anticipation clear in her eyes.

Beck let his jaw tense, his brows furrow. "Can we go up to Mason's room?"

Nora stared and was perfectly still for a moment. Then, Beck watched as a realization came to her. She closed her eyes and nodded. "Pete's mother would say this is a come-to-Jesus moment. Right?" She opened her eyes, and they were bright and glistening.

"I think so."

His mother nodded again and turned to head for the staircase. Halfway up, Nora suddenly stopped. She reached her hand behind her, and Beck readily took it and let her hold on and squeeze as hard as she could.

As if, she wasn't ever going to let him go.

Beck had never told his mother that when he was still a kid, in high school, sometimes at night after she'd gone to bed he'd go into Mason's room. The room had long ago been converted to use as a guest room. But Beck knew that a lot of what had been Mason's youth was packed in boxes stored inside his closet. When he and Nora reached the room, she stood in front of the door, in front of him, and waited, unable to move further.

Beck reached around her and opened the door, giving it a light push. Nora entered, and he was right behind her. As a matter of fact, Beck was less interested in the room than he was in his mother's immediate reaction to being there. She moved to the center of the room and slowly turned around. There were tears slowly running down her cheeks. Her chin quivered. His mother's mouth was tightly closed...and Beck knew that it was an effort not to let out the heart-deep anguish she might have been holding in since he was twelve. He reached out to hold her arm, not sure how steady she was, or if she could remain standing. His mother was feeling, maybe more profoundly then he had ever experienced, the horrible loss of that year.

"Mom..." Beck began.

A quiet whimper escaped her. The tears fell in earnest. Nora shook her head.

"I'm...so, so sorry... I..."

"Mom," he said again, this time coaxing her into his arms to hold her, lovingly, without anger. He felt her nearly collapse against his chest, her hands suddenly clutching at his shirt to prevent herself from falling, to prevent him from turning away and leaving her.

"I never meant to...to blame you, Beck. But I–I was crazed. I was hurt and angry and...my son was dead!"

"I have never been able to forget when you said it was my fault. It was Everett who explained that you were a mom who lost a child. In that moment, after Mason was gone, he said that's all you knew. But I thought...I thought you hated me for what happened."

Nora was frantically shaking her head against his chest. "*No!* No, no, no...that's not true. It was never true, Beck. But...I was... in so much pain. I didn't know what to do. I didn't know what I was saying. I told Everett, after we got back home, you'd never forgive me for what I accused you of. Everett said, 'He will. Give him time.'"

"I thought you loved Mason more than me."

If it was possible, she seemed to sob even harder. Beck maneuvered both of them a few steps to the edge of the twin bed and held Nora as he forced her to sit. He had to listen closely to hear what she was saying next.

"If anything had happened to you, it would have killed me. You are my firstborn, out of my love for your wonderful father. Mason was my son with Everett...and I lost them both. *None* of what happened was your fault."

Beck's relief was so great, he couldn't speak. He suddenly recalled Eden asking him how Everett must have felt, losing a son. At the time his stepfather was more concerned that Beck not blame himself. *It was an accident.* Exactly what Eden had said to him. And now, thinking about it, Everett had been the most stoic, had accepted the loss. But Beck knew that hadn't lessened the pain of losing his child, either. He rested his cheek and jaw against his mother's head, feeling the way her body heaved and quaked and trembled against him. In that moment he was reminded of his very first meeting with Eden that had led him to comfort her. And look where that ultimately had brought him. To now recognize the two most important women in his life. Beck let his mother cry. And cry. Years of regret and remorse, and love poured out that they could now share between them.

And forgive.

CHAPTER 16

"I really have to go," Eden said with as much charm and poise as she could muster.

She stood up from her seat next to her adviser and smiled at him kindly. He shook his head as he also stood, smiling in return. A handsome middle-aged man with salt-and-pepper hair and a firm but fair manner who was well liked by new students entering Georgetown Law and those about to graduate.

"I know you're off to some part-time job, or volunteering, or… You can't still be involved with a clinic, right?"

"No, I'm not. But…"

"You're late for another appointment," the professor said, walking her out of his office into the corridor.

Eden hitched the strap of her shoulder bag more comfortably as she also lifted the tote with her laptop and other sundry items. "I am."

"You certainly can't be accused of idleness. We're done, Eden. I wanted you to know firsthand that you were a great student, and I enjoyed counseling you. You're the caliber of hardworking, studious law student we always wish for."

"That's a nice compliment, Professor Adamson. I enjoyed the work, the challenge…"

"And you're glad it's almost over."

"Yes, sir." Eden chuckled, inching further away without appearing ready to sprint.

"Well, let me know if you need a recommendation. I'm more than happy to write you one."

"Thank you…" she said. She heard the *ding* of an arriving elevator cab and, with a vague wave to her faculty adviser, ran to catch it.

"I'll see you at commencement," Professor Adamson hastily called out before the elevator doors closed.

But Eden had already switched mental gears. She sighed in relief at her end-of-the-year evaluation being over and done with. When she reached the lobby, she called for a Lyft to take her to the Civil Clerk's Office. She groaned when she realized the time and inhaled deeply, hoping the hearing had not yet started as was generally the case with anything happening in the court system in DC. The Moultrie Courthouse was just a few blocks north of the Mall and Pennsylvania Avenue and, despite the late-afternoon time when she arrived, the entrance was busy with people coming and going, lawyers and clients, citizens with grievances unrepresented as they came to pursue justice.

Eden checked the time again and knew there was no point in rushing now. The hearing was bound to have started, and entering a hearing out of breath would not be good form, particularly for someone within reach of her JD. She took the elevator to the appropriate floor, only to find the corridor completely empty. There was no one standing around, waiting, chatting, excited with an outcome. Silent.

Eden began walking in one direction, checking the room numbers and the assigned cases posted outside the doors. She hadn't gotten very far when she heard voices gathering behind her, down the length of the corridor in the opposite direction. Eden turned and began walking to meet the dozen or so people leaving a room. She was only looking for one particular person…and Beck wasn't among them.

She casually stood aside to let everyone pass, no one paying attention to her, in any case. Whatever had happened must have ended on a good note. Everyone seemed to be in good spirits. Soon, they were all waiting in the elevator bank off the center hallway. Eden looked toward the emptying room as the door closed. She leaned back against the wall with nothing else to do now, but wait. The corridor went silent again. She considered her next move. Eden dug out her cell. She could send a text…

But, the door suddenly opened again. She drew in a quick breath of unavoidable shock as Beck exited. He seemed a little thoughtful and unhurried, and was also consulting his smartphone. She straightened from the wall and stood facing him, watching but doing nothing to gain his attention. He'd actually taken a few steps toward Eden when he looked up and saw her. He took a few more hesitant steps…and then stopped to stare at her with as many questions in his gray gaze as she held in hers.

"Am I… Is it over? Is it too late?" she asked. She hoped he could hear her, aware that her voice was barely above a whisper. It spoke of her anxiety, and insecurity, in the moment. It occurred to her that her questions had a double-entendre.

Beck slowly shook his head. "No. It's not. I gave my testimony." He took his time approaching her. "I'm pretty sure Raphael will get his release. There were a lot of people willing to speak on his behalf."

Eden was already moving toward him, focused on one thing.

The door to the courtroom opened again, and Zach stepped

out in a burst of energy…in the same way he'd first entered her life. Eden and Beck turned to regard him.

Spotting them, Zach grinned before giving his attention to Eden.

"You're all set. I'd say inmate 474392 will soon once again be Mr. Martin."

"Does that mean…?"

"It means I'm confident that the judge and parole board were impressed by what everyone had to say. And Raphael came across as sincere in expressing remorse for his part in a not very well thought-out crime." He turned to Beck, studying him before holding out his hand. "I was late. Never got a chance to introduce myself. Zach Milton. You're Beck Dennison. Eden told me about you. She wanted me to have your back in case they asked something you didn't understand."

"Thanks for the cover," Beck said.

Eden watched as Beck took the offered hand, and then relaxed with Zach's obvious openness and self-assurance.

"No problem. E called me when she knew she couldn't make it in time."

"Thank you," Eden said to Zach.

He smiled broadly at her. "Anything for you. I kind of enjoyed walking in. Pretty awesome."

"When you're prepared it feels good, doesn't it?"

"Sure does." Zach grinned with a tilt of his head.

Zach looked at Eden, back to Beck, and finally back to her.

"My work here is done," Zach intoned in a comical hero voice.

Eden laughed. Zach began walking away down the corridor.

"Zach, wait a minute."

She walked quickly to catch up with him. She was acutely aware of Beck standing where she'd left him. She knew he was carefully watching, appraising her approach to Zach, the smile she gave him, the smile Zach returned. She resisted the urge to look at Beck, knowing that her next move might be risky. But Eden was hoping she hadn't misjudged their initial, interrupted greeting. Their own intent.

"Thank you, Zach. You were really on it!"

"You don't have to thank me, E. I wanted to show I'm on my game. I wasn't going to disappoint you."

Eden swallowed, moved by his declaration, and all the implications behind it. She hugged him, wrapping her arms around his neck and reaching to kiss his cheek. With one arm Zach circled her waist, returning her hug. Then, Eden stood back.

Zach gave her one final smile. He gave his attention directly to Beck, raised an outstretched open hand in goodbye. He said nothing more and walked briskly to the elevator, disappearing around the corner.

It was a beautiful spring late afternoon. The kind of day that made Eden feel hopeful about anything and everything. And now that she and Beck had finally come together again, she knew she was going to push for what she really wanted. No better time than the present. They began walking, silently, down a street lined with freshly leaved trees. Eden tugged on Beck's hand, forcing both of them under the canopy of lush branches. They faced each other.

"I have to tell you—" she began, but he interrupted, their words crossing.

"I want to say something."

Eden blinked at him and held her breath again before speaking quickly. "This is important—"

"So is this," he interrupted again.

Eden realized he was bending toward her as if to whisper something low, as if to kiss her.

"Eden, I love—" Beck started.

"I love you," she rushed in.

"—you," he finished.

They'd both had the same urgency, the exact same words. Mutual sentiments. And with the words out, spoken to each other, Eden choked back a quick intake of air.

She briefly closed her eyes, feeling a faint dizziness as the full extent of her feelings for Beck suddenly rushed at her. She realized that she was experiencing what being in love really felt like. Overwhelming.

She felt Beck lay his hand against the side of her face, brush her lips with his thumb. She felt the pressure of his mouth on hers and a welling of joy. It was warm and tender and brief.

"What…should we do now?" Eden asked in a quiet voice.

Beck arched a brow, lifted a corner of his mouth in a rueful grin. Placed his hands on Eden's waist to rock her gently toward him. "What would you like to do?" he teased in a drawl.

Eden blinked at him. "Well…"

"Yeah. Me too."

Then his smartphone chimed. His expression was mildly annoyed by the unwelcome interruption, but Eden touched his chest.

"It's okay. Answer it."

Beck did, and his expression changed instantly with surprise and curiosity. "Mom. Hey! Everything okay?… You sound very excited about… What?… Really?"

Eden stared at him, enjoying the changes that came across Beck's face with the information he was receiving. His gaze focused on her briefly, letting his emotions show.

"Mom, that's fantastic..." Beck exclaimed, his attention now fully on the caller. "When?... For how long?... Wow... Mom... Mom, I want to hear all about it, but..." He chuckled. "No, not really a bad time, but...I'm with Eden..." He chuckled again. "'Hi Eden,'" Beck directed to her, pointing to his device.

Eden smiled and returned a silent wave.

"She's waving at you. Listen, I... You want me to come to the house? You want both of us to come?"

Eden nodded enthusiastically. Beck touched her face, stroked his thumb over her cheek. "Now? No, Mom. You don't get congratulated by cooking for us. We'll go out to dinner... Okay, see you soon... Love you, too... Bye."

Beck sighed, still grinning, as he ended the call.

"Your mother has some wonderful news she wants to share, and she wants to tell you in person, and she's wildly excited, and you have to go. I understand. I don't have to be there."

"She wants you to."

Eden grimaced. "That's really nice, but on second thought I don't think so."

Beck stared into her eyes. "You're not afraid you'll cry, are you?"

Eden was surprised that he made that reference, but she grinned and shook her head. "No."

"I'm not ready to leave you. I'm afraid you'll evaporate, or something."

Eden laughed at the ridiculous image that made. She shook her head, rubbed her hand against his short facial hair. "You go, Beck.

Nora sounds like she needs to be with you, whatever her news. I'll go home…and I'll wait for you."

His jaw tensed and he frowned, not convinced. "I just told you the most important three words of my life, and you're telling me it's okay to leave it at that."

"Just for now. A few hours. Don't forget I confessed the same three words." She quickly kissed him. He was about to respond, but Eden touched his mouth with her hand. "Tell your mother I'm just leaving court…true. And I want to be home and look forward to you coming, and you can't wait to come back…true. Right?"

"Right," Beck admitted.

"This is the right decision. I promise. And you won't regret it."

Beck hugged her, accepting her decision. "I believe you."

———

Beck lifted his mailbag and swung the shoulder strap across his chest. He adjusted the bag just behind his hip and turned to his mother. She was smiling at him in a way he was still getting used to. No longer tentative. No longer avoiding his own tentative gaze, questioning and unsure. Nora stretched out her arms to hug him, pulling him down to kiss his cheek, stroke his arm.

"I'm so glad you came out."

"That's great news about being included in the jazz festival in June."

"I couldn't believe it, Beck. And yes, I'm thrilled. I have no idea how the planners even got my name!"

He averted his gaze briefly and raised his brows when he looked at his mother. "However it came about, you're in."

"Yes, I'm in. You know, I'm a little nervous…"

"Don't be, Mom. You're a great singer. You have a regular gig, great notices and reviews, and fans. Who knows? Maybe you'll be offered a recording deal."

She scoffed. "I'm not going to hold my breath." The look Nora gave him had a touch of panic in her blue eyes. "You'll come to hear me?"

"Of course I will."

"And you'll bring Eden?"

"I'll ask. She's got commencement coming up, and I believe she starts a new job next month. I don't know what else is on her agenda. But I'm sure she'll want to be there."

"Sorry we didn't do dinner. I'll make it up to you. We got to talking, and…"

Nora gazed lovingly at him. "I'm so happy that we're doing that again, Beck."

"I agree. You have a rain check for dinner. Another time."

"And bring Eden."

Beck hesitated in opening the door and turned to regard Nora. "You really like her."

"I do."

"Mom, you only met Eden once."

His mother made a little moue of her lips and shrugged. "There's something about Eden. You said so yourself."

"I did," he agreed. "She's amazing."

"And?"

Beck thought for a moment, trying to gauge how much to reveal, how much to save for another time. But…what was he waiting for?

"I'm in love with her, Mom," Beck suddenly responded, his voice low and still, filled with his own surprise, and elation.

Nora frowned. "How come you don't sound thrilled to death?"

"I am, but…I guess I'm also a little scared."

"Oh. I think you just let Alia creep in."

"Maybe."

"Honey, I don't recall you ever telling me you loved Alia."

"Actually, I never did tell her. If I thought the relationship was solid and going somewhere, I probably would have."

Nora snorted. "If? Probably? That's putting the cart before the horse. The point is you never told her. Know what I think? You really weren't sure you wanted to." She opened the door and gently pushed him out. "Go tell Eden how you feel."

Beck hugged her and headed to his car. "I already have."

When her doorbell buzzed, it startled Eden. Not in surprise but in anticipation.

Beck stood on the other side, his eyes dark and sultry, the layering of his close-cut beard giving him the look of a handsome rogue. But he also suddenly appeared solid, and strong, and honorable—and the man of her dreams. Unexpectedly, Eden felt emotion and tears well up in her, blurring her vision, and making it difficult for her to even speak. She wanted to confess, again, that she loved him.

Beck's expression changed as he witnessed what she was going through, and Eden wondered if he understood…or was she being foolish? He stepped inside the door, closing it, removed his mailbag and set it aside.

"Do you need a hug?" he asked her. His tone was caring and soothing.

The same way Beck had been with her before they'd even

formally introduced themselves. That had set the stage, a standard. For Eden it was intuitive, confirming as they came together and arrived at where they stood now. Full circle.

"Yes," Eden expelled with a deep sigh.

She lifted her arms to him…and Beck walked into her welcoming invitation.

"It's been quite a day, hasn't it?" she whispered.

"I think it's going to have a great ending," Beck said, with a sigh of contentment.

"That's such great news about your mother," Eden said. She'd listened carefully, not interrupting as Beck explained the call and visit to his mother.

When he'd reached her place, they'd both been so distracted, so glad to be together again, that the conversation about Nora had not come up until they were seated for a takeout dinner at the dining table. Eden was still feeling somewhat giddy that the domesticity of being together finally felt so right and made her feel happy. She believed that any future of them together would eventually become part of a discussion. She'd waited a long time for a moment like this.

They cleared the table and refrigerated the leftover food.

They refilled wine glasses and went into the living room, taking post-dinner comfort together on the sofa. Eden curled into a corner with her legs drawn up, on an angle to face Beck. He slipped his arm around her waist and hauled her across the cushion until she was close enough for him to ease her back against his chest. Eden giggled girlishly at the maneuver and snuggled into the space between his chest and arm.

"I thought you said I was heavy as a cow," she reminded him, pouting playfully.

"Did I say that?" he asked, kissing her temple and rubbing his jaw there as well. "I lied."

Eden snuggled. "It's a good thing I'm willing to forgive you."

"It sure is," he said confidently.

"So, tell me. How did the organizers come to choose Nora for the festival next month?"

Eden let Beck tell her about the call from Max, sending in demo disks of Nora's singing and tapes of her live club shows.

"She doesn't know I had anything to do with it. And I didn't, really. It was her music, her voice, her presentation that got her selected. That's all I want her to know."

"Another thing," he said, his voice going lower with a new confession. "We had a long talk. A serious, emotional face-off about what happened when Mason died."

Eden drew in her breath, waiting. "Was it hard?" she asked.

"Not as hard as I thought it was going to be. It seems that my mother had been trying for a long time to figure out what to say to me. How to apologize. We both thought it was too late. She cried and said how sorry she was. I forgave her. We held each other, and…it felt so good to have it out in the open."

"Beck, that's so wonderful," Eden said quietly.

He tried to peer into her face. "You're not going to cry, are you?"

She jabbed him in his side with her elbow. "No, I'm not going to cry. I mean, I'm really moved by what you did for Nora. And it's so good that you were able to talk about what happened. I don't have to show it. I do have some self-control, you know."

She could feel his cheek draw into a smile. "You have amazing self-control where it matters."

"I learned from Everett. He was a kind man, but you didn't mess with him."

"Yes, ma'am. You have a love language that I'm hoping will rub off on me."

She was silent for a moment, trying to assign a meaning to his comment. She was thoughtful but didn't ask Beck to explain. He shifted, settling further into the sofa cushions.

"You haven't said what happened with you and Holly. I'm a little afraid to ask how that turned out. Was it a 911 between you two?"

"We didn't fight. I think we were both embarrassed about how we behaved that day. By the time Holly got back after her tour, we'd calmed down. We talked. We made up. She made promises and I made promises…"

"All is forgiven?"

"All is forgiven…and she's moving into her own place."

It was Eden's turn to reveal the latest developments in the saga with her sister. And as she had with Beck's story about his mother, he listened as she outlined the turn of events that would have her and Holly starting to live their own lives, finally respecting each other's space and providing adult autonomy.

"It's not like we'll never see each other, or that we won't have much to do with each other. I think there are ways that we both need to grow up. We need to stop depending on one another in the way we did when we were teenagers and had little choice. So…I offered to buy her a place of her own." Beck remained silent, just gently stroking her arm. Eden tilted her head up to him. "I don't know if I'm being too generous or trying to…you know…buy her off."

"It's not either of those, Eden. You were just recognizing that you and Holly have reached a point in your lives where you both really have to start standing on your own. Don't feel guilty for the fact that you now have the money to help make that possible. And it really is a good way to share some of your good fortune with her. It's not the car she asked for, but I think Holly knows her own apartment is a much better deal."

Eden laughed. "Yeah. She didn't turn me down. As a matter of fact, she said something I wasn't expecting. After throwing herself into my arms to thank me, she said, 'You're one in a million...and I'm so glad you're my sister.' I thought that was sweet."

"It was more than that," Beck said.

By mutual unspoken agreement, they had put off the obvious conclusion to the night. They could have headed for the bedroom and spent delicious, heated time in each other's arms, satisfying the gnawing need to make love and lie together. But they also understood that was a given and could wait. To Beck, it felt better, more comforting to talk quietly, snuggled together on the sofa. Catch up on all the recent drama in their lives, and realize they were beginning to entwine. There was no question or discussion that he was staying the night. After everything they'd been through, putting out brush fires, he and Eden had come up with a plan for themselves. The f-word...*future*...had not been spoken, but he knew it was suddenly on both their minds.

He'd taken their empty wine glasses to the kitchen and turned out the lights, comfortable that Eden had so quickly made a place for him in her life. And she had been totally selfless in her generosity of including him. He had to make sure that he told her again, before they went to sleep, that he loved her.

He headed to her bedroom, passing the open door of the bathroom and catching a glimpse of her already partially disrobed. Her back was to him, her face angled toward the mirror as she twisted and pinned her hair to the top of her head. Her arms stretched over her head gave him an alluring view of her slender back and down her legs to her bare feet. Beck experienced such a rush of desire that it caught him off guard and his throat tightened. Eden was down to her black bra, and hipster panties, emphasizing the indent of her waist. He slowly approached her from behind, slipping his arms around her waist. She gave him a sultry smile in the mirror as he draw her against his chest and began nibbling at the side of her neck. Eden tilted her head to accommodate the journey of his mouth down to her shoulder.

She drew in a shallow breath, relaxing, allowing herself to feel the hard, sudden evidence of his desire and intent against her lower back and buttocks.

"Beck," she whispered, her mounting passion quickly matching his own.

"Do you need a hand?" he asked, growling the question against her smooth skin.

Beck didn't wait for an answer. He deftly released the clasp of Eden's bra, and it dropped away and down her arms...into the sink. Her back arched naturally as his hands slid up her rib cage to caress and cup her breasts. Her eyes drifted close, and he heard the faint moan that breezed through Eden's parted lips. He pressed light, tickling, sensual little kisses to her jaw and neck, her shoulder, all the while massaging her breasts until the nipples stiffened between his fingers and Eden's head fell back on his shoulder. She willingly let him have his way.

Beck upped the ante when he let his right hand trail down her torso, feeling the sinew under her skin contract and move with the stimulation of his touch. He didn't stop, letting his hand slip beneath the band of her panties, and Eden's sharp intake of air indicated the depth of the pleasure Beck continued to draw from her. He had to tighten his hold on her with his other arm as the effects of what he was doing to her made her body begin to go limp against him.

Eden began to pant, blindly reaching around with her arms and hands in a futile attempt to touch him and return the favor of what he was doing to her.

"Not yet," he said, his voice guttural with trying not to lose control.

Eden whimpered. She lifted a leg and braced her foot against the ledge of the tub, making it even easier for Beck to explore and wander and stroke at will until he knew she was very close to the edge. Beck stepped back suddenly, out of the bathroom, and gently pulled Eden with him. There was no resistance, but neither was she capable of much independent movement now that her body was soft and open and her limbs loose and pliant.

Beck encouraged her onto the bed, and through drowsy eyelids, she watched him disrobe, his body showing he was as ready as she was to couple, to meld into each other's arms and let their desire for one another explode, taking them to another dimension. Eden positioned herself on the bed as Beck joined her. She reached her arms to him, welcoming him to her as he settled on her, into the space she made for him between her legs, on her stomach and chest.

The foreplay had been dispensed with, and they needed no more time to prep.

"I've been waiting all day," Beck confessed, the admission adding fuel to their desire.

"Me too," Eden added, her voice a shallow whisper of eagerness.

Beck eased into her with the guessing and delays of the afternoon quickly disappearing. Their bonding, the intense rhythmic rocking of their joined bodies and the breathy exchange of kisses, demonstrated more than could ever have been said with words.

CHAPTER 17

"Sorry you had to miss the celebration with your classmates. I hadn't thought about what your plans were going to be for commencement this weekend."

Eden squeezed Beck's hand. "They'll survive without me. And I don't think anyone would dare be upset that I chose you over four 3L friends and peers. No way did I want to celebrate this ending with anyone but you." She smiled up at him, knowing that the naked truth of her love made her eyes bright...and happy.

Beck grinned. "I'm glad I made the list."

"Not only did you, you're at the top. Besides, I'll still see everyone tomorrow for the graduation party hosted by the dean. I think that's enough togetherness after three years of slogging through classes and case work."

"You lie. You loved every minute of it," Beck challenged.

Eden sighed. "I did," she confessed.

They were doing a walk. Not exactly *her* walk. The evening and the occasion didn't call for something that athletic. The walk she and Beck were taking was meandering, slow. It was post expensive celebratory dinner, complete with champagne as closure to her law-school days. She'd received the official notice that she'd met the requirements to complete her JD and that, henceforth, she was officially in the last stretch to becoming an attorney.

"It's so funny that except for the first year, I've spent hardly any time in Georgetown at the university campus."

"Yeah, I know the law school is downtown, and that's why I thought a dinner in Georgetown would be nice."

"I'm glad you thought of it. It was very exclusive. Made me feel like a grown-up."

Beck laughed and pulled her to his side, an arm around her.

"You've been a grown-up since you were nineteen, Eden. I personally think you're seriously overdue for the fun stuff. You have a lot of lost ground to make up for."

They began ambling away from Georgetown Waterfront Park, the warm spring air giving them both an intense sense of peace and promise.

"Not sure how I'd do that. I start at Katherine Perkins's firm in June. No time to really kick back and do nothing. I have to begin prepping for the bar exams *yesterday*."

"Relax. I have it on the highest authority you're going to ace it on the first try."

"How do you know that?" she asked, piqued.

"I've seen you in action. I've gotten a firsthand glimpse into what you've been doing for the last three years. You throw yourself into everything you do. And I saw the program for Sunday. You're getting three…count 'em, *three* awards! The Dean's something-or-other, an achievement this, and advocacy that."

Eden turned her face to him and smiled, the night illumination making her eyes sparkle.

Beck stopped walking. He pulled out his smartphone and called up a number from the directory.

"What are you doing?" Eden asked.

"I have a surprise for you…and it's taking way too long to get to it. I'm calling for a car to take us back to my place."

She was not in a frame of mind to argue minor details. Her next commencement gathering was not until five the next afternoon. No need to rush to get up in the morning. Anyway, Beck would make sure that they didn't.

They entered his apartment thirty minutes later, and he turned immediately to her.

"I hate to make you take this off so soon…" He touched the bodice of her dress.

"I'll wear it for you another time." Eden kissed him quickly.

"Before you do, I want to introduce the first of my graduation gifts."

"Okay," Eden said, a little suspicion creeping in. "What, exactly, did he have in mind?"

"Ice cream."

Her eyes widened. "Seriously? *Yes.*"

Beck grinned. "You are easy to please. Where have you been for the last ten years?"

Together they went right into his kitchen to pull together all the paraphernalia, including a half-gallon container of ice cream from *Thomas Sweet.*

They kicked off their shoes. Beck removed his tie and opened several buttons of his shirt. He rolled up the sleeves. Eden put aside her shawl, her shoulders smoothly displayed above the neckline of her strapless champagne-toned dress. It was the second of her purchases, along with the fuchsia creation she'd worn to the Black Journalists gala the month before.

They'd fallen into comfortable routines and rituals that, very quickly, made Eden feel grounded as a couple, even though there had been no discussion about a future. She was not concerned. If one thing had become a certainty in her mind and heart, it was that Beck loved her, and he always found very simple and surprising ways of showing her.

Something as simple as ice cream. And after the ceremony on Sunday they were escaping for a concert in Rock Creek Park…and hamburgers afterward at Lucky Buns. Eden laughed, telling Beck the name was very unfortunate. Maybe they should go somewhere else?

They were just finishing the ice cream when Beck pulled a folded sheet of paper from his shirt pocket, carefully opened it, and frowned over the several lines.

"What is it?" Eden asked, craning her neck to take a peek.

Beck snatched the paper away. "My jam," he said playfully. "Be patient." He looked at the paper again. "So, the next surprise is that my mother wants you to attend the jazz festival she's in next month. I thought you and I should make it a road trip. If we fly, we'll get there too quickly." He peered at her over the top of the page. "Road trip?"

"That sounds romantic."

"Right answer. That's the idea. I want to show you something," Beck said, getting up from the table.

He took his sheet of information with him, but it made Eden smile. She had no intention of spoiling his game of revelations. She loved surprises, and Beck was good at that.

He quickly returned with a trademark sky-blue bag from Tiffany's. Eden stared at the bag, confused. Her mind suddenly went blank, and she had no idea what Beck had in mind, what he was up to. What had he gotten from Tiffany's? He sat down again and reached into the bag.

"I want your opinion. What do you think?" He withdrew a blue box from the bag tied with a white ribbon and pushed it across the table to her. "It's for Nora. To congratulate her on her upcoming show. She might get a recording deal. She could get more offers to perform. It's her moment."

Eden stared at the box, about four inches square. Too small for a necklace, too big for a ring. Eden untied the white ribbon and opened the box. Inside on a bed of a cotton cushion lay a shiny white-gold bracelet. It was about a quarter of an inch thick, unadorned...except for the inscription on the inside. She held it up but knew instinctively what it read. The same poignant epitaph Beck had tattooed on his upper arm in remembrance of his brother, Mason. But it began *For Mason, from Mom...*" with the rest of the quote as Eden had first seen. Heartbreaking, sincere, and so filled with love and regret.

Eden relaxed and began to tear up. The gift was astonishing, and she had no doubt that Nora was going to love it. Perhaps it will be another factor in healing the past. It was a process.

She looked at Beck as he waited, his gaze expectant and hopeful. "It's beautiful. She's going to love it." She got up and approached Beck to put her arms around his neck. "She's going to love it," Eden repeated, as if he still needed reassurance.

"I hope so." He reached into the bag and withdrew a second blue box. It appeared to be the same size as the first. He handed it to Eden. "This is for you."

He shifted from the table so that she could sit on his thigh. He held Eden around the waist as she unwrapped the second box, her fingers fumbling over the ribbon. She felt her heart begin to race as she opened the box with justified anticipation. It was not a necklace…or bracelet…or ring. Resting on the cotton was a star-tling glimmering pair of diamond earrings. *Her* earrings.

Eden stared at them. Her throat close and she couldn't even swallow, so great was her surprise. "Beck," she managed to get out. But it was said with a certain reverence. A certain awe. Eden touched one, as if to make sure they were real.

"These are the ones you were…*lusting* over, I think was your phrase. I wasn't sure, so I had to ask a couple of sales associates. Finally, one of them knew what I was talking about. Talked about you. You know, you're a legend in the…"

Eden slowly put her arms around his neck, resting her check against his. "Beck," she whispered again.

"I hope you're not going to be mad at me." Beck embraced her, stroking her back.

It felt so good, so comforting. He was being so tender. Being mad at Beck was the very last thing on her mind. If anything, he had just confirmed everything Eden had hoped would be true about him, that she'd conjured in her heart. "Beck…"

"I was hoping you'd have a little more to say. I know my name. I wanted…"

Eden turned her head and kissed him, full on. He immediately responded. Pulling her tightly into his arms. A hand caressed over the silky smoothness of her back and shoulders. He slowly withdrew.

"The thing is this, Eden. You're not supposed to buy something like diamond earrings for yourself. I know you love them, wanted them…could even afford them, now. But that's not the point. You were never going to allow yourself a gift like that, and you're not meant to. Where's the pleasure, the joy in that?"

"Diamond earrings…diamond *anything* is what a man, a lover, gives to a woman. But if I'm wrong, if I miscalculated or assumed too much…if I spoiled…"

"There's never been a man in my life who…who…"

"Loves you the way I do."

"I…don't know what to say."

"When I had the salesclerk wrap the earrings up, they were a little concerned that I was somehow spoiling your fantasy."

Eden shook her head. "No. No," she said, pulling back to look with feeling into his eyes. "Saying thank you seems really small. Not good enough."

"Eden, you ain't seen nothin' yet. There's a lot more love where that came from."

Eden felt filled with a love she never thought to have. Then, Beck kissed her tenderly, sealing a promise she knew he was going to keep.

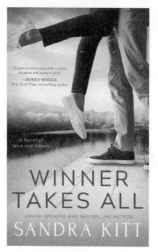
For a moment, when the text notification lit up the screen on her cell phone, Jean Travis considered ignoring it. But it was her work phone, and the incoming message meant it was from someone official, i.e., her boss, Bradley Clark.

Where are you? the message began.

About to leave, she texted back, heading down the corridor toward security and the exit.

Meet me at the pressroom. I'm on my way.

She knew this didn't bode well for the end of her day and the start of her weekend. Jean's silent response was to do as she was instructed.

Brad Clark was already waiting for her when she reached the converted conference room that also doubled as the pressroom. He appeared anxious, and Jean guessed that whatever was going on was important. The door to the pressroom was open, and there was a lot of activity inside.

"What's going on?" she asked, her attention drawn to the flurry of movement, equipment, and orders coming from inside the room.

"Press conference and brief broadcast in about thirty minutes," Brad said. "The mayor agreed to the broadcast of the current lottery winners. You're making the announcement and introducing the winners."

Jean frowned. "It's almost six thirty…"

"I know, I know. Someone dropped the ball, and everyone's gone for the day. You have to step in and do it. Local reporters and their crews are already here. The winners are in the greenroom. We already know who they are, but this is a big deal because of the Mega Million winning ticket. It's huge…" he said.

"Not funny," Jean murmured, accepting several pages from him.

"It's easy, should take less than an hour. I wrote up some guidelines. Here's a list of the current winners…" He gave Jean another page. "Make sure you emphasize that the mayor's office wanted to share the news with people in the city, letting them know that their neighbors really do become winners. They can, too, blah, blah, blah."

Jean grinned at Brad. "Have you ever bought a lottery ticket?"

"I don't gamble," he chortled. "My wife would kill me for throwing away money like that. Odds are too high. But…you can't win if you don't play. Wonder what ESPN's gonna do now?"

She was confused. "What do you mean?"

"One of our winners is a TV personality...almost famous..." While he spoke Brad's cell buzzed a notification. "I gotta take this."

"How much time before we broadcast?"

Brad looked at his watch. "Down to twenty-five minutes."

"Where will you be?"

"On my way home." He smirked, walking away and reading his text. "Do whatever they need you to. Stay until it's over. Call me if there are problems, and *only* if there are problems."

"Overtime, right?"

"Night. Have a good weekend..."

Jean watched him hurry away. She entered the pressroom to find that the reporters and film crews were pretty much set up. She then made sure the podium had a functioning mike.

She dug out a pocket mirror, checked her lip gloss, and absently fluffed her hair, then began to introduce herself to the reporters waiting to meet the lottery winners and tape the announcements.

The local networks no longer did a weekly five-minute drawing of lottery numbers. Everything was digital now, which cost less money and production time. For these occasional announcements, the winners were already known to the lottery commission. Only the public would be surprised when the names were called. Jean knew that all she had to do was interject excitement into the proceedings. She only had a minute to scan quickly through Brad's notes, to figure out an agenda for the announcement, to fashion an introduction—something cute and humorous—so that no one would suspect this was her first time.

Jean signaled to the security guard standing just outside the door. "We're almost ready. Please bring in the guests. Tell them to take seats in the front two rows quietly." She checked her smartphone clock. "Five minutes, okay?" she said to the waiting press crew.

She glanced around to find about thirty or forty people gathered in the back of the room to witness the announcement. They were fillers, like movie extras, there to lend authenticity to the moment. No doubt many were family members and friends, but mostly they were general public who enjoyed saying *I was there when*, Jean guessed. She got a signal from the reporters that they were all set. Jean took up a position at the front of the space, and camera lights suddenly flashed on. Just then, a side door opened and a number of people trooped in, momentarily creating a disruption. The bright lights for the cameras prevented Jean from seeing a thing beyond the podium. Then it went quiet.

"We're live," someone signaled.

Jean smiled into the cameras and began to talk.

"Hello! I'm Jean Travis, assistant director of Public Affairs at the mayor's office. I'd like to…to…" She fumbled and hesitated when she was distracted by another person making what could only be described as a perfectly timed grand entrance into the room.

Jean could detect a tall figure, a man, but couldn't see much else. He managed to create a stir and a brief buzz of whispering, taking his seat. Jean tried to cover her lapse.

"So much excitement," she said with a bright smile. "Thank you for being here tonight as we recognize the latest winners in our state lottery. And, of course, everyone wants to know—and see— who will walk away with the Mega Million prize that has grown over the past two drawings when there was no winning ticket."

Jean then had a chance to catch her breath while she read an official statement from the State Lottery Commission about the rules governing the program. Her attention was briefly caught again by the latecomer, who, incredibly, appeared to be giving her a covert hand wave. She ignored it and continued.

"So let's get to it! Like all of you, I'm excited to meet the lucky ones who will walk away with checks from the State Lottery, with numbers ending in a lot of zeros."

A cheer went up through the room. One camera turned to capture the seated group demonstrating their enthusiasm.

Jean smiled, and then she suddenly gasped.

The list!

She had not yet even looked at the winning names on the list Brad had given her. As smoothly as possible, she pulled the list from the other announcements. She briefly glanced at the names. The last name grabbed her attention. She recognized it. But from where?

"And now, our winners!"

Jean called the first name, including where he was from and the amount of the winnings. Shouts and applause erupted from the audience as an elderly man and woman came forward, broad smiles and clasped hand-pumps denoting their victory. Jean kissed the cheeks of the woman and man to interject a little human connection. A giant cardboard sign was passed to her, a replica of a check with the amount the couple had won. Jean asked them a few questions about how they planned to use their winnings. The gushing, excited reactions from the couple evoked laughter and shout-outs around the room. Then they retook their seats to another round of applause.

And so it went, down the list of names for the next forty-five minutes. By the time she called the fourth winner, Jean had her comments to a science, and everything went smoothly. But there was a heightened energy and anticipation, as everyone clearly wanted to know who had won the Mega Millions. Who was going to be set for life? She looked at the name again, and recognition finally sunk in. Jean knew this name. An unexpected catch lodged in her chest. She had to quickly swallow to get her next breath.

"Will Trick… Will, er… Patrick Bennett, please come to the front to accept your check."

She joined in the clapping for the winner, as she'd done for all the others. But this time she was more interested in who came forward. Out of the bright lights, a tall figure emerged. He was casually but smartly dressed in dark charcoal cargo pants, a black Henley, and a collarless, short black leather jacket. *Great presence*, Jean thought, keeping her attention on his approach, her smile fixed as her gaze widened with recognition. Jean reached out with her hand to touch his arm so that he'd face the camera in the right position. But he stunned her by taking hold of her hand and giving it a subtle squeeze…and not letting go. And he knew exactly how to position himself in front of a studio camera.

Jean made a discreet attempt to pull free, but Patrick Bennett wasn't having it. She gave in and tried to relax. Catching her off guard even more, he brought their clasped hands to his mouth and planted a light kiss to the back of hers. The audience loved it, cheering and whistling. Jean played it through and gave a faux blushing gaze into the cameras.

"Many congratulations to…to Patrick Bennett," she said with the right amount of enthusiasm and professionalism. "Mr. Bennett is the grand winner today of—are you ready?—*seventy-five million dollars!*"

There were whoops and gasps, and one audacious request from a female in the back of the room.

"I love you! Will you marry me? We're already here at city hall!" The room erupted into wild laughter.

"*Do it, do it, do it…*" went up the boisterous chorus.

Patrick Bennett, still holding Jean's hand, raised both in a kind of victory wave. He grinned broadly but didn't respond to the proposal. His free hand swept through his hair in a gesture that had Jean momentarily transfixed. Then she was able to extract her hand when she was handed the last cardboard check. Cameras flashed, dozens of cell phones were poised in the air, the glow of their blue-lit screens scattered throughout the audience.

Jean started the applause again, gazing openly at Patrick Bennett. It was an unavoidable sign of recognition between them. And then Patrick winked at her and murmured so that only she could hear, "Surprised?"

The quiet drawl of his voice made her stomach tense. That word, his tone, seemed much too intimate for the setting. She couldn't think of a thing to say. She just kept clapping and smiling.

Jean was so glad when it was finally over. She made a few concluding remarks, thanking everyone for coming and congratulating the winners again. As people got up and began moving around, many, if not most, headed to surround Patrick. She was curious about the familiarity with which people approached and spoke to him, as if they knew him. She covertly watched Trick. *Pa*trick. Jean had known him by the former moniker from the past. *Trick*. Jean gathered her things, absently chatting with some of the camera crew and making arrangements with the maintenance and security staff to have the room put back to rights.

She could just hear Patrick's deep voice off to the side, the easy way he chatted with everyone, even posing for selfies, which completely mystified Jean. He didn't know any of these people. What came across was a confidence and vibrancy to him, so unlike the other winners...just regular everyday folk who'd had a stroke of extraordinary luck. Perhaps this was one of the biggest, if not *the* biggest, moment of their lives. Patrick answered questions and accepted the good wishes of those around him with humility and a surprising grace, Jean considered. She kept stealing little glances at him, once catching Patrick doing the same to her. Her curiosity betrayed her once more.

Reporters continued to ask *How do you feel winning so much money?* questions, looking for cute, amusing, moving quotes for their profile pieces. She thought there might be an opportunity to use some footage for promo or marketing later on from her office.

The room finally began to empty out. She took a deep breath and approached the last few people, including Patrick. There was no way to leave without acknowledging him. Without remembering. Was he doing the same?

ACKNOWLEDGMENTS

A HUGE, heartfelt *thank you and* appreciation to Alexandra Gil, JD MLS, for supplying the law student's POV to my story. Also, thanks to Alexandra for the amusing insider anecdotes of her three years *as a law student.* After many years in the field of *law,* she then received her MLS to become *an academic* librarian in New York City.

ABOUT THE AUTHOR

Prior to breaking into the mainstream, Sandra Kitt was considered the foremost African American writer of romance fiction and was the first black writer to ever publish with Harlequin. Sandra is the recipient of a Lifetime Achievement Award in Contemporary Fiction from *Romantic Times*. Romance Writers of America presented Sandra with its 2002 Service Award, and the New York chapter of the Romance Writers of America with a Lifetime Achievement Award. In 2010, Sandra received the Zora Neale Hurston Literary Award.

A native of New York City, Sandra holds a bachelor's degree and a master's degree in fine arts from The City University of New York and has studied and lived in Mexico. A onetime graphic designer and printmaker, her work appears in corporate collections including the Museum of African American Art in Los Angeles. Sandra is a former managing director and information specialist in astronomy and astrophysics at the American Museum of Natural History in New York and illustrated two books for the late science writer Isaac Asimov. In 1996, Sandra wrote the last show script for the Hayden Planetarium, narrated by Walter Cronkite. A frequent guest speaker, Sandra has lectured at NYU, Penn State, Sarah Lawrence, Columbia University, and was an adjunct in publishing and fiction writing.

Sandra Kitt's first mainstream novel, *The Color of Love*, was released in 1995 to critical acclaim from *Library Journal, USA Today, The Black Scholar,* and was optioned by HBO and Lifetime from a script by Sandra. The anthology *Girlfriends* was nominated for the NAACP Image Award for Fiction in 1999. *Significant Others* and *Between Friends* appeared on the bestseller list in *ESSENCE* magazine, and Amazon has named *Significant Others* among the top twenty-five romances for the twentieth century.